World Fantasy Awards materials. Not for individual sale or resale.

ANIMALIA

SHAUNA C. MURPHY

BOOKS

COCO BOOKS and the HEART colophon are trademarks of Coco Studios.

Middle Grade / Fantasy / Mystery
Fiction / Fantasy / General
Young Adult / Fantasy / Mystery

In a school in Norway, students from around the world are taught the secrets of the Victorian-era world including animals' special abilities; involving a young girl, a dragon, and a mystery.

ISBN: 979-8-9880458-0-9

Printed in the United States of America

Illustration by Steve McDonald
Author photo by Jennifer Alyse
Interior Formatting by Katia Zuppel

First Edition

CONTENT RATINGS
Rated by readers on a scale of 0 – 10.
Language: 0 (None). Expressions are generally considered not offensive.
Violence: 3. Some violence including fighting, punching, and avoiding capture.
Drugs: 4. Prescription drugs and general pharmaceuticals are part of the larger plot of the story.
Psychological Suspense: 6. Protagonist has nightmares, including confusion and grief.
General Threat: 4. Protagonist faces threats and risk.
Sexual Content: 0 (None).

~Mercy is greater than judgment.~

ANIMALIA

1 - How To Trap A Monster 1

2 - Rumors Of Svalbard 8

3 - The Auditions 16

4 - The Things Of Pa 31

5 - Apothecary Bjørn 35

6 - The Sleigh To Svalbard 42

7 - The Monster Beneath Svalbard 50

8 - The Animalia Problem 62

9 - Five Houses 68

10 - Strange Favor 76

11 - Welcome To Animlia 88

12 - Ambassador Sunday 100

13 - Mind Sanctuary 122

14 - The Boxing Match 136

15 - Apothecary 143

16 - Grom's Changing 151

17 - Alejandro 158

18 - The Incident In The Night 172

19 - Fight Or Flight 180

20 - An Unexpected Christmas 187

21 - Dancing With The OlShields 193

22 - How To Fight A Monster 196

23 - SVALBARD'S SECRETS 205

24 - SERAPHIM'S LESSON 210

25 - THE DRAGON-MIND AND THE CRIME 216

26 - MYSTERY KNOT 223

27 - DRAGON INSTINCTS 228

28 - MAGNESIUM FOR MR. GROM 232

29 - CONCERNING ANIMALS 240

30 - PRESENTING GROM 247

31 - ROSE FRATERNITY 252

32 - MADNESS OF ANIMALIA 260

33 - BJØRN AND JUSTINE 267

34 - VIKTOR'S ULTIMATUM 272

35 - HUMAN VOICES 281

36 - LASZLO'S OBSESSION 290

37 - THE STORY BEHIND THE STORY 297

38 - THE HOME THAT'S NO LONGER HOME 303

39 - THE SORORITY OF EXCEPTIONAL WOMEN ... 308

DISCUSSION QUESTIONS 319

Q & A 323

ABOUT THE AUTHOR 327

SPECIAL THANKS 329

ONE

HOW TO TRAP A MONSTER

Night falls and the arctic moon rises.

I sit in the tavern cellar, at the card table. With one hand I tap the old wood table, with the other I fan my playing cards; jack, queen, king… My cards have a wink in their eyes, they tell me; *we can win.*

A dull candle flickers on the table between my opponent and I. It casts an orange glow over his long face, making him a tall jackrabbit: Viktor, the so-called smartest boy in town. *We'll see about that.*

Viktor counts cards, pulling from the deck. I should've known Viktor would play like a machinist, all math-minded. I frown out the cellar window – it's early autumn but everything is frosty cold.

His friends surround me on either side of the small basement. They shift, nervous, of course – we'll all audition for Svalbard School tomorrow – no one wants to talk about it.

My pet newt, Grom, runs down my arm – a lime-green swipe – and curls on the table by my hand. He licks my thumb with a scratchy pink tongue. My little Grom. I crack a smile at him.

The prize coins are set aside for the winner: Twenty whole kroner in the pot. *Blazes.* That'll feed Ma and I for two whole weeks. Winner takes them all.

And I'll win. For Ma.

I've won this game before – Carnivore Kingdom – a strategy game from our Nordic isle – a cross between deckbuilding and poker.

Focus. Focus.

Two hours of gameplay are sprawled in a maze of flat cards on the table between us. It's the last moves of the game. Time to close.

Step one: Assess my enemy.

Viktor is math-minded. My age, thirteen. Impulsive. Norwegian born-and-raised. An offense player. His parents run the machinist welding shop at the edge of town. He's wealthy. Deep purple rings circle his eyes – he stayed up late last night preparing his Svalbard School audition for tomorrow. He's tired.

He smirks at me knowingly, like his hand is so clever.

I smirk back. *My hand is clever, too.*

Step two: Enter my enemy's mind.

He doesn't need the money. He plays for pride. Pride makes you assume the worst in your opponent. Pride makes you anticipate attacks and not traps.

He bites his thin lower lip, thinking... Wood creaks beneath his heel as he bobs his leg – he's excited. So he *does* have a good hand.

Darn it.

I lock my gaze on him. "Draw."

His bluish eyes dance over mine and he chuckles with a wry smile. He winks at me.

Go ahead, Viktor, flirt – it won't work on me.

He pulls a card and taps its side – counting again. He relies on probability. He wins his games because he counts cards to calculate his next move. But I don't study cards. I study him. And I use something far more reliable – observation.

Probability gives chance, but observation is certain. I can test observations to find patterns. And where there's a destructive pattern, I can anticipate it. I can break it.

First, create space for the destructive pattern, allow him to use it. I set down a few low-value throwaway cards and Viktor's eyebrow flicks at me with this condescension, like I'm an obvious fool.

Step three: Anticipate attack.

Viktor lays down two Aces. Clever. He clicks his tongue and cocks his head to the side, like he's already won.

I tilt my head too, mirroring him.

His mistake: Thinking I play the game like everyone else.

I have my own rules, and I've predicted his Aces.

I lay down my Jack, Queen and King.

Viktor sets his jaw – his cheeks blush scarlet. I sense his heart quicken as though it's in my own chest: Panic.

Good.

Panic mixed with pride makes for poor decisions.

I carefully fold my hands under my chin.

That's right. Underestimate me. Miscalculate me.

The boys beside me whisper. They pass around a canteen of whiskey, like the game is getting good. Viktor's gaze darts around the crowded room. His pride can't handle it. He draws from his pile, weakening his hand. He lays down a Jack – cancelling mine – a counter attack.

Just like I thought you would, Viktor.

Step four: Block counter.

I forfeit my hand. I sacrifice my Queen.

Viktor bleeds into a wicked smile, like he's outsmarted me. He suppresses a laugh.

There's the pride I'm counting on.

He lays down his hand, preparing his next move – to take the game.

Step five: Reveal trap.

Instead of drawing, I turn over my trap card: Ace of Hearts.

The boys chatter beside me. I fold my hands over my chest. It's the best card in the game.

Under the rules of the game, unless he has a similar-value card – I win.

But he doesn't have a similar card, he's used up all his options.

I made sure of it.

His narrow jaw tenses. Wavy brown hair falls over his face and he leans onto the table, gripping the side. His steely eyes flick across the cards face-up on the table; counting again.

His behavior has patterns – he blinks repeatedly, like he's trying to wake himself – his lips move, muttering numbers, subtracting their values from the deck. He's calculating his probability for a certain card, if he draws. But he already knows his odds. Next to zero.

"Next to zero," I say, calm.

His jaw snaps shut and his face turns sour, like he tastes spoiled milk. "Yeah…"

The onlookers clink glasses and a few of them laugh.

Viktor forces a fake laugh, like he's unbothered, and stretches his arms high, smiling and shaking his head at the vaulted cellar ceiling, as though it played a joke on him. The room chatters, distracted – they pass around salted potato wedges. Viktor rests his hands behind his head, but his fingers flutter at the nape of his neck –

What in the –

In a flash he slips a card from behind his neck collar and swaps it for the one in his hand.

No one watches the game close enough – no one notices him cheat.

But I do.

My cheeks go hot.

Cheater!

I clench my jaw. He doesn't even need the money.

Viktor lays down his new card – King of Crystals.

I close my eyes. *No.*

"Oh… I guess, the game is a draw," the moderator says, chewing a potato wedge. "You each have ten seconds of wild play – whoever has the highest hand wins," the boy glances at his clunky machinist watch, which gives a subtle *tick… tick… tick…* "starting… Now!"

I hold my breath: *Focus.*

Viktor's arm surges forward.

...tick

His advantage: My weakened hand.

My advantage: His pride.

...tick

Use his pride against him.

...tick

Viktor pulls repeatedly from the deck, an attack position. But each time he pulls, by the rules of the game, I can activate a defense card I have turned face-down.

...tick

I flip each of my cards in response to his frantic attempt for an attack card. His ten seconds are up – I can respond.

I sacrifice each of my new defense cards – all ten of them. Each time I sacrifice, my overall points go up by one.

"TIME!" the moderator shouts.

I lay my cards down and fold my arms over my chest. I have twenty-one points. And he has twenty.

I win.

"She takes the game," the moderator says. "And all twenty kroner."

The cellar is silent. Viktor sulks at the leftover cards in his hands.

I run my fingers along my braided hair and twist it over my shoulder. Laughter bubbles in my chest but I keep a straight face. I slide the coins into my little purse. Grom sleeps on the card table. I scoop his green lizard-body into my dress pocket.

"She's a bit of a freak, isn't she?" a boy mutters behind me.

"Something ain't quite right wit'her," says another.

I turn to leave. They think I can't hear. I've heard everything they've said behind my back, all night. I fasten my purse to my side. Ever since Pa died, they've been afraid of me.

Fear makes people assume the worst.

I slip into my overcoat and duck out to the frosty night street.

In the snowfall, Sjosburg is a dream, my gingerbread village between forest and mountains. Fresh autumn snow speckles my coat and melts into the gray wool. God it smells wonderful, like peppermint. The shops glow with little icicles in the lamplight. I kick the powdery snow with my boots as I walk.

Alone at last. Thank God. And twenty whole kroner. *Ha!*

Grom crawls out of my pocket, onto my hand. "We won," I tell him. I nod my head in a big, obvious way. "Yes, we did."

He nods his little newt head back, imitating me.

"Good boy! That's right. We *won*."

Grom licks my hand – it tickles so much – I laugh so hard my sides hurt. He crawls over my coat and hides back into the warm pocket.

I turn the corner, the boys' voices fade away, but Viktor stumbles around the bend, chasing after me and calling my name; "Sunday, wait a minute! Sunn-daay!"

No...

I roll my eyes. *Some people can't take a blasted hint.*

"That was some good play," he slows to a walk beside me. "You even got me scratching my head there at the end."

I stop mid-step and turn to him. He has an intelligent, steady gaze. Freckles dot his eyelids. His lips are purple from the cold and his teeth a slight yellow from cigar smoke. I tilt my head, slowly, and slide my hand around his neck, down the collar of his shirt, and pull his extra card into the space between our faces. "Did you know," I drop my jaw with fake surprise, "that Viktor is a cheater?"

His eyes dim. He tucks his chin to his chest and brown wavy hair falls over his eyelids. He can't help it – a wide, wicked smile sets dimples into his cheeks.

He would be handsome, but he's a cheat. And horrible.

"You caught that move, huh?"

Idiot.

I turn to walk away. I care about Ma. Not him.

He slides in front of me, blocking my way. "You know, you might even be as smart as me."

"I'm *smarter* than you. I won."

"Ouch," he flicks a bushy eyebrow.

He steps closer to me. His breath mixes with mine in a white cloud. He's taller than me and I have to tilt my head way back to see him. His blue eyes have a golden-brown ring around the edges. He chews his lip and his cheeks go red and splotchy, suddenly. He takes a step back, awkwardly, and corrects his balance. "So… you auditioning tomorrow?"

"… I haven't decided."

"That's a load o' crock."

"Well, someone has to take care of Ma."

"But you worked so hard on it. You have to try…"

I avoid his eyes.

It's a game. Everything with him is a game. "You're still a cheater," I mutter, and I turn down the street, leaving him behind in the fog.

"Yeah?" he yells after me, "I'm the only one in this town who even talks to you!"

My chest hollows. As horrible as he is, he's right. When Ma overdosed and nearly burned our shop down, Viktor came. He helped. None of the 'nice-girls' came.

I turn the corner to the edge of town, by the forest. I stare into the dark, mangled tree-line, half-expecting someone to be there, but the twisted branches blur – all haunted – and I have to look away. Ma says monsters exist – but they aren't animals, they're just people who disregard others.

Years ago, everyone in town hunted the monster that killed Pa. They got so angry they slaughtered a boar – some random pig that had nothing to do with it. They raised it up in these trees and burned it alive.

…They should've burned me.

After all, it's my fault he's gone. The real monster is me.

TWO

RUMORS OF SVALBARD

Seven years — seven *years* since we last saw Pa. I watch Ma carefully from the side. She hums that same music-box melody she always sings and wraps candles with her long, beautiful fingers. No, she's not thinking of Pa, thank God. She hasn't noticed the date this morning, the anniversary of his death, sort-of...

"Did you change your mind?" she hums. "About the Svalbard audition today." She wraps candles and places them in the 'for sale' display at the window. She never looks at me when she asks important things. It's her tell. She forces peace in the home like she'd fall on a knife for it. I don't mind, actually. When she's like this, it's kinda nice.

"I don't think I'll audition..." I trim candle wicks, slowly, and wrap the ends with paper. "Wouldn't be accepted. Why try and be disappointed, right?"

Ma tilts her head an interesting way, like she sees something vague in the distance. She digs into her dress pocket and pulls out a few coins. "Why don't you fetch us some breakfast rolls from the bakery then. Just in case you change your mind."

She holds out three bronze kroner.

"…Really?"

Her eyes smile in half-moons. She nods and long curtains of brown hair fall over her knobby shoulders. "Can't be hungry on your big day."

My chest squeezes. "Thanks Mama."

She kisses my head and slides the coins onto my hand. She yawns, dazed, medicated probably. I swear her whole life is dream-walking. "You go on, I'll open shop. Take Grom with you. I can't watch him at the same time."

On the fireplace mantle, Grom's green newt-hands push out from the fabric nest and he smiles at me. My stars I could hold him forever. He scampers along the mantle and twirls. Good boy. I taught him that trick, to dance. Ever since I found him in that cracked newt egg two summers ago, I've trained him for the stupid Animalia audition… What a waste of time.

I scuff the wood floor with my toes.

A big giant stupid waste.

Grom leaps into the air – a lime-green swipe – and catches a gnat with his little pink tongue.

"He's gotten quicker lately, hasn't he?" Ma pulls open the shop curtains.

Quicker, sure, but *cunning* is more like it. Last week he spilled a jar of honey *on purpose* to attract more gnats so he could catch them. Crafty little lizard. He swallows his gnat and gives me sly side-eyes. I swear I can guess his thoughts.

I scoop him into my arms, step into my snow boots, and slip outside.

Oil-lamps glow like floating orbs in the fog. The clock on the church steeple moves its iron hands to 6:45 a.m. Aurora lights flow in the sky like yellow and blue ribbons, they cast everything in this hazy, underwater glow. Now that it's autumn, it's always a little dark out, even at high noon. Winter is constant darkness; summer is constant light… it's just the way of the Arctic Circle. The artisan dress shops across the street are gingerbread houses with deep sloped roofs, and beyond, nothing but glaciers and mountains.

I kick snow off the bricks, clearing a path. I gather my dress in a hand, hiking down the steps, but the twins shriek at me – *Caw! Caaaw!*

I roll my eyes. *Not again.*

I turn to the roof. Two crows, who I call the twins, scratch at our rooftop shingles. Ma patches our roof every autumn, and the twins love to pick at the wood plates she installs. They do it on purpose – to bother *me*.

I grit my teeth. I've told them to stop coming here. *Uh!*

Ma calls my name from inside, sweeping the floor. "Sunday – will you take care of them?"

Of course. It's my job to scare away the crows. *Ugh.* Nothing Ma does will make them leave. I fix my hands on my hips. "You know I'm really not in the mood this morning," I scold. "Do you see me coming to *your* nest and ruining things?" One of the crows tilts his head at me mockingly, and the other cackles.

I set my jaw. "If you don't leave now, I'll set the apothecary's dog on you."

The twins screech and chortle. They hop on the patched shingles, scratching them with their talons. They meet my gaze with a challenging stare; their beady eyes widen and they twist their necks at me with a stiff, insane gaze.

Taunting me.

"You think this is a joke, don't you?"

The twins snicker. They bob their heads and pounce on a shingle, prying it loose.

"Fine." I gather a few pebbles from the steps. I fling them at the twins –*one, two*– and they strike the tiles right by their talons.

Caw! Caaaw!!

The twins flap wildly, taking off into the air until they're nothing but smears in the dark sky.

Finally...

An arctic wind tunnels through the street and cotton-ball snow sticks to the gray sleeves of my coat. A Svalbard poster flaps in the breeze on a nearby lamppost. I step down from the brick steps into the foggy street. I brush my fingers along the cold dry paper.

Of course they're *auditions*, not applications, since no one knows how one person is picked over the other or why. But everyone knows that whoever goes to Svalbard becomes these things of myth – like Thomas Edison with his new lightbulb. Or Da Vinci, one of the best Artisans of all time. Pa told me, years ago, that Animalia teaches you the secrets of human and animal behavior – how to speak with authority and understand your place in the dominance hierarchy. He said Cleopatra was Animalia, she ruled an empire by understanding the secrets of human behavior.

Pa said he had so much fun at Svalbard, everyone in Animalia became family to him.

I slide my hand away from the paper and my chest sinks. If only I stood a chance.

If I could learn to be Animalia… It would be like… like I could learn about Pa, too.

A machinist hot-air blimp rumbles overhead, gliding over the northern mountains, carrying professors to Svalbard, no doubt. Wind whistles between the glaciers and – a faint *whispering*. Strange… I glance over my shoulder, toward the sound, but the cobblestone road is empty.

…Odd.

The little hairs on my arms prickle – no – someone is watching me. Definitely. Somewhere close. I tilt my head, listening with every nerve in my back: A winter owl cries on the church steeple, a rat scampers across the alley. I turn, slowly, into the fog, toward a patch of shadowed forest down the way. A gray, shapeless mass absorbs all my attention there, in the tree-line. The morning breeze swirls the pine boughs.

Someone is there…

The slanted edge of a skirt steps out from the tree-line, followed by her elegant sloped neck. A white waterfall of hair spills over her delicate shoulders, a snow tiger trails behind her and touches its nose to her hand: She's from Svalbard. Animalia.

The woman walks between snow-covered shops, closer. I glance over my shoulder – but we're alone in the street. Holy heaven – she's an angel, a moving piece of art, with soft cheeks and a pale blue dress swept back with a lace bustle. She passes and glances at Grom – and me – and smiles gently.

She slips into the fog and I stare at the place where her head used to be.

To be Animalia, like her… She must be in town for the auditions.

Don't dream. People like her are one in a million.

I breathe deep until my heart calms. You'll never be like her. I hold Grom close and step through the narrow brick-maze paths to the town bakery. I duck into the warm little shop and the scent of crushed cinnamon surrounds me. My gut hollows. My stars, if only Ma had been a baker.

I press my hand to the pastry glass and pour over the breads for sale.

The bakery boy slides apple-fritters on a tray. "So what – you're not getting ready for the auditions, like everyone else?" He wipes his hands on his apron. "You scared or something?"

"I – uh – hadn't decided yet…. Did you audition?"

"Last year everyone in my class did. None of us made it. But it's better that way. Svalbard is a cursed place, mind you. Sure we hear more about it, since we're the closest town to their compound or whatnot. But no one who goes there comes back the same. It changes you, changes the way your mind works." He says it with thirst in his mouth, like he hates and loves the very thought of Svalbard. I heard he auditioned for Artisan with his bakery cakes, and they dismissed him before he could even show them all. Poor fellow.

I point to the honey loaf, it's an apothecary-infused bread with warming herbs; clove and nutmeg to ward off the winter colds Ma gets. The baker-boy bags up the bread, "That'll be four kroner."

"I thought it was three." Inside my dress pocket, I rub Ma's three bronze kroner.

Blazes, Ma. We can't even afford one loaf.

"Is the sign wrong?" the boy turns his head around the glass case.

"No it isn't wrong." *We're just too poor to buy bread.* "I only forgot my coinpurse at home." I turn to leave and stop at the front door. "And, by the way, my father went to Svalbard. He was Animalia. So it can't be that bad, can it?"

"Yeah and look what happened to him," the boy scowls, leaning far over the glass, "he went and got himself killed by some animal."

My chest squeezes and I flick my head away. I rush out to the snowy street and force myself to suck in air, deep – he might as well've kicked me in the gut. I take the long way back through the alleyways, to avoid people.

I rub my chest. *Breathe. Just breathe.*

I swipe a tear from my chin with my mitten. *Don't think of Pa. Don't.*

Dawn breaks through the blue glaciers in the nearby mountains; a tiny crack of gold lights the sky. I keep my head down and turn the corner – their brown shoes come into view before their faces and I bump into two girls. "Oh, sorry," I mutter.

The girls are a few years older than me, and styled with nicer dresses. One girl is tall with thick flowing hair and the other is lanky with narrow features. "Oh look," the lanky one nudges the tall girl, "she's holding that newt again. What did I tell you about the newt?"

They laugh.

Not again. I can't do this again.

"Don't you think it's a bit *dirty* to have a newt, Sunday?" the tall girl talks down to me, like I should take beauty tips from her.

"Let me pass." I rub my nose.

"Oh, she's crying," the lanky girl says with fake-care.

"You probably heard I'm having a party tonight, for the auditions, and didn't invite you," the tall girl rakes her hand through her hair. "You know, I'd invite you, but you'd only bring everyone down," she flourishes her hands around my head. "We can't have all this sadness around us."

"No, we can't," the shorter girl laughs. "It'd be a waste of space, wouldn't it?"

"We wish we could help you." The tall girl half-smiles. "But you've always been this way, haven't you?"

I stare hard at their leather shoes on the frosty cobblestone. Tears burn in my eyes. I keep my head down, stiff, and I hate myself for saying nothing; I hate myself, hate myself, hate myself.

"Ah, there you are," a woman's voice lulls, calm.

Chills tickle my neck.

The girls' eyes widen at the woman, somewhere behind me.

A purr rumbles beside me and a tall white tiger brushes its head along my dress. Something light settles on my shoulder, wraps around me like a shawl – a woman's delicate gloved hand. *What in the* – a glossy curtain of white-and-brown hair spills over my shoulder, followed by the scent of lavender and arctic mint. I turn to her: It's the Animalia woman from the street earlier, the angel. Her icy gaze shifts from me to the two girls, "Tell me, what were you girls saying?"

"N-nothing," the lanky girl splutters.

The woman's presence is jarring, like a glacier – her fixed, cat-like gaze narrows on the girls, silence stings my ears, she tilts her head – "Then move AWAY."

Her voice rumbles in my chest – one thousand voices in one – and it's strange – like her mouth moves to a different shape than her actual words.

The girls stumble away down the road, afraid, like prey animals.

Gone at last, thank God. I sigh.

Her cheeks soften into a smile. "Don't resent them for it," her voice is gentle again, calm. "They're only afraid of you. It's in their instincts. They can't help it."

"Oh..."

She steps down the narrow alley and I move with her, tucked under her arm. "It's early and still dark out. How about I walk you home."

THREE

THE AUDITIONS

We walk through the foggy, twisting streets. Her white-gloved hand rests on my shoulder, light as a dove. She holds her head high, like she owns the town and everything in it. I swear. She's like someone from legend – someone people dream about being but know is impossible. Our feet crunch the snow. We pass the same buildings I've known all my life, but next to her everything is worn and old. The white tiger sniffs and ducks into random corners, he's not wild, exactly, but he definitely isn't tame.

"I wasn't crying because of those girls," I break the silence. "Those girls aren't my friends."

Her heart-shaped lips pull into a smile. "Are you auditioning today?"

"I thought maybe I shouldn't." I bite my lip. "For Ma."

"No?" the woman raises a slender brow. "And why is that?"

"Ma says Animalia is dangerous. She says Pa would be alive, if he hadn't been Animalia."

"I see," she stops at the brick awning to the candle shop and pauses with her head tilted at me. Over her shoulder, in the distance, two strange men stand huddled by an alley. They're dressed modern, like they're from a city. One, oddly, has a bowler hat with a red rose pin. They *followed* her.

"Did you know," I lean in close to her, whispering, "those two men are watching you, just there."

"I know," she mutters, without looking, "they've followed me for several days now. Don't worry. They won't bother you."

"Oh…"

"I knew Håkon Gråe, at Svalbard."

What the…

My mouth falls open. "You knew… Pa?"

Her eyes dim. "You pick up on behaviors, patterns, don't you? You see things others don't see. You notice when something is out of the pattern."

"…But I'm just –"

"Would you be happy if you stayed here, in Sjosburg?" Her expression is firm. Snowflakes stick to her hair in a glowing halo. Her expression isn't condescending, per se – but sharp. The question is a test.

"If I stayed…" my heart sinks. "*No*," I say, stronger. "I want to be Animalia, like Pa was. I've always wanted that."

Her expression raises slightly, like she approves. Her gloved hand slips forward and she helps me up the stairs to the brick awning – but before I can thank her, she slips back into the fog.

Gone again. Like some ghost.

I stare at the fog where the tiger's tail swishes out of sight. *Maybe she thinks I could be –*

No. I shake my head. *She was just being nice.* I step back into our shop, closing the heavy door behind me. I lean back onto the door and stare at the vaulted ceiling – fresh-dipped candles dangle from the rafters. I clutch Grom to my chest. He bites at the collar of my coat, puncturing it with his little teeth… *She knew Pa.* Some spark of fire sizzles in my chest.

I step out of my boots and dart into the backroom, shutting the door behind me so I sit on the stool, alone in the shadows. I light a candle and watch it flicker in the tiny workroom.

She went to Svalbard with Pa… No, she looked younger than he would be. Much younger. That doesn't even make sense. I shake my head. *Ugh.* People like her aren't real. I can't be like her, even if I tried. And even if I was accepted – someone has to take care of Ma and keep the shop open.

I lift a wick and dunk it into the hot wax pot, holding it there.

I could audition.

It won't reverse what you did to Pa.

I flick my head. Don't–listen–to–that–voice… Blazes! That blamed voice again – it's like a monster. It whispers again, deep in my chest: *You killed your father.*

I clench my jaw at my own reflection in the window. She won't distract me today.

I dip the candle into the hot wax pot and hang it to dry with the others. My reflection in the window blurs with the frost outside, making my face a slant moon – she leans toward me, whispering: *You're a monster.*

Ugh. I shake my head and dip another candle into hot beeswax – *dip* – and cold water – *dip* – hot wax.

You know what you are.

Don't react – she'll only get worse. Steam blurs her face in the glass. The scent of honey froths in the air. "You're wrong," I drape the candle into the wax-mold. "No one thinks I'm…"

… a secret monster.

I miss the pot edge and hot water splashes my hand. *Blazes!*

I pat my hand with a cloth. *For Saint John's sake, Ma.* Can't we get a boiler that works?

I click the machinist boiler off and sag over the workdesk – I frown through the window to Sjosburg beyond: Brick chimneys and oil-lamps line the empty autumn street, dusted with snow and pine needles. That Svalbard woman is probably gone now. Gone forever.

Ma's muffled voice echoes along the floorboards between my bare feet, talking to someone in the storefront. The day's first customers must be in.

I wipe my hands on a dry rag and hang it on the hook.

If she knew your secret –

"But she doesn't," I snap back at my reflection. "I'm fine."

But if she knew –

But she doesn't!

She would hate you.

I squeeze my eyes shut… Breathe. Just breathe.

She'd rather you were dead, and not Pa.

"Stop it!" I shriek at her.

Sunday glowers back at me in the glass.

No. Not Sunday. Not me. The monster.

I swat a stray tear from my chin. I tie off the candle wicks.

I could still audition… I could try.

By my dipping station, I pasted an old photograph of Pa holding me as a child in the snow; he opens my hand and fills it with flowers, to feed a deer. Pa told me, on that day, not to be afraid of animals. That animals can sense your fear. But he also said they can sense love, too. Pa was everything Animalia should be; bold, smart, caring for animals. He had these wide, strong features. Blondish-hair, golden-blue eyes, like mine, and still this sort of graceful way about him.

You'll never be like Pa. And you'll never be Animalia.

"…Sunday, love?" Ma calls me from the storefront.

My eyes go wide. No.

No, no, no.

"Sunday, you all right?"

Hide Pa's picture, quick. I set a bucket in front of Pa's photo – Ma is so blasted sensitive – any stupid memory of him will make her cry.

The steam-boiler *clicks* noisily and powers off.

"Love, is that you? Did you get the bread?"

No, Ma. We don't have enough money.

I pinch my fingers to my nose. "… No, but I'll pick some up later."

Ma's elegant swan neck rises from nowhere, turning the corner beneath the stairs into the backroom. Inky, mushroom-brown hair drapes her face in a permanent frown. "You all right, dove?" Her hazel eyes gaze through me. "I heard a sound…"

"It's nothing," I lie.

Liar.

"You look tired."

I nod at the wood floor between her worn shoes. "I'm fine. I – *uh* – decided I'll audition today after all."

I did?

I don't remember deciding that.

She half-smiles, "That's great honey… Well, we should get you ready then, shouldn't we?"

"Yeah…"

"I'm glad you'll audition. You worked so hard to train Grom."

I duck under candle reams – she reaches out to hug me and I fall into her thin arms. She whispers in my ear. "I'm proud of you, no matter what."

She hikes up the stairs to the attic and I follow her. The dirty hem of her dress bobs as her heels kick the cotton bustle. For heaven's sake – I shouldn't be doing this. Blazes! I'll humiliate myself again. My hands tremble. This blasted audition. We pass my small bed and my old sketches of Animalia alumni that line the wall – Saint Francis of Assisi, surrounded by birds. And Cleopatra, of course, with a royal headdress and a dark cat.

I sit on the stool and watch Ma's reflection in the long dressing mirror. We're an odd pair.

"We better enjoy the day, it only happens once…" Ma combs through my stringy hair with her fingers. She twists the strands into a braid down my back.

"Thank you." I mutter. "For helping me."

"Mmm."

The monster claws in my mind: *You're a burden on her.*

"I – I think I might have a chance. To be Animalia."

Her dark brows draw up in a glazed-over look. "Course you do."

I bob my foot on the old stool.

"Feeling nervous?"

"No."

I glance sideways at the monster's reflection, reappeared in the attic window – her cheeks sink in – hollow, like she's eating me alive: *Pa is dead because of you.*

I snap my gaze away. She can't distract me. Not before my audition.

"You have no reason to be nervous," Ma squeezes my shoulders, her eyes are sad. "If your father made it into Animalia, maybe you can too. It's possible."

…It's possible.

It's possible. Possible.

I stand. Ma tugs my corset and ties it down in a clean line. She leans over my shoulder and fastens the layers of stiff yellow fabric over my narrow hips. It's the nicest dress I own but the fabric is cheap – it snags as Ma pulls it. I bought it with my card game winnings, for special occasions, but if I'm accepted into Svalbard I'd get an allowance, which I could send home to Ma... To help keep the shop open.

Ma hums and buttons down the back of my dress. My chest squeezes. She's so good to me. I shouldn't want to leave home. But I do.

"You're so quiet. I don't think I've ever seen you this focused."

"I'm not focused," I splutter, and blush. Stupid.

Outside the attic window, on the cobblestone street, girls chatter:

"Five years is so long to be away if you're accepted, though."

"It's only thirty miles north. You can come back over summer."

"But the school in the middle of *nowhere*."

"Imagine the professors. From all over the world."

"I'm auditioning for Artisan, how 'bout you?"

Ugh. I frown down at my yellow dress; I'm a ragdoll next to the girls in the street – my dress hangs with gaps around the shoulders. It's all a waste anyway. I'll only get rejected, like everyone else. But Ma never talks about that, she always encourages me. My stupid dreams.

Once, the local tutors told her I was 'out-of-touch.'

They're probably right.

At school, during lunchtime, sometimes I walk along the graveyard meadow, and if I'm lucky I find all kinds of animals there. A pair of jackrabbits lives by Pa's gravestone, and for a while I fed them bits of corn husk, so they'd learn to trust me. Now they run to me whenever I'm near. They have the softest ears. Last week I spotted them following me through town. Sneaky little rascals.

Ma kisses my cheek with thin, cold lips. She pulls the last layer of my dress overhead and fluffs the bustle so it falls in a waterfall down the back of the yellow skirt. Grom coils himself into a bright green curl in my arms. I make the sign with my free hand for him to turn and dance, instead he bites my finger playfully.

"Stop that," I scold him.

He bites harder, eyeing me; a challenge.

Little monster. He has the temper of an alligator.

I roll my eyes, "Stop biting."

He leaps to the dresser, toward a flickering candle. He presses his snub nose into the melty wax and warms himself by the flame. *Good grief.* I shake my head at him. He loves fire. It's his second-favorite thing after Ma's fake gemstone earring – I've tried taking it from him but it's become his plaything. He scampers to the fake purple gemstone, holds it secure in his tiny hands, and rubs it with his flat nose again and again.

"Don't get him excited. You'll wear him out," Ma fastens the last layers of my bustle. "Let him relax. He knows what to do. There – you're ready. We better head out."

"Right…"

I slide Grom into my arms and hurry down the stairs to the candle shop.

Ma ducks into her room and slaps around her bed, searching for something.

My gut dips. Not again… She's looking for chloral – ever since Pa passed, she's addicted to it. She snatches the small blue bottle from her bedsheets and sniffs it – her shoulders soften, she makes a sound, almost a purr – and takes a swig with her head thrown back, like it's whiskey. Ugh. In her bedroom, antlers hang from the walls… all of Pa's old things. She just keeps them there.

"Can we go?" I press. "We'll be late."

She whips her head back, chugging. *For heaven's sake.*

Ma closes shop and we leave, walking down Main Street arm-in-arm. I frown down the narrow street. The sunrise splashes white-gold onto the mountains above us, it catches the light sideways on the icy sloped roofs, making them blue. Grom sleeps in my coat pocket – *please let him be ready.*

"…You know, Ma… If I get accepted, I could use the allowance from Svalbard to help keep the shop open."

Ma clenches a hand behind her back.

She knows I'm right. She needs me to help run the shop – without me we'd run out of money, who knows what would happen.

"We're lucky to live so close to Svalbard, aren't we?" Ma gives me a weak smile. "Maybe the selection committee will recognize your name and they'll know your father was alumni, and it'll increase your chances."

Church bells echo through the main square and Apothecary Bjørn turns a blind corner and bumps into Ma. "Excuse me, Ms. Kjersti, and Sunday," he bows his wavy brown head and his tall body bends far over. His curious, ocean-eyes meet mine – and a glimpse of a gold necklace dangles beneath his grey cloak – along with a bundle of dried lavender, and a handkerchief embroidered *'J. S.'*. His rosy cheeks pull into a strange smile, but he breaks away and drifts down the street into his brick apothecary shop.

…Odd.

He looked happy about something. Probably some new potion he's making. He's a Svalbard apothecary, after all, he's like magic. He could heal a broken tree if he wanted.

Ma and I hike up the creaking wood steps into our small local school. Silence rings in my ears. I stare at the wide auditorium doors at the end of the hall where auditions are held. Ma squeezes my hand. We walk.

Breathe.

You can do this.

Girls wait in line ahead of me, ready to enter the audition room. They're all so put-together, better than me; lace petticoats and bright colors, wide-brimmed hats. An aged woman – a volunteer with the school – sits slumped-over in a chair outside the auditorium door. She says, blandly; "When you enter, a timer will start. You'll have two minutes to present to the committee. Just walk to the 'X' on the floor. If the bell sounds, exit the stage."

"Right," I say.

"Two minutes?" Ma mutters, "How can they decide?"

The woman looks away.

The girls in front of me tap their leather shoes and squeeze their arms. It's obvious what programs they'll audition for by the way they act; a girl in a pink dress holds an art portfolio, she hums to calm herself – she'll audition for Artisan. Behind her, the toughest girl in town clenches her hands into fists, her face turns red with nerves – Warbringer. The girl behind her carries a small glass terrarium and fiddles with the plants inside, arranging the details perfectly – Apothecary. The artisan-looking girl gives me side-eyes, like she's noticed me staring at her. I flick my gaze away. It doesn't matter, anyway. They aren't my friends.

I'd rather be friends with animals.

The line grows shorter – my gut clenches and Ma pulls my sleeve, "You know, you don't have to go in. If you don't want to."

"I'm fine. I'm going."

Be brave. It's possible. Possible.

One girl enters through the door, then another. They return to the hall again and they look deflated, like something's been stolen from them. Even their bright colors are dull.

Not encouraging.

A boy mutters behind me. I turn: It's Viktor. He rakes a hand through his wavy brown hair. He whispers to himself, rehearsing what he'll say about the little machine he made. Of course Viktor wants to be Machinist, he's a math person. I turn, to wish him luck –

"– Sunday Gråe," the volunteer calls. "It's your turn."

I freeze. My eyes go wide. I'm not ready. I'm not.

My heart sinks beneath the dusty wood floor.

You can do this. You can.

My pulse pounds in my ears. I step through the dark doorway and my legs prickle, numb.

They'll hate you.

I step over creaking floorboards, into shadows.

You aren't meant for Svalbard.

Focus. Focus.

I brush past red velvet curtains onto the stage. A spotlight shines on an 'X' on the wood floor; I stand on it and the auditorium swallows me in darkness. I blink into the shadowed theater seats, at the glint of shapes in the first row – the silhouettes of the selection committee. Sweet heaven. My heart twists up my throat.

It's them.

At their table below, candles flicker beside parchment and inkwells. They mark numbers beside a list of names.

A Svalbard woman with a slicked-back bun frowns at me. Orange candlelight glints off her jade earrings and the beading on her kimono. "Program you're auditioning for?"

Oh no. She sounds strict.

"Um… Animalia?" My cheeks warm. It came out like a question. Stupid.

The committee mutters among themselves. The five of them shift under robes and pearls, silk neck-scarves. Like royalty.

A woman at the panel sits straighter, half-concealed in shadows. She adjusts herself with a white wool shawl around her shoulders and folds her delicate hands under her chin, studying me: She's the Animalia woman from earlier, the angel.

Adrenaline pumps in my ears.

Now. Now is the time.

Grom pokes his little green head out of my chest pocket, blinking at the spotlight above. I almost apologize for him and I pull his salamander-body out of my pocket. I spill him onto my palm and I pinch my fingers above as a sign for him to dance.

Grom licks his lips absently.

The artisan man on the committee clears his throat, loudly.

Grom reaches for my finger with tiny green hands, confused.

Tick… tick… tick… The clock on their table counts down each moment lost.

"Please," I whisper to him, and make the gesture for him to dance again.

Tick... tick...

Grom half-turns, half-convinced by me.

...Tick.

Grom watches my hand shaking and my eyes water and his scaly head tilts, sad for me. He scampers up my arm to my shoulder and licks my cheek, giving kisses.

The animalia woman stands and white hair swishes down her back. "Might you introduce us," she says, slowly, "to this creature?"

"Oh," I come closer so she can see. "This is Grom. He's a pygmy newt."

"Is Grom your pet?" Her shadowed face is framed with lace and pearls.

It's a trick question. It has to be.

"Well... Grom is – a friend."

Her hazy gaze narrows on me – not with condescension, per se, but assumption; "Animalia doesn't *own* animals. We don't *train* them. We are caretakers of the natural world. Cultivators. Protectors. You can measure a person's character by whether or not they are attentive to the needs of their animal. Remember that, Sunday."

"...Yes, ma'am."

She leans in, toward Grom and into the light, revealing her full, angelic face; studious cat-like eyes, dark eyelashes, and silky white-and-brown hair which falls like curtains around her high cheekbones. She holds a delicate wool shawl around her bare shoulders and sweeping blue dress. Behind her, the snow tiger lays on the floor, chewing its paw.

Her eyes touch mine – I hold my breath – but she sinks back into the shadows –

Bzzzz!

The brass bell rings and I jump.

Grom crawls down my sleeve and into my pocket.

The auditorium blurs. My heart pumps in my neck.

I fumble down the stage and pass Viktor in the shadows. He's ghostly pale and stiff, like a boy caught doing something wrong.

The auditorium door squeals, closing behind me and I can't help it – I stop the door with my foot and peer back through the crack, watching Viktor's miniature train machine roll around him on the stage. The square flaps turn over one-by-one so the train turns yellow, but one of the flaps gets stuck over a wheel and the little train falls head-first. Viktor scrambles to prop it up, but the bell sounds and he runs offstage, passes me, and pushes through the door.

I step through, into the bright light of the hall, and hug Ma.

"How'd it go?" Ma turns me by the shoulders so I face her.

"…Don't know," I shrug. "Nothing went right, really. But, somehow, it was good."

She nods firmly. She holds me and her brown hair falls in waves by my cheek. I rest my head on her shoulder and stare at the yellowed, curling wallpaper behind her.

Odd that behind these walls, sit the most elegant people in the world.

Ma holds me by my shoulders and places her forehead on mine. "I'm so proud of you."

I squeeze her hands on my shoulders. "I think…" I bite my lip. "…I could be Animalia." My chest stings. I shouldn't have said it out loud.

Saying it is like making a promise. It gives hope, makes it real.

Ma kisses my forehead. Her eyes shine and it warms me.

It's possible. I could be Animalia.

Ma takes my hand and we head out, into the snowy street, but she hesitates, "I'm going to go ask Apothecary Bjørn for something – I'll meet you back home later. You should go have fun. Celebrate with your friends."

My *friends*?

Well… I have the animals.

"Right, see you later." I wander down Main Street, passing bakery stands from the afternoon farmer's market. The scent of the street lingers in the breeze, just-baked sourdough bread and smoked cinnamon buns. I use one of my kroner to buy a stack of corn cakes from a market stand and tear little pieces, feeding Grom.

I drift off toward the meadow, outside town, and all is quiet.

I kneel down in the blanket of snow. Alone, at last. I close my eyes and let the sun roll over the sky until it dances low on the horizon. I sense – without needing to look – the blue and orange light of the sunset through the mountain glaciers. The tender underside of a butterfly's wings as she settles on a cold rock. The quick hop of a rabbit. The cry of a winter eagle overhead.

I tear pieces of corncake and extend them out in front of me.

I close my eyes and tilt my head, an eagle screeches in the breeze – the wind turns, suddenly, and the eagle swoops down fast and perches on my arm.

I hold my arms out, stiff. The eagle adjusts his grip on my arm with heavy talons – his dark glossy eyes find mine – he pecks at the corncake in my hands and flaps away with huge, heavy wings.

I rip a piece of corncake and lunge forward – white rabbits come around me, eating from my hands. A doe emerges from the tree-line, and her faun – they sniff the air, drawn to the scent of corncakes. I feed them, speaking sweetly to them as they eat – the doe licks my palm clean and the animals return to the tree line, retreating to their homes for the night. The sun sets gold and hazy on the meadow, casting everything in warm light.

But behind me, I sense, not the steps of an animal, but the heavy steps of someone uninvited, walking behind me into my delicate world. I turn to him and the weight of his gaze is heavy on me. He drops his basket and scrambles awkwardly to pick it up: Viktor.

"You were spying on me!"

"I swear, no," he splutters, "I'm only here to fetch berries for jam. It's one of my chores."

I fold my arms. "Berries are on the *other* side of town."

"Yeah but they been picked o'er."

Ugh.

I kind of glare at him, and soften, slowly. It's not his fault, I guess…

My hair falls around my shoulders in loose stringy waves. The pins have pulled loose, and I was never one to fuss about the way I look, anyway. He probably thinks I'm some sort of wild person but who cares.

He stands there, watching me with this cautious look. "…Word 'round town is people saw you walking with that Animalia woman."

I flip my head back to him. "So?"

"So be careful of her, Sun. They say she steals men's hearts and buries them alive. She's a killer."

"That's a load of nonsense."

He steps closer. "I'm just trying to look out for you."

He watches me, still. In the dusk light his skin looks gold and his eyes sharp blue. White skeleton leaves stick to his grey wool coat. "You know," he mutters, almost to himself, "I think you're the most beautiful person I ever knew."

I shake my head at him. Teasing, always. "What do you want?"

He doesn't laugh. He's serious. "…Nothing."

His expression is soft, his body relaxed. His cheeks are splotchy red. He reaches for my hand, kind of clumsy. His fingers touch mine – they're cold, dry. Wispy snowflakes drift between us and swirl.

My heart flips and I turn away, leaving him behind.

I walk down the meadow and rub my hand. I don't know why – it feels like the end of something. A lump rises in my throat. Stupid. I don't care what he thinks.

Not for a second. Not at all.

I wander into the twisting brick streets of town. I duck into the bakery and pick out two honey-coated loaves of bread. The sweet kind Ma likes for breakfast, toasted with jam. I buy them with my card game winnings.

I cradle the bread in one hand, and Grom in the other, and approach the awning of our candle shop, but something white flaps in the wind, fastened to the side of the door. I step up to it and pull the crisp white envelope out, turning it over: It has my name on it – scribbled with an elegant hand: *Sunday Gråe.*

My heart thumps in my throat. *My stars.* This is it.

I dart into the shop. All is dark except for the fireplace light and a few flickering candles on the living-room table. Ma must be in bed.

Perfect.

I spill Grom onto the table and crouch over the envelope. I rip it open.

Ms. Sunday Gråe,

Svalbard School for International Excellence is pleased to offer you admission to our Animalia program. Animalia is a select program offering the finest education of animals and living species in the world. It is a five-year program with students from all across the globe, and should not be entered unless all five years will be completed. Upon completion, all Animalia students will be admitted into the acclaimed Svalbard Alumni Society, and will have our full support in their endeavors regarding the conservation and cultivation of the natural world.

Please note: Scholars in this program are allowed one animal companion to join them as their sole responsibility.

Please see the included list of supplies. You can collect these items from your local apothecary.

Warm regards,

Dean Justine Seraphim
Dean of Svalbard – Head of House for Animalia

FOUR

THE THINGS OF PA

I sit by the fireplace in my nightgown and stare at the hissing blue flames.
I knew I'd make it.
I smear a tear from my nose.
I knew it.
Grom sleeps, curled like a green lizard in my lap.

Ma yawns loudly down the hall and bumbles toward me, drunk with exhaustion. "You won at cards?" She stumbles to the bread on the table – with one hand she rips a chunk from the loaf and folds it into her mouth, with the other she pats my head, "Good girl."

I turn my head away.

She chews, slowly. "…What's on your mind?"

Pressure builds in my chest. I stare hard at her bare feet beside me.

"You knew I'd be Animalia," my voice is thin. "You knew I'd be accepted. But you let me doubt myself."

She holds the sides of her nightgown, bends over and sits by me on the cushions, facing the dim fire. It casts a sideways, red glow on her slender face. Shadows fill her hollow cheeks. "So perceptive, little Sun. Just like your father." The fire spits and crackles. She hugs her legs to her chest, holding herself in a ball. She balances her chin on a kneecap and her eyes go distant and glassy. Her silence is a betrayal. "…Sunday, by the time you were five you knew what birds were outside your window by their song. When you were six, you'd tell me what animals were around by their tracks in the snow. When you were eight you could pick up details no one could see – a feather, scratch marks, a scent in the wind – you'd tell me how animals behaved, just by a walk in the forest. That's uncommon, even for Animalia. So yes, I knew. And now you know what you are," she shrugs. "You're just like your father."

I pinch my brows. "It's like you aren't even happy for me."

"It's not that – it's just," her thin lips tense. "Animalia can be dangerous. Sometimes I think, maybe your father would still be with us, if he never went to Svalbard. He was always going out into the woods alone. I thought so many times it was dangerous, but of course I never said anything. Maybe, if he'd been a metal-worker, or some other profession… I just want you to be safe. That's all."

I frown at my hands. Talking about him is like talking about some miracle – not the fact he's gone – the fact he existed at all. He was a miracle out of all men. He was both powerful and kind – *both* at the same time… Being loved by him – it changed Ma. And he loved me enough I swear I can still hear his voice sometimes in my head… but I hear the monster more.

"Here," Ma loosens the clasp of her necklace and lowers it into my hands, "you should have his old key, take it with you to school." I absently trace my fingertips over the cold silver ridges of Pa's old key which Ma looped onto a necklace chain. She found the key in Pa's overcoat hours after he died. Who knows what it's meant to open. "It'll remind you of him."

I clutch the key to my heart.

I lean in and rest my cheek on her knobby shoulder. Her silky brown hair fumes with gardenia and chimney smoke. I close my eyes. She plays with my hair, running her fingers through the frayed ends. God I love her so much.

That night, I dream of Pa.

I sprint, slapping around in the dark forest, leading Ma to where I last saw him – where Pa was attacked.

Everywhere I look the forest twists into a maze. Haunted creatures sit in the branches above, watching me. I turn, pulling Ma through the forest. Dr. Laszlo, our old town apothecary, trails behind us like a huge brown bear, panting in the dark.

Pa's body lays in the snow at the bottom of a basin, bent at an off angle. We slide down the slope and kneel beside him.

Ma screams.

Blood seeps through Pa's waistcoat, into the slush. His icy fingers clutch five winter roses.

"It was a monster," I shriek. "I *saw* it. Like a wild dog. It attacked me and Pa saved me from it. And I ran."

Dr. Laszlo stands above me, frowning behind a thick mustache. His gaze sharpens on me, he adjusts his gold spectacles. "Is that *really* what you think?"

I nod hard.

He purses thin lips at me. "It wasn't a monster, little one. There are no bite marks from any animal. He must've slipped on a rock and hit his head. This other sharp rock pierced his gut, when he fell."

"No!" I hold Pa's cold hand. I pull myself close to him and place my head on his chest. I listen for a heartbeat… But his eyes are closed, his face pale.

"It's our anniversary tomorrow," Ma flicks her head away, like she's in physical pain. She hugs herself, as though to keep from bursting. She slaps a hand over her nose. "To think he'd gone to get me roses."

"NO!" I shriek. "It was the *monster! I saw it!*"

"The fear is confusing her," Dr. Laszlo mutters to Ma. "She's creating things in her mind – monsters and imagined things. Guilt is hard to live with. If she hadn't wandered out at night, your husband would not have gone out looking for her, and slipped and hit his head."

"But it was the monster…" I beg. "It was *here*."

"The monster is psychological," Laszlo tells Ma. "She's in shock. Confused."

I imagined it…

"Fine…" Ma sniffs, and speaks soft enough so she thinks I can't hear. "But please don't say that – we'll tell the town it was a monster that killed him. Some animal. I don't want her to live with this."

"Very well," Dr. Laszlo agrees, and kneels down to me. He holds my hand with two of his. His brown eyes are kind – he has glowing bronze skin, and a special warmth about him. He pats my shoulder. "Remember that, Sunday. It was the monster, not you."

No one else but me.

"The monster is to blame," he holds my shoulder.

I am a monster.

"That's right. Only the monster."

A secret monster.

FIVE

APOTHECARY BJØRN

I wake and bolt upright. I sit in a nest of cushions by the fireplace. Soft morning light shines on the frosty windows. My acceptance letter is crumpled in my hand. I curl over and pinch my fingers to the bridge of my nose – *ugh*. What I'd give to kill that memory.

Grom sleeps in the nook of my arm. He holds his tail and his scaly belly rises and falls with each breath. My little Grom.

I place him on a pillow and fold the blanket. I have only one day to find the supplies I need for Svalbard. One day till I make the journey to school and my life changes.

To school… Svalbard is *my* school.

I unfold the supplies list and smooth it on the low table:

ANIMALIA SUPPLIES
One ticket on the Arctic Sled to Svalbard Circle.
Sturdy boots.
A lantern.
Outer layers for snowstorms.
The animal companion of your choice.

A crystal bell.
A blue ribbon.
Gardening gloves.

<u>BOOKS BY ALUMNI</u>
"*Thinking Creative*," by Thomas Edison.
"*The Animal Kingdom and Our Kingdom*," by Her Royal Highness, Queen Victoria.
"*The Wild and the Tame: A Construct*," by Taniko Mundi.

A laugh bubbles in me. It's too good! I roll the list into my dress pocket.

"Mom, I'm going to the apothecary," I call up the stairs to her. "To get supplies for school."

I gather my bag, slide Grom into my jacket pocket, and turn to the door.

"I can come," she splutters, "I'll help."

"It's all right, I'll be back."

She knits her brows at me. "You know Bjørn is more private than Dr. Laszlo was years ago. Bjørn barely opens shop to people outside his little circle. Don't let him turn you away. If he tries to send you home, just keep asking for what you need."

"…Right."

I wade through the snow to the small apothecary shop down Main Street.

Odd that an apothecary would have anything needed for Animalia.

I stop outside the brick shop, with frosty windows and a polished wrought-iron store sign:

BJØRN'S APOTHICAS
Little green vines with red berries curl over the iron sign.

I step up to the door and knock.

Thud. Thud. Thud.

The door creaks open and a tall, composed, bohemian-styled man frowns down at me. He folds his hands over his chest elegantly; Bjørn, our new apothecary. His eyes flick to my shoes and up again and he starts to close the door, "*No-new-clients.*"

"Wait!" I press a hand to the door – I lunge, and my foot slips. I fall hard on the ice, right on my side. Bone-aching pain strikes my hip and I hold it, groaning. From the steps below I wince up at him – his face is upside-down from my view and disapproving.

"Please –" I splutter, dizzy. "You're from Svalbard."

"And-why-would-you-like-to-know?" He speaks fast, with a drag in his mouth, like he's intelligent without trying. "I don't have the drugs your mother is looking for, so sorry to you and good day."

I roll onto my knees. I must look like a beggar. "*Please.* I need supplies –"

He waves a hand, "We all need *something.*"

"Yes, but –"

He yawns, closing the door, "Find it yourself."

"*Please!* I'm going to Svalbard!"

Bjørn pauses in the door gap. His eyebrow flicks up, and he pushes the door open.

I stand and compose myself. I hand him my acceptance letter and supplies list.

He plucks the parchment and scans the list with a darting gaze. "…So you're lucky enough to have met *Justine* – the new dean."

I wipe hair from my face with my wool mitten. "Um… her name is Justine?" I wrap Grom in my jacket, but he pokes his little green head out, just below my chin, and shivers in the frosty air.

Bjørn cracks a smile at Grom. "Well come in, then. It's cold out."

My jaw drops.

It worked.

I step, slowly, through the old doorway.

Warm, dusty air fills me. Exotic plants and vines drape from the ceiling, over the stairs, around cabinets. The air fumes with lemongrass and sunshine. Colorful birds flutter in a large atrium in the back. He must've traveled all over the world. The shop is much taller than it is wide, and tiny wood drawers are stacked up the wall; drawers that must hold herbs and minerals…

My mouth hangs open. Of course he's so secretive. Something so precious; others wouldn't understand it. Bjørn turns to me and gently folds his hands across his slender chest. He chews a toothpick in the side of his mouth. His steely gaze flicks around my face. "…So what makes you think you deserve to go to Svalbard?"

I tense. "… I suppose… I don't."

His dark eyebrow flicks again. "You don't deserve it?"

I clench my hands in front of my dress. It's a trick question. It has to be. "Just yesterday I didn't even know I was Animalia."

"*Ah.* Don't know who you really are, then." He pulls the toothpick from his mouth and points it at me in a jab. "That's the problem."

"I just don't know. If I'll fit in at Svalbard."

"Sure you will," his ocean-eyes shine and he turns over his shoulder, rummaging through glass bottles. "You're Håkon's girl."

I hold my breath. "You knew Pa?"

"Of *course*. He's Svalbard alumni. You'd be hard-pressed to find alumni who haven't heard of him." He frowns over his shoulder at me as though that were obvious. "… Don't you know about your father's work?"

My cheeks go hot. "Ma doesn't talk about him much. She says Animalia can be dangerous."

Bjørn laughs, his eyes catch the light of the chandelier and creases appear around his thin cheeks. "Do you know how many poisons I've cured as a physician? The infirmities I've been exposed to. Or how many diseases the human body fights every day, *hmm?* Life is dangerous. Embrace it – if you don't, you won't live."

I press my hand into a tight ball. "But Ma always said… Maybe Pa wouldn't have died, if he wasn't Animalia. If I wasn't –"

"Stop that," he cuts. "Don't talk like them. You're a Svalbard girl now. You're not some ordinary girl in the world, as if that were so wonderful," he twirls a hand in the air, like the idea is ridiculous. "You are *Animalia.* Playing small won't help you follow his legacy, will it?"

Moisture glosses over my eyes.

Not now. Hold it together.

I lower my head.

"*Ahh...* Yes." Bjørn rubs his chin. "What happened to him was so unfortunate. They never did catch that monster who killed him, did they?"

My heart rises to my throat. I glare at the wood floor.

Don't think of Pa. Don't.

He leans onto his wood desk, inching closer. "You know, the moment I heard that story I thought something was off about it. Animalists are trained to handle dangerous predators. No. It wasn't some hog in the woods that killed him. It was different. Whatever the monster was. Different."

I am the monster.

Heat burns my forehead.

A secret monster.

Bjørn rummages through his supplies, reading bottle labels, gazing down from his long nose, "Dr. Laszlo was your town apothecary back then – so if he was there that night, then everything that could've been done to save your father was done. That can comfort us."

But not me.

I am the monster.

My throat closes. The air grows thick and hot.

Breathe. Breathe.

"Maybe Ma was right. Maybe Svalbard will be too much… Maybe it's better if I don't go."

"And maybe the sky falls," Bjørn snaps. "And maybe you're worse than everyone. And maybe you're better. And maybe that doesn't really *matter*, does it?" He steps closer, tilts his head. "And maybe it's not all about you, is it?"

"I'm sorry," I mutter. "I'm just nervous."

He sits on the side of his desk. "You know, Svalbard is not a – *safe* place." His expression darkens, "some people who go to Svalbard can't handle it – some people *are* broken by it – they become twisted in on themselves –" he taps his head with a long forefinger. "All twisted in their mind."

I am twisted in my mind.

"Some of them drop out, and use the knowledge from Svalbard to do hateful things."

I've done bad things.

"But you're Håkon's girl. Now that isn't *you*, is it?"

But it is me.

"Maybe one day you'll catch the monster that killed your father. And that will give you the confidence you're missing now, hmm?"

"I'll find the monster," I say to the floor. "I'll kill her."

Bjørn raises an eyebrow at me, like I puzzle him. He pulls out a ball-shaped, crystal bell. "Know what this is?"

I shake my head.

He chuckles. "For a girl who holds a reptile, you know very little of them." He holds out the crystal bell, sways it, and Grom's dragonesque slit-eyes follow the movement. Grom reaches for the bell with tiny green salamander hands and prods it with his nose, squeaking with delight.

"And the list said a blue ribbon," I press. "Why a blue ribbon?"

"You'll find out at Svalbard," Bjørn waves a hand and holds up a strip of blue silk fabric. "This shade of blue, this icy, light-blue. It's a calming color for many animals. It's the house color of Animalia. We'll use it today for marking Grom."

Bjørn stamps Grom's little blue collar with a fabric press, giving it the symbol of Svalbard; a mountain and crown. He withdraws an ink well and inscribes the collar; *Animalia – Omnivoria – Monstrum – Dragonia – Gråe.*

"And here –" he turns to a separate, dusty drawer, and pulls out a silky blue necklace with crystals that dangle along the band like dripping icicles. "For you as well."

My cheeks warm. I pull it from him and drape it around my neck. I catch my reflection in the mirror behind him. Crystals are expensive... I pull my hair aside and the crystals splay along the neckline. Like a queen.

Bjørn kind of smirks at me as I brush my fingers over the beautiful, jagged crystals. His deep-set Nordic eyes shine like he knows something I don't. "Here – this is a pin for Animalia. Clip it to your coat tomorrow for orientation – so it's easier for the professors to sort you all, at first."

I take the silver pin – it has a tree on it – but no animals. "A tree?"

"The Tree of Life. House symbol for Animalia."

I reach deep into my dress pocket for the kroner I've saved to pay him, but Bjørn swats my hand away. "Please, Svalbard will pay me. I'll have the rest of your supplies sent to you at school." His tone is warm but also says, *'we're done'*.

"Oh. Right." I stumble out the door and scuff my boot on a step.

He shuts the door behind me and I stand outside in the cold – laden with gifts.

"He was so kind," I whisper to Grom. "But he barely smiled."

SIX

THE SLEIGH TO SVALBARD

If Pa could see me now.

Ma and I wait by the sleigh stop on the edge of town where the supplies caravan comes once a week. The Arctic sleigh trail is rare and expensive, but Ma saved up the funds, just in case I got accepted. Ma waits behind me, she holds one of my heavy bags with two hands. The sun kisses her cheeks under the turquoise sky. She wears a yellow button-down business gown for the occasion. Her cheeks are flush, her eyes glint green. Her wide-brimmed hat flutters in the wind. She is a painting.

My heart rises to my throat... Leaving her. The money she scraped up for me. I ready my suitcase when someone clears their throat behind my ear.

I turn – Viktor smiles down at me. His blue eyes shine behind a rim of wavy brown hair. "You didn't think you'd see me here, did you?"

"You came to send me off?"

"I was accepted."

What? I gape at him.

"I'm going to be a real Machinist."

... Machinist? Him?

He smirks at me.

I turn away and link arms with Ma.

He leans over to my ear, "Guess we're the only smart ones in town after all."

I roll my eyes and hold Ma's arm. Still… Having him at school might be nice. Viktor looks out for me, sort of. In his own way.

"Sunday," Ma pets my hair on my shoulder, "promise you'll try to make friends at Svalbard. That you'll – leave some things behind."

Leave things… behind? "What d'you mean?"

"I just want to see you smile again. Happy." She twists my hair into a sun-kissed curl over my shoulder. "Maybe you can find your smile there."

"Sure… All right Mama."

The church bells chime – noon – crows flap from the steeple – and the sleigh convoy screeches on the ice, turning the distant corner.

I frown at the brown blur on the horizon. "You hear that?"

Ma follows my line of vision.

"It sounds like howling." My gaze sharpens on the animals pulling the sleds, "they're… wolves. Ma, see? Instead of sled dogs."

The wolves run fast – big as bears – pounding the ice toward us.

The convoy turns a corner – *screech* – and a dozen mint-blue covered sleighs slice into the ice and pull to a stop in front of us. I stumble back. The sleighs are huge, all regal with Artisan welding. The wolves pant and nudge each other lovingly.

Holy heaven. Actual tame wolves.

A stately woman with rust-colored hair and a forest-green dress steps off the helm of the largest sleigh and pushes between the wolves to me. "Right, find your house sled – each program has their own sled."

That voice… My pulse rises to my throat. She was at my audition.

She's a Svalbard professor.

She really doesn't *look* like a teacher. She's full-faced, elegant and young, with an emerald long-sleeve gown and dark pinstripe gloves. Her auburn hair wraps around her head in a pinned-up bird's nest, fastened with pearls.

I hobble closer with my suitcase. Behind the fogged sleigh windows, the silhouettes of students shift inside.

My throat tightens. *This is it.*

Ma kisses my head, hugs me, and I approach the sleigh with the Animalia symbol – the Tree of Life, so it's called. The same as the pin Bjørn gave me, fastened to my coat lapel.

I turn back to Ma. My heart flips.

The woman with auburn hair calls, "Boarding," and rings a large brass bell.

Viktor winks at me and steps into a sleigh with the symbol of a hammer: Machinist.

My gut dips. Now is the time. I pat my pockets, I have everything I need; Pa's key, extra coins… I press my hand to my breast pocket… It's empty.

My gut dips.

Grom.

I turn to Ma, wide-eyed. "Where's Grom?"

I drop my bags and search down the brick platform, and a lime-green swipe darts sideways across my vision – Grom. He climbs up the bustle of the Svalbard woman's dress.

"Grom!"

He scampers over her shoulder, drawn to the bell in her hand.

"Grom, get back here," I run to him and tug him from her sleeve, but Grom clings harder, and I have to pull his little claws from her dress cloth one-by-one until he pulls loose. "I'm so, so sorry…"

She shoots me a warning look with thin red brows, "Departing in thirty seconds!"

Ma follows me, carrying luggage. "Mom!" I reach out to her, and we load my luggage onto the sleigh. I hug her. This is it. The goodbye.

"I love you," I splutter, and step onto the sleigh.

"Five seconds!" the woman calls.

The wolves shake their manes. Bells clank on their harnesses. I grip the sleigh railing and lock the door in place behind me.

"I'll come back!" I cry over the noise. But the sleigh lurches forward and Ma's waving hand disappears behind me, into the fog.

"I know!" her voice fades into the distance, "I love you!"

I stand in the sleigh doorway, frozen. Out the window, Sjosburg falls out of sight, replaced by tundra. My chest tightens. I turn, heaving my bags up the steps, and start down the short hallway.

The sleigh interior is wood with a silver runner down the center. A boy reads on the empty bench beside me. He's a slight boy with fine, handsome features and dark hair tied up in a bun atop his head. He sits in a separate chair by the window. He has a potion pin on his lab-coat; he must be a first-year apothecary.

…Safe enough.

I slide onto the bench and sit opposite him in the small space. I pull out the circular bell and Grom hugs it.

I sneak a glance at the apothecary boy. He reads with his legs crossed and head tilted, like he's deep in thought.

Perfect.

Svalbard will be a new start. I have to make a good impression.

I slouch and frown sideways out the window – our sleigh climbs higher into the snowy mountains. I slide my hand into my dress pocket and turn Pa's old key with my fingers; it's cold and glossy. Pa would be proud. The crisp white hills smear into darker, stormy mountains. I close my eyes – visions of Pa burn into my mind:

Pa limp in the snow.

Ma rocking him in her arms.

I am the monster.

I snap my neck aside and –

Tap – tap – tap!

I jerk awake.

Someone knocks on the column next to our bench. I glance over. A round face emerges around the corner, and a short girl with curly brown hair and a toothy smile steps out. "Can I join?" she asks, loudly, and waves as though I don't see her. "I'm Animalia."

Oh no.

Her honey-brown eyes dart from Grom to me.

"Oh... fine." I pull my feet in so she won't trip through the aisle. The stout girl strides past, her face glowing, all smiles and approval, "I was looking for someone in Animalia. I couldn't find *any*. Just you. I can tell by your lizard," she squeaks, like she can't contain her joy, and I spy something tucked under her arm: a little pink butt. "What is –"

"Oh –" she stumbles. She sits across from me and turns the little pink animal around in her arms. "This is Rosie. She's a teacup pig. She's a hairless pig and won't get much bigger than this. She's my chosen animal. You know, how we each choose an animal."

The little pig blinks at me, and snorts.

"I live on a farm," the girl situates her glasses on her face as though they're too big for her. Her glasses are odd – with multiple lenses – and she swipes them off her face quickly and into her bag, like she didn't really need them for vision at all. "I'm Oria, by the way. People call me Ori. And Rosie is my pig."

"Oh."

"What's your name?" she asks, holding her little hairless pig square in her lap.

"...Sunday Gråe."

"Like the day of the week?" she says, as though I were joking.

I turn and watch the wolves run outside the window.

Make friends. Ma said try and make friends.

"Yup," I turn back to her. "That's my name."

"Oh... That's fine, Sunday is a nice name." She has this big, unashamed smile.

The Apothecary boy keeps his gaze locked on his book, but his ears flush pink. He's listening to us. His mouth parts open and his gaze floats up to me, "Sorry," he splutters, "but did you say you're Sunday *Gråe?*"

My smile dims.

His brown eyes light, kind and warm. "So you're the daughter of Håkon Gråe?"

Oh no.

My gut sinks under the bench. "…How d'you know–"

"He's the Animalist, right?" the boy adds quickly, "I'm Hikaru, by the way. I didn't mean to interrupt. It's just, you look like his pictures. Is it true he worked with tigers? He had created a whistle, apparently, which could draw animals to him. It was like – an animal whistle. Everyone in Apothecary knows him. Is it true he was killed by a monster? Did you see it? He's in my book, here –" the boy extends his textbook to me with Pa's picture and I can't – I snap my head away.

Heat fills my face. My throat closes.

Don't think of Pa. Don't.

The floor spins. *Breathe Sunday, breathe.*

I lower my head into my hands. The sleigh rails screech against the ice. I close my eyes and I'm on the forest floor again – my head pounding, screaming up into the forest branches above.

I am the monster.

I squeeze my hands until the feeling passes, and slowly sit upright again.

Oria's eyes widen at me, "woah…"

A secret monster.

The boy slowly pulls his book back to his chest, like he regrets everything.

Oria turns to the boy sharply, "You can't just ask people things like that."

"I didn't mean –"

She scowls at him, "And you're Apothecary I assume. So why are you in the Animalia sleigh?"

"Uh… The Apothecary sled is full."

Liar.

I press my thumb to the space between my eyebrows until the muscle relaxes. Ori's brown eyes flash sideways at me, like she's determined to fix me and be my friend.

Please, no. Don't even try.

My heart sinks.

Ori sets her elbows on her knees and leans over to me. "So where are you from?"

I pinch the bridge of my nose. "…Sjosburg."

"Oh that was close, then. I'm from far away. From Barbados originally, born in the Caribbean, but my family moved to Ohio, can you believe it? In America. I grew up on a farm, that's why I love animals," she leans in closer, whispering, "you know – I haven't found any other Animalia. I think we're the only first-years that got in."

I half-smile. "That can't be right."

"It's true though," she nods. "The program is really selective. I mean – secretive, too."

I pet Grom. He licks my finger and bites it with his gums.

Rosie, the teacup pig, sleeps on Ori's lap. Sweet creature – her folded pink ears flinch in her sleep. The pig has its own Animalia collar, a light-blue ribbon around its neck with the inscription; *Animalia – herbivore – porcus – swine – Moss.*

…Perhaps Ori isn't so bad.

Maybe she's good.

"Isn't it great we can keep our animals," Ori adds. "Imagine what we'll learn," she brushes curls from her face and ties her cropped hair into a sloppy bun atop her head. I open my mouth to reply but something bright shines out the window, reflecting the sun. I squint through the glare: it's a glacier. And between the glacier and the mountainside sits a compound – no – a *palace* – a stone structure from another time, with great medieval towers and a wide wall surrounding the whole massive, icy complex.

Svalbard School.

Chills prickle my legs.

Ori side-smiles at me. Holding our animals, we inch close to the frosty window beside Hikaru, who pretends to study. Ori slides down the bench right beside his chair, leaning over the side and into his space. "How can you be studying right now?" Ori snaps at him, "Look where we are."

Hikaru lowers his textbook, hides his smile, and joins us, craning his head toward the window. Side-by-side we gape at Svalbard.

My breath fogs the glass. "Is it even real?"

"I knew it'd be great," Ori and I exchange a hopeful look.

Hikaru's mouth hangs open.

"Welcome home," Ori says.

Svalbard is a fortress. A sanctuary. My home.

SEVEN

THE MONSTER BENEATH SVALBARD

Ori cranks the window handle and pries the glass open.

Arctic wind floods my hair, my coat – peppermint and pine fills me. I tilt my head out the sleigh window and Grom squeaks with delight. Cotton-ball snowflakes stick to my hair. Sweet heaven I was made for this. Grom shivers in the wind and I wrap him under the flaps of my jacket and rub him. The wolves pull the sleighs around a slope and into a gothic courtyard.

The courtyard is mythic; something out of history. Stone statues line the snowy clearing with sculptures from every culture; Alaskan carvings, Celtic knots, Indonesian totems. Great stone angels surround us, with a halo of snow around their grey heads. They frown with sad marble eyes.

The Artisans who must have set foot here… Hokusai and Da Vinci…

The frozen faces of history's figures pass overhead; emperors, queens, czars…

My gut hollows. *I'm not ready for this.*

The sleigh pulls to a halt by an arched entryway. The other students step off.

God, please help me.

I heave my suitcase in one hand and hold Grom in the other, stepping into the courtyard. I stare up at Svalbard. The school is half-covered in fog, as though floating on a cloud, like a dream, with strange towers and walkways disconnected, floating in every direction.

The sleigh-driver steps off and swats her hands on her green velvet dress. She weaves through the first-year students like a hawk and her beak-like gaze settles on us. "You two," she commands with a Welsh lilt. "You're Animalia."

I nod.

"Come up," she waves us toward the wolf pack leader – a tall wolf with a white chest. "...And you may call me Professor Anning."

"Do you teach Animalia?" Ori asks, rosy-eyed.

"Not exactly," Professor Anning says, amused. "I'm not a head of department. I teach some Animalia, some Apothecary."

Anning places a hand on each of our backs, looking over the line of wolves down the sleds. "See these wolves..."

Ori reaches out to pet one and Anning swats her hand away. "They are *not* for petting," Anning snaps. "They are not *pets*. This is a courtesy they're offering us. We keep their region clear of poachers, and they protect the compound from trespassers."

The pack leader watches me from the side. His crystalline, piercing gaze is something wild.

The wolf softens, blinks, and turns away.

"*Hmph*," Anning grunts, "I see you've met the pack leader. Come – let's get you settled."

Anning pushes open the thick front doors of the school and students pour inside.

I step slowly into the cavernous main hall. I pass under crystal chandeliers and wide renaissance paintings that stretch across the lofty walls. The main street of Sjosburg could fit into this one large, dusty room alone... It's shadowed and old. It should feel haunting, but it isn't.

It's like... standing in a faded memory.

Other girls keep together, friends already – Artisans – they move on and leave us alone.

I reach out to touch a cluster of gold-flaked candlesticks attached to the wall – every detail ornately brushed in gold paint; little leaves, cherubim… The gold is glossy and cold.

I hold my breath. Amazing. Like walking through a jewelry box from another time. I reach my hand out toward an Artisan oil painting, the detailed brushstrokes, and Anning shouts; "Do NOT touch the paintings."

I recoil my hand. My cheeks warm.

Stupid… Of course we shouldn't touch paintings.

"All right you two," Professor Anning claps her hands behind us.

Ori and I turn.

"Follow me."

We follow. We are small.

Small next to her and the stairways, sculptures, empty ballrooms…

"You are *not* to venture off alone," Anning says curtly. She turns a sharp corner and sweeps the floor with her dress. Everything she says is a rule, some law not to be broken. She's strict, but she doesn't feel like a bad person. She feels good.

We follow her under stained-glass windows. "Only select students from around the globe are chosen to study at Svalbard…" her voice echoes in the vast, open spaces. "But Svalbard is more than a school, it is a *society*. And as apprentices of the society, you are required to keep the secrets of Svalbard safe from the rest of the world," she turns to us. "Can we trust you not to speak about what you learn here?"

Ori nods passionately.

Anning walks on, leading us under archways of Egyptian hieroglyphs and Japanese calligraphy. "Svalbard has kept the world safe for centuries. When the black plague broke out, Svalbard apothecaries constructed breathing apparatuses. When the Silk Road was threatened by bandits, Svalbard warbringers kept trade moving freely. Graduates have negotiated peace, cured deadly diseases, saved animals from extinction, created world-renowned art. We keep secrets safe from a world that cannot handle them. These same secrets would destroy those who are not trained to use them." The heels of her shoes snap as she glides over the tiles, but she speaks with her jaw clenched. *Interesting...* Anning is at home here, but under pressure.

Behind Anning's back, Ori widens her eyes at me, her expression says; *this lady is so strict.*

Anning twirls a hand in the air, "Animalia is not some magic thing. Animalia teaches *empathy*. Teaches how to understand both human and animal behavior. It is psychological, examining dreams, patterns. But we are still scholars. And as you grow in your studies, you'll find your ability to comprehend animal behavior will increase. You will understand not only *what* your animals think, but *how* they think."

Anning gathers golden candles from a table. "You girls need to get settled in," she hands me the base of the candlestick, "six doors down on your right are stables, you can gather food there for your swine, Oria. Collect whatever extra supplies you need for your animals and meet me back here. I'll get the bellboy for your luggage."

... Bellboy?

She turns and her pinned-up red hair disappears around the corner.

We both stare at the space where she used to be.

"Did she say five doors down, or six?" Ori says.

"*Um...*" I bite my lip. "Six doors. On the right."

I pace down the hall, counting ornate doorways until I find the sixth one – it's a secretive, small stairway of stone – like a dungeon. "This must be it."

Ori frowns into the dark, cold stairway. "That can't be right."

"It is."

"I'm not going down there."

I set my mouth. Odd she would leave us here alone.

Maybe this isn't the right way...

No. This is right. I take one step down the stairway, then another, and Ori groans, following.

I pause. My hair stands on edge.

Something is down here. Some animal... It's too dark to see, but I...

feel them.

I leave my luggage on the step and shove my candles forward, lighting the steps down the narrow stone stairway – it's a dungeon – we have to walk single-file to fit. With each step down the air grows cold, musty.

"Can't we go back?" Ori whines. "It's so nasty here."

"Well… She said it was a stable, right?"

An animal is nearby. I'm sure…

My candle barely lights the steps below which spill into a dirt pit with a flat floor – and I strain in the dark, looking for the animal until a shadow slithers across the floor.

What in the –

Something moved.

I hold my breath.

Ori grabs my arm. "Something's down there," she hisses in my ear. "Something moving!"

I press my pointer finger to my lips, telling her, *'shhh'.*

"You go," she whispers, pushing me.

I stumble down the next step.

This was a mistake.

My heart pumps.

It's just an animal. Only an animal.

I lower myself to the dirt floor and cling to the wall. In the opposite corner, a strange slumped-over figure sits, rocking itself.

I stop. Chills prickle my spine. A worn lounge chair faces a dim-lit fireplace, casting long shadows behind it. The figure crawls into the chair, slumped at an off angle. On a side-table, a wooden mule cup sits on a porcelain tray. Sour smoke and rancid food wafts in the air. I cup my hand over my nose. My eyes water.

God, no.

Someone's *living* down here.

We shouldn't have come.

I crouch low with my candles, searching for the way back.

The man slumps over the wood chair. With one hand he toys with the mule cup, with the other he grips his neck. He thrashes his head and I stumble back, into Ori.

What the blazes...

But the man tenses. He knows I'm here.

He growls, "Is that you again, Justine?"

My heart pumps in my throat. Ori grabs the sleeves of my dress.

The man turns, his head bent at an angle, his eyes glazed over. On the floor beneath him are markings of some kind of map, symbols poured with wax all around him. In his chair, the man sits in the center of the wide wax octagon, and at every point in the octagon is some kind of item; a knife, an animal bone, a potions bottle. All the edges pull into one point in the center.

The man growls at me. "I won't tell you a thing, Justine."

Ori clings to me, whispering, "He's talking to you."

Beside my feet, a book lays open on the dusty floor, showing sketches of animals.

"JUSTINE!" he bellows. His voice is one-thousand voices in one. "I know you're there."

"I – I didn't mean to," I splutter.

The man's lip curls like a dog. "You think you can replace me."

Ori grips my shoulders.

"...Yes," I lie, softly. "I – I think that."

The man sets his jaw, like he's surprised by my answer. He softens, "You're different now," his voice is aged and thin. "Perhaps you've learned your lesson then. Fine. I'll tell you this once, what's to happen with them. I know how he thinks:

As memory fades, their trace is gone.
Both man and beast,
Tastes air like death – to an animal's mind."

I focus, memorizing the words.

Air like death...

What does that mean?

I bend down to the filthy ground, slowly, and slide the small book toward my lap. I slip it into my coat pocket.

The man's jaw snaps shut. "Don't bother me again, Justine."

Ori pulls my hand and we sprint up the stairs. I gulp for air, tripping over steps and running until we surface to the main hallway. I cough, clearing dust from my lungs.

What in the world...

"What was that?" Ori splutters.

Anning turns the corner in a sweep of green fabric and folds her arms at me, scowling. "I suppose you girls think you're clever, wandering off."

"No ma'am," Ori splutters. "We got lost. Sunday thought it was the stable, and then – it wasn't an animal, it was a person and –"

"Wait..." Anning's face narrows. "Who did you see?"

My heart floats to my throat. "A man," I mumble. "It was my fault. I talked to him. Ori didn't. It was my idea to go."

Anning purses her lips. "Didn't I say not to wander off ?"

"Yes, ma'am," we say.

Her emerald-eyes accuse me. "You are not to tell *anyone* what you saw. Is that clear?"

We nod.

She waves over someone across the hall and a slight Irish boy in a tweed flat cap hobbles over to us. He takes Ori's bags, and mine.

"Thank you," I say.

"Don't speak to him," Anning snaps. "You're not in Sjosburg anymore Ms. Sunday."

The boy pauses half-way through taking my bag. He meets my eyes. His soft cheeks have orange freckles and his expression lifts slightly, it says; *thank you.*

"Eoin," Anning snaps at the bellboy, "Take Oria to her new room."

The boy nods once, a quick bob of his sideways cap, and he limps into the distance with Ori at his heels. She looks back at me once, turns a corner, and disappears.

Anning rubs her forehead. "You'll have to explain yourself now..." She walks the hallways briskly and I follow her without question. She takes me an interesting way, through an optical illusion between a painting and a dip that conceals a narrow hallway. We slip through and hike a narrow, ornate stairway with artifacts from different cultures and times.

Anning stops, oddly, mid-step. "This is where I leave you," she bends close, and whispers, "go to the fifth door on your left, knock once, then open… good luck."

My heart thumps in my chest. *I'm already in trouble?* But I only just got here.

Grom stares up at me, limp in my breast pocket. He smells my fear.

Blame-it. Why can't I be like everyone else?

I pass ornate doors and pause at the last one – a gem-blue door.

Ma…

If only Ma were here.

Breathe, just breathe.

I grab the brass knocker and swing it.

THUD.

I jump. It thunders in the quiet hall.

My hands shake, I grip the door-holds and push.

Please don't let me get kicked out of Svalbard…

I push my weight forward and the door creaks open.

A breeze tunnels through an open window and icy air slices me.

A decorative water pool quivers in the center of the circular room. The marble floors shine like snow. The archways twist with romantic sculptures. The paintings look Italian. The furniture French. On a table beside me, torn parchments flutter in the wind; their pages are thin and worn, with elegant lettering; like Sanskrit.

A vast window covers the far wall. Outside, jagged mountains spear the horizon.

I suck in through my teeth. I shouldn't be in a room like this. My dusty shoes. My faded dress. My sweaty hair.

"Yes?" sings a soft voice.

I straighten.

A woman sits up from behind a chaise sofa and her white braided head raises above the light blue pillows. She faces the window, away from me, watching the mountains beyond.

It's her.

She gave me my acceptance letter: the dean, Seraphim.

Purring rumbles from under the sofa and a thick white tail bumps from under it.

The snow tiger strides out, circles me once, and returns to her.

She slips her fingers through his dense white fur, over his head, down his back... Intimate. She tilts her head, listening, and stands. Her eyes meet mine and everything is winter, porcelain, war.

I step back.

I don't remember deciding to do that.

I'm a child – she is a queen.

Her dress rolls in silken waves as she walks toward me, it's edged with white lace and a bustle of light blue fabric thrown back; a floating angel. She folds her hands in front. Her expression is light and expectant, the same look she had during my audition, but her eyes dim. "What did you do?"

"What?" I splutter.

Her frozen gaze flicks across my shoulders, my face, like she reads everything I ever did. "You saw the man underground, didn't you?"

"I –" my heart rises to my throat. "I didn't mean to."

"Tell me," she presses, "what did he say."

"He said...uh..."

"It's all right," she softens. "Try to get the exact words out."

The words pull straight from my gut:

"As memory fades, their trace is gone.
Both man and beast,
Tastes air like death – to an animal's mind."

Her expression lifts slightly. Not pleasure, per say, but thrill.

She turns away. Her shoulders slope as she walks, and she glides toward the mountain-facing windows. Her fingers touch the glass.

"...I understand you perfectly," she mutters, to no one in particular.

Perhaps she's forgotten I'm in the room... Perhaps... I can just leave now...

I turn awkwardly toward the door. All kinds of letters and official documents flutter on her desk. A shipping crate lays half-open with a brand marking the side: *Bjørn's Apothicas.*

She turns and strides back to me, between the chaise lounge and the worn texts. She rests her hand on her tiger's head as he bends over, gnawing on a bone.

"I admit, there are certain hazards of my occupation, and having a student like you around could be so helpful when it comes to... *communicating* to the others here. But as Dean of Svalbard, my job is keeping our students *safe*. Promise you'll never go back down there again."

"Yes, ma'am."

"Very good."

"And ma'am –"

She raises a brow to me.

"Um, that man. He was like an *animal.* The way he moved and everything."

"Oh?"

"It's just. It reminds me of something I saw years ago. There was this... monster in the woods. It moved almost the same way."

Her eyes darken. "You sure you've seen him before?"

"No... It just felt. The way it *felt.*"

"You know, I haven't formally introduced myself to you, Ms. Sunday," she smiles gently, "I'm Justine Seraphim, Dean of Svalbard, Head of House for Animalia. Do you know much about Animalia?"

The way she talks to me – like she's speaking to a child.

I shake my head. I know nothing next to her.

"Animalia is more than knowledge, it's a process..."

I squeeze my fingers behind my back. "Oh..."

"It's founded on The Book of Animalia. An ancient text. It holds all our house secrets. However, Animalia is deeply psychological; we examine dreams, we watch behaviors and patterns. Some observational abilities can never be taught. One must have certain sensitivities to learn what we teach here. You simply have the empathetic abilities, or you don't."

I bite my lip.

She steps closer. "Have you ever spent so much time with a friend that you start to speak like them, pick up on their little mannerisms, or understand their perspective in an intimate way?"

I nod.

Her eyes dance from Grom to me.

"Animalia is the same. So you and your animal will start to understand one another, share perspectives, characteristics…" she leans over to Grom in my arms and tilts her head to him.

Grom mirrors the movement, tilting his little head back at her – and out of nowhere he growls at her, swatting the air between them with his claw.

"Grom, stop it," I catch his claw and secure him to my chest. He pushes against me, sniffing the air, angry.

She smiles sweetly at him, "Dragons are cunning, suspicious animals. Lethal. They have dreams, often very telling dreams. They're also defensive and proud. They're obsessed with fine, expensive things, like bells and coins, which is why they have a reputation for *stealing*." She gives me an accusing look, as though referring to me. Like I somehow have already done something wrong.

"Oh – I'm not – Grom isn't a *dragon*–"

Grom growls, extending his neck toward Justine and thrashing around.

"They are cautious, loving creatures, though no one would guess it…" Her pale pink lips pucker as she speaks, like she's talking about *me* now, not Grom. A necklace dangles from her throat – diamonds and sapphires – like shining stars. So elegant. Her perfume oils froth in the cold air; mint, rose, pine, lavender. God she smells wonderful. Like heaven. Her cheeks flush peach. Her eyes are glaciers. She is a moving, breathing painting. Her hair is white but she isn't aged, her cheeks are soft and round. And who knows where she's from – she has no accent, nothing noticeable about her background. "Dragons are of a reptilian classification in Animalia."

"But… Grom is just a newt."

She almost laughs, "Sunday. You aren't a child anymore. Don't lie to yourself about what you are."

…What I am?

"Monstrum Dragonia," she leans on the back of the sofa. "Grom is a dragon. No they aren't *extinct*, as the world understands. Only endangered. Grom is young now but he will become an apex predator."

Grom is a… *dragon.*

No.

The white tiger rests on a cushion beside her, chewing its paw.

No. She's wrong.

She folds her delicate arms, "And so you will learn and grow to understand the mind of your animal… A predator's mind."

I stare down at my dirty shoes and avoid her eyes.

She said that like it's a horrible thing. But her tiger is a predator.

It can't be that bad.

Grom rests belly-down, limp in my arms. He's tiny and innocent. Not some kind of –

She steps toward me and a clean, bare foot moves out from the lace hem of her dress. "Dragons can sense things," she presses, "details. They're crafty. Problem-solvers."

Her head stays perfectly still. Her face is a porcelain mask.

My cheeks warm. "…You mean *me* now, right?"

She softens. It's an artificial movement for her. "I could use a girl like you as a second pair of eyes for me."

What in the heavens –

"You could use… me?"

Please let me go. Let me…

She walks away toward her desk, and turns back, "You must be tired and hungry. At the bottom of the stairs you'll find a guide to your dormitory, where you'll have plenty to eat."

"Thank you, ma'am." I bow and almost run for the door.

"And Sunday," she frowns.

I turn.

"Never come here again."

EIGHT

THE ANIMALIA PROBLEM

I close the door behind me and press my back to it.

Grom sinks his tiny teeth into the fabric at my sleeve and pulls. He growls like a dog, thrashes his head and rips the fabric.

Grom is a… dragon?

No.

Dragons went extinct a long time ago. Everyone knows that.

"Stop it," I snap at him. "You're ruining my dress."

He turns, taking me in with intelligent, dark-eyes – he flicks his head away spitefully and chews my sleeve again.

"I said stop –"

"*Gnnnar!*" he whines.

"Stop it now."

"*Tsssss…*" he hisses, lowering his head.

Dragons are supposed to be the worst. And that's not Grom… Grom isn't aggressive like that. He's a newt.

Grom buries his head in the crook of my arm, and eyes me from the side, like he's ready to pounce. I swear he can guess my thoughts.

I set my jaw at him. "Don't you dare."

He pounces at my chest and I grab him and pin him down there.

"Gnnaaar!"

I hold him to my chest as I walk. I'll get answers.

He flails around in my grip until I reach the bottom of the stairs and the frail servant boy, Eoin, waits for me. He bows to me as though I somehow deserved that.

I open my mouth to speak, but I snap my jaw shut. I shouldn't.

I've learned.

We walk across marble floors and empty ballrooms, dusty pianos, golden harps.

We reach the main hall and he leads me down the center corridor, which branches into five red-carpeted stairways. He takes me up the rightmost stairway. Blue tiles shine between the marble railings.

My head spins. I've held my breath this whole time.

Breathe.

The path spills into an iron spiral staircase. I hike the spire, and the curved stained-glass windows cast colorful light onto my arms. The stained-glass shows strange creatures; a zebra with a red chest; a bull with a single horn.

Animalia.

We stop at the top of the spire, facing a dead-end wall, and Eoin turns to me. He talks to the iron step between my shoes. "I'll leave you here."

His footsteps echo down the rusty steps of the tower.

...Where in God's world am I?

I face the empty wall which holds only a mirror. Nothing else.

"But there's no door." I whisper to Grom.

Grom scampers down to the floor, attracted to his reflection in the mirror. There's an inscription below it:

> *Never to mind,*
> *those who try to enter here without an animal's mind,*
> *will find more bitter than hate,*
> *a rescue that will come too late.*

A riddle.

Grom sniffs the mirror and tilts his head. He places a small green claw on the smooth surface and his reflection does the same.

"It's your reflection, Grom. It's just you. We're different but the same, see?" I set my hand on the other end of the mirror and –

CLUNK.

What the –

Something heavy behind my reflection swings. Two sides of the mirror press into the wall and the center pieces slide open, revealing a dark stone passageway.

Woah.

Grom scampers up my arm and I peer through the shadows… Holding him secure, I duck through the walkway and into a lounge.

I gaze up and all around; sky-blue curtains line tall cathedral windows. A fireplace crackles to the side of the circular room; the air froths with burnt pine; silky light-blue pillows lay everywhere. Fit for a queen.

This is where I'll live?

It's a dream. A box of chocolates lays open on the table beside a chessboard with marble animal chess-pieces. Two large enclosures are fixed to the opposite wall, filled with blankets and toys.

One is inscribed: CARNIVORE

The other: HERBIVORE

Where in the world –

Ori jumps from the sofa, holding her pig. "You made it!"

I gawk at the ceiling; glass chandeliers, silver sculptures…

If Ma were here she'd say this is excessive.

I press my fingers to the bridge of my nose.

"What happened to you?" Ori holds my arm.

I avoid her. Pressure builds in my chest.

If only I could go home. I need Ma. I need…

"Forget about that guy," Ori squeezes my arm. "He can't hurt us now."

"I'm fine," I mutter.

Ori hugs me. It's so abrupt it catches me off guard and I step back. I tense, and slowly soften into her shoulder. Her curly hair smells sweet, like lemons. But she pulls away awkwardly, and the moment passes.

Somewhere in the hours of the day, I guess, we became friends.

"Sit down, relax. Let me get you a drink," Ori offers, and sits by the fire. She lifts a glass goblet and fills it with warm fruit wine, "drink it. Don't worry it's not *real* wine. It's mulled. No alcohol." Her warmth is jarring next to everything else in this frozen place. Even the walls stick to my skin. Renaissance paintings of bears and baboons frown down at me.

Ori studies me. "So, what happened to you?" I've never seen her not-smiling.

"Nothing," I mutter.

She scrunches her slender brows.

"It's just – the man in the basement. I've *felt* that way before."

"When?"

"When I –" I grit my teeth.

When I killed my father.

My throat closes and I have to look away. I stare absently into the fire. My hand brushes the fold in my coat pocket where I slipped the book from the basement.

What if he comes looking for it?

I shut my eyes and the man from underground fills my mind – the curve of his back – the growl in his throat – and I'm suddenly seven years old again, screaming for my father in the snow.

That man killed Pa.

I clasp my hand over my eyes and rub my brows.

No. No, there was no man that night. No monster.

I imagined the monster when I hit my head that night. It was my fault Pa died. Only mine.

Bjørn said some people can't handle Animalia.

> *… They get all twisted in their mind.*

Maybe my mind is twisted, too.

I turn the goblet of plum-colored wine in my hand absently.

"He was so strange," Ori taps her arm. "You think he was on drugs or something?"

The fire spits and cracks. "Or just some sort of monster."

She slumps, stares into the fire with me. "…I suppose it's a Svalbard thing."

"Did you hear what he said?" I ask.

"I heard him all right," she scoffs, "didn't understand a word though. I just figured it was some local language. Like that's why you understood it and I didn't."

I frown at the fireplace…

But he made perfect sense to me. No different language.

…Odd.

"Orientation is in an hour," she yawns.

"Oh."

"And. I've been figuring things out," she kicks her little heeled boots onto the short table between us. Her pinstripe dress splays over her knees to the wood floor. Her style has odd colors – purple and brown – it reminds me of a place far from here. A loud place with colors and money and character. I don't imagine her in a farmland, like she told me. I see her in a city, making deals with people on the street, setting things to her advantage.

Strange…

I press my thumb between my eyes.

Ori reclines with her hands behind her head, smug.

I can't help it. It's like an instinct. I can sense things about Ori: She's smart.

Smarter than I'd thought. Crafty. Always-listening.

Perhaps we're all a little like our animals. Once, I heard pigs are social creatures. They're curious, outgoing, intelligent…

… *Interesting.*

"What do you mean, you're figuring things out?" I reply, cautious.

She bounces her foot as she reclines, like she hears music no one else can. "Because I know things. I've discovered some things."

The fire crackles.

"I know we're the only two Animalia students admitted this year," she has a knowing side-smile. "And guess what. In this entire dormitory, there are hundreds of beds. But only five students are here."

"So?"

"*So?*" she scoffs, leaning forward over her knees. "What do you *think?*"

"Where are the other students?"

"There are three boys here. Older, fifth years. They're in their room."

"You met them?"

She nods. "Don't you want food?" She sets a platter with grapes and cheese between us. "A snack? ...Nothing?"

Footsteps pound down the stairs and three boys spill into the lounge. Oddly, they all look a tad like their animals; one has cat-like features, another tall and lanky, and one with bird-like features. The lanky boy comes up to our snack tray, he holds a marsupial – like a monkey. The boy blushes, shy, like the creature he holds. The tiny human-hand of the monkey grabs a grape from the platter and pulls it into his small, monkey-mouth.

The monkey's eyes flash up to me, and down.

... So intelligent.

The boys chatter, leave, and shut the door behind them.

Ori bubbles into laughter, "You should see your face."

"Have you ever seen a monkey like that? It's a slow-loris. I've only seen them in books."

Ori shrugs. She checks her bulky machinist wristwatch. Her family must have money. Ma and I could never afford that. "It's time for orientation," she sighs, like she's bored already.

She can't be bored. This place is too wonderful.

"I set your things down in your room – well it isn't just *your* room is it – it's *our* room."

"Oh," I stand with her.

"Come," she hooks me by the arm. "We're the only Animalia girls. We're going to be the talk of the school."

NINE

FIVE HOUSES

We step down the grand staircase and enter the hum of chattering students entering the dining hall. I search for Viktor among them and catch his wavy brown head bounding along with the other Machinists. He stumbles along the side of the group, trying to keep up.

Interesting.

Not so important outside of Sjosburg, are you Viktor?

Warbringers enter from a narrow hallway, with sheathed knives swinging from their belts. They dress in strict military uniform, but they don't have strict manners, they argue and laugh and tease each other. A group of Artisan students join from a separate stairway; some of them hold musical instruments; cellos, flutes, and some carry art supplies. They stride around in patterned dresses and giggle like they're holding secrets, clinging to each other.

My gut sinks. I'll never be like them.

Ori and I follow them into the dining room – it's a vast, circular ballroom – with a spherical glass ceiling and columns with angelic sculptures. Outside the glass windows, polar aurora floats in the night sky, swaying in atmospheric blue ribbons.

Circular banquet tables line the room for the Svalbard houses – the wood tables have a painted stripe down the middle, green for apothecary, red for artisan... A professor sits at each of the wide circular tables. Pine boughs line the tables, like Christmas.

Machinists sit at a nearby table – huddled over little contraptions, screwing bits into their latest inventions. Leather tool pouches swing from their belts and they wear dark colors, probably to hide the grease stains smeared over their shirts. A few of them have – not spectacles – but welding goggles with many lenses.

...If Ma could see this.

Viktor sits hunched over a metal gadget. At least he's here. He stands, walks to me and stops me with a hand to my shoulder. His gaze draws low, dark hair hangs in waves over his eyes, "What's wrong?"

Blazes – I forgot how he can see right through me, "It's nothing."

"You're scared of something, I can tell."

"Everything is new here, that's all."

He folds his long arms across his chest, "...People are bothering you, aren't they? They're just jealous of you, Sunday. They want to get close to you so they can use you, you know. I could see it coming a mile away." He shakes his head, pulls away, and sits down at the Machinist table beside the others. He slaps his old watch onto the table, turning a screw into it.

I pass the Warbringer table, and one of the boys – with tan skin and hazel eyes – happens to meet my eyeline. He stares at me, and winks.

What the –

I flick my gaze away. My cheeks warm.

Maybe Viktor is right. Maybe there's something about me others notice. And they want to use me, or something...

Ori squeezes my arm. Her chin hovers by my shoulder as we walk. She studies the other houses, too.

We pass the Apothecary table, and some of the students wear long off-white laboratory robes over their clothes – like monks. They curl over books, studying already. Hikaru sits there, studying, and pretends not to notice us.

The Artisan table sits in one big cluster, all draped over each other, hugging as though family. Less students sit at Artisan than any other – only thirty or so – not like the other tables which have at least one-hundred. The program must be selective. One of them plays a violin in the corner – a local melody from our home-isle; the tune should comfort me, but it burns a hole in my chest.

There's no going back home now.

Ori and I sit at the empty circular table in the back of the room with a painted blue stripe, for Animalia. The three Animalia boys sit opposite us – they're fifth-years and close as brothers.

The regions they're from are obvious by their animals: A parrot; a bobcat; and a slow-loris.

I grimace at the empty seats beside us; there's enough for dozens of Animalia, but they're all empty.

The other tables chatter and make friends. If only I could sit with them.

"Sit with *me*," Ori pulls my arm and slides me closer.

Professor Anning turns the corner and sits at the other empty Animalia table, adjacent from us. Our eyes touch – and she rips her gaze away. She pours herself a cup of tea.

"Odd..." I mutter.

"What?" Ori whispers; her chin hovers over my shoulder.

"It's Anning," I turn and whisper to Ori – but I stop. Ori hovers inches from my face – I know how it looks. Like we're friends. But I only met her today. I keep a little distance and mutter, "Do you know anything about Anning?"

"*Yes,*" Ori's eyes light. "I've heard about her."

Of course she has. It's like Ori is constantly sniffing people out but never thinks of it. "...Anning is an *interim* professor," she leans closer, whispering, "she *isn't* Animalia. She has no animal. No creature."

I prop my elbows on the table and rest my chin in my palm.

...Not Animalia?

"*Yes,*" Ori coaxes. "So you get it now. I heard she studied fossils here, when she went to school. *Fossils.* She was *Apothecary.* So why couldn't they find a substitute who's actually Animalia?"

Anning fiddles with her hair in a persnickety way, pinning up the auburn strands in a neat little swirl.

"But what does that mean?" I ask Ori, "She can't teach us?"

"It means we have no *real* professor. And. It means there's a reason we're alone at this table."

"I don't want to be alone at this table."

"But we *are,*" Ori presses. She glances around the room, huddled by my shoulder. "Why so sad? I sort of like it."

"How come?"

"Look," she tugs at my sleeve. "They're watching us. The other houses. We're the *only* Animalia. The only ones chosen out of anyone in the world. They see us differently."

I follow her gaze to the tables around us – the faint glances of Artisans peering over their shoulders at us. Talking about us. Our animals. Our insular way.

"We're special," she whispers in my ear.

I turn to face her directly. Her soft cheeks pull into a smile.

Something about it – all of it – doesn't sit right. "Is something wrong with the others who auditioned?"

"Something's certainly *right* with us," Ori says, flirty, with an impish smirk. "Animalia is special."

A pit carves in my stomach. I should tell someone. About everything. All the little things that are off.

But Anning warned me not to say anything.

DONG –

A great bell rings and Grom leaps from my shoulder. Heads turn, followed by echoes of '*shhh*'.

The professors clap mildly, and I crane my neck over their heads – a snow tiger paces in with heavy steps, followed by a swish of royal, mint-blue robes brushing the floor. A scholar's sash lines her neck. Her presence is some force of nature. Like sitting beneath a predator: Seraphim.

She stands at the podium in the center of the room and nods to her left and right, acknowledging the professors.

Her eyes touch mine – I tense – I'm the only one in the room who isn't clapping for her. I snap my gaze away and clap grimly like everyone else, to blend in. I set my eye-line to her blue silk shoes, not her eyes.

"Beloved students," she says, calm. "Welcome back to Svalbard."

I risk a glance at her. White fleece dangles from her neckline. Animalia doesn't use animals for clothing so… So she must have known the lambs, somehow.

"I am Justine Seraphim, Dean of Svalbard. Your previous dean, Raj, retired early this summer, and congratulates you all for the work you've accomplished under him…"

The students break into huddles, whispering:

"Raj left?"

"Why would he leave?"

"The alumni picked *her?*"

"This year will be special at Svalbard." Seraphim leans onto the podium. "It is one of our biggest recruitment years yet – and we've admitted many new students from across the globe."

Sure… Admitted to every program except Animalia.

The students cheer.

I don't clap. The room swallows me. The students are so confident. So deserving. The best of the best…

They made a mistake admitting me.

"As usual," Seraphim says, "breakfast will be served in your dorms, lunch and dinner will be in this dining room. And I have a special request for all of you…" her voice grows low and strong; "stay away from the west entrance hall and the entire west wing of the compound."

"The west wing," Ori hisses in my ear, "that's near the Animalia section of the school. Where we were earlier –"

"This is for your own safety. Anyone found wandering in that area will be subject to review, and expelled from Svalbard." She says it with a smile, as though it were not a threat.

Silverware clatters, and Eoin, the scrawny Irish boy, lays plates out for Ori and I and sets pots of steaming vegetables on our table for dinner.

"Introducing, our world-renowned professors," Seraphim gestures to Anning, at our table, who stands.

Seraphim announces, "Professor Mary Anning. Interim professor of animal anatomy and fossil studies."

Anning's face breaks with a flash of discomfort.

Ori tugs my sleeve. Brown corkscrew curls fall around her face as she leans onto me, "Told you," she hisses, "she's interim – *temporary*."

Seraphim gestures to the Artisan table, "Professor William Cortez, Head of House for Artisan." A lanky, disheveled man with a rouge silk neck-tie stands from the center of the cluster of Artisans. Gold jewelry lines his fingers, his cheeks are scruffy and his hair wild. If I saw him outside this place, I'd think he were some sort of collector of fine things. The Artisan students clap and whistle for him.

"Professor Ari Suri," Seraphim says, "Head of House for Machinist." A tall, elegant woman in a kimono stands. My stomach dips. She sat at my audition. My stars she's beautiful. Her kimono is beaded with gold…

Red neck-tie, blue gown… Of course. The house colors of Svalbard.

Professor Suri bows to the Machinist students, and her graying black hair sweeps to the side in a dark, glossy waterfall over her shoulder. The Machinists cheer and clap for her.

"Dr. Istivan Ketto-Laszlo," Seraphim announces, "Head of House for Apothecary." A burly man in an off-white lab-coat stands. His smile is a flash of white under tossed brown hair, but he still looks annoyed, somehow.

I grip the table's edge. It's… *him*.

Our town apothecary when Pa died.

Dr. Laszlo smiles at Seraphim and his gold-tanned cheeks draw up with dimples. He cleans his gold octagonal spectacles with a green handkerchief. The Apothecary students clap politely for him, but no one really cheers – Apothecary is the most serious, academic house.

"Professor Marie Seacole," Seraphim says, "Head of Warbringer." A woman in a dark uniform-dress stands. Gold military awards glitter on her breast pocket. Her silky black hair is pressed into a bun. The Warbringer students stand and salute her. Seacole waves a hand, "At ease," she calls in a Jamaican accent, and the students sit.

Seraphim rests her arms on the sides of the podium. "And I am Head of House for Animalia." She nods toward our small circular table and I hold my breath. I make my face go slack, expressionless. "Centuries ago, the founding scholars of Svalbard left a vision for this education – and though tonight is a celebration, each of you should also be aware –" her eyes touch mine – "Svalbard is meant for *successful* students, only. The first year is the most challenging. Those who are unwilling to do the work will fall behind, and if they do, they'll be expelled."

The students stir.

"Svalbard separates houses by design. We eat separately, sleep separately – for the sake of your studies – you'll become very close to those sitting beside you."

Ori glances at me with side-eyes, like it's good news.

"But under my leadership, Svalbard will be different," Seraphim puffs her chest. "This year, we will integrate. Halfway through your first year, each of you must present a project, partnering with someone from a *different* house."

Someone whispers: "Is she allowed to do that?"

Her sapphire eyes shine. "But I'm sure you're hungry," she raises her hands – an imperial gesture – "ex fide fortis."

"What?" I ask Ori.

"The Svalbard motto, Latin: *Strong through faith.*"

Everyone grabs silverware and slides food onto their plates; grilled vegetables with herb oils; potato-halves and berries; crumb-cake and nougat. I scoop grilled zucchini onto my plate, more than I'd dare take at home.

I sneak a glance back to the podium – but she's gone.

"*Mmmm…* Smell that?" Ori chatters. "I could eat this whole table I'm so hungry."

Anning passes behind me, and I stop her – "Professor Anning?"

Anning turns, slowly, and her beak-like gaze hardens on me.

"Oh... I was just wondering. Where are the other Animalia students?"

Anning's eyes flick to Seraphim's tiger pacing the edge of the room. She hesitates, and slowly, she pulls her pointer finger to her lips, mouthing, *'shhh'*.

I freeze.

My eyes go wide. I squeeze the table edge.

Anning turns, leaving me there. My fingers go numb. The room spins; students laughing, food steaming, Grom growling...

Whatever is going on, someone doesn't want me to find out.

But I will.

TEN

STRANGE FAVOR

The bell rings, dismissing us to our dorms for the night.

Students pass in a blur.

I search for Viktor in the crowd – he's talking to Professor Suri – but he notices my watching him, wraps up his conversation, and comes straight to me.

He raises his bushy brows at me. "All right," he folds his arms. "Something's really wrong...What is it?"

"Nothing." I lie.

"You know I see through you," he tilts his head, "all these other pomp people won't – but I do." He bounces his fingers on my arm, beside Grom, playing with him the way he used to when Grom was newborn. Grom sniffs Viktor and recognizes his scent – his little tail flicks up – and he leaps for Viktor's chest.

Viktor catches Grom and cradles him like a baby.

It's odd. With Viktor here, in this elegant place. He almost feels like a gentleman.

"I'm fine," I say. "Only saw some strange things. That's all."

Viktor sucks his cheeks in. "...People here knew *him*, didn't they?"

My chest sinks.

Yes. People here knew Pa.

My throat closes, I nod my head. And he knows what that means.

Fire lights in his eyes – and he snaps his head around like he'd break something if he weren't holding Grom. "Screw 'em, Sunday. You aren't here to suck up and do a dance. You don't have to be their friends. You just have to pass your classes."

"I know," I swallow.

"They didn't even *know* him," he snaps. "These people. Pretending to be all important. They don't even know you."

"I just think… Maybe I'm not cut out for this. Everything here. Maybe it isn't for me."

Grom leaps back into my arms, sensing my sadness. He crawls to my shoulder and cuddles my neck.

"Don't do that, Sunday. You worked years to get here. You were *obsessed* with Animalia. Always drawing those dumb animal sketches in class."

I stare at my shoes. My cheeks go hot.

"And now you want to give it up – just because a few people are getting weird about your father?"

Grom licks my cheek, giving kisses.

Viktor softens, steps closer. "Screw 'em all," he mutters. "You're here for *you*." He pulls a bit of beef jerky from his pocket, unwraps it and feeds a piece to Grom. Brown hair falls over his dark eyelashes. "This guy has gotten feistier, huh?"

"Yeah," I mutter.

Because he's not a newt.

"You know," Viktor sighs, crosses his arms. "You and me – we haven't been buttered up like the rest of them here. We know the hard life, don't we? They'll never understand you, Sunday. You won't 'fit in'. But why would you want to? They're all fake, talking about each other like they're all 'specially selected'. *Pussh.* Just let 'em rot. They're all jealous of you, anyway. Believe me. You're more exceptional than their lot, and not because you go to school here. And if you need someone, at least you have me."

Ori steps forward sharply, "And *who* exactly are you?"

Viktor keeps his eyes trained on me, not her. "I'm the only one... who really knows Sunday Gråe." He walks back to the Machinist table and leaves me there with Ori.

I deflate a little.

"...*rude...*" Ori mutters.

It's true though. He's the only one here who really knows me.

Ori's been nice, but only while it's in her advantage to be my friend. I can already tell she's the type to play social games. She wants to be liked by everyone – no matter the cost.

"Who was *he?*" Ori scowls at the place where Viktor stood.

"I know him from Sjosburg."

Ori rolls her eyes. "Well he was *great*," she says, stiff. "So can we leave please? Jeesh."

We leave but Anning stops us in the hallway. She frowns down at us with her beak-like gaze. "Sunday Gråe and Oria Moss. You're needed in the wardrobe room. For uniforms."

Ori and I exchange a look and Ori arches a slender eyebrow. "Uniforms? Is it really that hard to tell what house we belong to?" Ori leans toward Anning with some cheek. "I mean, there are only *two* girls in Animalia – me and –"

"*Now,* please," Anning waves us away.

Ori laughs. She scuttles off and grabs my hand, sliding it up her arm. I return her smile – to be polite – but I unlink my arm from hers because, well, I only met her this morning.

We follow a sign directing us down a spiral staircase and into the wardrobe room.

Ori and I walk cautiously down the steps – deeper and darker – until we stand in a large dressing room.

A stout Norwegian woman hangs jackets to dry and steams dresses from a wire-hook. "Sunday Gråe?" she calls with a sing-song lilt – a local accent. Her eyes smile like Ma's. I come right up to her and make a little bowing gesture – I don't know when I learned it. Other students do it. It feels right, in this place.

"I'm Sunday."

"Good," she sets down her steaming iron. "Up you go, on the platform."

I stand on a circular platform – mirrors surround me in a half-circle. I glance back at my reflection; stringy hair, limp arms, drab dress. I'm still a Sjosburg girl; from a village of tiny shops, a poor candle-maker's daughter.

"I'm Agnet, the housekeeper here," the woman eyes me up and down. She wipes her hands on a washcloth that hangs from her waist. "I'm the keeper of the compound. I keep the castle, mind you, not the students," her gaze wanders to Ori, "and what're you doin' here?"

Ori reacts with a complicated head gesture, "Can I stay?"

... I can't be alone. Not again.

"Please let her stay," I beg. "She's my friend and I don't know the school well yet."

"Fine," Agnet fiddles with my dress, "she can stay while you're measured. But there's a curfew after hours."

Behind Agnet, the Irish servant boy, Eoin, steams dresses, pulling out the wrinkles. He hangs his head in a permanent bow, but he sneaks a look at Ori from under his cap, like he thinks she's pretty.

Ori sits on the step beside me, fiddling with her pig.

"You're much too small," Agnet pulls at my sleeves and fiddles with the ties. "I'll be back."

The way she says it... It's like she's used to fitting one woman in particular. All around me, the gowns are only one size.

"Sunday," Ori says quickly, "what was in your supplies list for school?"

"Don't know," I shrug, "I visited my apothecary who said – *uh* – he'd have them sent here... What was on yours?"

"General things," Ori softens, "but my Ma and I had to go shopping. She measured me and special ordered the clothes for me. We had to pay through the nose for the uniform dress. I already have mine."

"Oh."

Ori's gaze settles on the servant boy around the corner. "Hey, you."

The boy does a double-take.

"What're you doing here? You just work for the school or something?"

My eyes go wide and my cheeks warm. Ori is too bold.

He pauses sweeping the floor, "I... don't know." He frowns at the ground and walks away into a backroom.

... Odd.

Agnet parts through colorful gowns toward me on the circular platform. I shiver, half-dressed, clutching my overdress to my corset and bloomers. Agnet tosses my old dress into a bin for washing. She wraps measuring tape around my waist, my shoulders... and chatters in a thick Nordic accent, "So Animalia, is it? For the past three years none have been chosen for it, or perhaps they were chosen and dropped out shortly. Forced out. Couldn't keep up with the work, mayhap. They're gone now."

My gut turns. "Why'd they drop out?"

Agnet shrugs. "Here one day, gone the next. But if anyone is going to drop out, it's in the first quarter of the first year – mark my words – we'll be lucky if we keep one Animalia student that steps off that sleigh."

My chest twists. I hug my arms. *Please, God. Don't let me drop out.*

Agnet watches me deflate. "That won't happen to you though."

"So where are the other students now?"

Agnet tilts her head at me, curious. Her pale eyes are empty. She taps my chin with her pointer finger once. "Now don't you worry your little self. It's your first day. A big day, and you'll do plenty fine. You'll carry on the Svalbard traditions. The secret knowledge."

"Secret knowledge?"

"Oh yes," Agnet chatters, as though it were obvious. She pulls a dress over my head. "Do you think the world would be able to handle the knowledge Svalbard has? No, no. How many people would kill to learn the strategies the Warbringers know? But they can't handle it. They don't have the *character* to handle it. They don't consider that Warbringers must first study peace strategies for a whole year. Then self-defense, then weapons, then social strategy, and finally war methods. People always skip to the last step. They disregard the whole. They want the power without the obligation, you know... The result without the responsibility..."

The Irish boy mops the floor. Oddly, he absorbs all my attention while Agnet chatters. He wears his face like a façade, permanently passive, like someone out of a different time and place, sunk into Svalbard, dissolved into the walls. His pants are faded and his freckled cheeks dull. He should be in a pub with friends. Not here.

Ori is slick. She passes the freckled servant boy and whispers: "*In Animalia. Meet us there. One hour.*" She dashes off up the stairs and the boy watches her leave, speechless. His ears turn peach and he scrubs the floor.

"Finished," Agnet sings.

I snap back to my reflection in the mirror.

Holy heaven.

I turn here and there and the dress bustle follows my movements; plush ivory fabrics fold over royal mint-blues. The gown is a variation of what Seraphim wore earlier. And they call it a uniform.

I could be, like, some smaller version of her...

"And these were ordered for you," Agnet loads my arms with heavy, beautiful gowns. I crouch down and splay them on the red carpeted floor; gowns for lounging; formal-wear; summer; winter; travel. *Oh!*

They're perfect.

"And I almost forgot," Agnet carries a box from the side of the room. "This package also came for you."

I glance at the tag on the shipping box:

Ms. Sunday,
Good luck at school. Make us proud. And remember, home is only a short way away.
Apothecary Bjørn

"How much do I owe you?" I ask. "For the things."

"*You* owe *me?*" Agnet laughs, waving a hand. "I take orders from Dean Seraphim. Only you, these gowns. I have to say, you're lucky you won favor with a woman like that. I don't know what makes you special, but good on ya. Oh – and also she told me... This necklace."

She strings out a necklace; it's laden with what look like gold fish scales – and the flaps drape together into a net. It's Egyptian-looking. I hold my breath. I carefully take the necklace from her and fasten it around my neck so the weight of the gold scales press onto my collar bones. "Is it an antique?"

"None of my business," Agnet shrugs. "Like I said, I take orders from above."

I gaze up into the lofty beams of the room; beside the glass ceiling are windows into what must be the Dean's office I visited before... Only, it didn't feel like an office. It was Seraphim's personal space. Just like this wardrobe room feels personal... The dresses around me, they could all belong to Seraphim.

Chills roll down my back.

She's doing this for me because...

Maybe because of Pa.

Or because... she wants to use me, somehow. Like she said.

Agnet stops me before I leave. "And Ms. Sunday. Best not tell anyone what I told you, about the other Animalia students. Things can be... touchy sometimes, at Svalbard. The professors are really the ones who should be tellin' you those things. Not me. I've worked here for years but I'm not alumni or anything. I'm not *from* Svalbard School, you understand. I don't even live in the compound, really. I have my own place up the mountain."

"Sure, right," I slowly pace up the stairs, carrying my new gowns, "I won't tell."

My head spins.

The Animalia students disappeared...

I walk and the thick fabric of my new dress trails on the steps behind me in a fluffed bustle. I hold about seven folded gowns at least, with Grom sitting on top. They must've cost a fortune.

I turn the corner and – *wham* – bump right into Dr. Laszlo, dropping all my gowns.

"Oh!" he kneels down beside me to collect the gowns. "I apologize Ms. Seraphim. I think we both turned at the same time..." His eyes meet mine and his face falls. "Oh," he draws back, "I thought you were the dean," he chuckles and stands awkwardly.

My face warms. I gather the gowns from the floor quickly and stand.

Dr. Laszlo straightens his lab-coat. He's an older man now than years ago when he was our town apothecary but, behind his gold spectacles, his face is flush and boyish. "Well, you and Seraphim are certainly very *alike*, aren't you?"

He must have started teaching apothecary here shortly after Pa died.

For years, I wanted to thank him. For helping Ma and I that night. But I never got the...

Dr. Laszlo cracks a strange smile, straightening his spectacles at me – "ah, I almost didn't recognize. Young Ms. Sunday Gråe," he bows curtly, "so grown up – after all these years. I hope your mother is managing well."

"She's fine," I lie.

He frowns at something down the hall. "Well, good evening," he steps around me quickly, muttering to himself in what must be Hungarian.

... Strange.

Mistaking me for Seraphim. *Me?*

I shake my head and keep walking.

Seeing him is like walking in a memory. The only one who helped us try to save Pa.

Dr. Laszlo, my secret hero.

I'll see him again, and, if the moment is right, I'll thank him properly. Yes.

I enter the Animalia lounge, and Ori waits for me. She gapes at the folded gowns in my hands. "What on earth," she gasps, "look at all those silks – and velvet! How'd you get them?"

Seraphim gave them to me.

"I don't really know why," I admit, setting the gowns on the chaise lounge.

"They aren't making you pay for them?" Ori gapes.

"No."

I could never afford them.

"All right," Ori folds her arms over her chest, frowning at me like I owe her something. "Who do you know?"

"I told you, I don't know anyone here."

"But your father was Animalia."

My face turns hot. *Papa was...*

I snap my face away from her. A rock turns in my throat and my eyes water.

I tighten my jaw.

Not here. Not now.

"I... I don't have," I choke. "Anyone."

Ori sits back, slowly. Her frown changes, it's deeper, like she's sorry she asked.

I force myself to breathe deep and sink into the sofa.

Ori stares into the smoldering fireplace and her curly head snaps back to me. "What did that man say to you? The one in the dirty basement?"

"He said –" I bite my lip. Anning told me not to talk about it. "I – *um* – don't know."

"So you didn't understand him, either?" she presses forward, eager. "I thought so. It wasn't English! I thought, maybe you knew that language because you're from around here – these Nordic *northern* places," she pats Rosie in her arms, "but I didn't want to ask and be so rude. It was a creepy sound, right? All growls, like a madman. Maybe he thought you'd understand. His language, if that's even what it was."

"Right..." I say, blandly.

"Strange. Not like any language anywhere in the world."

...But I understood him. Every word.

Sure the interaction was odd, but he sounded normal.

Something must be wrong with me.

Oh no.

My gut dips. I *knew* that man. It's all... connected, somehow. "Ori? What if you were capable of something," I ask, slowly, "but you didn't know you could do it?"

"Like what?"

"Like maybe, bad things, things you've done before."

"Good grief," Ori laughs, "don't look so down. People here are strange. So what? You don't have to be all tortured about it."

"…Right."

A knock echoes on the far door – THUD, THUD, THUD.

We straighten.

"Who was that?" I splutter.

Ori just smiles.

She runs to the stone door and pushes it open. The hinges swing and the Irish servant boy, Eoin, ducks in.

I sit up. "He shouldn't be here."

"*Why?*" Ori teases, rolling her eyes. "You can't talk to a servant boy?"

"That's *not* what I meant."

The boy patters in. His pants are still wet around the knees from washing floors.

"Come, sit here," Ori pats the sofa beside her.

The three of us sit in a semi-circle around the fireplace.

"So tell us who you are," Ori presses, "why do you work here? Don't you have family?"

The boy shifts in his seat. He peers over his shoulder with wide, paranoid eyes, and presses his hands together in his lap, "I can't remember," he admits. When he speaks, he has a thick Northern Irish sing-song lilt – like Belfast.

"I wish I knew…" he says, slowly. "But I don't even know where I'm from."

I frown at him, "But it's obvious."

Ori turns to me. "It is?"

"You're from North Ireland, somewhere. Maybe Derry."

"How would you know?" Ori furrows thin brows at me.

"My Ma is Irish."

The boy stares at the wood floor between Ori's slippers. "I can't remember if I have a family."

Fire lights in me. Something about him irks me. He doesn't *remember?* "Fine," I snap. "What *do* you remember?"

85

Ori shoots me a meaningful look that says; *'Don't sound so rude.'*

I set my jaw… It's not like me. To speak harshly like that. But I can't explain it. He doesn't match up.

Eoin presses his hands together, stares into the fire; "I remember standing out in the cold, in the mountains here – I was freezing, it was just earlier this month… Then there was this woman – the dean, Seraphim. She saved me, she put her coat around me and brought me into the compound. She said I could earn my living here, until I could remember. That's my only memory."

"That was recent," Ori says, "this fall?"

Eoin nods. "I only remembered my name, really. She set me under the housekeeper, Ms. Agnet."

"So Seraphim *found* you?" Ori pries.

Eoin nods.

Ori rests her pointer fingers to her lips. She reclines deep into the sofa and gives me side-eyes. "We like you, Eoin. We think you're all right. You can be friends with us."

I pinch the bridge of my nose… *Goodness' sake, Ori… Speak for yourself.*

Eoin fidgets. He's weak. Feeble.

Pathetic.

Perhaps the fear of getting caught in our dorm finally set into him. "I – I'll be leaving now," he stumbles to his feet, and trips once as he leaves out the door.

Ori stares at the place where his blondish-red head used to be. She pets Rosie mildly. "That boy… What an interesting creature," she says. "He's like one of those dogs you adopt from the shelter. No memory. Just an empty little soul." Ori places her pig in the 'Herbivore' enclosure and tucks her in with a blanket.

"What a day," I say, blank-faced. Grom sleeps in my arms and I cradle him. Poor Grom. His tail hangs limp with exhaustion. Maybe if he sleeps well, he'll feel as though he's still home.

I should place him in the 'Carnivore' enclosure, but not tonight. Tonight I need to watch over him.

I carry him up to our new bedroom – and my jaw hangs open.

The bedroom is… Huge.

The whole candle shop could fit in here. Two king-sized beds frame either side. Ori has already unpacked by her bed. She's fitted her side with her things; striped purple-and-white bedsheets and a bulky machinist clock that makes a light *tick-tick-tick* by her nightstand. She set out a photograph of her family – they're dressed like an elite family, and her father looks familiar, like maybe I've seen him in a newspaper or something – but Ori catches me looking and slides the picture away, hiding it in a drawer.

I set my things by my bed. It has light blue curtains which drape around the sides of the frame. A little wood plaque sits on the pillows with my name engraved on it: Sunday Gråe.

I arrange my things on the dresser by my bed. I don't have much, really. Just Pa's old key and my deck of playing cards.

I loop Pa's key onto twine and dangle it from the mirror. I shrug out of my overcoat and my hand bumps into a lump in the pocket – the book I took from the man underground. Of course – good grace it's filthy – I wipe the dust, showing the inscription: THE BOOK OF ANIMALIA.

I glance over my shoulder – Ori lays turned away in bed, she hasn't noticed anything. I slip the book into an empty drawer in my dresser.

"Goodnight," Ori mumbles, and turns out her lamp.

All goes dark – starlight streams in from the wide windows beside me; beyond them, icy mountains line the horizon. The howl of wolves echoes in the wind. I shed my overdress and crawl into the cold, starchy sheets.

At last…

My bones sink into the mattress.

Grom patters over and nudges his way between my arms.

"I love you," I whisper to him.

He licks my palm with a scratchy tongue. He understands.

ELEVEN

WELCOME TO ANIMLIA

A great archway looms over me – with an iron gate – shouldered by two lion statues with an inscription:

EX ANIMA – VIDERENT

Chills roll down my arms.

So *this* is the Animalia compound.

If Pa could see me now.

I push the doors open, slowly, and step into the dome aviary.

The room is a giant glass sphere, large enough to host trees and all kinds of shrubbery. Warm air hugs me; hummingbirds and winged insects swirl above. My jaw drops.

A big blue butterfly flutters down to me. I raise a hand and it lands ever-so-softly on my fingers. The air is thick, heavy with moisture – it's tropical, like a rainforest. I grin everywhere I look; cardinals hop along tree branches, bees kiss flower after flower. And in the canopy beyond – monkeys swing tree-to-tree. Songbirds whistle along the glass ceiling.

Ori waves me down across the way, "Sunday!"

I balance the blue butterfly on my fingers as I walk to her.

Professor Anning cracks a smile at me, "Wonderful, isn't it?"

I nod.

Anning rolls up her sleeves. "This menagerie, girls, is a secret. It's reserved for Animalia students only. You are to guard its secrecy. If you ever see anyone here, unescorted by a professor, who is not Animalia, you must inform me immediately."

"Yes, ma'am," we say.

"Just so. You are not to enter any other program's compound unattended."

"Yes, ma'am."

"Perfect. Now let's tour the grounds." She paces around the perimeter of the atrium and we follow. We pass green vines and hardy orange blooms, every strange, leafy thing imaginable. "Animalia is charged with keeping species alive from every corner of the world. Graduates of Animalia are keepers of living things. We consider it our professional obligation, to be caretakers of the garden that is the earth. When a species becomes in danger of extinction, we shelter them here. The atrium is usually kept solely by the Animalia students, who care for the animals here, but since we're so short on students I will be tending to them, as well."

"But you aren't Animalia," Ori says, and forces her voice to sound sweet, unassuming. You'd never think it was an insult. But I know better. Ori wants information. Wants to test her.

Anning turns, slowly, facing us directly. She is a tall mother bird. "No, I am not," she tilts her head, cautiously. "But you still have much to learn from me, understood?"

"Yes, ma'am," we say.

She turns and walks ahead. Ori and I exchange looks behind her back.

Ori whispers to me, close by my shoulder. "If she were really Animalia, she'd be more fun."

"Animalia students have heightened ability to control fear, and to manage the fight-or-flight impulse," Anning turns back to us with a warning look. "You are highly-sensitive, as well, so you girls will tend to have better hearing, seeing, and sensing ability than others at Svalbard." She turns a corner and leads us down a stairway to an underground exhibit. Ecological landscapes sprawl on either side; we peer through the glass windows where different animals live in the arenas. A sandy space is marked 'savannah'.

"The Savannah Exhibit," Anning starts, "home to our precious ligers. Half-lion, half-tiger. No they aren't 'myth.' Many crossbred creatures are mistaken for myth. If introduced to the wild – unfortunately – they would be poached. We'll keep them here until we can reintroduce them – with the help of alumni – back to the wild."

"That's what alumni do?" Ori patters behind Anning.

"One of *many* things they do."

A liger follows me as I walk, sealed away on the other side of the glass. I return his gaze – his dark lion-eyes mean to tell me something.

Anning chatters on but I don't listen. I touch the glass. The liger brushes its neck against the place where my hand rests on the glass.

… *Amazing*.

"Sunday," Anning yells down the hall. "Keep up."

I run to catch up.

She leads us by a vast water tank. "Oceana," her voice echoes along the black tile. "A place for all water creatures," she brushes her nose a bit with the back of her hand and suppresses a smile. "Water creatures are… Somewhat of a specialty of mine." The way she says *Oceana*, with pride – it's like she's saying her own name.

I stare into the deep, dark water. My eyes glaze over, I turn to move – *THUD* – a tentacle snaps along the glass barrier, right by my face.

I stumble away.

Grom clutches onto the blue fabric of my dress. He growls at the tentacle.

"The giant squid," Anning laughs, as though it were obvious. "Another animal thought extinct by the world, which we have preserved here, with *great* effort. Come – this way."

I gape at the face-sized suction cups until Ori pulls me by the arm. Anning brings us to a metal door – like on a submarine – and she wrenches it open. Snow flutters in and dusts my shoes. "After you," she holds the door open for me.

I hug Grom to my chest to warm him and step outside with Ori. We stand in the snow, squinting into a large, fenced-in arena.

Anning yells over the howling wind. "Look there!"

I squint, following the line of her pointing. In the distance, across the alpine meadow, elephants stomp the snow – only they aren't elephants. They thrash their heads and their tusks sweep the snow – thick brown fur sways from their long, sloped backs: Wooly mammoths.

Holy heaven.

"I thought they were extinct!" I beam at Anning.

"Yes, of course," she shouts back, grinning in the wind. "That's what we've told the world. Could you imagine if they knew?"

Ori beams at me with pure joy.

"Yes…" Anning says. "They're happy here. One day, maybe, we'll let them wander as they have before. For now, we're watching over them."

The mammoths toss in the snow. A young one, half the size of the others, runs and plays in the snow. She holds her mother's tail.

My heart rises in my throat.

… Ma.

If only I could see Ma now.

There's so much hope in Animalia. So much wonder. If only everything in the world were kept safe, like this.

Anning leads us back into the warm atrium.

We sit on a bench below a tropical tree. Butterflies land on us as she tells us about the ways of living things and the interconnectedness of the animal chain. "To preserve the animal chain," she says, "is to preserve our own lives, as well." The way she talks about Animalia, it's the way a food connoisseur would talk about a dish they loved. She isn't Animalia herself, but she knows all about it. "Remember girls, Animalia is not magic. There is no *magic* out there. This is real. Real risks. Real abilities. Real responsibility. You will learn to listen to your animals and be empathetic to their needs. Some of the most skilled Animalia can attune themselves to the perspectives of their animals – like strings singing the same melody. *Hmm?* But those concepts are not for first-year students."

My face crumples. In tune with Grom? How?

Anning swats a hand in the air, "Never mind."

She gives us this assignment: To dig through individual glass tanks – filled with caked mud – until we scrape up fossils. She hands us a research form to fill out and excavation tool kits, like tiny dental instruments. It feels like an Apothecary assignment, somehow, not really Animalia. She turns to leave and adds, with a little cheek, "You can't be afraid to get your hands dirty, girls."

I smile at her fiery red hair as it disappears behind the tree line.

She's all right.

Ori and I work for hours, digging with fine little forks and brushes – careful not to damage any bones. I dig up what looks like an angler fish, and I can tell Ori is jealous. She dug up something strange – a nautiloid, according to our encyclopedia – a large, extinct shellfish. Ori huffs and groans over the bones. Clearly she isn't used to hard work.

Grom plays on the rim of a tree root while we dig. He and Rosie touch noses now and then.

The atrium is heaven. Bluebirds settle beside us, watching us. I sense their attentiveness. Their twitchy movements make sense, somehow, their conversation of chirping and song. Friendly creatures.

Ori checks her clunky wristwatch. "We'd better wrap up for the day."

"Right," I slap my hands on my apron, wiping off the mud.

Anning returns to us and huddles over our work with her intense beak-gaze. She reviews the marks on my paper. "Girls, I can see by your work that you were distracted," her hawk-eyes shoot across the bones of my angler fish and the shell of Ori's crustacean, "you'll have to write a report tonight, to follow-up on your work here. Please review the animal you've excavated in *Victor's Animal Encyclopedia*, and tell me the exact function of the body's design for its environment."

"Yes, ma'am."

She marks our research papers. She gives Ori a C, and me an A-. She turns and leaves.

Ori gapes at my paper. "Why do you get everything special?"

I try not to smile. *Because I'm naturally good at this, like Pa.*

For once in my life. I'm good at something.

I fold my smile into a grimace for her. "Don't know," I shrug. "We did the same work."

❧

That night we sit by the dorm lounge fire, cross-legged, and finish schoolwork. Ori eyes me from the side. She leans over the low table to finish her report. I've already perfected mine:

The Angler Fish

The Angler Fish is a deep-sea dwelling fish. It is not extinct. It is a predator. It has various projected bones from its head which have a bioluminescent light for the deep dark spaces of the salty sea. It uses this multi-colored light as a lure to attract smaller fish and invertebrates that it can eat. Its sharp teeth are designed for piercing the tough flesh of other dense, deep-sea fish...

"What are you writing?" Ori whines, craning her neck over to my report paper on the table. "I wish we'd had the same animal. Then it would be easier."

"How would it be easier?"

"Never mind," she rolls her eyes. "*Ugh.* I wish we didn't have an Apothic teacher. No wonder apothecary students are stressed studying all the time. It's like we can't have a life."

Something behind Ori stirs, catches my attention – my eyes narrow on it.

What the blazes –

I grip the neckline of my dress. I lean in. Something moved behind the distant, blue-velvet curtain. Chills touch my spine. I drop my pen and it falls onto my lap.

Ori frowns at my pen. "What are you–"

I point to the bump behind the curtain.

Ori follows my finger to the shadowed space beside her. Her brown

❧ 93 ❧

eyebrows raise.

I stand.

She stands.

Slowly, we approach the lump behind the curtain.

I set my jaw. *Someone snuck in.*

Fire lights in me. I grit my teeth, grip the blue velvet cloth, and toss it aside, revealing the Irish servant boy, Eoin. He jumps.

Ori drops her jaw. "What are you doing?" she hisses at him. She smacks him a little with the back of her hand, as though they were friends.

"I just –" he stammers, "wanted to see what you're doing."

"Well come on then, sit," Ori says, exasperated. "And don't scare us half to death."

"I'm sorry…"

We sit.

I glare at Eoin. I don't mean to. Something about him is off… His pants are worn around the knees from scrubbing floors, but the hem of his pants has a tuft of white fur stuck to it, thick fur, like that of a snow tiger.

No, that can't be right…

My head spins. Eoin is somehow connected to Seraphim.

All my senses focus on him: Eoin's green eyes are distant, dull. His blondish-red hair is disheveled and grown-out, but the edges are sharp; I'd say about six months ago it was cut by a professional barber. Eoin comes from money.

But is that true?

I bite the inside of my cheek.

It's true. It sits in my bones; I'm certain.

Eoin comes from money. And Seraphim is keeping a tight eye on him.

Eoin eats our cakes and cookies. He snarfs them down like he's never tasted food. I watch him until I can't bear it any longer. "Eoin," I ask, trying to make my voice sweet.

He snaps his head up to me.

"When were you going to tell us… how you got inside?"

"Huh?" he says.

"What?" Ori says.

"The mirror-door," I say, slowly, so they can understand. "The riddle. *Only one with an animal's mind…* It won't open to students who aren't Animalia."

"Oh…" Eoin says.

"That's right," Ori says, wide-eyed. She taps her pen and gives me an approving look. "It won't open to anyone who doesn't have *'an animal's mind.'* That means Animalia."

"I dunno," Eoin blinks.

That's true. He doesn't know… But maybe I do.

My senses sharpen. I lean forward with my elbows on my knees. I study him: His lip is peeling, but not from dry air. Only the bottom lip peels. He picks at it. He's nervous. His shoes are worn but they're mint leather. Expensive. And two sizes too big still. Bought in advance so he can grow into them. Eoin comes from a lower-upper class and frugal, image-conscious Northern Irish family. I'm sure.

… It worked. I did it again.

Eoin is not who we think he is. He's far from a servant boy.

He avoids my gaze. His cheeks blush peach. I'm staring too hard.

I try to soften. "It's all right, Eoin," I press my hands in my lap. "We're going to find out who you are, eventually…"

He blinks at me and recoils a bit. He took that as a threat. He looks like he's about to cry.

Ugh. So weak…

I tilt my head with a forced gentleness, "I promise," I add, stiff, "we'll help you."

He nods lowly.

Ori raises a brow at me. She snaps her book shut and the sound makes Eoin jump. "Well we've finished our papers," she announces. "See you later Eoin."

We say goodbye to him and he retreats back into the castle, somewhere…

I glance out the lounge window. The fifth-year Animalia boys play in the snow outside the complex. They throw snowballs at one another. Their animals chase each other in circles; like brothers.

Ori yawns, tucks in Rosie for the night, and saunters up the steps to our room.

"Ori," I bite my lip. I used her nickname, not her full name, Oria. I don't know when I took to her nickname, but I can tell she likes it.

She stops mid-step above me and turns. "Hmm?"

"Have you noticed? The boys are all fifth-years. That means all the other new students from other years dropped out, or something."

"Oh," she wobbles on the step, sleepy. "Sure. I suppose the others dropped out. That's what Anning told me, anyway."

"Oh…" I knit my fingers into a knot.

Why would so many drop out?

Because they didn't drop out. Something happened to them.

I pace up the steps to our room when –

"Help!"

I pause. "Did you hear that?"

Ori yawns. "What?"

"Someone shouting. Outside. In the distance."

We stand still, listening.

"Help! Somebody!"

Ori and I sprint down the steps to the window. Outside, one of the Animalia boys races through the snow and back into Svalbard. My heart pumps in my neck. I squint my eyes, it's dim outside, dusk, and snow swirls through the air. "Where are the other boys?"

Ori presses her hands to the window. "Where'd he go? I can't see him!"

"We should call Anning."

Ori eyes the emergency bell, which is rigged to ring Anning and Dr. Laszlo, the emergency team.

"Wait," Ori says. "We don't know if it's really an emergency."

… She's wrong. It's an emergency.

Wham!

The lounge door swings open and the Animalia boy bursts in. "Help!"

he trips over himself and falls to the ground, hugging his slow-loris with one hand. "Get help, quick."

I run to the emergency bell on the opposite wall and pull the rope – *Dong! Dong! Dong!*

The Animalia boy crawls forward, toward the fireplace, and weeps. He moans, wide-eyed, rocking back and forth as he holds his slow-loris to his chest. *"No, no, no…"*

"Where are the others?" I yell.

"No, no… no…"

I sweep beside him and place my hands on his shoulders. I make him look at me. "Where are they?"

He stares into the fire. "It wasn't human."

I frown at him. *Human?* "…Then… What was it?"

He shakes his head. Tears crease along his eyelids. "It's coming after me. I'm next. I know I'm next…"

"You are *not* next," Ori says, her hands on her hips. "We're going to help you."

I study him. The terror inside him. His trembling hands. His frizzy hair pressed back with a woven tribal band. The animal that clings to his neck like a frightened child.

… He knows something we don't.

"What happened to the other students?" I press. "Why aren't there more in Animalia?"

His eyes go cold. "They always told us they dropped out. Our friends dropped out. Without ever saying goodbye. Why wouldn't they say goodbye?"

Wham!

Anning bursts into the lounge in her nightdress. Her hawk-gaze pierces me. "What happened?"

The boy shivers, dazed, and stares into the fire.

Dr. Laszlo sweeps in behind Anning. His brown hair is disheveled, like he just woke up, and he wears a lab-coat over his dark nightclothes.

"The boys were all playing outside," I stand, "then I heard screaming and they ran, and we don't know where the others are – it's just him now."

Anning's face falls. Something shifts in her green eyes, not surprise, but dread.

Laszlo saunters to the window and glances outside. "They must've seen a wild bear."

"It wasn't a bear," the boy snaps. "I'm Animalia. I know the difference. It wasn't an animal. It was a *monster*." The boy shivers, petrified, holding himself and muttering; "I knew I wasn't imaging things... I knew it was only a matter of time... I didn't forget... I knew I was..."

"Please, doctor, take care of this one," Anning tells Laszlo. "I'll look for the other boys."

Dr. Laszlo adjusts his gold octagonal spectacles, kneels beside the boy, and pulls his arms gently on either side to help him stand. "Up you go, there, there. We'll get you some soothing herbs, you'll forget this was ever a fright..."

Thank God Laszlo is here. Everything about him is so... fatherly.

The boy trembles, leaning onto Laszlo like a child.

Laszlo places one hand on the door, and turns over his shoulder to me. "And Ms. Sunday?"

My cheeks warm. "Yes?"

"Thank you," he smiles with white teeth and tan cheeks. "For ringing us."

"Oh... no problem."

"Do let me know if there's anything I can help with." His Hungarian accent makes his voice soft, romantic, "Or if you notice anything suspicious. My office is a short walk away."

"... I will."

Laszlo leaves with the boy and shuts the door behind him.

The fire crackles. We stand in silence.

Ori frowns at the space where Laszlo stood. "... Well that was horrible."

I follow Ori up the stairs toward our room, and glance out the window. But instead of seeing Anning in the snow, Seraphim is there. Her tiger steps lightly beside her, sniffing. She traces the boys' tracks in the snow.

... Odd.

Anning must have told her. About the missing boys.

Seraphim stops walking, and slowly turns around to me above her, like she could sense my watching her. She does not smile.

My gut dips. I shouldn't watch her. I flick my gaze away.

Ori and I turn in for the night. I arrange my things in my space so they're more comfortable. I organize them the same way I had at home.

Ori slips into bed, and I double-lock the door to our room.

...Click.

I've been holding my breath. I force myself to exhale.

"Don't worry," Ori mutters to me. She turns out her lamp and our bedroom goes dark. "The professors will figure everything out and make it right. That's what they do."

"...Right..."

I rest my head on the starchy pillowcase. I hold Grom close.

If only I believed her – but she's wrong.

There's a monster in Svalbard. And I know it in my core. It's connected, somehow, to Pa.

If only I could tell Ma...

There's no regular postal service coming in or out of the compound. No way to write home. But if I could.

My heart thumps and twists. Moisture lines my eyes.

If I could. I would tell Ma everything.

TWELVE

AMBASSADOR SUNDAY

A snowstorm falls thick and heavy on Svalbard and the days blur. It's an especially cold winter, with constant darkness in the Arctic Circle. It's obvious which students have come from warmer climates – like Ori – she shivers and whines about the lack of sunshine. She talks about the Caribbean Islands nonstop.

I curl up by the fireplace in our lounge, warming my feet. I scribble on a piece of parchment and write to Ma, even though I'll never be able to send it to her.

It's more of a diary-entry, I suppose.

Ma,

Is it true a monster really killed Pa? The more I think about the night he died, the more I think – maybe I didn't imagine the monster there. Maybe something really was hunting him.

I can't sleep. There are things I've seen here that make me question that night Pa died.

In my mind I've been hearing more and more, that voice that's like a monster, and she tells me she hates me. It's worse now than ever. How do I get rid of her, Mama? At night it's the worst — the things I've seen jumble together. Was I wrong to think I killed Pa? Or was I responsible too?

I have to find out more about the man I saw in the basement, and if he really is a monster. If I figure out who the monster is, somehow, I think I could live with myself, and understand why I am the way I am.

I press my head to the note, crumple it and toss it into the fire.

I take Ori's arm and we walk side-by-side toward the Animalia Atrium.

"Have you seen the boy?" I ask her in the hall, "the one from the attack that was all terrified a few nights ago?"

Ori shakes her head absently. "The boys are on a different schedule. Maybe our paths haven't crossed."

My gut dips under the wood floors. She's wrong. "Something happened to them, Ori."

Ori's face falls, and for a split moment fear flashes in her face — but she quickly wipes it away. "*Don't worry so much,*" she rolls her eyes. "*Jeesh.* You're scaring me. It was just a wild beast or something they saw. We'll just be careful not to go outside the school complex."

"…Right."

We enter the Animalia atrium. Birds sing and dive over us. Sunlight filters in through the glass ceiling and the green blur of Anning's dress turns the corner. She waits for us, arms folded. She doesn't scare me anymore, she's softer than she lets on. With the three of us working so closely, it's hard not to be familiar. She could be my aunt.

Every day in the atrium is a new lesson, some precious secret; a near-forgotten creature; an ecological secret; a method for saving animals… It's more amazing than I could've imagined.

I sit on a bench and toy with my notebook. Ori starts her work for the day, cataloguing footprints of various mammals. My mind wanders, I can't help it, I scribble pictures of the vines, the butterflies… I write another note to Ma.

Ma,

Animalia is so wonderful. It's like the beauty of everything, all living things. I think I know why I loved Animalia so much before, even though I could never say exactly why... it's like I sense this invisible thread, holding things together, animating them. There's this design in the signature of living things. I think that's what it must mean to be Animalia, to understand the design. And to see things others won't see.

Anning taught us that plants will only grow according to the size pot they're in. She said to understand how to care for something, you have to treat it as though it isn't broken, or maimed at all, and instead to allow space for things to grow into the fullness of what they can be... She said we have to see the fully healed version, the fully grown future, to treat things in the natural world as they should, so they can be what they truly are, underneath. It's funny to think about. But I feel like there's space for me here, too. Like maybe I can be who I'm meant to be.

"Ladies," Anning announces, strolling toward us. "I have news."

We sit on the rim of the garden's stone edge.

"I'm told it's time you learn… the basic *psychology* of Animalia. Even though I myself am not Animalia, I will do my best to teach you."

"Who told you what we have to learn?" Ori asks.

"Why can't someone from Animalia teach us?" I ask. "Like Seraphim?"

Anning folds her lips into a grimace. "Dean Seraphim is… *uh*… busy."

I deflate. "Oh…"

Anning clasps her hands together. "Animalia uses empathy to ignite the subconscious mind, which excels in understanding behaviors, motives, connections. Today we will test the type of empathy you have with your animal counterparts."

"With Grom?" I say.

"A test?" Ori frowns. "But we didn't study."

Anning bites her thin lower lip. "The test will help you understand your mental strengths and weaknesses."

We trail behind her to a wide, dark room behind the atrium. I peer into the room from the side – a wall separates each half from the other. Both sides of the room have several low stands, with different items on them.

"Again, Animalia is not some 'magic thing'. It is a trained practice which takes extreme mental fortitude. That is what we are testing; your empathetic strength, and your corresponding subconscious ability. Oria you first, dear, place Rosie on one side of the room, and enter the other side yourself. You won't be able to see your animal – that's the point. But we'll be able to see both of you. The goal is to test if you and Rosie select the same item."

What happens if we don't?

…Does that mean we aren't Animalia?

"All right," Ori bounces Rosie in her arms a few times and gently places her on the opposite side of the wall.

Anning holds a Machinist stopwatch. "You have one minute to try and select the same item as your animal."

Ori stands on the opposite side of the wall, separated from Rosie.

Anning presses a switch on the gold stopwatch. "Begin!"

Tick! Tick! Tick! Tick!

Ori frowns at the items in the bowls before her.

Rosie trots up to the objects, sniffing them. Finally, Rosie sets her snout on a bowl of soybeans. She starts eating.

Tick! Tick! Tick! Tick!

"Five seconds!" Anning shouts.

"I don't know!" Ori yells. She paces down the wood floor, turns around herself, and finally picks up the bowl of soybeans.

"TIME!"

"*Ugh,*" Ori groans. She steps down from the platform with the bowl of soybeans, flustered, and brushes curls from her face.

"Well done, Oria," Anning says.

Ori does a double-take. She spins around to see Rosie trotting toward her, with soybeans on her snout. "We picked the same thing?" Ori squeals. "I knew it!" She gathers Rosie in her arms and swings her around. "We did it. Yes – yes!"

Anning marks her notebook with a feather pen. She returns to the room, and resituates the objects, rearranging different items.

My heart rises to my throat.

"Don't look so worried," Ori says to me, rocking Rosie in her arms. "Don't overthink it."

Easy for you to say. You have a pig. Of course it chose food.

Grom yawns at me in my arms.

What would Grom pick?

"Sunday," Anning taps her stopwatch. "The test is ready for you."

My pulse pounds in my skull. "…right." I step up to the platform and set Grom down behind the wall. It's too dark. I can't make out the shapes of the objects.

I walk around the wall and stand on the opposite side. My steps echo on the wood floor.

"Ready, and–" Anning pulls a switch and lightbulbs turn on, illuminating the objects in front of me. "Start!"

Tick! Tick! Tick! Tick!

Everything blurs.

Focus, Sunday. Focus.

Five stands are in front of me, each with a different object;

A crystal bell,

A blue ribbon,

Golden scales,

A bowl of walnuts,

And a knife.

…What on earth?

I step closer to the objects. The test has to examine something. Some trait.

It's a mind-riddle.

Grom. What would Grom pick? What does he want?

Tick! Tick! Tick! Tick!

"Thirty seconds!" Anning calls from the side.

My heart thumps.

A crystal bell, what does that mean? Playfulness. Grom is playful.

The blue ribbon – comfort?

Golden reptile scales – scales are for protection. Defensiveness?

Walnuts – food. Pleasure.

A knife?

Tick! Tick! Tick!

Please, no, no, no.

"Don't overthink it!" Ori shouts from the side.

"Shhh," Anning hisses at her.

Maybe I am overthinking it.

I close my eyes. I slow my breathing. I listen…

I listen the way I would listen for animals in the meadows; listen for birds, rabbits.

I sense Grom behind the wall. He sniffs at the objects. He bites at the blue ribbon, then drops it, uninterested. His tiny feet patter along the wall, and I follow him on the opposite side, eyes closed. He stops walking.

I stop walking.

His heart is light and flutters with excitement… *Thrill.*

Thrill?

I open my eyes. I stand in front of the small knife.

Tick – Tick – Tick!

"Five seconds!" Anning shouts.

The knife? Really?

I gather the small, delicate weapon in my hands. Its blade is one-sided and sharp as teeth. It's engraved on the side with the Animalia house symbol; the tree of life.

"Time!" Anning yells.

I step down from the platform with the knife in hand.

Grom steps down from the other side. He carries the knife in his mouth.

… He picked the knife. Out of all of them.

Grom.

"Oria?" Anning says, calm. "Will you go back to the atrium and fetch my notebook? I've forgotten it."

Ori's eyes flash around the space between us. "Sure," she turns away with Rosie.

Anning presses her finger to the bridge of her hook-nose. "Do you know why you picked the knife?"

"*He* picked it," I splutter, stepping down to her. "Not me. I just thought, maybe he wanted this one."

Anning gives me a sharp look. She rips the knife from me, and from Grom, and sets them aside. She pulls a blue ribbon from her pocket and hands it to me, instead. "People will ask you what item you picked – and when they do, you'll say that Grom picked the Animalia ribbon. Don't tell anyone that your subconscious mind is violent. Don't talk about the knife. Not about anything disagreeable."

"Why?"

Anning's thin lips tighten. She marks my test paper with a fountain pen. "I am writing that you both selected the blue ribbon."

My arms prickle, numb. "Did I do it… wrong?"

"What do you think?" she snaps her head up. "The tests show you the nature of your psychology. The motives of your mind. Oria is at Svalbard for pleasure, obviously. But you are here because you crave *vengeance*. You are ruthless. And it will only get worse the longer you bond with the dragon. You will dream *dangerous* dreams. See things no one else sees. But not only that – your animal is a monster. *That* is dangerous."

"No. *Please*, Ms. Anning. We aren't dangerous."

"*Please, Sunday,*" she mimics, condescending to me.

Grom watches me from below with dark glassy eyes.

Grom is… *Dangerous*?

The air goes stale around me. "But, isn't danger… in his nature?"

"Wake up!" Anning snaps, slapping down her pen. Her eyes go wild. "Your subconscious mind is bonding with a *dragon*. Don't you get it? People will see you as a threat. They already see you as a threat. You think people admire strong people, *huh*? They don't like it when you're strong. They don't like it when you're smart. When you're different, when you're bold. When you don't conform. When you have power and speak your mind in truth." Her eyes widen, eager, like she's speaking from something personal.

I step back.

"Animalia is a house of *predator* and *prey*, understand? And what predator is stronger than a dragon? There is a dominance hierarchy here. We don't teach animal dominance until the third and fourth years, but already your dragon wants dominance. He wants to fight. You are vulnerable and young now, and *now* is the time when it would be possible to stop you. Weak people *hate* strong people. And you will be stronger than everyone. Get that through yourself. You must pretend to be harmless, as long as you can. There are far more weak people than strong in this world. And the weak manipulate to elevate themselves. They lie and accuse and condemn. They play the victim and then kill. People don't understand real power – they will search for blame in you even if there is none. They won't challenge you outright. They won't say it to your face. They'll come together and slit you in your sleep."

I clutch Grom to my chest. *What in the hellfire –*

Anning softens, like she realizes she's gone too far.

Someone at Svalbard is threatened by me?

.... Who?

Ori isn't threatened by me.

My gut twists. The only other person in Animalia is Seraphim.

Fire lights in my chest. It's her.

But Seraphim isn't against me. She gave me all my nice clothes. She knew Pa. She's been looking out for me.

Then again... I don't *actually* know her.

I don't know Anning's motives, either. After all, she isn't Animalia.

My gaze narrows on Anning: Her rust-colored hair is frayed and sloppy. Her eyes are bloodshot from caffeine; black tea. A faint aroma of Earl Grey seeps from her clothes. Her cheeks are dry and creased from stress. Ink stains smear her fingers, but they're not fresh. The ink is dry, faded.

The smears are about eight hours old.

Anning stayed up all night writing something.

Something important.

There's more going on she won't tell me.

Ori stumbles back into the room carrying Anning's notebook. "Sunday? You all right?"

I snap my head away to the marble floor.

"Sunday isn't feeling well," Anning says. "Walk her back to the lounge."

Ori cinches her brows at me, like she's concerned. "… Sure."

I skip dinner.

I sit in the Animalia lounge, alone. I slide Grom into the 'Carnivore' enclosure. He claws at the cage and whines, begging me to let him out. "You're dangerous to be around," I tell him. "That's why you have to stay in there."

Ori enters the lounge and slides a plate of cake and a goblet of juice onto the table beside me. "I had Eoin get this for you, especially, from the kitchen. Since you're skipping meals now."

"…I don't want it."

Ori half-smiles, like she expected I'd say that. "Fine. I'll just give it to Rosie."

Ori sits on the floor beside me and hugs her knees to her chest. She lowers the cake down to Rosie, who licks the frosting eagerly.

"Sunday…" Ori sighs, "I know you can't sleep at night. And I know you're obsessing about the man we saw in the basement. But I just think –"

"Wait –" I hold her arm. "Does Rosie usually do that?"

By our feet, on the floor, Rosie keels over, thrashing and flinching.

"ROSIE!" Ori gathers her up and frantically searches all around for water.

I rise, perfectly still, and watch Rosie's seizure soften until she hangs limp in Ori's arms.

Ori fills a baby bottle with water and nurses Rosie back to health, slowly. "It was just a passing seizure, or something."

I turn away to the fireplace. The flames whip high and sparks graze my skirt. "The cake was poisoned," I say, flatly. "Someone knew you'd give it to me."

"The cake was not *poisoned*," Ori wipes hair from her sweaty forehead. "For heaven's sake, Sunday. You're paranoid."

I turn back to her. "But you saw what happened. Rosie only licked the frosting, but what if I'd taken several bites of that cake? Someone is trying to kill me."

Ori rolls her eyes. "*Oh please.*"

"Wake UP!" I snap. "Someone in Svalbard is coming after Animalia. It took the boys and it's coming after us now. We have to find the killer."

Ori stumbles backward. She clutches Rosie to her chest. The way Ori looks at me, with fear in her eyes – it's the same look Anning gave me, it says; *you're a monster.*

The following morning, I sit by the washbasin, alone, and clean my feet.

I scrub them raw.

Cleaning them like this – it's comforting.

Through the washroom door Ori fusses over what to wear. She always lays her clothes out the night before. God knows why. Every time she changes it again in the morning.

I stop scrubbing. I force deep breaths. *Why am I so irritated?*

Anning's words echo in my mind: I'm dangerous. A predator.

I set my jaw.

She's right. Maybe I am dangerous.

My heart sinks.

…A monster.

On the marble floor by my feet, Grom chases a horsefly. He snaps his teeth at it, growling.

I dunk my head in my hands. *Am I changing?*

I could tell every detail about Anning. And it wasn't a guess, I knew what she'd done, where she'd been.

I could never do that before.

I stare at my face in the dressing mirror… Purple rings line my eyes from lack of sleep. I'm a skeleton. A shell.

"Sunday?" Ori calls from the other room. "What's wrong with you? We have to go-*ooo*. Class is starting. You've been washing your feet for like, two hours."

If only I could sink into the tile floor – and take a bath and never get out…

I throw my clothes on and step into my shoes. Ori grabs my arm and pulls me. We hurry out of our dorm and jog, her brown corkscrew curls bounce as she runs. "I'm really glad your feet are clean for class," she fake-smiles. "Even though we're running late. That just makes my day."

Maybe Ori sees me as a threat, too…

Inside the Animalia Atrium, Ori and I sit in front of Anning.

I stare at the grass beside Anning's dark green dress. I can't look her in the eye. Not after what she said…

"This year is not like previous years, with the houses so separate," Anning tilts her head an interesting way. "Our new dean is setting into effect an *ambassador* program. The program selects one student from each house to visit the other programs, as an ambassador, and to educate the other programs on what it means to be – in our case – Animalia."

"There are only two of us, though," I say.

"Can I go?" Ori says.

"We've already decided on ambassadors for each program. Sunday Gråe will be the ambassador for Animalia."

Ori deflates.

"Don't worry, girl," Anning pats Ori's shoulder. "The other ambassadors will visit you and you'll have time with them one-on-one."

Ori smiles wickedly at me, like she got the better end of the deal after all.

"So…" I mutter. "What do I do?"

"Come with me," Anning waves.

I follow Anning through strange medieval stone passageways. We stop in a high, circular room with windows all around and mountains beyond. A few professors recline on velvet lounge chairs, reading books from the circular shelves.

It's a professor's lounge, and they've brought their chosen ambassador student with them.

I stand close to Anning.

The other ambassadors are these fifth-years; older than me, polished, more confident.

"Are we all here?" Dr. Laszlo says. He rolls up the sleeve of his off-white lab-coat to check his wristwatch. His carefully trimmed, downturned mustache gives him a permanent frown. Behind his gold spectacles, his eyes are hazel and handsome. "All of us, except Seraphim," Laszlo jokes. "She's off on her *own* business, as always."

Only Professor Cortez, the Artisan, laughs. Strangely, his arm is bound in a sling.

"Did you hurt yourself, William?" Anning asks.

"Freak accident," Cortez chatters. "The ladder broke while I was painting the ceiling. Should have died, really, but a student was working on a tapestry below me, which broke my fall. And also we have the worlds' best doctor here."

Dr. Laszlo bows a little and scans the room from behind his gold spectacles, "Very well," he mutters with a Hungarian lilt, "We'll each visit day-by-day, 8:00 a.m. Counter-clockwise."

Counter-clockwise...

What?

I follow Laszlo's line of vision to the map of Svalbard on the wall. The house complexes are situated in a circle, almost like a clock, with each section in an adjacent part of the circle. Symbols are above each of the program's sections; a suit-of-arms for Warbringer, a gilded harp for Artisan... Of course. The houses are situated strategically around each other.

I frown at the map – I've seen these lines before, these symbols.

In an instant I'm back in the basement again – looking over the strange man and some kind of ritual he'd made – the symbols, they were arranged the same way with dripped ink and wax – in an octagon, just like the map of Svalbard.

Anning squeezes my shoulder and I tear my gaze away. My expression must look too intense. I soften my cheeks. I pretend to be interested in what the professors say. I act dull, naïve.

...Others will see you as a threat.

"Perhaps if we're lucky this will be the only year it happens." Laszlo complains.

Odd Laszlo is so annoyed. Maybe he takes his teaching time with Apothecary that seriously... Or mayhap he likes his privacy. That's more likely.

Perhaps I can find out why he's so touchy... Just how I did with Anning.

My eyes narrow on Dr. Laszlo; he has clean fingernails, scraped clean with a tool. His cuticles are bleeding – brutal. His mustache is trimmed but the backside of his head is unkempt. He's image-conscious but part of him doesn't care. Bruises line his wrists, encircling them. His watch is too tight? No. His wrists were bound by something recently...

Odd...

I pet Grom absently on my shoulder.

Laszlo's gold watch has Hungarian words etched on the outside, and a glass interior – he comes from wealth. His lab coat is hot-pressed, but the ends are still wrinkled. He did it this morning. He was anxious. He rushed.

I glance up again and Dr. Laszlo walks closer to me, like he could sense my studying him. He bends over to Grom, his hazel eyes are hungry, intelligent, like he'd dissect Grom with a scalpel. His expression toward me is cold, medical.

Chills rush through me but I don't look away. I won't.

Anning clears her throat, loudly, and Laszlo steps away from me and smiles – a wide, handsome smile. "I see you're still tending to animals, Mary." He winks at Anning and walks away.

…Interesting.

My fingers are pinched, so hard my fingernails have dug into my skin. I force myself to unwind and spread my fingers. I open my jaw to make it relax.

"I think it's pleasant," the Machinist professor says: Professor Suri; her voice is soft and hopeful. She tidies her kimono and sweeps stray dark hair behind her ear. Jade earrings glint beneath her jaw. "Things like this never happened with Dean Raj, did they?"

"Well not much happened under Raj, at all," Cortez says blandly. His Spanish accent is smooth, warm. He kicks his foot back against the wall, smokes a pipe. He certainly looks Artisan. He fits in perfectly with the room; the renaissance paintings, the sculpture busts. He's a standing piece of art. A statement. His disheveled hair and scarlet necktie would make anyone else look ridiculous, but it looks right on him, somehow. He chuckles, "Raj didn't have much imagination, did he?"

Professor Seacole, the Warbringer, shoots Cortez a warning look, like he's said too much with students present. "Enough talk," she snaps. "Off you go."

Cortez leaves with a student following in his wake, carrying an art portfolio.

"This way," Anning presses a hand to my back in a new direction. We tunnel down a northern stairway and into an austere hall. The air chills, colder the deeper we go and Anning opens a gate which spills outside into the snowy main courtyard.

I wrap Grom in my jacket to warm him. The faces of the courtyard statues are glossy with ice, and they frown down at me; Grecian warriors, Algerian fighters, South American soldiers…

We're headed to Warbringer.

The relics should be inspiring. Only – *blazes* – they aren't.

It's like a graveyard.

We cross the frosty courtyard, heading to a fortified building – the most secure area of Svalbard. Great walls surround the building and Anning pushes a lever in a special code at the gate to open it. Up – Right – Left.

I memorize the code.

The gates swing open and we enter the huge Warbringer compound; we pass a strange archery range and training grounds and Anning opens the main doors to the black building.

I step in and my jaw goes slack. It's a… *war museum*. A great hall with exhibits honoring the warriors of the past. Weapons and uniforms line the walls in glass cases, coming from every culture and time around the world. I follow close at Anning's heels as we pass the glass cases, filled with maps, histories… Anning turns a corner and pushes open the double-doors to a sit-down classroom.

A hundred Warbringer students face the front of the room. An older student at the front of the class stops her lecture. She erases the chalkboard with military diagrams, bows abruptly to Anning, and sits in the front row.

Anning strides to the front of the class. "Good morning, Warbringers."

"Good morning, Professor Anning," they reply in unison.

I jump.

Holy Heaven… Everything they do is regimented.

"As part of Dean Seraphim's new orientation program," Anning speaks over the room, "we will be implementing a new ambassador program. The goal is for you all to ask questions freely from a student of a different house. This –" she turns to me, "is Sunday Gråe. She's an Animalia student. You may ask her anything you wish."

Their stares harden on me. Their frowns. Their pressed uniforms and shorn hair.

One boy, in particular, can't stop smirking at me. I've seen him around school. He sits in the front row and has short, light brown hair and doesn't sit at attention, like the others. He kind of smiles at me.

Just ignore him.

Creep.

My jaw clenches, but I force myself to soften, to appear relaxed.

A younger girl in the back stands and asks me a question. "So do you train animals?"

"Oh… No," I try to sound pleasant. "That's not what we do at all." I exchange a glance with Professor Anning, who flicks her head as though I should elaborate.

"We protect animals," I say, "we focus on conservation and ecology."

The tan, brown-haired boy in the front row kind of smiles at me again.

… What a total ratbag.

But the creep swings his arms forward, and speaks up; "So what's that creature on ya shoulder?" he asks, loudly.

I glare at him, which makes him laugh a bit. He sounds Scottish, but he looks Spanish – his skin is sun-kissed; but his uniform is creased and smudged with dirt. He's a sloppy Warbringer.

"This is Grom," I say to the classroom.

"Yeah but what *kind*," the boy presses, then gives me an expectant look, "is he a lizard?"

A few people laugh in the back.

My cheeks warm. "He is *not* a lizard."

"*Ohhh*," the boy says, and circles his head a bit. Teasing me.

I grit my teeth.

… Idiots.

A girl in the front row, about my age, asks, "He looks friendly. Is he a newt?"

I soften. She has warm eyes and smiles at Grom. She turns a bracelet around her wrist which has strung-together dreidels.

"Grom is a green-tree dragon," I say. "He's only two years old."

"Can I touch him?"

I tense. "*Umm*… Fine. But only you. No one else."

I set Grom on her desk. He keeps his distance from her, but when she holds out her hand, he touches her fingers. That means she's kind. He wouldn't do that with just anyone.

The class breaks out into whispering:

"It's too big to be a lizard."

"Dragons don't exist… everyone knows that."

"Don't ask me, ask the girl with the dragon."

Great. Now I'm 'the girl with the dragon.'

The tan boy in the front pulls his fingers around his strong jaw, like he's sizing me up.

I square my shoulders. I can't put my finger on it. They annoy me. All of them. Fire lights in my belly. I'm not afraid of them.

I say, loudly, "Any more dumb questions?"

"Yeah," the brown-haired Scottish boy says, with a wide smile, leaning over his desk. "I have a dumb question."

The boys around him laugh.

I scowl.

"Can he breathe fire?" the boy teases.

I tense. I'd never considered it before. "I – I don't know…"

Blazes. I should know that.

The boy's smile dims.

Anning interrupts sharply, "Dragons are not like the *myths* you hear about them."

I soften.

Thank God Anning is here.

The Warbringers hush, listening. "Not all dragons breathe fire," Anning says, "but the green-tree dragon, if given a specific diet of crystals and other minerals – can produce gasses in their stomach, which will result in fire. When these gasses build, they must release them."

The Warbringers stare at Grom – a fire-breathing weapon.

My gut dips.

Just weeks ago, Grom was my little newt, not some fire-breathing dragon.

"The existence of dragons, for example, is one of the many secrets in Animalia which we guard and protect. And we are expecting you –" Anning stares them down face-to-face, "–each of you– to protect those secrets. Understand?"

"Yes, Professor Anning," the Warbringers say in unison. They sit with upright posture, eyes fixed on the empty space above her head.

"You will not tell anyone what you've learned today," Anning says.

"Yes, Professor Anning," they repeat.

"We'll be leaving now," Anning ushers me under her arm, and I swipe Grom from the girl's desk, who whispers, "*thanks.*"

I pass the tan boy on my way out, his mouth rests open, as though he would speak to me, but he thinks better of it and slumps back into his chair.

Anning and I exit the compound and wade through the snow side-by-side. She pats my shoulder, "Good girl," she sighs, "those things can be exhausting."

"Thank you. For explaining Grom."

She smiles at me from the side. Red hair curves around her high freckled cheekbones. She looks younger when she smiles. Maybe now is a good time to ask her about the missing Animalia students. But... She told me to keep quiet about it. I lower my eyes.

"I'm off to an appointment," she whisks away. "See you tomorrow, then."

"Right."

I watch the green bustle of her dress turn down the snowy courtyard.

I stand, alone, in the quiet yard. Cotton-ball snow flutters around me and sticks to the blue fabric of my dress.

I should go back to Ori.

But Anning left tracks in the snow. A trail...

... I could follow that trail.

After all, Anning is hiding things.

The sooner I find who is behind all this, the sooner I'll have peace.

Wind whips my blue dress around my ankles, my hair blows free in it – snowflakes dance around my neck.

I should see what she's hiding.

I step toward her trail.

She knows about the missing students.

I follow her footprints down a hidden part of the courtyard. Statues of Animalia frown down at me; Cleopatra's eyebrows arch at me, disapproving. St. Patrick holds a sculpted snake in his hand, and a cross in the other; his sadness tells me: Turn back.

I ignore him, too. I turn a corner to a small door. I place a hand on the cold iron, and push.

Cre-eak.

I peer into the empty hall.

Red carpet lines the wood floor. Dim lanterns hang from the walls.

I step lightly onto the carpet and inch down the cold hall, toward the end where Anning's voice echoes, muffled. "There's nothing out of the ordinary that I notice about either of the girls."

I stop:

"Fine. Then how did the professors respond?"

Chills touch my spine. It's Seraphim.

I hold my breath. I press my back to the wall, listening to her around the corner:

"As expected…" Anning says, dull.

"And the girls too?" Seraphim asks quickly.

"… Normal."

"House staff?" Seraphim presses.

"Nothing unusual," Anning says, slowly.

"There has to be something, did you talk to the boy?"

"*Er* – his mind is still gone."

"And did you send the letter with all the specifications?"

"Yes. It's being made."

Seraphim's tiger purrs – its pink nose comes into view around the corner. It sniffs the ground beside my feet. The wood floor creaks under the weight of its massive paws.

I hold my breath.

Please. No, no, no.

My gut drops. This was a mistake.

It can smell me. *Blazes!* I shouldn't have come.

The women, suddenly, go quiet.

No.

"…That will be all today, Anning."

"Will you be heading out of town again?"

Outside, wind moans quietly.

"...No," Seraphim says, soft. "No, today I'll be in."

"Very well." Anning's footsteps recede down the wood hallway.

I grit my teeth. I can't walk away now and risk being heard.

Please don't find me... Don't find me...

I squeeze my eyes shut. I sense – without having to look – the low rumble of breath in the tiger's chest around the corner. And the gentle footsteps of a woman turning the corner, toward me.

I open my eyes and Seraphim stands over me.

No!

My heart hammers in my chest. I gape at her.

She is a marble statue – an angel. Her expression is neutral but her hands are tense by her sides.

Adrenaline kicks my chest and I strain to breathe. "I'm sorry," I splutter. "I – didn't mean to."

She presses in close toward me, ever-so-slowly. Her voice is low, "You've been spying on me." Her face hovers in front of mine. Her breath has notes of lavender. Her eyes are watery and haunting, "haven't you?"

"No, I haven't."

Her dark eyelashes flutter up and down, around my face. My back presses to the wall. One of her slender eyebrows curves up. "You're lying to me."

Her expression goes stiff, it's subtle – like she's holding back a predator inside.

God help me.

Anning's words suddenly make sense. Seraphim is the apex predator. Seraphim is the alpha. I am not. I cannot threaten her dominance.

... Pretend to be harmless, as long as you can.

Grom squeals and runs up the hem of my dress. He buries himself in my dress pocket – his green tail flops out the side.

I swallow hard.

Lie.

She'll know if I lie.

"I – didn't mean to come here."

Her head tilts to the side with cat-like focus. "You're lying again," she says, slowly. "You want something from me. You're *hunting* for something."

Her icy gaze pierces me. She reads every twitch of my expression. "What item did you choose. In the test with Anning?"

My heart pumps in my throat.

Anning told me not to say… She told me not to…

"I – I…"

Her jaw tightens. *"What item?"*

"The blue ribbon," I splutter.

Seraphim's eyes dart around my face. Her grip tightens on my wrist. "Lying again."

The tiger growls, sensing Seraphim's anger.

Tears glaze over my eyes, everything goes glassy. "I didn't mean to… I only…wanted answers…"

Seraphim pulls away from me and crosses her arms over her chest. "I will get answers out of *you*." She turns away, walks down the hall and commands, "COME."

Her voice resounds like only hers can – I obey without deciding to, and follow behind her. Tears burn on my cheeks.

It isn't like me – why in the blazes did I have to spy?

Seraphim opens the door to her office.

I stumble in, toward the sofa and clutch onto it. "Please, Ms. Seraphim. I –"

"QUIET," she snaps, one-thousand voices in one. "SIT DOWN."

I sit.

Grom rolls out of my pocket, terrified. I cradle him in my arms.

Seraphim turns away, softly, toward her window and the mountains. "You lied. Do you know why?"

"It isn't like me." I splutter.

Seraphim fixes her hands on her hips, frowning at me. "I know."

She… knows?

The tiger laps water noisily from a nearby bowl.

"You just *had* to challenge me, didn't you?" Seraphim presses her fingers to the low bridge of her nose, like she has a headache. "Your subconscious mind is already out of control."

I hold my breath.

"I'll be frank with you Sunday, you're talented, maybe too talented for your own good. And right now, your instincts are dominating you. Your *spirit* must dominate your actions. If you're swayed by every passing thought, every tempting little idea, the dragon-mind will control you, instead of you-it. Understand?"

The casual way she says it – like she's speaking from experience. She glares at a painting of a tiger on the wall beside me, like she'd rip it in half.

I lower my eyes. "I always have that voice there, in my mind, accusing me."

"You tolerate that voice because you can't tell truth from lies."

It's true. I never really understood what happened with Pa. "Part of me thinks, Pa died because of me."

"Sunday," she sighs, shakes her head. "You didn't kill your father."

She doesn't know that.

"Go to bed," she dismisses. "Off you go."

…Bed?

Outside the window, all is dark. Stars hang low and bright.

We've been talking longer than I realized.

I hang my head and turn to leave. "…Thank you. For helping me."

"And Sunday," her eyes are clear, sad. "You didn't kill your father… I did."

THIRTEEN

MIND SANCTUARY

It's like waking from a nightmare to a worse nightmare. The floor spins.
She can't mean that. She couldn't have killed Pa.

Seraphim folds her arms across her chest. Her cheeks are slack, sad.
"Years ago, someone had been hunting Animalia – killing them off one by
one. I'm sure you've noticed our house is short on students. Whoever they
are, they have access inside Svalbard, to harm our students and professors,
which is why I'm dean now. I was appointed to protect the students. But
every time I get close to finding the culprit – I reach a dead end."

"So... you were trying to stop the monster, years ago? That's not the
same as *killing* Pa."

"Yes, but it's been my job to find the killer."

"But if I hadn't gone out – he'd still be alive."

She chews her lip at me. "I'll be straight with you Sunday, until you
settle your guilt about your father's death, your subconscious mind will
crave vengeance. You'll never use your dreams and abilities correctly. Until
you forgive, you'll be double-minded."

"But still – something is out there – whatever was after Pa is after me."

"*Yes*," Seraphim coaxes, as though I were a child. "Now you understand.

Whoever is behind these disappearances is attacking in intervals. And the next attack will happen tomorrow night. I don't know where. But you know what you can do to *actually* help?"

"What?"

"Stay out of this. Because if you get involved, you'll be hunted, too."

"But can't I help somehow?"

The tiger brushes its neck against her mint-blue gown, then collapses on a blanket, licking its paw.

"You can pay attention to one thing," she sits on the sofa beside me, "– Animalia call it the *mind sanctuary*; it's only your subconscious mind, the part that dreams, highly intelligent, always active but rarely noticed by anyone who isn't Animalia."

I grip the velvet sofa beneath me.

"The mind sanctuary is your innermost home in your mind. And Animalia decipher it through dreams."

"Why would that help?"

"The mind sanctuary speaks, long into the night, and even in passing visions in the day. But you've silenced and crippled this part of you. Let me guess, you haven't been able to sleep."

"… No, not really. But if I do, I dream."

"Pay attention to what you see there. The mind tells many things. And if you see anything concerning the monster. Tell me."

I slip through the Animalia lounge and into my room for the night.

Everything is dark except for one lantern by Ori's bed. She hangs her head over a book, keeps to herself.

Rosie sleeps on a special pillow by her nightstand.

The wind moans outside. I set my things down.

Normally Ori is chatty and I can't get her to stop.

I slip into my nightdress. Svalbard should be home for me, but still I feel… watched. I slip my fingers over *The Book of Animalia* in my spare drawer... But no. I took it from the man underground and I can't risk Ori seeing me with it now. I'll take it out later tonight. Once she's asleep.

I roll onto the starchy sheets, recline on the bedframe, and set Grom on my comforter.

"So," I break the silence, "how was your day?"

Ori slumps over her knees in bed, marking her notebook with an ink pen.

I make my voice extra soft, "Was it... bad?"

Ori shrugs. She slaps down the pen and snaps her head to me. "Did you know – people have been admitted to Animalia the past *four* years. None of them stayed in the program. They failed, or something, and dropped out."

I busy myself petting Grom. There's a bite to her voice that's all toxic; "It's like – they set us up for failure, right? I was assigned *impossible* things today. Why do they expect us to know things they aren't teaching us? All these *secrets* of Svalbard that are like – how would I *learn* that?"

She's frustrated. I understand that.

"Do you miss home?" I try.

She scowls out the west windows, to the icy tundra beyond, "... Sometimes."

"Maybe when you return home to Ohio over Christmas break, you'll feel better."

She turns to me, slowly. The light in our room is dim – I can't quite make out her features – but I swear, in the sideways lamplight her features narrow – she glares at me. "I'm not going home for Christmas...." she says, darkly. "And I'm not from Ohio."

I grip the sheets under me, frozen.

... *What?*

Her eyes go dark and her shoulders slump forward.

My heart pumps in my neck, "... You're not from..."

"I'm from New York."

"But you said –"

"I lied," she says, flatly. "And I'm sure you'll judge me for that, but I don't care. I'm from New York, and before that, Jamaica, and before that, Barbados… *Uh!"* she grabs her knees, clenches her jaw and frowns out the window. "All my parents wanted was for me to go to this stupid school. And now look – I'm failing – I'm only two months in and I'm failing," her head melts between her knees. She grips her curly hair in her hands. "All I wanted was to graduate here. There's no way I'll graduate when all the others haven't."

Our eyes meet. There is hate in her. She turns away.

Ori and I are different… Maybe too different.

"…You can look down on me if you want," she mutters. "I'm sure your little town here in Sjosburg has been nice and *pleasant,"* she softens, shakes her head. "I don't mean to sound harsh, I just – do you know what it's like to be the 'pig girl' in New York City? I tell everyone I'm from a farm because at least then it makes sense – *God knows.* I wish I was from a farm."

She groans and rolls her eyes.

My heart sinks. I almost had a friend.

Almost.

"My dad is Italian," she explains, "my mom is from Barbados. They met here at school. Both Machinist. They fell in love. When they graduated, they got married in the Caribbean and moved to the U.S. They built railroads there – *railroads* – and made a fortune – and they tried to teach me to be Machinist. But I hate machines," she groans, rests her head on the backrest, and corkscrew curls fall over her shoulders. She stares at the vaulted ceiling. "I hated school. Bad at every subject. Except when I found Rosie here."

Ori smiles sideways at her pig, resting under the orange lamplight.

I clutch my fists around my sheets. Heat rises in me. I've tried to make Svalbard home. I've tried. But I can't trust anyone here, not even Ori.

A lump turns in my throat. She was almost my best friend.

"I first saw Rosie at the World's Fair," Ori says, soft. "My Pa had hit me because I had made him look stupid. He'd been drinking," she leans forward on her bed, elbows-over-knees, and talks with her hands, as though to make me understand, like this type of thing is typical, "he usually doesn't do that. He was only hitting me some of the times…"

Ori leans back again, "But in this one section of the World's Fair, there was a circus. I wandered alone through the animal stalls, and there was Rosie. She was born premature, filthy, she'd been abused by the animal keepers there – thrown aside. She was all bruised from getting hit. I just loved her. I wanted to take her home and tell her she was all right, that she still had a purpose. That she was still worth something. And that she shouldn't die. The circus-lady there said Rosie wasn't for sale but I threw every cent I had at her and the lady just accepted my money and turned away, and I took Rosie home. I've taken care of her ever since. When I was accepted here I was so relieved, you know. It was finally my chance to prove I was worth having. Smart. Like the rest of my family. Useful, you know. Like machines are useful. I just love Rosie to death."

I bite my lip. So that's why Ori constantly wants friends. Wants people around. Why she's jealous for affection.

We're nothing alike.

Her nice new watch and trunk full of gowns makes sense now. She comes from a Svalbard family. Prestigious. Wealthy.

"You didn't have to lie," I say, softly.

"Well what did you want me to say?" she melts. "Are you perfect? So you've never said something you wish you hadn't?"

My gut sinks into the mattress. I have… I lied to Seraphim. I didn't mean to. I just wanted answers.

But Ori lied so casually, so easily.

"We've all had to adjust to our surroundings," Ori says, "to survive."

I soften.

But she lied. She may have lied about other things, too.

Ori lowers her head. She turns out her lamp. "I'm sorry."

"…All right."

I sink into the cold folds of my bed. My heart twists. I almost had a friend.

I frown at the wood beams on the ceiling and they spin. I squeeze my eyes shut and press them with my fingers.

I can't trust anyone.

Maybe not even myself.

My God.

I curl into a ball and squeeze my knees to my chest. No, no, no.

You are not the monster, Sunday.

Think about what's real. What you've observed.

Two things are clear: There's a monster in Svalbard.

Second: Whoever the monster is, they're connected to Pa's death.

Ori makes soft slurping sounds into her pillow, fast asleep.

Now. Now is the time.

I slip out of bed in my nightgown. I snatch *The Book of Animalia* from my drawer and rush down the stairs to the lounge, in the dark, and duck into the old coat closet.

I lock the door behind me and light a candle inside.

I'll stop the monster the same way I win at cards: I'll get inside my enemy's mind.

I close my eyes.

Focus, Sunday. Focus.

The strange events pile over me: The poisoned cake; the white fur on Eoin's trousers; the boys gone missing – their voices echo in my mind:

"It wasn't an animal – I'm Animalia. I know the difference. It was a *monster.*"

He didn't say man. He said *monster.*

Dr. Laszlo's reassurance to me as a child: "It was not *you* who killed your father, Sunday. Only the monster."

Always the monster.

Anning's warning: "There are others who will see you as a threat."

And Seraphim, "Animalia is founded on ancient, secret principles, laid out in *The Book of Animalia…*"

That's it.

I flip through the pages. I hover over the animal illustrations until I find the same symbols from the man's drawing, underground. I rush out into the lounge again and grab the objects I need; candlewax, ink well, a bottle of wine, a small knife, a map of Svalbard.

I duck back into the closet and close the door.

Perfect. I lay out the map. It has the same octagon-symbol as the map of Svalbard in the professor's lounge, with the house symbols; hammer, tree, sword, harp, mortar-and-pestle... Connected, they form an octagon around the entire school.

Think, Sunday. Think.

Recreate the symbols. I spread the map wide over the floor and drip ink over the floorboards in the shape of the octagon. I use twine to mark the sections of the map.

What if this monster was after Animalia, yes, but also after all of Svalbard?

The first attack was the Animalia boys. I press a pin into the Animalia section.

Then a couple weeks ago, Professor Cortez had an 'accident' and almost died.

It's a pattern, moving counter-clockwise around Svalbard, and the next step in the octagon is Warbringer.

Counter-clockwise...

What if someone wanted to bring down all of Svalbard – they would attack the heads-of-houses, one-by-one. To make it discreet.

Seraphim said the culprit was attacking in intervals, and that tomorrow night something horrible would happen.

That's it. Tomorrow night, the attack will be in Warbringer.

I wake to light flooding my face. My eyelids flutter open and Ori stands above me in the doorjam of the coat closet.

I slide a few pillow feathers from my hair.

Ori fixes her hands on her hips. "You've lost your mind, you know. You're actually a wild-person."

I prop myself up on an elbow. "I know where the monster will attack next."

"*Ugh*," Ori pulls me to my feet. "C'mon."

Ori and I rush through the halls to the Animalia atrium and Ori is quiet all class. She doodles on her notebook while Anning shows us various rare birds; eagles, falcons, osprey. We feed a flightless bird called 'the dodo'. It whines with warbled squawks as he approaches me. He's a squat, waddling sort of creature with a protruding scoop beak and tiny wings. It tilts its head at me, eyeing me from the side with a stiff neck. We take a feather sample... It would be fun but Ori lowers her head, works in silence. She swats tears from her cheek when she thinks I'm not looking.

We finish and go upstairs to our room to prepare for winter banquet. It's strange, with her so quiet. She was so excited about winter banquet, just days ago. She ties up her hair quietly, scooping it like a fountain atop her head. She shoves gloves up her arms and adds a rosy blush to her olive cheeks. I tie my hair half-up and wear my nicest dress; a blue shade with silver folds and my crystal necklace.

I enter the circular dining hall with Ori; it's decorated for Christmastime, with pine boughs, red ribbons and Artisan sculptures. A giant tree was cut from the wild and towers over everyone in the center. I sit at the Animalia table. The other houses' circular tables are full of life; the Artisans play dreamy folk music – and couples dance together. I stare at one of the girls dancing; her pointed toes, delicate turns.

Their laughter is jarring next to the silence in me.

Ori wanders around the edge of the room, pouring apple cider into her glass.

If only I didn't have to sit alone.

There should be others here, in Animalia...

I scoop Tom Kah soup into my ceramic bowl.

Ori sits down by me, but says nothing. She barely sips her soup. Her face is slack, sad.

Ma always told me friendship is a choice. That you have to choose your friends wisely. And that it isn't always easy.

I set my spoon down. "You know, Ori," I soften. "I forgive you... For what happened last night."

She lowers her head, "… thanks…"

I stand to leave but – *"Hello, hello!"*

I turn, wide-eyed: It's the Warbringer boy who teased me. *The ratbag.* He's tall and tan with a fresh-pressed white military uniform and wide smile. He would be handsome but he has the pride of someone who's never grieved a day in his life.

He strides up to our table like he owns the world.

Arrogant.

"Well *hello*," he says with a Scottish lilt, and slides onto the curved bench across from us.

Ori nearly chokes on her pumpkin bread.

He's here to tease me. My cheeks go hot. *I won't let him.*

"I'm Alejandro," he gives me a toothy grin, like he's a friendly neighbor. He extends a hand to Ori, and she blushes, blinking, and shakes hands with him.

"Oria Moss," she says with a flourish and adds, with fascination, "are you… a *Warbringer?*"

"That I am," he bobs his head.

Please.

He reaches out to shake my hand, and I hate myself for returning the gesture, shaking it without thinking.

"Just thought I'd see what you fine ladies were up to today since –"

"Studying," I say, curt. "We've lots of work to do."

"Good on ya," he says. "Well if you're sick o' studyin' the friends and I got some games goin' on laytah' tonight." He clenches his hands into fists and punches the empty air next to him.

"*Er…* boxing games?" Ori guesses.

He gives a big, obvious wink.

Ori beams.

"We can't come," I say. "We have homework."

He tilts his head and smirks. "You're a bit icy 'round the edges, aren't ya Ms. Sunday? Maybe I should call you *'Icy Ms. Sunday'?*"

I clench my jaw.

Under the table, Ori kicks me.

"We'd love to come," Ori gushes. "That sounds fun and we'll stop by if we can."

"Right as rain," he stares absently at the space between Ori and I, "it'll be 'round midnight. Bring the warm clothes." He taps the wood table with his pointer finger, as though he hears music in his head. "It's the field on the north side of the complex. North of the war museum, mind you. The code to the gate is 'up – left – right' but you didn't hear that from me." He stands, waves to a friend, and walks off.

Ori turns to me, slowly. "You didn't tell me you *knew* people."

"I don't."

"Why were you so mean to him?"

"He was mean first."

She raises her slim eyebrow with an expression that says: *You can't be serious.* She draws herself up. "We're going tonight. I don't care what you say. I'm not missing it for the world."

I roll my eyes.

Across the dining room, at the Machinist table, Viktor stands with his back to the wall, watching me.

I flick my gaze away.

Too late.

Viktor edges around the evergreen tree toward our table. "Hey," his voice is quiet. I have to step closer to hear him. "That bloke was bothering you, wasn't he?"

Ori scoffs at him and sits at the bench beside me.

"Yeah he was a little," I admit.

Viktor's mouth tightens. "You need me to go beat him up for you?"

I never noticed before, but Viktor's nose is handsome, it's sloped at an interesting angle. His thick brows draw low toward dark blue eyes. His hair waves long and disheveled, sloppy – his chin and cheeks are narrow.

"He isn't bothering us," Ori interrupts.

"He's just some jerk," I mutter.

"Why do you care anyway," Ori snaps at him, "it's not like you could beat up a Warbringer."

Viktor tilts his head an interesting way. "No," he admits, softly, still looking at me, "but I could build a gun and shoot a Warbringer. That would do the trick."

Ori's face is all horror.

I lower my head and press my lips together to hide my smirk. It isn't funny. No. I shouldn't laugh.

Viktor and I exchange a mischievous look, like we can guess each other's thoughts. Something about him, his dark humor, his lazy way – it's home. He raises his hands out to me, to ask for a dance, and I move forward without thinking, joining my hand with his. He slides his other around my back. Heat fills my face – *blazes* – my cheeks must have color now. He pulls me in. We turn slowly around the hall, joining the other couples. His eyes dance over my face like he wants to say something but is holding back. The song is wistful, sad. We slow to a stop and he pauses with his hand on my shoulder, tense – I swear he's about to say something important.

He softens, shakes his head. "I have something for you." He reaches deep into his worn trouser pocket and pulls out a little newspaper-wrapped gift box. "An early Christmas present."

He… got me something.

I pull apart the wrapping paper and open the box: I pluck a small iron figure from inside and place it on my palm: It's a tiny music box, with a sculpted iron figure of Grom on the top.

"Made it myself. Just turn the little crank here on the side. It'll play for you."

I crack a smile. "It's perfect."

"It plays a little lullaby. I didn't write the tune. One of the Artisans did. I told them about you, and Sjosburg, and they wrote it."

"A lullaby?"

"Because I know you miss your Ma. And you don't sleep at night, do you?"

My cheeks warm. "Thank you."

He nods, turns away, and joins the other Machinists.

"Ugh," Ori scoffs. "What a creep. I dunno why you talk to him."

I toy with the music box in my hands. I brush my fingers over the welded replica of Grom.

"It isn't that impressive, anyway." Ori adds. "Trust me, I've lived with Machinists. They make one little thing for you and then think you owe them something. Ugh. Never trust a Machinist."

"Maybe he isn't perfect," I mutter, "but it's home."

"Fine. But you're still going to the boxing game with me tonight, right?" *Blazes. I'd already forgotten.*

"Sure. I'll go." *But only to test my theory about the monster's attack pattern.*

Ori beams. "*Yes.*"

On our way out of the dining room, I stop Anning and ask, "Is it allowed for students from other programs to sit with one another?"

Anning's face is a mask – a permanent half-frown with thin lips. She tilts her head back, "Under Dean Raj – *yes* – students wouldn't mix. But with Seraphim, well, she doesn't mind what *you* do."

"What?"

Anning stares at something behind my shoulder. I follow her gaze and turn. Seraphim's tiger walks the circumference of the hall. Behind the tiger, Dr. Laszlo nods at Anning.

… *Odd.*

Laszlo's lab-coat sweeps behind him and he disappears down the dining room.

I turn back to Anning. "Where did the Animalia boys go? Ori told me, you said they graduated, but that can't be right."

"Well, after the night they saw the monster, Dr. Laszlo treated the one and sent him home. Back to his homeland. The others graduated, and everything is fine." Anning walks away, mildly, leaving me among the crowd.

I set my jaw. She's hiding things.

And the way she said it; 'She doesn't mind what *you* do.'

…What does *that* mean?

After the banquet, I rinse my hands in our washroom. I force Grom to rinse his, as well, which he hates unless the water is steamy warm. I force his green hands under the dripping water. He fights me and makes growling noises.

"Well do you want to be filthy or clean?" I snap at him.

"Gnnar!" His complaining and snarling has gotten worse since his teeth have started to grow in. His claws are sharper now, too, and sometimes they poke me without his meaning to. I towel-dry his little claws with a handkerchief and swaddle him in it. I roll his crystal ball into the cloth and he bites at it with his nub teeth. He whines all the while. Complaining. *Ugh.* He knows I hate it when he whines like that.

He's been cranky lately. Impulsive.

I stop mid-step.

Impulsive. That's exactly how Seraphim described me.

That I couldn't control my own mind.

I squeeze my eyes shut. *No, no, not again.*

That I can't trust myself.

I'm a monster.

I flick my head to the side. Stop it, Sunday. Stop.

A secret monster.

Seraphim's warning surfaces to my mind: *Until you forgive, you'll have turmoil in yourself, you won't be able to use your gifts fully…*

But I can't forgive myself.

I lean over the sink, toward the mirror.

My reflection stares back at me in the glossy surface – her eyes are cold, accusing. Her clothes are flashy and arrogant. Her hair is swept back like Seraphim's – unauthentic. Selfish.

…A secret monster.

She leans close to me, whispering; "I *hate* you."

"Sund*a-ay!*" Ori calls. "What are you doing in there? You've been washing your feet for like – two hours."

I turn away from the mirror.

Snap out of it.

I towel-dry my feet and enter our room. Ori lays belly-down on her bed, smiling – she holds a notepad, sketching the dodo bird. We do our homework in silence. I crank the music box Viktor gave me and it plays this haunting, beautiful melody. It's like he's with me.

Once, when we were kids, I came down with Scarlet Fever. Viktor was the only one in town who noticed I wasn't at school. It was so lonely. Viktor waved at me from the street outside the attic window. He made a snowman there, in the street in front of our shop. He talked to me through the window. He said I should pretend the snowman was him, so I wouldn't feel alone. It was months until I could see anyone else.

I squeeze my eyes shut and press my forehead to the little music box. I could listen for hours. I hold Grom in one arm, prop myself on an elbow, and sketch the dodo with my free hand. At no particular point Ori says, briskly, "Now I know why I'm in your life, Sunday."

I pause, pen-in-hand, "Why's that?"

She ties her hair in a sloppy bun atop her head. She flashes an impish grin and shining, beautiful brown eyes. "I'm here to make sure you have a life," she speaks from behind a loose corkscrew curl. "You don't have to thank me now, trust me, you'll thank me later. When we go to the boxing match."

FOURTEEN

THE BOXING MATCH

I sit on Ori's bed and groan at the clock on her nightstand. The hands point to 12:00 midnight.

Ori wears her best dress for the boxing match, like she's going to another party.

"You should wear your hair up," Ori tells me. "First impressions matter."

"I'm not going for them."

She puffs her lower lip at me, mimicking me.

"I'm only going to test my theory about the Svalbard map."

Ori rolls her eyes, "Oh yes, the *monster* again." She steps into velvet shoes. "Don't you want to enjoy it here? We live here now."

I situate the music box on my dresser, beside Pa's old key and my old playing cards. "We can't be caught out after hours."

"*Jeesh*, we won't get caught."

"The other students went missing, remember?"

"They *graduated*," Ori chatters, squirting perfume on her neck. "Don't be so afraid."

Fire lights in my belly. "I'm *not* afraid."

Ori turns to me with a flirty brow, "Then prove it."

Heat fills me. It's the dragon-mind – the agitation – it focuses me; coconut and vanilla waft around me – Ori's perfume is from the Caribbean. A gift from her mother. Ori smiles at me and a gap shows through the side of her teeth – her father hit her there, repeatedly.

"Sunday," Ori snaps. "Cut it out."

I rip my gaze away.

"Sometimes it's like you go somewhere else," she sets her hands on her hips. "...Are you coming or not?"

"...Coming." I slip on my overcoat. It's a rash decision, going out after-hours. It came from the dragon-mind. But...

My lips curl into a smile.

...I don't care.

"We'll be quiet," Ori whispers, and links arms with me. We pass the Animalia lounge and clank down the iron stairs. We pass wide halls and cross the snowy courtyard. We huddle together for warmth and I enter the same code Anning entered: Up – Left – Right –

– *click.*

Yes.

The gate swings open.

We shuffle in, checking every which-way and slip by unnoticed.

I run in the snow, laughing and tripping, and Ori clasps a hand over her mouth to muffle the sound of her own giggle. We pass an archery range and a weapons shed...

Cheering echoes faint in the wind.

"That's it!" Ori pulls me toward a great white tent which rises down the tundra. Pricks of light expand into oil lanterns which hang from the sides of the tent, and the songs of fiddles grow louder. I hold open the white canvas tent flap and duck inside.

A hundred Warbringers surround a low boxing ring. Artisans play fiddles in lively jigs, and Warbringers throw coins into jars by their feet. They shout at the ring, drink ginger ale, and make bets on the fighters.

Grom perks his head up from my coat. He crawls up my braid and onto my head for a better view of the fight.

"Come *on*," Ori yanks my arm and pulls me through the crowd, to the boxing ring.

Alejandro fights in the ring.

His opponent is an older fifth-year student with a wide tattoo of a Himalayan tiger across his muscular back. Sweat and blood roll down Alejandro's chest. The boys are trained. Their footwork is quick, their jabs aimed. There's a strategy to the game. Like cards. They search for each other's weaknesses.

Grom leaps onto the wood edge of the boxing ring. He growls at the boys fighting and scampers along the ledge, excited.

Alejandro groans with each punch – *one, two* –

Ori grabs my arm. I agree. The fight is brutal.

I would be startled, like Ori, but fire rises in me. The dragon-mind – I'm like Grom – I want the fight.

Focus, Sunday.

I snap my head aside. Tune out the music. The chaos.

Control your impulses, like Seraphim said.

My lips curl into a small smile.

… But why?

Focus, Sunday.

The monster will attack the Warbringers tonight – the monster will try to make it look like an accident.

I won't let that happen.

Alejandro uses his opponent's momentum; he folds him over his knee and dislocates his jaw – *smack!*

Ori recoils.

I lean in.

Alejandro is a good fighter, but his weakness is his playfulness. He thinks this is a game.

It's not a game.

Warbringers cheer for Alejandro. They've placed money on him.

Alejandro thrusts the heel of his hand to his opponent's nose – *crack* – nose broken.

He can win.

Maybe he's not as horrible as I thought.

All is chaos. Warbringers pound the muddy ring.

Ori and I stand out in the crowd of them; our colorful gowns, our subtle manners…

The more I relax into the dragon-mind, the more I love it. Even my hearing is sharper.

The Warbringers behind me whisper: "…Dragon girl."

"Don't be so loud, she'll hear you."

"Only two in Animalia."

I edge my way along the stands to Professor Seacole, who watches from her own distinct chair in the wood stands. I pull Ori along to follow me.

There has to be something here. Something missing.

Professor Seacole watches the game, leaning back in her chair like it's a throne. She rests her chin in her hand, studying her fighters.

I stand behind Seacole. I glance down to the gap between her boots and the opening in the wood stands below. Something moves there. I crouch down, slowly, and Ori leans over, "What are you doing?"

A brown blur crawls onto the hem of Seacole's dress: A spider.

"Look," I tell Ori.

We peer closer. It's a thick brown spider with a red hourglass on its belly – poisonous.

"It's a Red Recluse." Ori's jaw drops. "How'd it get here? It's a tropical spider."

"Someone must've planted it," I peer under the stands to the empty gap below, but no one is there. The spider scuttles up Seacole's dress, over her back, toward her neck, "Quick!" I hiss to Ori, "We have to catch it."

I slap around the stands until my hand finds an empty ginger ale glass – I snatch it and hover over Seacole's back.

Ori slides in front of Seacole. "Professor, please – don't panic. Just. Don't. Move."

Seacole straightens, "What the –"

I slap the glass onto her back, surrounding the spider. I pull a handkerchief from my pocket and flatten it over Seacole's neck – in one quick swipe I slide the glass and the spider onto the cloth and remove it from her back.

Seacole stands and snaps to us. "What foolery is this –"

"It's a deadly spider we saw on your back," Ori splutters, "please, we're Animalia, we know what it is."

Seacole frowns at the red-and-black spider concealed in the glass.

"… So you think just because you're Animalia I should trust *you*? What if you planted this on me?"

My heart skips a beat – "We didn't mean –"

"Then why do things go wrong whenever Animalia students are around, hmm? How would a poisonous spider just *appear* on me – if you didn't place it there first?"

"Please," I beg, "We think –"

"Your house is cursed. All of you are. If it were up to me your lot would stay away from us. I'll excuse your nonsense this time, but it'd better be the last."

"Thank you, ma'am," Ori curtseys.

Seacole sits back down, stiff. She grips the arms of her chair, like she's alarmed by something else in the arena – not just us.

Ori grabs my arm, "How did you see the spider?"

"Because I anticipated it."

Anticipate my enemy. Just like cards.

And it confirms my theory. Whoever the monster is, they're attacking the houses in a pattern.

"How would you kill a beast?" I ask Ori.

She frowns. "… I dunno."

"Cut off its head."

The monster is targeting the heads of houses, not just the Animalia students.

I watch the spider writhe and jump inside the drinking glass. It attacks the places where my fingers touch the glass. "Someone stole the spider from Animalia."

"But the atrium is locked for people in other houses."

Snow swirls around Alejandro. In the lamplight, sweat shines on his back in a slick orange gloss. Alejandro hunches forward and jabs – *one* – *two*. His opponent backs away as the blows strike him and he loses his footing, exposing his gut.

Alejandro can finish him now.

Half the Warbringers chant for Alejandro: They shout his nickname:

"ALEC!"

"ALEC!"

"ALEC!"

But Alec's gaze draws up and to the side, strangely, to Ori and I – his hazel eyes touch mine and widen, surprised. His lips turn into a smile – bloodied saliva drips from his mouth. The spare moments of distraction are enough for his opponent to regain his balance.

Alec smiles stupidly at me and his opponent strikes him in the face – *wham.*

I flick my gaze away.

...*No. Still a fool.*

The bell rings. DONG.

One of the girls bellows, "Time!"

The cheering fades. Coins are exchanged. The Artisans pack their instruments and leave with everyone else.

Alec sits in the mud, slumped against the side of the ring.

A Warbringer girl, the kind one who held Grom the other day, stands beside me: Jael. She helps Ori prop Alec into a sitting position. I stand over him.

"I won, didn't I?" he mumbles, eyes-shut.

"Not exactly." I say.

"Rats," he gives me a toothy smile. He looks horrible. All blood and mud.

"I'll take him," Jael says, and slings Alec onto her back like he's a sack of wheat. Her arms are strong, the same blue bracelet with dreidels shines on her wrist. She's collected and calm. No forced niceties. Nothing fake.

She leaves with Alec slung over her back.

Ori and I start out, leaving the tent. I step out, but my gaze is drawn to someone's silhouette looming outside the tent flap. If I weren't Animalia I'd never notice it, but the shadow absorbs all my attention. The tiny hairs on my arms stand on-edge. I stare.

In my hands, Grom stares, too.

It's a lithe shadow. Not the strong figure of a Warbringer. It's out of place here.

The slight figure slides around the back of the tent, quickly, and past the opposite opening. He peers into the tent and I catch a glimpse of him full-faced: It's the servant boy, Eoin.

His green eyes are faded and his lips are blue. He doesn't wear a coat.
What the –
He must be freezing.
Chills crawl over my neck.
"Sunday," Ori pulls my arm, "let's go."
Eoin backs away, into the snowy wind.
Perhaps I should tell Ori…
No. It could be nothing.
We leave the grounds swiftly and I check over my shoulder for him.
We cross the courtyard of statues, and I glance over my shoulder again.
I don't see him following me. No… It's more than that.
I *feel* him.

FIFTEEN

APOTHECARY

The next day something is wrong.

I can't focus. Can't think.

They'll never understand you.

I tweak my head, like I would fling her voice out of me. Whenever that voice accuses me, it's like I can't think clearly – everything blurs – nothing makes sense.

Anning walks me through the halls to my next ambassador visit – the Apothecary laboratory. She gives me a questioning look, "You feeling all right, girl?"

"Yes," I lie.

No. I'm not all right... I'm nothing like you people.

I open my mouth wide, forcing my jaw to relax.

Grom squirms in my hands and I clench him in my grip, making him stay still.

I kick the silk hem of my yellow dress as I walk and the lavender bustle sweeps behind me. I shove my white gloves up my fingers but they constantly pull loose. Ugh. I've tied up my hair in this half-bun, letting the underside of my hair fall like curtains around my shoulders, but I hate this look on me. It looks soft. I wear the crystal necklace Apothecary Bjørn gave me. Perhaps wearing it, I'll fit in with Apothecary.

Grom squirms free from my grip and sits atop my shoulder. He's grown larger now, heavier, and a long green tail curls over my shoulder. He slings his tail like a whip, flicking me 'without meaning to.'

I roll my eyes at him.

He groans with his throat in garbled dragon-speak.

Visiting other programs is always this, like, event, and now I have a reputation following me, with people calling me 'dragon-girl' in the halls and wherever we go. Their curiosity about Grom, about me... *Ugh*. And the apothecary students are the *worst* – they look at Grom like he's something to dissect.

Idiots.

Apothecary is the most dull, most '*academic*' house.

I turn my head and stretch the tense muscles in my neck.

What the blazes is wrong with me?

It isn't like me – this irritation. It's the dragon-mind – or something. We walk to the south side of Svalbard, the halls grow colder here, darker. It's part hospital; the floors shine with sterile white stone. We pass under hydroponic herb gardens that line the walls with leafy-green vines; like walking in a life-size terrarium. Paper labels line each row; dill, parsley, thyme, maca, cocoa, celery...

Grom gawks at the rows of colorful fruits as we pass; green, pink, blue...

We pass under an archway of thin trees and Grom grabs a small orange kumquat fruit from the branch. He holds it with two hands, taking big bites of the little citrus.

We duck into a laboratory. The apothecary students all wear white lab coats over their clothes and they tinker with terrariums on their desks.

Grom drops the orange kumquat fruit. It falls from my shoulder to the floor.

– *thud.*

It rolls between the students' desks. They watch it.

Grom chokes – hisses loudly – and falls to the ground –

"Grom!"

He flails, seizing and writhing. He scratches at the white tiled floor with his claws.

The students stand and back away from him.

I scoop Grom into my arms but he reels with pain, shrieking.

"Help!" I cry.

Dr. Laszlo sweeps beside me and snatches Grom. He lays Grom on his back with medical form, under a lamp which faces the apothecary students. He pushes Grom down on the silver tray.

I grip Anning's arm.

Grom screeches. His tongue curls and foam bubbles from his mouth. I clasp my hand over my nose. I can't watch.

Dr. Laszlo sheds his long white lab-coat and grabs a pair of silver pliers. He addresses the class: "What kind of pain might a creature have from digesting a kumquat? Anyone?"

Grom flails on the table, kicking and crying.

A young boy in the back row pipes up, "Kumquats are very acidic, Doctor."

"Indeed," Laszlo watches the students from behind the shine of his gold spectacles. "So an alkaline substitute is the best organic option we have, is it not?" Laszlo pulls dried kale from a cupboard beside him – and with long silver pliers – he attempts to shove the green herb down Grom's throat.

Grom panics. He bites the pliers with his tiny teeth, growling.

"Little monster," Laszlo swears loudly.

I run to Grom and soothe his sides with my fingertips. I stroke his bloated little belly. "Give it to me," I pluck the kale from his pliers. I prop Grom up and gently feed him the herb.

Grom holds onto my fingers with little green hands, eating the kale. He chews – and swallows. Little tears seep from the creases in the scaly skin between his eyes. His breathing evens, soothed by the herb, and he rolls into my hands, limp.

Dr. Laszlo rakes a hand through his thick brown hair and sets down his pliers. "Exceptional. Well done, Ms. Sunday."

He speaks so the entire lab can hear. "I haven't taught much on animals yet, for obvious reasons, but the lining of a dragon's stomach is highly alkaline. Especially the green-tree dragon. It's rare, to have a creature which requires such alkaline foods to maintain pH balance," he paces the empty space in front of his students. He's harsh-sounding, but he commands respect. I'd trust him with my life. "When the dragon ate the acidic fruit, the delicate alkaline lining in its stomach began to deteriorate," he smooths a hand over his short facial hair… "Anyone have an idea *why* this might be?" he scans the classroom – his student's heads are bowed over their papers, scribbling. "No?"

The young, slight boy in the back speaks up again, "Because dragons' stomachs produce an amino chain-reaction which can create fire." I crane my head toward the boy. His hair is drawn up into a black bun atop his head. He's the quiet boy who sat beside me on the sleigh to school: Hikaru. He wears a yukata beneath his lab coat and pushes spectacles up his nose.

Smart…

My gut sinks. He knows more about dragons than I do.

Laszlo gestures us forward and Anning lectures the class about Animalia – and the important work we do saving endangered species…

I cradle Grom in my arms. He turns away from the class, toward my breast pocket. He drools on my sleeve.

Anning finishes her speech and no one asks me any questions.

Thank God. It's over.

I turn to leave with her but Laszlo moves – quickly, silently – and grabs my wrist. My heart skips a beat. His fingers are cold. It's a subtle gesture, but it feels loud.

He places something soft in my hand: Tea bags.

Why would he –

I flush.

"Brew this," he mutters in a Hungarian lilt, "then wait till room temperature. Then a bath for the reptile."

He releases my wrist.

I break away and walk arm-in-arm with Anning. My heart pounds in my chest.

We leave the lab and I glance at the paper packets.

Green Tea
~ Thailand's finest herbal blend ~

Anning sends me back to my room and I set Grom on a pillow. He groans as he tries to sleep, shifting on his bloated belly.

I turn the green tea packet in-hand... Kind of him. To give it to me.

Odd that I trust him more than anyone here. Maybe it's the history I have with him. It's almost like... he's family.

I find a porcelain basin and boil water.

I tip the kettle over the green tea leaves and the steaming water pulls through the herbs. The mixture wafts with mint and eucalyptus.

On the pillow beside me, Grom's little ears flick. He sniffs. He crawls toward the basin.

I test the water with my pinky... Nice and warm.

I scoop Grom into my hands and slip him into the mint-green bath.

He splashes and slithers around, surfacing by the edges. He drinks the tea as he swims, and smiles at me with his tongue hanging out. He tunnels and spins in the water like a green ribbon.

I splash my fingers in and he swats at them playfully. "That's all you needed, wasn't it?"

Mist froths from the basin, steaming the windows.

I step into the washroom and wash-up as well, and when I return, drying my hair – Grom taps the edge of the porcelain bowl with his little fingernail. His tapping means: *I'm ready to get out.*

I scoop him out of the water, which has gone a tad cold, and dry him with a washcloth. He nudges my cheek, giving kisses. I place him on a pillow by the fireplace and he curls his tail, holding it, and yawns, falling asleep.

Ori knocks on the door for me. "Sunday," she calls. "Someone's here for you."

I frown.

For me? This late in the evening?

I step down the stairs, into the lounge and give her a questioning look. "Who?"

Ori tilts her head toward the main door. "They just keep knocking, asking for you."

THUD – THUD – THUD.

I jump.

"Sunday, open the door dammit."

I tense: Viktor.

He shouldn't be here.

I swing the door open and the mirrors turn aside, revealing his tall lean figure and tossed hair. His hands are stained with oil. Welding tools hang from his belt.

"Finally," he groans, and glances over my shoulder. "Woah, it's really nice in there."

I step to the side, blocking his entry.

"Why can't you just let me in," he dips to the side, trying to pass me, but I step in front of him, blocking him again.

"Other houses aren't allowed in here," I say, stiff. "It's late. What do you want?"

"Who says I want anything."

I fold my arms. "What do you want?"

"Look," he leans on the wall, like he still wants in. "I'm gonna be honest with you–"

"Good," I cut.

He sets his lip. "I'm not doing well in the program, Sun," his voice is quieter now, like he's ashamed to say it.

"So study harder," I say plainly. "Don't waste your time with me, study and ask your professor how you can learn more."

"It's not that *easy*," he thrashes his head. "I'm last in my class. *Last*."

"So?"

"So help me make up for it."

I fold my arms over my chest and lean back against the mirror door. I frown at the ceiling and shake my head. "What would you want me to do?"

He slumps forward with his hands held out to me, "The marks of grades are inside Professor Suri's desk. In the first drawer. It's unlocked. I just need you to look out for me while I add a few marks to my grade. So I don't get kicked out of school," he searches me with blue eyes – like his argument makes sense. Like he's justified in it.

… *Cheater.*

"That's the worst idea I ever heard."

Viktor's cheeks touch red with angry blush.

"Who do you think I am?" I snap. "Some criminal to help you cheat your way through school, while everyone else works hard?"

That does it.

Something in him snaps. His eyes go wild. He lunges to duck past me – predictable – I grab his arm and as he moves forward and I fold it behind his back, trapping him against the wall. I grip his arm, squeezing. I'm stronger than him. I have the fire of a dragon in me.

"The hell is wrong with you," he yells.

I should let him go… But – he should be punished first.

He's weak. Wrong.

I tighten my grip on his wrist. My fingernails dig into his arm.

"Sunday –" he thrashes. "Cut it out."

I force the fire down. I will myself to step away from him. I unclench my fingers and let him go.

He backs away from me and cradles his wrist in his hand. He looks at me with fear, like I'm a stranger. A monster. "What the hell did they do to you?" He backs away. "This place is changing you."

I fix my jaw at him. "Why, because I'm strong now?"

"You aren't yourself."

"Maybe this is who I really am."

"This is *not* who you really are."

"I'll say who I am."

"Fine," he draws himself up. "Do whatever you want. But I won't change."

"Clearly you won't," I cut. "Because you're still cheating."

He snaps his head away and runs down the spiral iron stairs – his feet clamber until he reaches the bottom.

I turn back into the lounge and shut the door behind me. *Ugh.*

…Maybe I was too hard on him.

I clench my jaw. I was so angry – and I stopped him so easily. It's like it came from deep inside me, or something.

Ori sits on the sofa by the fire, encyclopedia-in-hand, and watches me, wide-eyed.

"I suppose you heard that?" I say flatly as I pass her.

She nods.

I hike up the stairs. "Well… sorry."

"Sunday," she turns over her shoulder to me. "I think… You did the right thing… Not letting him cheat. And I'm glad."

"Thanks." I rub my head. "Goodnight."

"Night."

SIXTEEN

GROM'S CHANGING

I lay in bed, frowning at the wood beams on the ceiling.

I slip out of bed and walk to the French doors. I turn the handle, and step out, barefoot, onto the frigid balcony. It's frosty cold but who cares. Arctic, purple rings line the sky; the atmosphere's aurora. God it's beautiful, like heaven. Snowflakes stick to my arms and hair. In the distance, a doe strides beneath a line of pine trees.

Pa loved deer. They're peaceful, like him.

… How very different I turned out to be.

My chest squeezes. Maybe he wouldn't be proud of me now. The way I am.

The doe wanders into the distant tree-line and disappears.

"You seem off today." Ori spoons granola into her mouth and ties up her hair.

"Huh?"

She laughs. "Never mind."

I rub my eyelids. What a night.

I thumb through the fine dresses in my closet. I drape them over my chest; let's see… which necklace matches which gown – *blazes* – none of them are good enough – *ugh* – fine. I settle on the nicest dress I own. The one I wore when Dr. Laszlo mistook me for Seraphim.

Grom bites at my bedsheets, puncturing tiny holes in the silk. I hold him down so he sits still and pry open his mouth with my fingers; teeth nubs grow into his gums.

New teeth. New energy…

I slip into my light blue dress and tie the bustle behind my back so it falls and trails along the floor. I fix the gold-scale necklace around my throat.

Ori and I walk side-by-side through dusty ballrooms toward the Animalia atrium – to study. Grom bites the gold scales of my necklace, tugging.

Of course… The gold scales are *dragon* scales.

Grom sinks his little teeth into the necklace scales, teething. I stroke my thumb along his little back as he chews.

Bjørn must've known Grom was a dragon when he gave me the necklace.

Blazes. Was I the only one who didn't know?

Ori carries Rosie, her pink snout rests over the crook of her arm.

Rosie sneezes at Grom and Grom growls at her.

Ori gives me side-eyes.

"What?"

"I think you're becoming more dragon-like," she teases.

"Is that so," I say, flat.

Ori's smile fades. "Well don't we start to share the perspectives of our animals?"

I clench my hands. Fire lights in me.

It's none of her business how I am.

I roll my neck. It's so tight.

My cheeks are hot. Feverish. Sweat drips down my back.

… She should mind her own business.

It's not me. All irritated like this. Ori is my friend.

Control it, Sunday. Push it down.

Ori frowns at me. "Are you… all right?"

Control your thoughts.

"Fine," I lie. "Just a headache."

"…You get a lot of headaches, don't you?"

We pass under stained-glass windows and toward a lofted study space in the Animalia atrium. The mosaic glass shows wildlife; it's like a cathedral of animals – the colors speckle Ori's face in reds and blues.

Ori frowns at the white tiled stairs as we hike into the high places of the atrium. "It's common lore that dragons love jewelry. They love wealth. They need it."

"So?"

"And so do you," she says, like it's obvious. "All morning you've been pouring over your jewelry, looking at it like it's food. You're obsessed."

I roll my eyes. If only she knew my life in Sjosburg – the scraps of food I ate growing up – the winters I had to share a bed with Ma to keep warm.

"I'm not someone who's obsessed with jewelry. Trust me."

"But you are now," Ori insists. "You've changed."

I fix my jaw.

It's true. It did take me a minute to get ready this morning. I couldn't help but look at all the fine things.

I… had to.

Ori purses her heart-shaped lips at me. Her expression says: *You know I'm right.*

Maybe she is.

We sit in the high study space of the atrium. Beside us, marsupials swing from branch to branch in the tree canopy. "So who were you," Ori asks, cautious, "before you came here?"

"Dunno," I shrug and lay back on the sofa. "I liked animals."

"Yeah but what else?"

I bite my lip, "Well… cards I guess. I always win at cards. Here let me show you –" I whip out my old deck from my dress pocket and splay the thick, long cards over the wood table between us. I show Ori the card names, the values. "The key is to use empathy, to win. To understand your opponent. If you know who you're dealing with, how they think – you can anticipate what they'll do."

Ori concentrates on the cards, puffs her lips. "That's like what you said about the monster though."

"Yeah… Yeah I guess so."

"So you anticipate how they'll attack, then what?"

"Then you have to set a trap for them… Ori you're a genius."

Her face brightens with a toothy smile, "I am?"

"Yes, that's exactly what we have to do. We have to set a trap for the monster."

"How?"

"Every opponent has a weakness, some character flaw. Maybe it's arrogance. Maybe they underestimate you. A trap doesn't have to be complicated, it just has to allow them to use their character flaw to their own downfall – the problem is I've felt so blocked lately, in my mind–" I stop, card-in-hand. Anning's red head turns the distant corner, next to someone with tossed brown hair and a lab coat: Dr. Laszlo.

In my arms, Grom growls at Rosie. Dr. Laszlo passes and smirks at our animals like they're up to no good. "Having trouble with your beasts?" he stops, folds his arms and gives us a warm smile.

He could be my favorite person at Svalbard.

"I think *Grom* is the real beast," Ori teases back. "He's a bad influence on Rosie," she coddles her pig in her arms. "Rosie wouldn't do anything wrong on purpose, would you girl?"

Laszlo draws up, intrigued. "Is that true, Ms. Sunday? Is Grom a beast? Would he disobey you?"

It is careful conversation.

Laszlo is intelligent.

"Grom is independent from me," I reply. "He can do whatever he wants."

Laszlo's expression is all pleasure. He removes his spectacles for a moment, cleaning them with his lab-coat, and smiles to his chest. With his glasses gone his features are striking, sturdy cheekbones and a strong jaw. "Very true, Ms. Sunday," he replaces his gold octagonal spectacles on his long nose. "But don't Animalia students have special empathy for their beasts? Don't they share a mind with their host?"

Fire flickers inside me. "I wouldn't call myself a host."

Ori glances back-and-forth between the two of us, like she's confused about how the conversation turned so serious.

"*Ahh...*" Laszlo banters. "Then what would you call yourself?"

I square my shoulders. "Animalia."

Dr. Laszlo laughs. His hazel eyes are so kind and his smile so genuine, I want to laugh with him, too. But he laughs at me, not with me.

I dig my fingernails into my palm.

Don't speak. Control your impulses...

Laszlo studies me. It's a doctor's gaze. He takes in everything about me.

If only I could speak, scream.

Don't speak. Push it down.

I shrink under his gaze.

His gaze darts down to my hand, tense at my side. "Well... Seraphim would be proud of you, with an answer like that... Good day, ladies."

"Good day," Ori says.

Ori gathers our things, hooks arms with me and we leave the atrium, toward the dining hall.

But the way he looked at me, like he could fix me... Out of all the professors, maybe he's the one who actually could.

Ori rests her head lightly on my shoulder and I squeeze her arm where it hooks through mine. I don't know when we became close. But we are.

Thank God for Ori.

At dinner in the circular dining room, I bounce Grom on my lap. I feed him stuffed grape leaves. At the table beside us, the Warbringer girls arm wrestle and Jael catches my eyes from across the table. She folds her arms on the table, she wears a black uniform-dress, like all the Warbringer girls. She leans in and says, "Where are the other Animalia now?"

I shrug at her, "We don't know."

Jael twists her dreidel bracelet. "You think you're next?"

Chills prickle my arms.

She's right.

It sinks into my bones. It's only a matter of time before the monster – whatever it is – gets us, too.

Jael straightens. She's a true warbringer; the talk of a threat makes her taller, stronger. She brushes a curtain of dark glossy hair over her shoulder. There's a glint in her eye, like she knows something I don't. She opens her mouth to speak, but great bells chime down the hall–

DONG. DONG. DONG.

Seraphim strides between the tables. A thick diamond necklace shines around her neck.

That jewelry. Where the blazes does she get those things?

The dining room goes still, watching her. She rests her hands on the podium, and announces; "Starting today we'll begin a new project, required for every student, to collaborate with someone from a different house."

Whispers echo along the tables.

If only I were like Seraphim. Confident. "You'll each be assigned a partner, and will create a project that reflects attributes from both houses. This collaboration has never been done before. But I believe it's important to understand one another…" Her eyes are a dreamy bluish haze, and bright.

I turn away.

"This education is not to be taken lightly. Whoever stays must demonstrate commitment. It takes a serious mind to live as a Svalbard graduate. The knowledge of Svalbard is precious. Not for the selfish, or cowardly of heart."

Maybe I imagine it, but she looks directly at Viktor when she says 'cowardly.'

I hug myself across the middle. I am *not* a coward.

I'll fight to stay.

After dinner, Ori and I check with Anning to hear who we're paired with for the new collaboration assignment. Anning leans on the doorway frame, tucks her loose red hair back, and withdraws a parchment from her pocket. She unfolds it, reading; "Sunday Gråe is partnered with Alejandro OlShield. Oria Moss is paired with Jael Tal."

Ori just smiles at me. She'd probably pick Jael out of anyone in the school.

And I'm paired with the one person I can't stand.

Perfect.

Anning turns away, but I stop her. "That can't be right, can it?" I say, almost to myself.

Students stream past us, leaving the dining room on every side.

"What's not right?" Ori asks, butting in.

"The odds we'd both be paired with people we know."

Ori shrugs. "Dunno," she smiles. "But I like it."

Seraphim's white tiger strides along the hall, between the students and around Anning, his white shoulders flex with each heavy step.

"How were the pairs selected for the project?" I ask Anning.

"The draw is random," Anning says mechanically.

It's a rehearsed line. "Random? Really?"

Anning walks past the tiger and out of the dining room.

Seraphim is watching her.

Seraphim is watching me, too. And changing things.

SEVENTEEN

ALEJANDRO

I eat raspberry porridge in the Animalia lounge and spy a note with my name on it, slipped under the mirror door.

> *At Dr. Laszlo's lab early this morning for a nose adjustment — long story. Let's meet at 11:00 a.m. in the lenai room for the project. It's the big garden room behind the main ballroom.*
> *Cheers!*
> *-Alec*

Ori plucks the note from me, reading it.

"I don't want to go with him," I groan.

"What's gotten into you?" she rakes a brush through her corkscrew curls.

"I just don't want to deal with a partner assignment right now."

Ori sets down the brush. She rests her hand lightly over her mouth, watching me, and twists her lips into a wicked smile. "You *like* him, don't you?"

"No," I splutter. "He's ridiculous."

"...But that's kinda nice, huh," she searches me with warm brown eyes. "...*I'm* ridiculous."

"Sometimes," I chuckle. "Sometimes you are. That's true."

We both laugh.

"Fine." I sigh. "I'll meet up with him later. For the assignment. I have to find Anning now anyway."

I follow Anning across a quiet snowy meadow to the Artisan mansion – on the north grounds.

The mansion flaunts welded spires, smoking chimneys and frosty curved windows. Anning pounds the iron door knocker and we're welcomed by a timid first-year artisan holding a fiddle.

I step into the welcome hall and I'm wrapped in the bittersweet aroma of fireplace smoke and paint oils. Artisans exit their studios and various living rooms and follow us around a corridor to a large fine art studio.

Ten students stand at their canvases in the midst of a still-life painting class. They each paint a different angle of a fruit-and-flower bouquet. Professor Cortez circles between the students, checking their work and hovering over their shoulders to give them adjustments to their colors, their lines.

If I wasn't Animalia... living here would be a dream.

Artisans file in behind me, holding various instruments; I can tell what their concentration is by the tools they hold; sculptor, dancer, architect, composer...

They sit on apple boxes on the floor, their assembly in this room is something rehearsed, like they've done it a hundred times for Professor Cortez.

Cortez hugs Anning a moment too long and she steps up and starts her lecture about Animalia. I half-listen; the dragon-mind distracts me, it crawls in the back of my mind.

Forgive, Sunday... let it go.

Whenever I relax like this, things appear in hyper-detail. I notice connections I'd never see before; the delicate brushstrokes on the paintings around me, the gentle way the girls whisper in each other's ears. The knowing glint in Professor Cortez's eyes.

The Artisans clap as Anning finishes. Conversation fills the studio, followed by music, and one of the younger girls pulls me aside. She carries her sari as she walks with me, and gestures in sign language. She pulls me toward an easel and turns her painting toward me: A still-life showing a cup of green tea and chopsticks.

I smile. "Pretty."

She bites her lip at Grom in my hands, and then me, and pulls me toward a bookshelf in the back of the studio room, away from everyone else. She peels through the art book, flipping pages until her fingers slide onto a watercolor print.

"See?" she signs, turning the book toward me.

I gather the wide book from her, cradling it in my arms. The watercolor print has a wide, pale-green dragon painted in soft brushstrokes. Hindu symbols line the sides of the pages. I can't read them.

"What does it mean?" I ask.

She gestures to Grom on my shoulder, then to the wide, spiraling green dragon on the page. She runs her fingers over the calligraphy translation at the bottom; fortune, fire, cunning, dreams…

"Fortune?" I ask.

She nods and her short hair swings around her ears.

My cheeks warm. I'd never considered the history of other dragons before.

Grom presses a little green hand to the watercolor drawing of the dragon.

Did Grom have a family?

I always assumed they were gone. Killed by something. But they must've been around, at some point. However rare they might be.

I run my fingers down Grom's scaly back.

But when I found him in his cracked egg, he was alone.

He would've died without me…

Behind the girl, an Artisan boy pushes his spectacles up the bridge of his nose and clears his throat – he joins me to read the text. He holds a top-hat, a satchel full of books, and strokes the stubble on his chin. "To be exact," he trails his finger along the symbols, "various cultures have created art which suggests the dragon doesn't trust others easily, and does not accept friendship readily. Ancient prints suggest that fortune comes to those few who can befriend this creature. The dragon symbolizes prominence, it is a lover of wealth. The green-tree dragon has an active mind, it dreams and schemes, it has a vast memory. It will never forget a day of its life."

My gut sinks below the dusty wood floor.

Does not accept friendship easily, active mind…

It might as well describe me.

"But it also mentions," the boy says, "because the dragon denounces evil and wrongdoing, you must be careful not to suppress its instincts too much. If you do, you'll find yourself tolerating evil…" the boy scratches his head. "Well, that's odd."

"Yeah," I mutter. "Odd."

I stand in the lenai, surrounded by an indoor courtyard.

I wait for Alejandro on a bench and rest my head back toward the curved-dome glass ceiling. The sunlight shines warm on my face, like sitting in a greenhouse. Grom scampers in the pansies and radish heads below.

I press my fingers to the bridge of my nose. How do I forgive myself when I don't even know if I'm to blame for Pa's death?

A lump rises in my throat. I hunch over and stare at my blue shoe bouncing impatiently on the brick path. It's five minutes past our meeting time – I turn to leave but his voice echoes down the courtyard. "Oi!"

I roll my eyes. I glance over my shoulder and he waves at me, flailing his arm in a huge motion until he slows to a stop beside me.

I fold my arms at him and he smiles at me stupidly. A wide bandage covers the bridge of his nose. His eyes are glassy, like they've watered from pain.

I frown. "Is your nose all right?"

"Oh the shnoog," he rolls his eyes, as though he'd forgotten about it. "Got in a fisty-bump with me friend last night. Ol fun. No harm. Doc'o Laszlo had to crack it or it'd stay all bent ya know," his gaze goes distant, "he's a bit ruthless, that Laszlo," Alec smiles in spite of himself. "I 'spose it just hurts more each time I get it cracked by him."

"...I see," my gaze drifts down to Grom; he bites a stick and rolls on the ground.

"He's a little might, idn't he?"

"Yeah," I smile at Grom. "He gets bigger every day. And his teeth are growing in."

"Well I'll be darned," his mouth hangs open a bit. His body is so tall and relaxed, everything droops off him.

Grom scampers around Alejandro's leather shoes and pounces on them. "Oi!" Alec laughs – but the laughing hurts his nose and he pinches it lightly, his eyes watering. "Little tyke's got spirit."

I pull Grom up and bounce him in my arms as I walk. "So what's your idea for our project?"

Alec strides beside me with long legs. He slides his hands deep into his pockets and his jaw juts forward. "... Dunno. Was hopin' you knew to be honest –" he sniggers with thin lips, "actually I just wanted to talk to ya. Now I have an excuse to see ya. Ya' know? Now that we're partners. I don't need an excuse."

My cheeks warm. I fix on the brick pathway.

... No. This is going to be worse than I thought.

My heart pumps. I clench my jaw. Fire rises in me. Grom crawls up my arm and nudges my cheek, sensing my anger.

Why can't people just leave me alone?

Control the dragon-mind. Forgive.

Forgive, Sunday, dammit!

Ugh!

I stop walking and turn to him. "I forgive you, for your assumptions about me."

Alec's eyebrows raise, taking me in. He turns his palms up to his shoulders, "Oi, no – I'm here for the project Ms. Sunday. I mean no disrespect. I only think you're a bit of a class act, aren't ya? Sides, I like spendin' time with you. You're the *dragon girl.*" He gives me a big, obvious wink.

"I see…" I turn away and walk through the courtyard, passing white star-shaped flowers and lime-green vines. Alejandro studies me with side-eyes while we walk, careful. He sucks in his cheeks like he's swallowed a lemon.

I stop. "What do you mean I'm a class act?"

His eyes are afraid. I've never seen him look scared. Not in the boxing ring. Not around school. "…Well you are," he presses at last. "You're a kind of put-together lady. And you're generous – and it'd be my talent to sniff out a good person – trust me, I have a good sniffer – and you'll be a good one."

My eyes flash down to the gauze plastered over his long nose, "You sure your sniffer isn't broken?" I wander aside to a bird fountain and let Grom crawl off my arm to it – he splashes and plays in the water.

"Plus," Alejandro folds his arms and quirks his head. "Just look at your dress."

"What about my dress?" I snap.

"Easy, easy," he pats his hands on something invisible in the air, "I just mean your dress is better than anyone else in school. Better than my dress, better than some of the professor's dress. Mind you – you're not arrogant like someone with wealth – so what're you? Where are you from? You're different. See wot I mean?" He tilts his head up and strokes his neck with his fingers, and he sucks in his lower lip, studying me.

I stare at the red brick path between his worn leather shoes. I'd never considered how I look to other students. But the dresses were a gift, I never picked them out.

"Yer from this here Nordic isle," he says, slowly. "Aren't ya?"

I tense.

How'd he guess that?

"Aw don't be so scared," he waves a hand. "I'm from the isle, too. Course we only moved here bout twee' years ago. We lived in Scotland. Me Pa was from Brazil by way of Spain – he was a regular Spanish-style Don Juan if ya know what I mean. Me grandfather was Don Alejandro. Me Pa was always sailin' about as a Warbringer on one of those big cargo ships 'round Cape Horn. He isn't with us anymore, but I always imagine him sailin' off into the sunset. And me Ma was also a Warbringer, from Scotland. We lived in Scotland most mah life but now with me at school, the family moved too, they live just southeast of here. We're local folkal."

He must live close then. Only a sled stop away.

"Our house is bout ten miles south-east of here. How bout you?"

I turn away and fiddle with a yellow bell-flower. It's none of his business where I've lived. And telling him – no doubt – would be telling everyone at school, the way people talk.

"*Hmm*," he sighs, filling the silence. He has a wry smile. "Mind you Sunday, if you ever decide to tell me yer secrets – I am as *confidant* as the sky."

...What does that mean?

He hunches over, smiling with a pouty lip. His cap is crooked and he smells like cigar smoke – I open my mouth to ask him if he broke the rules and brought a pipe to school – but I think better of it.

Perhaps, in some small way, I can trust Alejandro.

I wander to a nearby apple tree and preoccupy myself with picking a ripe apple.

"Now," he clasps his hands, loudly, "what're we goin' to do for a project... *Hmm*... You know," he gives me a sneaky smile, "it would do you well to get your lil' dragon breathin' fire already. Since he's growin' teeth now n' all. He'd make a nice weapon."

I turn sharply. "Grom is *not* a weapon."

"I know, I know – but he is... Just a little bit, idn't he?"

I scoff under my breath. I turn away and pluck another apple from the short tree.

"I know, you're a mama now. And you're protective. But one day this little guy's gonna grow up. And he needs proper training." Alec clenches his hands into fists and makes a sturdy boxing punch.

I roll my eyes.

... *Warbringers.*

"Every mama wants to protect their lil tyke," Alec coaxes, leaning around the tree and into my line of vision, "but every dragon's gotta grow up somehow. If yer overprotective, they go *soft.*"

"I am not *soft.*"

He laughs, pinching his nose again as though the movement gives him pain, but he can't help it. "Oh, oh, I know yer not soft, Ms. Sunday," he talks with his hands. "*Yer* anything but soft, aren't ya. You're a real rough-and-tumble girl."

I watch him from the side.

...No. He's not teasing me.

He sits on the park bench and crosses his long legs. He tilts his head back and lets the sunlight hit him in the face. He rests there, for a moment, and snaps his head up again, "All right – I'll make a deal with ya."

I slowly sit on the bench beside him, and he looks pleased.

"I propose," he says, with gusto, "we make use of my idea of a fire-breathing dragon."

Ugh.

"Unless –" he adds, with a long pointed finger. "You think o' somethin' better – more practical and all that – after the Christmas break." He gives me a wry look. His tan leathery cheeks pull into a smile. A bruised purple ring encircles one of his eyes. There is a dip in one of his earlobes, like it's been clipped on something, but it looks right on him, almost better that way.

I haven't thought of any project ideas yet, but I will. "Fine," I extend a hand to him. "Deal."

He shakes my hand firmly.

I stand to leave but Grom leaps from my shoulder into Alec's arms.

"*Oi!*" Alec catches him. "Little rascal."

Grom pushes Alec's chest playfully and Alec tickles and wrestles him back.

"Careful!" I reach forward.

Grom bites Alec, swishing his tail – and Alec pokes him back, teasing. I soften.

Perhaps this is good for Grom.

Perhaps... If Grom trusts Alec, maybe I can too.

The following day I visit the Machinist wing with Anning.

The Machinist lab is like standing inside a clock. It's a wide, metal-made complex filled with all kinds of gadgets and welding tables, and above the archway to the front door there's this engraving:

> *The greatest weakness lies in giving up.*
> *The most certain way to succeed is to always try just one more time.*
> *– Thomas A. Edison, Svalbard Machinist*

The Machinists whisper as I enter:

"Dragon girl..."
"That's her –"
"Only two in Animalia."

I search through the students – all in welding aprons and smudged with grease – and Viktor appears behind the farthest welding table – he sulks over spare parts and cranks something with a wrench.

Our eyes meet, but he looks sad, and turns away.

Maybe I was too hard on him.

All the Machinists work on intricate contraptions; coiled electrical engines and batteries.

Everyone but Viktor, who sits in front of scraps.

I shouldn't have turned him away like that.

Anning speaks about Animalia, but the Machinists fidget with screwdrivers and welding wands as she speaks – they eye their inventions and bite their lips, like they're on a deadline.

Anning chatters about the animal kingdom and Professor Suri works quietly at her desk, probably for the private railroad company she owns. She twists her dark hair and fastens it with a jade pin. Her forest-green kimono is pristine – no grease stains or signs of wear. Gold coins are piled on the side of her desk. She sips a cup of pink floral tea and spreads out her business plans, as though reading the morning newspaper.

I catch a glimpse of one of her papers: BUSINESS PLAN, LOCOMOTIVE.

Professor Suri tears open an envelope with her name written on it in cursive. She flips open the letter. I crane my neck over to spy the words; *'hunting,' 'make contraption,' 'be aware,' 'Svalbard would lockdown.'*

At the bottom, the letter is signed; *Justine Seraphim.*

What in the –

Professor Suri turns over her shoulder at me, like she can sense my gaze, and I step behind Anning again.

Seraphim is warning the professors about something.

My heart sinks. I should warn Suri, too. Machinist is next in the octagon pattern around the Svalbard map – the monster's attack pattern. I turn back to her, but too late – she's gone.

Anning finishes her lecture and the Machinists snap back to work, clanking and welding their metal contraptions. Everyone except Viktor, who toys with his engine like he wants to snap it in half. I step around the welding tables to his work station alone in the back. He tightens a screw with a wrench.

"Viktor," I try. "I'm sorry for how I acted. I didn't mean to be harsh."

"Yes. You were," he wipes his sleeve over his forehead, leaving a dirty smear there.

"I don't know where it came from."

"I do," he slides his wrench into his work belt and fixes his hands to his hips.

"…what do you mean?"

He plants his hands on the welding table and leans forward, close to me. "It's this place. This school. It's changing you, me, everyone."

It's true. It's changed me, being here. "But maybe some changes are good."

"*Pssh*, please," he waves his hand up and down my dress, "– all this fuss and pomp, this isn't you."

"Maybe it is, though. Maybe I like–"

"Sunday, *listen* to yourself. You've never cared what others thought. You never had to present yourself and tame yourself."

"I – guess it's just part of, being at school. Learning. Growing or –"

"It's not that," he snaps. "We have to leave before it changes us permanently."

I soften. "Maybe I'm just growing into… who I really am."

His expression goes dark. "There are other ways to honor your father's memory than putting up with all this and becoming some kind of servant to Svalbard."

His honest, cold stare is too much – I snap my face away.

"I know," he says softly, and he comes around the welding table to me, a little awkwardly. "Animalia is all you ever wanted." He places one arm around my shoulders, and with the other he holds my wrist. His presence is sweet, comforting. I swear he could hold me forever. "It's not your fault," he whispers. "But we *have* to leave this place. It's time." He squeezes my arm. "I'll take you with me."

Him holding me, it's familiar. Like family. His long fingers are cold and steady. I rest my head on his shoulder and melt a little. His shirt smells sweet, like cigar smoke. Leaving would be easy – I'd be away from the monster – away from my past with Pa – away from my studies and everything. But there's no way I could forgive myself for leaving Svalbard, or Ori. Every day learning Animalia, it's like learning about who Pa was, and who I could be.

I turn to face him – his ocean-eyes are sincere. "I can't go."

That night, in my room, I towel dry my hair from my bath.

Ori lays belly-down on her bed, reviewing her notes on the Arctic Puffin.

I yawn, sitting on the edge of my bed – but something pulls my attention. The little peach hairs on my arm stand on edge: *There's something outside.* I close my eyes and listen with every muscle in my back. The wind howls outside in a coming storm. Only the wind.

But that same blasted inner nudge turns me toward the window. I can't help it. I *have* to look outside. I walk to the window and rest my hand on the cold, frosty glass.

What the –

Something *is* down there! In the snow. A shadowed figure trudges on, leaving Svalbard. I hold my breath; his tall narrow frame, slumped shoulders, tossed brown hair: It's Viktor, pacing into a thick snowstorm. He's headed west, toward the distant train station. He can't leave.

What a fool!

It's too far to walk. He'll die in the storm.

No, no, no…

I grip my throat. I have to save him. I push through my dresser and throw on my thick winter coat.

"Where are you going?" Ori cries. "Sunday! We agreed no going out alone at night!"

I don't care. I slam the door behind me. I rush down the stairs, fly through the lounge, and clamber deep into Svalbard. The marble halls are empty, cold. I run through the wide, silent ballrooms and my footsteps echo loud as explosions on the floor.

I strain in the dark. *Darnit!* I can't see a blasted thing. I should've brought Ori's lantern.

I turn around, alone in the dark ballroom. My heart pumps in my neck. Above, a dusty crystal chandelier creaks and slowly rotates. Like in my nightmares.

Keep moving…

I dart into the west wing – it's banned – but it's the fastest way to Viktor. He can't leave Svalbard. He'll regret it forever. I dash through a narrow passageway heading west. It must lead out of school. I turn the corner, but instead of a hallway I stand in a kitchen. All is quiet. Something *reeks* – like rotten meat left out way too long. I gag and clasp my hand over my nose.

My gut dips. *This can't be right.*

I run in the dark; I pass cabinets, knives, pantries. But the only way out is a darker, narrower corridor.

I frown down the shadowed, quiet space.

The exit could be just down that way.

For Viktor… For Viktor…

I step slowly down the shadowed hall. My heart thumps.

Why?

Why am I doing this? Why am I afraid?

I stop.

Why did I stop?

Heat flares in me. The dragon-mind. It stopped me.

It senses something.

I listen to it. I stand, wide-eyed in the dark, searching… it's probably nothing.

But… something *is* there.

A faint dark outline – a bent-over figure. It's doubled-over and stretched out with its hands on the floor. The person is frozen that way – at a demented angle, completely still.

What the –

Chills grip me. My heart turns.

No, please…

The person is alive – but not moving. It's shaped like a man but positioned like a beast on all-fours. A ragged brown cloth is draped over its head and limbs.

The monster.

No – No – No –

Its hands lay flat on the carpeted floor. Its bare feet and ankles show under the tattered brown sheet. It's bent forward at a painful angle with its back contorted – it knows I'm here – it thinks it can disguise itself.

I hold my breath.

It is like the angler fish. It's camouflaged and won't move until it's close to its prey.

The dragon-mind rises in me. I grit my teeth.

Think. Think.

I have to move – quick! But I can't run. If I run, it'll know I've seen it and chase me.

I walk away, briskly, back the way I came from, into the hallway, to the kitchen.

My heart thumps in my ears.

Move! Quick!

I pause in the doorway and turn over my shoulder – but the figure, still bent forward at a painful angle with its hands and feet on the ground – the figure is somehow *closer* to me.

How the –

It picks up its hands, ever-so-slowly, sliding them across the floor. The movement is so subtle it'd be invisible to anyone who didn't look for it. It's cunning. Demented.

The figure slides its hands closer. Its head hangs low to the floor.

Its feet drag toward me.

It will catch me. It will.

My God –

The dragon flares inside me. Adrenaline pumps into my limbs: I am a predator, too.

I will outrun it.

EIGHTEEN

THE INCIDENT IN THE NIGHT

I run, frantic for a way out. My shoes clank on the wood floor.

He'll know I've seen him. That I'm running from him.

I will die.

Sprinting, I glance over my shoulder. The monster hunches-over, crawling fast like a dog in the shadows, louder and closer.

"Help!" I scream. But my voice echoes into the empty places of the west complex.

It's too dark to see.

Which way?

My hands slam into a dead end. "No!"

I wrench the door handle but it's locked. I pound the door. THUD – THUD – THUD!

I move to the next door. I try the knob; *click.*

Also locked.

Please, God. Don't let me die.

"HELP!" I shriek.

I glance over my shoulder. The strange figure, cloaked in rags, is bent sideways at an off-angle beside a chair and it freezes, as though to blend in with the kitchen furniture.

It thinks I don't see it: It's insane.

"HELP!"

There's one way out – on the opposite side of the room. And the monster blocks my path to it – I can stay here and die, or try to break free and fight it.

Fight.

The dragon rages in me: I'll do whatever it takes.

Fight!

The monster is twice my size, but I can buy time.

I have to try and pass him.

I leap once – lunging for the opposite wall, but the shadowed creature lurches from its place – leaping – and pins me to the floor.

– WHAM!

"NO!"

His knees press me on either side. His thick hands bind my throat.

The figure's face blurs with cloth and it thrashes its head like a dog. I wrench my arm out from under me and wedge my fingers into the dark places where his eyes should be. The figure shrieks and bites my fingers. Blood smears my hand and he bites down on my fingers harder. Blood drips on my face.

He pushes his hands over my mouth and nose, suffocating me.

I can't breathe. I can't –

He thrashes his head in a demonic blur; brown, red, black, red: I writhe on the floor – my lungs clench for air – but his fingers grip my nose – his knees bind my arms.

I can't breathe.

My lungs contract. My vision fades to black at the edges.

Someone help – help me God – help –

His hands grip my hair and wrench my head to the side. Something pierces my neck – his teeth.

– Don't let me die.

His arms are planted by my face – his forearm is thick and marked with an ink pattern – and another shadow rises above the man: Someone stocky with corkscrew curls – Ori. She holds a heavy kitchen pot overhead and swings it once – hard – like a bat over the monster's head.

CRACK!

The creature's head slumps at an angle, and he rolls off me.

"Hurry!" Ori yanks me to my feet. I trip – and grip her arm, gasping for air as we run – through the kitchen – laundry rooms – empty ballrooms.

I stumble and lean into her as I run, limping.

Thank God, Ori. Ori. Ori.

I glance over my shoulder. Nothing's following us. We run up the Animalia tower stairs – through the lounge – and reach our room.

My hand shakes as I slam the door and lock it behind us.

I – almost died.

Ori hugs me. I squeeze her arms and rest my head on her shoulder. My body aches. I sob into her hair like a child. Blood from my face smears her nightgown.

She holds my shoulders at arm's length. "What *was* that?"

I hold her hands where they rest on my shoulders. "It was him. The monster."

We hug. I cry into her curly hair. She uses French lemon shampoo – it smells so good. Like cake. Sometimes I use it, too, even though I never asked her to. I know she's noticed I use it, but she never mentions it to me.

My heart turns. I don't know what I'd do without her.

"Thank you," I say. "For everything."

I limp to the washroom and clean out the scrapes on my neck and arms – they aren't deep, but I can't stop shaking as I pull the washcloth over them and smear blood from my neck and arms.

I slide into bed and stare out the window, into the dark early morning starlight – but someone knocks on the Animalia door.

THUD – THUD – THUD.

I jump in bed. My heart pumps. "Who was that?"

Ori sits up in her bed and lights a lantern.

In my nightgown, I patter down the stairs to the lounge. Ori follows me, she holds my arm. All is dark.

Slowly, I peer through the look-hole: It's Professor Seacole, the Warbringer head-of-house.

"Should we let her in?" Ori whispers.

Please don't let this be bad...

I open the door a crack for her.

Seacole sets her hands on her hips. She's so strong, with thick arms and awards pinned to her chest from the Crimean War. She frowns down at me. "The dean wants to see you."

No...

"...All right," my voice is small. "We'll get ready."

"Not her," Seacole says. "Only you."

Ori and I exchange a look of dread.

No... don't make me go alone.

Ori is the only one I trust in the whole school.

I retreat to our washroom – I slap water on my face and throw on my overdress. My hands shake as I tie up my hair with a blue ribbon. Ori sits on the rim of the bathtub and watches me in silence. It feels like the end of something. Softly, she says, "Come back."

I nod.

I scoop Grom from my bed and hold him to my chest, cradling him while he sleeps. I won't be separated from him. He's my one comfort.

Seacole waits for me in the archway. My chin falls to my chest and I follow her through the halls. The Warbringer students say she's kind, but she doesn't smile.

"Where are we going?" I ask.

"You'll see."

We pass Eoin, the freckled servant-boy, who absently mops the ballroom floor. His eyes glaze over, he hunches with the mop. Chills prickle my arms.

Eoin could be the monster.

Eoin isn't right in his mind. Maybe he's on drugs, or something...

Behind Eoin, Professor Suri gives sharp orders to Agnet, the housekeeper, instructing her about the school ventilation system. *Please notice me.* But none of them do. None of them feel my silent cry. Our footsteps echo through the tall, open spaces of the main hall. Seacole turns north – the same direction of the incident.

Pressure builds in my chest.

Please, no… Don't make me go back.

Warbringers pass in the hall, they tease each other on their way to their 5:00 a.m. early morning exercises – their cheer is jarring next to my own agony. Alec laughs among the chatty students. He walks with his arms swung around the other boys. For a moment our eyes touch – he breaks away from the group, and takes a step toward me, then frowns at Seacole. He stalls behind his friends. "…Sunday? What's wrong with–"

"Back to your business," Seacole snaps at him.

We continue on, and I glance over my shoulder at him receding in the distance.

His light is something far away from me. I'd never belong in his world, with friends like that… With cheer and laughter and safety.

I belong somewhere else. Somewhere cold, alone, kept away.

Seacole and I turn a sharp corner toward a hidden, ornate black opal staircase – around the corner from the Animalia atrium.

Seacole stands at the rim of the stairway, she looks over my head as she speaks, "She's down there."

My heart sinks.

I step down the strange stairway, slowly. My shoes clack on the slippery dark stone. Pottery and paintings of animals are embedded into the alcoves beside the stairs.

I went out after hours. Seraphim will punish me for breaking her rules.

I reach the bottom and pause at the dark wood double-doors. The plaque beside the door reads:

<u>Animalia Catalogue Library and Museum</u>

I lightly brush the cold silver handle with my fingertips. *She'll kick me out of Svalbard.*

I close my eyes.

God help me...

I knock once, loudly. Someone sniffles beside me and I jump – Anning sits at a cataloging desk beside Professor Cortez, the Artisan. *Why is he –*

He whispers something in her ear and they laugh. She stands – a swirl of moss-green velvet – her voice is a strained whisper to him, "it's not like it's an easy book to misplace, *The Book of Animalia*, if it isn't in the Animalia collection it should be in yours, all that artwork..."

Cortez flicks his disheveled head in my direction and Anning's jaw snaps up, like she just noticed me staring at her. Her neck stiffens and she breaks, "Well go on. She's waiting for you."

"Oh..." I whisper. "Right."

I turn the handle and the dark door creaks open. The library is an ominous half-cave room, with sleek black tile and filtered green light from above, where windows meet garden spaces hosting different species of reptiles. Strange objects surround me – metronomes, animal traps, chains. Chills touch my spine. *What in God's world...*

Seraphim sits at a raised desk, with spirals of books behind her. *Blazes.* She's like some great judge, sitting there like that. She scratches an ink quill along a piece of stationary.

Grom hides in my overcoat and pokes his salamander-face out from the lapel.

"Come in," Seraphim says flatly.

I obey.

I walk, slowly, up the few steps to the awning in front of her.

She pushes her papers aside; her eyes are distant, cold. "Sit."

I obey.

In the corner, the snow tiger bites its paw and chews it.

"Were you going to tell me," she sighs, smoothing down the dark folds of her dress, "what you were doing in the west wing last night?"

"I'm sorry. I didn't mean to."

"You broke the rules."

A hole burns my chest. "…I know."

Please let me stay at Svalbard.

"It was an impulsive decision, wasn't it?"

I deflate.

"You don't 'mess around' with my rules, Sunday. You obey me."

"I don't know what I was thinking. I saw –"

"I know what you saw." She props an elbow on her desk and cups her chin in her hand, taking me in; she's rested, secure. The scent of crushed lavender seeps from her pores. Her shoulders slump with a feminine swoop. With the cave and columns behind her she's formidable; someone out of time.

How very different I must look.

"Viktor is gone," she says at last. "He made it through the storm. He caught the train early this morning, to Sjosburg."

"How do you kno–" I stop. "… Thank you."

The snow tiger yawns – his casual groan is so violent Grom crawls back into my coat.

Seraphim stands, she paces by the nearby enclosure window. Her shoe heels strike the marble floor and echo along the glass spherical ceiling. She passes rows of books between glass cases of colorful, tropical insects and snakes. "Such beauties…" she whispers, running her fingers over the glass. She frowns into a floor-length enclosure with rainforest plants and – judging by the plaque below – some dangerous animal, too.

She stares into the enclosure, motionless, for like, an eternity.

A large diamond necklace rests beneath her throat. It shimmers as the light hits it…

Others will see you as a threat… Make yourself seem harmless…

I step beside her, facing the dark glass enclosure. "Ms. Seraphim," I venture a whisper. "I promise not to break any more of your rules."

Her eyes narrow on the shadowed trees behind the glass.

"…What are you looking for?" I ask, quiet.

"I am trying to decide whether or not to expel you."

My gut squeezes, my heart pumps in my neck. The question is a test.

A searching.

It has to be.

"I've made progress," I beg, "I can learn to control myself, I really can. My abilities, they can get sharper. My instincts can get sharper."

Seraphim folds her arms over her dark velvet chest. Her focus narrows on the shadows between the plants. "And what happens when your instincts are sharper?"

"What do you mean?" I splutter. "I can be stronger in Animalia. I can see things others don't see and know things they won't."

She chews her plump lower lip and brushes her fingertips over her necklace. "Sharper... Stronger..." she shakes her head. "You have no idea how you sound. You sound like the people we try to stop." She turns to me. "You are *ruthless*. You've proven you're dangerous. And since you've avoided an honest test with Anning, you give me no choice. I will test you now, here. If you pass, you can stay in Animalia. If you fail, you're no use to me – you'll be expelled and will never be Animalia. You've used up your chance to do this test the easy way – this will be hard."

NINETEEN

FIGHT OR FLIGHT

The glass cage beside me is dark, only shadows of tropical trees. My hands tremble on my coat. "I'm not afraid to go in there."

"You should be," Seraphim fixes a dead rodent to my coat. "The creature in there, it loves to eat these rats." She readies the iron handles to open the enclosure.

"Don't you think it isn't fair, sending me in smelling like bait?"

Her smile twists. "Welcome to the food chain."

She's trying to put fear in me. "I'm not afraid. I'm Animalia."

"Not yet you aren't," she snaps. "You're a student, nothing more. A fragment of your father." She leans in. Her eyelashes flick around my face. "And I see fear all over you. Fear creates a chemical response in the body, called adrenaline – it spurs a fight or flight response. Animalia know to control that response – but look at you, you're trembling."

"But I'm not–"

"The test is simple," she cuts. "There is an emergency knife at the opposite end of the enclosure. If you harm my animal, I'll expel you from Svalbard. If you run from the enclosure, I'll expel you from Svalbard. If the animal attacks you, well – use your imagination."

That doesn't give me many options.

"My father taught me not to be afraid of animals," I rub my arms, "he taught me every animal was God's creation."

Seraphim's eyes narrow, "Just because these animals were created by God doesn't mean they won't kill you. We are all plagued by the demands of an imperfect world." Seraphim pushes open the enclosure gate, pulls me forward and through the doorway, and slaps the doors shut behind me. She steps away into the shadows, watching me.

Palm branches brush my shoulders as I walk through the cage, in near-darkness. My breaths echo in my ears.

Remember your training.

I turn. Everywhere I look is some haunted shadow; tropical vines, roots, shadows of my own face reflecting in the glass. Adrenaline pumps in my chest, my eyes go wide and my pupils constrict, adjusting to the darkness.

What animal would be here?

Release the fear, release it.

Fight-or-flight sets my every muscle on edge.

Let the fear move through you.

The details of the cage swarm my mind – insects snap around my shoulders, roots twist beside my feet.

I close my eyes. *Focus.* Pa's voice fills me: *Animals can sense your fear. Release the fear.*

I sense, without having to look – the bitter scent of animal fur looming in the damp air – the weight of something hanging from a branch behind me – and its deep intention: To kill.

My heart hammers – I am prey.

I turn to the distant shadow of the creature, half-concealed behind a palm frond; and two beady dark eyes stare back at me.

It senses my fear.

Pa always told me, that like animals, there are people who don't mean us well – people are among the most ruthless in all creation.

I re-angle my head to the empty space by the glass where Seraphim stood.

But she's gone…

The emergency knife shines in one corner of the cage and opposite it, the door sits ajar, tempting me to run.

I could grab the knife, just in case.

No, she'd kick me out of Svalbard just for taking it.

I close my eyes again. *Breathe.* My heartbeat slows. I slide the dead rat from my shoulders and roll it toward the creature. A peace offering.

I look up again and the shadowed animal is closer, frozen-still right above the dead rodent with stiff, insane eyes. It doesn't even glance at the rat, no, its eyes are fixed on me, hungry. Its intelligent gaze stares deep into me. A human-like hand grips the branch beneath it. Its silhouette is terrifying, long arms and strange legs, it's something hunched, something… abused.

What in the…

Is it even an animal? …A baboon? A monkey?

Pa always told me nature teaches us boundaries; some things will kill you if you give them the dominance to. We have to be rooted in who we are and speak with authority over the natural realm. Boundaries must be established. Doors must be closed.

We stare into each other – the invisible cord between us is electric. It's a testing; who has more authority. I am bigger, but that doesn't matter, the baboon is stronger, cunning, pure chaos.

My gut dips.

Heaven help me.

I glance at the way out – I look back again and the monkey stands closer now, frozen on a nearer branch – close enough it could leap out and attack. "I don't want to hurt you," I warn it.

It stares at me with rigid insanity. It will kill me.

Pa's voice lives in me: *Stronger.* Speak with all of who you are.

"I don't want to hurt you but…"

Too weak, still. Its human-face goes slack, its dark glossy eyes roll back – *what the blazes* – I step back. Something's wrong with it, like it's been through some kind of drug experiment, its head is lumpy, tortured…

My heart pumps. It steps forward, stalking me, claiming dominance.

The knife. I need the knife – no – the door is closer.

Too late –

A brown flash leaps at me and the monkey grips my neck – I scream – its hands bind my throat and it thrashes wildly, I wrench my arm up and around its hairy back, pulling its fur and – *wham* – I slap it down on the stone floor.

It slithers into the shadows on all fours, like it feels no pain – hiding in the dense trees.

I glare around the dark tropical thickets. It ripped my dress and scratched my shoulder. Blood seeps into the fabric. It could be anywhere. I close my eyes – its presence is something jarring, chaotic – it's right behind me. I open my eyes and turn again – it's camouflaged with the palm frond beside me – it leaps at me again, and I crack my hand like a bat, swinging down at it midair and casting it to the floor. I pull in breath and speak with all my body, "THAT IS ENOUGH."

The monkey huddles on the floor, wide-eyed.

"BACK AWAY," I demand, pressing forward.

The monkey curls over in a bowing posture, it huddles back and retreats from me, into the shadows, hissing under its breath.

"STAY DOWN." I am one-thousand voices in one – I am my father, I am part of all creation.

My heart drums to a steady rhythm and I collect myself.

I am rested. Strong. Sure.

My body buzzes with a kind of alertness. I stare at the empty place where it used to be.

It isn't until she stands behind me that I even notice she's there: "Come," Seraphim says.

I turn and she opens the door out for me.

Every bone in my body wants to resent her, but I can't think of her at all – new strength surges through my body – that *voice* resonates still, deep in my chest. I walk through the dark stone library and every nerve in me sings, electric.

I follow her through the archives; she speaks, explaining how she had rescued the creature from a chemical testing experiment – her voice sounds as though it's underwater – stronger inside me is Pa's voice, *my* voice.

Seraphim pauses by a manuscript shelf. "What I am about to tell you, you must never tell anyone."

I nod.

"Animalia is a house of authority. Not everyone understands the animal kingdom. It is about status – function – a place in nature, in the food chain. There are some who think of Animalia as adopting a *lower* perspective. They think we're less than human." Her eyes drift up toward the columns of manuscripts. "We don't *conform* to animal instincts. You've just demonstrated that." She pulls a large, ancient manuscript from the shelf. She tucks the book under her arm and pulls me to the dark chaise lounge that faces the glass reptile enclosures.

We sit side-by-side. She opens the book in her lap. The moment is strange, something from a dark dream. It's odd. I understand her. I'm more relaxed than ever, more myself. She speaks to me like I'm an equal – not some dumb student; "Have you ever had a moment, where you thought you knew something, *sensed* something, though you had no real evidence of it. Like an instinct."

"Yes," I say. "I am drawn to certain things, without thinking. Like how I looked out the window and saw Viktor leaving Svalbard."

She nods, slowly.

"Once, I saw someone following me," I say, remembering Eoin, the servant-boy. "Only I didn't see him. I *felt* him, behind me."

"*That*," she leans forward, "is Animalia." She brushes her fingertips down the book's smooth paper, over the inky inscriptions. "No one taught you Amafi, Sunday. But you speak it. The language is learned through Animalia instincts. No one can simply *use* the language unless they're truly Animalia."

"Right, but how would I use it?"

Seraphim laughs – a sweet, high-chimed chuckle. "But Sunday," she leans in and grips my shoulder, "you're speaking it right now. With me."

I pull away. "No I'm not."

"Think about it, Sunday. What did you say to me, just now?"

I frown. The words I just spoke – the actual *words*. "Well I said…" my gut flips. It's the same haziness I have if I've repeated a word over and over – it's lost significance and transformed, slipped from my mind. Become something strange. Just like the words in our conversation.

My fingertips rest lightly on my chin.

Her lips twitch into an approving smile and she pats my shoulder. She slides the book on the table. "The best thing you can do is trust me, *hmm*? Just how you've learned today that authority must be respected, now you know – don't break my rules."

I nod.

"Your Christmas break starts tomorrow, but for your protection I won't permit you to return to Sjosburg."

"I can't–"

"You won't be safe there."

"But – "

"This monster is intelligent. It would find you there. Other enemies of Svalbard would find you there, too."

It would *find* me?

"Besides, you have work to do. I'm sending you away with charts for your study, you'll research the mind sanctuary and the meanings of your dreams. Understand your dreams and you'll understand this monster. I'll send for your protection over the Christmas break, with the Warbringer boy, Alejandro. It would be wise for you to secure a connection with a Warbringer, especially a young one that is still forming his strength. Yes. Warbringers are loyal. It will serve you later in life."

The way she says it… Like even relationships are strategy.

She stands and turns to the animal enclosure – the baboon slithers between palm fronds. It sits on a high branch and rocks itself back and forth, like a child.

"This 'monster' that's hunting you, it comes from a group of men that hate Svalbard, and especially Animalia." She brushes her fingertips across the book on the short table in front of me. "Their fraternity is called the Rose Society," she turns the book to face me, which shows illustrations of a rose and odd symbols. "This is their mark. The upside-down rose. The brotherhood all have this mark. You saw some of them when I first met you in Sjosburg. Remember?"

I bend over the ink print. "I've seen this symbol – it was on the person's arm, whoever attacked me."

"Let me guess. The person you saw didn't *feel* quite human, did they?"

I dab my nose with my sleeve. "No, they didn't."

"After you're done researching the mind sanctuary, report to my office. I'll have new instructions for you."

I bow my head a little. It isn't something I do, bowing. But it feels appropriate, somehow. "Thank you."

TWENTY

AN UNEXPECTED CHRISTMAS

I pack for Christmas break, folding my dresses into my travel trunk.

Ori sits on her bed, slumped over her knees, fiddling with one of her bracelets.

"I won't be gone long," I say, folding. "Just a few days, really."

"I know you've been going through a lot," Ori says, softly, "besides being attacked."

I tense. Ori's social sensitivity is sharp.

I turn to her. "I wish I could take you with me."

"You don't have to tell me all that's going on in your head," Ori chuckles and sits cross-legged. "I just hate being one of the only ones staying behind at school over the break."

"They'll have a Christmas feast," I try to sound hopeful. "Others will be here, too."

"Some of them..." Ori rolls over on her bed and lays belly-down. She props her chin in her hands and shakes her head. "Wouldn't want to go home, anyway. It's better here, even if the school is empty." She clears her throat, trying to act brave, but her voice shakes. "I just hate being left alone, with that monster here."

I set my lip. "Just promise you'll be careful…"

Ori's eyes narrow, misty. "It has to be that man we saw underground, the first day we came here, don't you think? It *has* to be him."

I snap my luggage shut. "Just stay locked in here as much as you can. Promise you won't go out at night."

"Promise."

I button my overcoat around my dress. "Over summer, maybe we can even travel together."

Ori pets Rosie in her lap. "Bring some taffy back from town, will you?"

I walk to her bedside and squeeze her hand. "I will."

"Here," she pulls a little pink bracelet from her wrist and slides it onto mine. "This is for you. I made two. So we have matching ones."

"…pretty."

She hugs me and I hold her tight. Somewhere over the weeks, Ori became family. "I'll be right back," I sniff. "With taffy."

Ori rubs her eyes. "Kay."

I walk through Svalbard, out into the courtyard, and down the Warbringer compound foyer. I hold my suitcase and pass rows of weapons; medieval iron spears, stone axes…

Professor Seacole rises from the staircase with Alec behind her, dressed in a black clean-pressed uniform, she mutters something to him and Alec salutes her as she walks off.

Seacole's steps soften down the stairs and Alec turns to me with a wry smile. "All right," he folds his arms. "What'd you do?"

"Nothing."

"*Psshhh.* I'm supposed to protect you from wut – nothin' for no reason?"

"I didn't do anything."

He taps his foot and tucks his chin under at me. "What'd you do, Sunday," he sings, "What'd you do-ooo."

"Fine. I – I fought a monster."

"*Oohhh,*" he sniggers into his palm, like I've told him a joke.

"I'm serious," I insist.

"Oh. Right I know ya are. Ol' Seacole here wouldn't have me protecting for nah."

"I still don't see why they're putting me with you."

Alec opens his arms wide, like he would hug the world, "Cause I'm the best at wut I do."

I roll my eyes.

"Nah really. I'm the best in me class. The best in mah house." He pokes the air in front of him. "Thas' why they put me with you." He tucks his chin to his shoulder, like he can't contain his laughter. "You're made of tough stuff. Takin' on a monster. So there might be a monster comin' after me – I'll be on tip-top alert."

Alec pays for a dogsled caravan from Svalbard to a nearby train stop and we board the train for a short ride on a red steam-engine, headed for Alec's hometown. I walk down the train hall in search of a compartment. Passengers whisper as we pass. They sneak glances at my fine clothes and Alec's military uniform; it's like we're something of myth to them, something strange from a faraway place they'll never understand.

The train lurches and I find a seat by the window for us. Grom and I cuddle and I bounce him on my knee. Grom places his nose on the window, watching the topsy-turvy snow hills pass. The sun sets sideways and low over the jagged horizon, making the vast basin shine silver and blue. The other passengers stare at us, whispering, it irks me. Like they're monitoring me. Any one of them could be some enemy of Animalia. Like Seraphim said.

Ignore it.

I chew a cinnamon stick and watch farms pass; Scotland cattle; reindeer… The train climbs over mountains and bridges.

Alec reclines across from me with his eyes shut, like he's exhausted from school.

"So if something bad is about to happen to me, can your Warbringer instincts tell?"

Alec opens one eye to me, then closes it again. "Nah, it doesn't work like tha," he kicks his heels up on the bench, beside me, "being a Warbringer is like – if there's someone round who has bad intent, I can pick up on it – and anticipate that n' all. The only thing is I haven't caught on to one goin' around hunting you in the night like you say. So whoever they are, either I haven't seen 'em, or they're able to mask themselves, somehow... But you're safe with me. And safer now that we're further from school."

The train lurches to a stop.

Rows of homes are built up the hillside, with line over line of sagging shingled roofs and Tudor windows. Snow slopes off the sides of the houses like frosted gingerbread homes.

We step off the train and folk music echoes from the Christmas market. Children sell bakery buns – cinnamon sizzles in the wind.

Their laughter. Their warmth – so different from Sjosburg.

I buy a bag of Marionberry taffy for Ori and roll it into my luggage. *I'll be back soon, Ori.*

Alec walks me toward a hill with a narrow trail winding up. A sweet log cabin with a thatched roof is tucked into the forest there: "Thas' it. Home sweet home," Alec takes my luggage and carries it for me.

I hike up the snowy forest trail. This place... It's like the same dense, haunted forest around Sjosburg. An owl screeches – the branches rustle – I jump and turn over my shoulder.

Alec turns and nearly drops the luggage. "*Jeesh.* Relax, will ya. Yer makin' me nervous."

"...Sorry."

We pass a dirt-and-wood boxing ring just outside the front porch. Alec props open the cabin's heavy circular door with his foot, and holds it for me. I duck through the wood doorway, slowly, and warm, yeast-filled air clings to me; just-baked bread, sugar cookies and pine. A small fire crackles in the stone fireplace and pine boughs drape along the cabin windows as decoration. A young girl with messy curls sleeps at the bench beside a low table. Family antiques line the walls and windows.

My heart swells.

If Pa were alive. Home would've been like this.

Alec nods to his red-headed sister sleeping on the bench, "*Er* – this is *Samantha*, but Grandma and I call her Snuggy. Cause she's snuggly. And – you thirsty? You wan' a water?"

"Oh – yes, please."

The girl wakes and runs to Alec – he picks her up and twirls her around, attacking her with little kisses on her cheek.

Alec sets my suitcase by the stairway and addresses the house, loudly, "Got a mate from school a'right. So nobody say nuthin' about *you-know-what!*"

A strong-standing aged woman strides from the kitchen and sets bread on the table: Alec's grandmother. She slaps her hands on her apron and gives me a big hug. She rocks me in her arms, as though I were family and not a stranger at all. "Welcome back from school sweetness. Make yerself at home." She holds me by my arm and squeezes it.

"Oh… Thank you."

I set Grom down on a cushion by the fireplace and he curls his tail under, ready for sleep. Alec's little sister twirls around in a worn dress and when she turns, smiling at me, puffy white scars shine over her ear and down the side of her tan neck. Her hair twists in wild red spires over her forehead and around her shoulders and she leans on Alec's worn pant leg – her hazel eyes flash up to me. "Is she from Svalbard too?"

Alec pats her head by his hip. "That she is, Snuggy."

"Sit, please," his grandma tells me. "Dinner's all set 'n ready to go."

I sit next to Alec at the table. Candlelight flickers over pine boughs and red flowers. *My stars* – it's a dream. I dunk fresh bread into jellies, Spanish-style cookies, chocolate pudding. They laugh at everything – full of witty comments. They talk with their hands, their eyes shine. Alec's grandma went to Svalbard as a warbringer fifty-some years ago. She extends a hand to me across the table and squeezes mine. "We're so glad you could come."

She's *glad?*

Snuggy turns to me, fork in-hand and tells me she will be Artisan. She pulls me into the kitchen and shows me her decorated sugar cookies. She tells me she's been baking all day, folding fan-tans, rolls, gingerbread.

Alejandro stands and taps his glass with a silver spoon – *ting* – *ting* – *ting!* "Ah'right everybody," he announces, with one hand over his heart, "it's time for Snuggy to present – the first gift of Christmas!"

Snuggy flashes an impish grin and runs into the other room while Alejandro pulls out an old violin. He props it on his shoulder and plays a strained *O' Christmas Tree.* Snuggy runs back to the table with wreaths draped over her arms and hands one to each of us at the table. Alec places the wreath on his head and I laugh – but the others do it as well. The wreaths are designed like crowns, meant for wearing like hats, topped with small candles: Advent crowns.

Snuggy drapes one around my head and lights the little candles on top one-by-one.

I hold the crown with a hand, so it won't fall.

I don't belong around love like this. If they knew what I did to Pa…

It's like sampling something I could never really have. A taste of what life could've been for me. No matter how many times I've tried to have a life like this, it ends the way it always does.

This warmth isn't my lot in life.

TWENTY-ONE

DANCING WITH THE OLSHIELDS

I don't remember the last time I laughed like this – so hard my sides hurt. Alec's Grandma stands and claps her hands. "All right, that's quite enough of stuffin' ourselves."

"I dunno, Grandmama," Alec slumps in his chair, his hands on his belly, "I don't think I'm stuffed enough."

"You're stuffed as a Christmas goose – it's time to give sommat back."

They slide jellies, nuts and berries on wood trays.

"What are we doing?" I whisper to Alec.

He fills a tray with me. "Goin' all into town. Fetcha coat."

I slip on my overcoat and Alec hands me a tray, heavy with cakes and cookies.

I follow Alec out of the house and we all carry our trays in a little procession down the winding snowy path. Our wreath-crowns glow like fireflies in the midnight forest and steam rises from the hot cakes on our trays; sugar, vanilla and pine waft in the breeze.

Reindeer raise their heads – sniffing cinnamon in the air. An arctic fox, white as snow, scampers across the trail – he blends in perfectly – no one notices him but me.

We reach the bottom of the hill, into town. All the Tudor-roofed shops are decorated with pine branches and red holly berries. Music echoes faint in the wind; fiddles, flutes and bagpipes. Alec's grandma leads us to a small inn on the corner and the music grows louder. She takes our wreath crowns as we duck inside.

The warm, dim-lit pub is alive with people; half the town at least, laughing, dancing jigs.

The musicians catch sight of Ms. OlShield and cheer. She waves me over and I place my tray at the table beneath the musicians. The neighborhood children flood the trays, they squeal with delight and scramble for the honeybuns, grabbing fists-fulls of hazelnuts.

A few kids hug me, too. I shrug away but they keep hanging off me – and by the fourth hug I stop resisting, I just hold them back.

The musicians play an impromptu jig:

> *"The OlShields are a very good family,*
> *A very good family, a very good family.*
> *Cakes and cookies for everyone here, everyone here, everyone here.*
> *Ms. OlShield is full of good cheer, full of good cheer, full of good cheer.*
> *Merry Christmas and give us a beer!"*

The children hold cookies between their teeth and dance. They prance around in worn shoes and clothes, twirling in quick jigs.

The drummer counts down – "Four, three, two, one!"

The bagpipes strike up, followed by drums and flutes and they sing:

> *"Cinnamon, raisins, thyme and whiskey –*
> *now's the time to sing and cheer –*
> *Christmas comes here once a year..."*

Alec twirls his little sister. He's so tall and lanky next to her, I can't help but laugh at his dancing. He has to bend way over to reach her – he picks her up and twirls her toward me. They each grab one of my hands – we prance in one direction – then turn and go the other. My cheeks hurt from smiling so much. Alec kicks his legs up high – and squats down like a frog.

Squat – kick – leap.

Children surround him and imitate his silly jig.

I take a break and retreat to the corner, to catch my breath. This isn't like me. No.

But… maybe it could be.

A harpist comes forward, playing a slower tune. Her hands pull the strings like she's weaving a tapestry. The children clear away, back to their families and everyone chatters around the sides of the room.

The harp plays like a music-box, with a tune from an older time on the isle. Alec leans against the stone wall beside me. He takes my hand and we dance slowly. His clothes smell sweet, like pine needles. White scars line the side of his neck… I'd have never noticed unless I stood close. His features are noble; his gaze firm. He has wide cheekbones and a set jaw. There's something upright in him: like he'd stand and fight when everyone else turns away.

"Thank you," I say. "For letting me stay with your family."

"I think they're the ones who are thankful," he nods to his sister, who sits on a table holding a glass of milk – she kicks her legs over the edge, smiling at us.

This place. The people. It's too good to be true.

He watches me from the side. "Things'll be all right, Sunday. You'll see."

TWENTY-TWO

HOW TO FIGHT A MONSTER

That night I dream I stand in my bedroom at Svalbard.

Nighttime aurora cast an underwater glow onto the wood floor. Outside the window, stars glide over the tundra. A deer walks out there, in the snow.

Pa's favorite animal.

"… Papa?"

"You keep looking for your father," Ori mutters behind me, darkly. "But you forgot me."

I turn to her bed. She slumps over her knees and shadows crawl over her face in a blur. "You shouldn't have left me."

"They told me to go—"

"I didn't want to be alone," she sobs into her hair. "Now I'll die because of you!"

"You're *not* gonna die."

Ori turns sideways, where shadows gather in our room. The shadows crawl over her skin and hair, pressing her down until she's dissolved into the dark folds of her bed.

"Ori?" I sprint to her bedside. I slap around the sheets and under the covers.

She's gone.

"ORI!"

I wake and bolt upright.

What the —

My hands clench my neck. I pry my fingers loose and feel around in the dark; pillow, blanket, table, fireplace...

The OlShield's living room.

...What a nightmare.

I sag into the pillows and rub my eyes until my focus settles on a strange shadowed figure, crouching low beside the sofa.

No. It's just pillows.

But the shadowed figure moves, slowly, crouched and doubled-over in the dark.

I clutch the blanket to me. My heart thumps in my chest and the figure crawls ever-so-slowly toward me.

No, please. No.

I turn to roll away and Alec's face pulls from the shadows. He holds his pointer finger to his lips, giving me the '*shhh*' sign. "Easy, easy. It's just me."

"You scared me," I hiss. "I thought you were... Something else."

He clutches wrapped gifts to his chest and winks. "I'm a Santa Claus."

He sneaks gifts under the Christmas tree boughs and sets down a little box with my name on it. "C'mon then," he whispers over his shoulder, "let's give us some coffee and a fire."

I sit by the pillows in front of the fireplace and hug my knees to my chest.

Alec carries in steaming mugs of coffee and snickerdoodle cookies and places them on the fireplace hearth. He bends over, reaching with long arms into the fireplace and lighting it. "I'll have to chop more logs this afternoon..."

he sits cross-legged by me. He stirs the fire with an iron poker, "You know, I heard you just now."

"Hmm?"

"In your sleep, you were tryin' to speak but you were strangling yourself. You were callin' out for your Pa. Did you know?"

Yes, I know.

"Oh… you heard that, huh?"

He tucks his lip in. "Maybe you need to see Dr. Laszlo about it."

Sure. See the very doctor who knows I'm responsible for Pa's death. "I'll be fine…" I balance my chin on my knee, "did you get gifts for your sister?"

He nods once; a big swoop of his head. "Art pencils n' things. She's studyin' to be Artisan n' all. Her audition isn't for years, but my *goat* she's practically one of 'em already."

I half-smile.

Sapphire light peels over the snowy mountains and icy glaciers, casting the room in a dark blue glow.

"…Alec?"

He turns.

"What happened to her? Your sister."

"You mean the scars on her," he tilts his head and brushes the back of his fingers down the side of his face.

"Yeah."

He rubs his neck. "*Well…* She was small. We were runnin' all along the hills here. But Snuggy – she got a little carried away, tripped and rolled down the slope of the hill. There's a train that runs at the bottom of the ravine. She fell – Ma and Pa could tell she'd hit the train. She couldn't stop herself. I ran as fast I could. My parents were Warbringers. They always taught me – to run toward danger, toward the unknown. Not to be afraid. I leapt for me sis right in time, and I held her to the hill away from the train. But Pa and Ma had run from another side, which had a bit of a cliff – they couldn't get around the cliff in time, and so they got caught in the grill of the train, you see. They got swept under. I saved me sis, but the train skimmed us both. It got her neck and the side o' her face. It got my arm and back a bit. But we're both alive today, you see…" his eyes go distant, staring into the fire. He bends a knee to his chest and slings an arm over it. "That's when I decided to be Warbringer. I don't want to be afraid of nothin' and I used to think – if I'd been faster, better trained, maybe things would've turned out different."

Alec has lost so much, even more than me – but he handles it so much better than me – but…

But he's not responsible for his parent's death. That's why.

He scratches the back of his head. "Me and sissy have to live with the memory of it now." He rolls up his sleeve, showing scars that line his arms. He unbuttons the top of his shirt and shrugs his shoulder out, showing puffy scars down his shoulder and back. "But it's my sis who needs a mama and has jus' me. And so my nan raised us here. But it isn't the same as it was."

I think I'd be too afraid in that type of situation, to do much of anything."

His eyes narrow. "How come?"

"Do you ever think you could've saved them?"

"Sure. But that's my inspiration. I'll be the best Warbringer in the world, and the people I love will always be safe."

The fire spits and crackles. There's a shine on the brass shovel beside the fireplace and my reflection twists in it, I look like something hateful.

His brows crinkle, like he's studying me.

"I'm different than you, Alec. I'll never belong in your world, with a family like yours. No matter, even if I might want it."

"…why's that?"

"We're opposite," I frown at my reflection in the brass shovel. "You saved your sister with what you did. But my father is dead because of me…" I turn to face him directly. "I'm not what you think I am, Alec."

"I'll decide what I think," he says, calm.

I sag over my knee. "When I was young, I disobeyed him. And so he died because of me."

Alec draws back, slowly. "…But that's just a child's mistake. That's not murder…"

"If I'd done the right thing, he'd still be alive."

"That's not the same as *killing* him."

"How did you do it then? How do you stop thinking about the day they died?"

"Aye. I've thought about it. But I let it motivate me to be the best warrior. If the same thing happened today, I'd save 'em all. Your father's life can motivate you to be great in Animalia. Ya gotta be free, not lettin the horrors keep ya all afraid for years."

"But I can't control my ability in Animalia – my instincts come only when I'm at peace and if I'm not – it's like I don't even understand myself. I can't control my mind, it's like I'm torn in two. I don't know what part is me and what part is limiting me. And… I do blame myself for his death." My arms tense around my sides. "I hate myself for it."

Control it, Sunday…

Control it – or it controls you…

Alec squeezes my arm, as though to wake me. "You have to let him go, Sunday. Ya gotta forgive yourself. It's givin' you all these nightmares. You're all closed off from everyone. Not trusting anyone – *hmm?* I can see it. You're strangling yourself in your mind. You're stoppin' your own voice from speakin' out."

I shouldn't have told him.

This was a mistake.

"So what should I do, huh, since you dealt with it so much better."

His brows draw up high, like I surprise him. "You never see clearly lookin' back with your face full o' guilt. You only see clear if ya forgive. Move forward. Get your head out of your own mind and into helpin' others around you."

"That's what Seraphim told me. Like my mind can't problem-solve if I don't forgive."

"Yeah, thas' right."

"But how can I forgive myself when I don't trust myself?"

"O' *course* you can trust yourself."

"No," I snap. "No, I can't. There are things I can do – that I don't even understand – like speak this strange language, or find patterns in people and know their secrets."

"That's why you're at *Svalbard*," Alec pushes back. "You're there to get past who ya are so you can see who ya could be. And use yer abilities in the world. Ya don't find yerself by diggin' a crazy hole in your own mind. You find yerself when you enjoy others and serve 'em with your life – that's what makes ya whole." He turns his palms up to me, like he'd hug me if we were closer – I'd think the gesture a joke coming from anyone else – but his golden-brown eyes are sincere.

Maybe I was wrong about him. Maybe he can discern people well, not because he's condescending, but because he's kind.

Interesting.

Alec's eyes have purple rings under them from lack of sleep – he stayed up all night wrapping gifts for his sister. His fingernails are bitten down to the skin – a nervous habit – he's stressed about something. His fingers are disjointed; broken in multiple places from boxing: He uses boxing to cope with his anxiety.

Fire crawls over my mind.

Don't scrutinize Alec.

"It's like I see details others don't. I make connections between them. I find patterns and I see a network of these associations – and all of them together create something new."

"That's yer ability," Alec presses, "just forgive, and you'll succeed. I can tell."

I frown out the window to the purple night sky. My key is… forgiving.

Grom crawls to my lap. He nibbles on my snickerdoodle cookie. "Animalia is like this miracle to me." My gaze wanders to the Christmas tree – the colorful, humble paper ornaments. I twist Ori's purple friendship bracelet around my wrist. "I shouldn't have left Ori there. All alone."

"We'll be back soon." He warms his hands over the flames. "You sad to be missin' Christmas with your Ma?"

I nod. "Of course, sometimes it's like she forgets each memory days after we make it."

"Forgets her own daughter?"

"…Yeah. She's addicted to this drug, chloral. After Pa died, she started taking it, 'for her grief' but it's like it makes her empty all the time, like instead of feeling pain she feels nothing, remembers nothing. It's kinda like I lost her too, when Pa died."

"This drug, chloral, what is it?"

"Some apothecary concoction," I shrug, "Ma sniffs it and after she drinks she falls asleep or she'll walk right by me, or forget to close shop or blow out the…"

Wait a second.

Alec cocks his head. "… what?"

I rest my fingers on my chin. "Remember how I told you about the man Ori and I saw in the basement, and the strange things he said: *Memory fades, and their trace is gone…*"

"You think he's talking about a drug?"

"Chloral is poisonous to animals if they're exposed… Odd, I think, somehow, the monster is connected to that drug."

Alec chops firewood outside with a heavy axe. Grom leaps from my arms and scampers around the pinecones. "We'll be goin' back to school soon today," he slings the axe and splits a thick trunk. "I know you're worried about Ori."

I nod.

"And I want you to –" he adjusts the axe in his hand, like he's angry with it.

"What?"

"I don't trust everyone at Svalbard. Just keep me in the know all right?"

"… I will."

"Come," he plants his axe in the dirt and ducks into the wood-hedged boxing ring. "I'll show you some things. Self-defense."

"All right…" I carefully duck under the wood hedge and into the ring with him and he positions himself beside me. "Right," he says over my shoulder, "if this monster attacks you, go for the vulnerable parts of the body. The best is the eyes." He air-punches the space beside me. Keep your shoulders up. Good, yeah, like that – and second best is the gut." He steps in front of me and slaps his belly. "Knock the wind out of 'em. You can even kick 'em in the gut. That'll give you time to run away."

I jab the air a few times with flimsy arms. Teaching me this isn't worth much, honestly. "All right, I think I got it."

"And let's try this – maybe the monster binds you again the same way." He grabs me from the side, locking my arms together. I squirm to budge loose but no-use. He's too strong and towers over me. "Easy, easy," he mutters. "Now instead of pushing back, twist your wrists, and all at the same time, push down-and-out."

I inhale sharply, clench my hands into fists, and throw my hands down all at once, breaking loose. Alec stumbles away with a big grin, "That'll get 'em."

On the train ride home Alec stretches his legs onto the seat beside me. He bends his lanky arms behind his head and reclines, closing his eyes. His shoulders slope boyishly and his lips part open, exhausted, and somehow innocent-looking.

How'd someone like him get so obsessed with fighting?

I pet Grom in my lap.

"…Alec?"

"Oi?" his eyelids flutter open.

"…Why do you fight? Boxing, I mean."

He rubs his eyelids and sits forward with his elbows propped on his knees. He puffs his lip at me like it's a strange question. "Why do I fight?"

I nod.

Out the window, snowy hills pass in a blur. He taps his lip with a finger. "When you're fighting, you're not just fighting to win," he says, slowly. "You're fightin' for yourself, because… Because you're alive."

Of course. In the Svalbard ring he took hit after hit, and never backed down.

"Feels like you got somethin' in you. Somethin' that won't die."

Interesting.

"And *also*," he stretches his long arms. "One day I'll be the best boxer in the world."

I chuckle. Not because of the dream, because of how he said it. Like it's already true.

He leans forward to me, like he's letting me on to a secret, "Even if I get beat o'er in the ring now. I learn. I get tougher. You'll see – I'm gonna win me some award money and get mahself a house of my own."

"I don't doubt it."

I twist the friendship bracelet around my wrist and the purple strands shimmer in the light.

Hang on, Ori…

I'm coming.

TWENTY-THREE

SVALBARD'S SECRETS

"I can't go into the Animalia dorms, anyway," Alec leaves me at the iron stairs beneath the dorm rooms, "I'll meet ya and Ori at lunch."

I sprint up the iron stairs to the Animalia lounge.

"Ori?" I search around the lounge.

Dust glitters in the orange lamplight. Wind howls outside.

"Orr-ri," I sing. "I got taffy."

I swing open our bedroom door.

What the —

Everything is chaotic. Ori's clothes drape over the furniture, a bowl of porridge goes stale by her bedside, the curtains are crumpled and pulled down over a window.

… Odd.

Below her bed, Rosie oinks at me wearily. Her snout is dry and pale.

I gather her frail body up in my arms and she folds into my chest, limp. I give her a little biscuit from my bag and she chews it slowly.

Ori would never leave her alone without food.

My gut sinks beneath the red rug. *No, no, no…*

She's here. She has to be.

I run down the stairs with Rosie and Grom. I sprint through the halls and wrench open the double-doors to the Animalia atrium. "Ori! Come out!" I pass the various sections; savannah; oceana; menagerie.

Nothing.

... She's somewhere else. I'll ask a professor.

I sprint down the halls toward the dining room. I turn a corner and bump into someone tall wearing a lab-coat – *wham!*

I stumble back, apologizing, and Dr. Laszlo turns to me, straightening his glasses.

"Oh – Doctor, have you seen Oria? I can't find her."

He frowns at me, like I'm panicked for no reason. "Well she probably changed her plans," he smiles. "She probably felt homesick and decided to take a visit."

I shake my head. Clearly he doesn't know Ori. She'd never go home over break.

"You seem upset," he rests a hand on my shoulder, "step into my office, have a cup of tea, it'll soothe your nerves."

He's so kind.

I bite my lip. Ori is still out there, somewhere. But I can't be so rude and deny a professor. "Oh. Sure, thank you."

He smiles at me; his teeth are white and his eyes clear. "Don't worry, she'll show up." He holds the door open and I step into his expansive office. The place is half library, half lounge. Logs crackle in the fireplace. The air is thick with the scent of a forest: Cigar smoke, mint, pine. Cozy rugs, plants, and sofas sit to one side, and the other is disheveled with work stations, lined with skeletons and surgical tools.

He sets a tea kettle over a burner. "Please, sit."

I sit.

Glass cases surround me, filled with syringes. Smoke fumes from the fireplace and Grom hides in my jacket; his nose is too sensitive for strong smells.

Laszlo pours me a cup of tea and places it on a saucer with a slice of lemon.

"Thank you." I take it from him. Maybe now I can finally thank him for helping Ma and I, years ago. With all the patients he's treated over the years, we're probably just another family to him, some vague memory.

Laszlo sits on the chaise lounge opposite me, cross-legged, and balances a saucer on his knee. He squeezes the lemon into his cup and gives Grom a studious look; "Monstrum Dragonia."

I fiddle with the warm porcelain cup in my lap. "What?"

"The scientific name for dragons," he stirs his tea, "they're classified among monsters."

"Oh…"

"I once had a patient," he peels lemon rind with his fingernails, "called Paracelsus. He had a wife that was obsessive. His wife would control every little thing he did, poor fellow. He went a little mad. He became silent, then aggressive. One day, he killed his wife. He struck her with a rock. Brutal, animalistic man – though he didn't know it, himself. So, Paracelsus had the mind of a monster, as well."

…Why is he telling me this?

"Thankfully I was able to help him," Laszlo cleans his spectacles with the edge of his lab-coat. "There are ways of stimulating the mind. Calming the inner-beast."

Chills prickle my spine.

Is he… hinting at my condition? Like… he can help me?

"I confess, I have a weakness for monsters. Typical drugs aren't as effective on them, so I've researched these people with animalistic minds. But finding a true species of monster is rare." He winks at Grom in my arms, coughs, and clears his throat. "Monstrum Dragonia used to be a plague to these Nordic isles," he leans way back on the sofa. "When they learn to breathe fire, well… they certainly are an apex predator."

Of course. That's why Alec wanted Grom to breathe fire for our project. "Professor," I ask, softly, "would you happen to know how I might go about helping Grom breathe fire?"

Laszlo laughs at the ceiling, a wheezing sound. Tan lines crease around his eyes. He rolls his head and his legs spread wide. "Now why on earth would you want that?"

"It's an experiment."

"A *dangerous* experiment," he warns, with a handsome smile. He sucks a long drag of tea. His voice strains suddenly, serious, "there are dangers to growing with a dragon. Mind you, no one in Animalia will tell you this…" his voice strangles, he curls his hand into a fist and his face crumples, "Remember, Sunday, don't trust just anyone. Your dragon will grow – and so will you…" he coughs and pounds his chest with his fist, like the tea went down the wrong pipe. His breaths strain.

…Odd. He must have a condition. He rakes a hand through his thick, speckled brown hair, but his hands tremble.

If Pa were here, he would've been friends with Laszlo.

I trust Laszlo more than Seraphim.

I dig my fingers into my palm… But Seraphim is my head-of-house, she must know where Ori went.

Laszlo bends over in a coughing fit – he strains so violently he stumbles to the side and hobbles to his desk, slapping around his herbal supplements.

I set my tea down. It's rude I didn't drink it, but he needs privacy. I duck out of the awning, shut the door behind me and sigh.

Ori.

She has to be somewhere normal – like the dining room. A lump twists in my throat.

I shouldn't have left her.

Moisture lines my eyes. My hands tremble. I run to the dining room and search along the circular tables – they're all packed. All except the Animalia table, which is empty. The students eat jams, curry, and pumpkin bread. The Machinists play with their new tools, the Warbringers have made a catapult out of spoons and shoot nuts off the end. Anning wearily gives orders to Agnet, the housekeeper.

I rush to her. "Professor, have you seen Ori?"

Anning frowns at the floor, as though she hasn't thought of Ori for years. "Oh… Oria Moss. No. Haven't seen her."

What? "Not the whole break?"

Anning's gaze is distant, her eyes, which are usually hawk-like, gaze absently into the distance.

Heat flares in me. I see through her: Her eyes are bloodshot, but her skin isn't dry. She's had plenty of sleep. Her pupils are dilated: Drugs.

Ugh! I should've known.

Anning is on drugs.

Her dress is frayed and torn at the bottom, she's stumbled over the edge repeatedly with lazy steps... She's been drugged for days.

Useless.

"By the way," she mumbles, "Seraphim wants to see you. I'll take you to her now."

My gaze drifts to Alec, surrounded by his Warbringer friends. They share souvenirs and Alec passes around leftover cookies.

"Wait," I tell her, "I need to see someone first."

I rush to the Warbringer table and grab Alec's shoulder. "Ori's gone," I splutter. "She disappeared."

Alec whirls around. "Easy, easy," he pats the air. "Are you sure?"

Please.

"I'm positive," I press. "I found Rosie all alone." I push Rosie toward him and she barely opens her eyes. "I have to go—"

Alec grabs my wrist. "Woah. Remember we said we'd figure this out together. Did you tell the dean?"

Anning yells over the chatting students; "Now, Sunday."

"They're taking me to her now," I pass the pig to him. "Take care of Rosie, will you? I don't know what Seraphim will do to me."

Alec tucks his chin under, "Sunday – you're talkin' nonsense. They're not takin' you away."

I leave him with Rosie laying in the crook of his arm.

Anning pulls me out of the room.

It sits in my bones: Everything is about to change.

TWENTY-FOUR

SERAPHIM'S LESSON

I stand outside Seraphim's office.

I shiver in the frosty air, it's like standing in a meat locker. The ornate blue door stares back at me, daring me to enter.

I hate this door. She is behind this door. Chills crawl down my arms.

I knock.

Thud. Thud. Thud.

"Come in," chimes a woman's voice.

I push the heavy door and it creaks open. I step into the circular office. She sits at her desk, opposite me. She brushes a sleek waterfall of white hair over her shoulder and pushes her papers aside. "Come," she waves me forward, "sit."

I obey.

She folds her hands under her chin, studying me – I swear she sees through me. Every move I make, every glance...

Pressure builds in my chest and bursts, "Ori is gone."

"I know," Seraphim says, calm.

"What?"

"She's been gone all break."

"Where is she?"

"…We don't know."

My mouth hangs open.

"What we *do* know," Seraphim re-angles her head, "is she was taken in your dormitory."

Heat rises in me and my throat closes.

Ori asked me not to leave her alone.

Now she's gone because of me. Just like Pa.

It's my fault she's gone.

I squeeze the chair beneath me.

I… killed her.

Seraphim's eyes narrow on me, like she can read my thoughts. She stands, "You won't be staying in the dorm anymore." She walks beside the window and her blue gown sweeps the floor. She sets a hand to the glass, "You'll stay down the hall from me, here, where it's safe."

"Here?"

She waves a hand.

"Please," I grip her desk. "Just tell me. Where do you think she is?"

Her eyes flash down to my hands on her desk and I slowly remove them. "You'll have to *leave* Svalbard, Sunday."

"But I –"

"Svalbard is no longer safe for Animalia students, and you are the last one. Would we keep the program open for one student? You can stay the night in my special room, and then leave."

I stare at her, wide-eyed.

Leave Svalbard?

My heart thumps in my ears.

No…

"But –" my voice is a strangled whisper. "It's been my dream. To be Animalia."

Seraphim leans on the window frame and folds her arms over her chest. "You'll go back to your hometown in the morning. It may not be safe for you there, either. But it'll be better than here. I can't watch out for you constantly." She turns away, brushing through scrolls on the nearby shelf.

My breaths are loud and heavy in my ears.

Do something. *Think.*

I stand. I take one step toward the door and stop.

I can't leave.

I *won't.*

Adrenaline kicks my gut, squeezing my neck and arms. I turn back to her. "If I work for you, can I stay? You said before that I could help you."

The corner of her mouth twitches in a smile, but her lips purse again. She stands tall and presses her hands behind her back. "Why would I take on an apprentice like you, *hmm?* You've spied on me, lied to me, and exercised idiotic judgement against me."

My throat closes. I did judge her wrongly.

How'd she know –

She walks to me, slowly, like a predator. "What's worse, you cannot control your mind."

"I'm sorry."

"You're impulsive and self-seeking."

"But I'm trying. Please. Teach me to be like you."

Please God, let her like me.

Her shoulders melt. "If you want to stay and learn Animalia," she says, carefully, "you must agree to work for me only. Do you agree?"

I stare.

It worked.

"Of course," I splutter.

"I'll entrust you with private errands and in exchange I'll teach you to control your mind. Do you promise to keep what we discuss a secret?"

"Yes, ma'am."

I killed him. I killed Pa.

"Stop that," Seraphim snaps. "Sit up. Listen."

I sit up.

"Stop feeling sorry for yourself," she snaps. "I don't feel sorry for you."

"…You don't?"

"Because there's nothing wrong with you. You are *not* a monster. You *choose* who you become."

I lower my head.

"Your character is judged by your *actions*," she folds her arms and leans back. "Your false shame is an inverted pride. You're still thinking of yourself only. You blame yourself. You hate yourself. All about you." She leans forward, softens. "I've seen my share of *real* monsters, Sunday. Trust me. Monsters feel no shame, no guilt about their brutal actions. Now that isn't you, is it?"

I shake my head.

The way she talks – it's like she's told herself these things before.

"I've been trying," I wilt, "to get rid of the voice that blames me – I can't force it away."

"You can't fight hate with hate. The more you hate that voice, the more you expand its authority in your mind, the more you fear it. The only way your spirit can have greater authority, is by operating in mercy. Forgiveness gives birth to grace, mercy, self-control, peace, wisdom, increased ability… But when you let hate fester inside you, it's like poison in your gut. Your subconscious mind will wither and distort."

Seraphim's tiger sits beneath her, poised with its head tilted, mirroring her.

Seraphim is a master, really. My best hope.

I lower my head. "Thank you. For helping me."

"You're welcome," she stands. "And now you will help me with something."

"… All right."

"Give this message and this tincture to Professor Seacole, the Warbringer." She withdraws a letter from her dress pocket along with a tiny glass and hands them to me. "Tonight at ten o'clock, Seacole will be at the bottom of these stairs here. Give it to her then."

I take the letter and the little bottle and slip them into my dress pocket. Odd… Such a simple task. Why can't she do it herself?

She's testing me.

She strides down the room, opens the doors and waves for me to follow her. We pace down the ornate hall and she turns an interesting way; she sweeps open a glass-and-marble door and I step inside.

It's a queen's quarters, with white rugs and sprawled floral arrangements of ivory and blue – the living room is wide, with a bedroom beyond – the doors to the washroom are open and a porcelain tub sits beside wide glass windows. Candles are everywhere. Paintings of various dragons line the walls in every color; blue, gold, silver.

…Odd.

If Seraphim thought I'd only spend a night here, why decorate it this way?

"Do you like it?" she asks, warm.

I turn over my shoulder. I'd almost forgotten she stood there.

"This will be your new living area. And remember not to venture out more than necessary, especially not at night."

I gaze up and all around; crystal chandeliers sparkle in the dim light. Paintings of white lions roar down at me from the artful curved ceiling.

"You are to keep this door locked, understand?"

"Yes, ma'am."

"Here is your key," she hands me a heavy gold thing. "I'll have your luggage sent here from your old room."

Serphim leaves. The door shuts with a *click*.

I stare at the white door where her face used to be, and stand alone in the wide, circular room. Outside, a snowstorm moans.

It's all a strange dream. I pace around the room, brushing my fingers over the dusty table, the velvet chaise. I walk and walk and walk. I sink to my knees and sit on the floor, empty. The purple bracelet Ori gave me shimmers on my wrist.

Pressure builds in my chest and bubbles in my throat. "I'm sorry, Ori."

It's your fault she's gone.

I twist my neck and rub it. Forgive. Let it go – forgive, *blazes!*

She'll die because of you.

I stand in a flash and push past the furniture. "No, no, no," I stop in front of the full-length dressing mirror, where my reflection glares at me with the heat of the dragon. Her eyes are creased with dark circles, she growls – *"I hate you."*

Tears spill through the creases in my cheeks. My hands wrap around my neck.

Heat lights in her eyes. She steps closer. *"You killed her."*

"I didn't mean to!" My hands tighten on my throat. "– I loved her – I did."

"You *hate* her!" she screams. She is close enough now that she can hurt me. She grips the wood chair beside her and throws it like a bat at the mirror – it cracks the reflective surface into fragments, bounces back and strikes me in the head –

Wham!

I wake on the floor. Wood fragments surround me. My reflection in the mirror is cracked into a thousand pieces; a purple bruise circles one of my eyes.

I stand and press my hands into the sharp fragments, they bleed, and I feel nothing.

Moonlight shines on the hot blood in my hands, making them purple and toxic-looking.

I've been distracted. Distracted by Alec. By Seraphim. Not anymore.

I kick the glass pieces away, into the corner.

I have to find Ori.

I tuck the room key into my pocket and leave down the hall – I am going to the place where she was taken.

TWENTY-FIVE

THE DRAGON-MIND AND THE CRIME

The Animalia lounge is dark. I light lamps one-by-one up the path to our old room.

It's like walking in a nightmare. Deathly quiet and haunted. I turn the knob to Ori's bedside lantern, sparking it to light. Grom squirms and claws at me until I release him and he darts around the floor, sniffing, growling. *Blast – it's freezing!* The air prickles my skin but my forehead is slick with sweat. *Calm yourself. Focus on Ori.* I breathe deep – fire lights in me – the dragon's mind – *focus, focus.*

I crouch to the gap beneath Ori's bed. A rug lays on the wood floor, but it wasn't there before.

What in the –

I pull the rug aside. Scratch marks line the wood. … Odd.

Marks from an animal?

No.

The marks are dull – they were made with… fingernails. *God, no.*

My gut turns. I snatch the lantern and lower it to the floor. The marks are letters. I tilt my head so they turn right-side-up.

R O S E

… Rose?

Ori wrote this. No doubt. The scratch marks are quick, frantic. She must've known someone was coming for her. Scratching the floor was her last message. Rose. Rose. Rose.

Rosie. Her pig. What else could it be?

But why would she –

I shake my head. Someone covered her message and the marks. Who?

There was a scuffle, bits of her curly hair were torn and lay on the floor. The doorknob on the door to the room is new. The same design, but polished, I remember specifically because the old brass knob was worn near the bottom from constant use. It's new. Someone replaced it, to change the key to the lock, in order to get in, but when?

The dragon-door in the lounge is designed to open only for someone in Animalia. But our personal room here should've been secured… unless… unless someone wanted to hide that they broke in, so they changed the knob and the lock entirely.

Who has maintenance access in Svalbard? Agnet, the housekeeper. Eoin, the servant boy.

Why would they change it?

I lower my head close to the floorboards. Dried wax lines the boards in a steady drip toward the washroom. Ori must have run with a candle lit in her hand. I follow the drip-line through a doorway to the washbasin.

The washroom is a mess. Linens and hand towels lay in heaps. Ori was searching for something, frantically… What was it?

The lemon soap bar sits on top of the towels. One end of the bar is mashed down, like she rubbed it down, for some reason.

My foot touches something cold and wet. A puddle. Ori must've taken a bath before she was attacked…

If I were Ori.

I walk through her steps.

What would I have done?

I turn the faucet and hot water fills the bath. Steam clouds the mirror everywhere except the streaks of lettering where Ori used soap to write on the glossy surface.

Chills prickle my legs.

Yes!

Smart, Ori.

Yes, yes, yes...

Steam fogs the mirror and the letters appear clearer–

IT CAME FOR SUNDAY'S KEY

My... key?

Key, what key? Not the key to the room, the person had already broken in.

Unless...

I scramble to the bedroom and slap around my dresser, looking for Pa's old key – I always kept it looped on a necklace, as a memory from him. The chain is there, but –

My jaw drops. Pa's key is gone.

If I were Ori – where would I hide it – what would I do if I knew someone was coming for it? If I didn't have much time. I duck back into the bathroom and flip over Ori's lemon bar soap. The underside is mashed and bumpy. I claw at it and dig into it, pressing the soft yellow folds to the side, until a glint shines through the buttery soap.

I hold my breath.

I wipe away the thick soap, revealing Pa's key.

Yes, Ori. Yes!

I snatch the key and bolt out of the dorm – I run through the dark halls, sprinting through corridors. It's almost ten o'clock. Seacole will be expecting Seraphim's letter delivered from me.

I slow my steps, approaching Seraphim's staircase, and calm my breaths. I turn the corner – Seacole waits at the bottom. Her frown makes her an iron statue, in full-clad military uniform with her dark hair pressed into a bun. She's designed for war. I hand her the letter and the small lavender-filled tincture bottle.

Her iron gaze finds the blood in my hair and the dirt on my arms. She swipes the letter from me, breaking the seal and opening it on the spot. Her brown eyes scan the faded ink, which shows faintly through the backside of the thin paper. I shouldn't look, but – I make out the cursive lettering: *'watching,' 'drug.'*

She swirls the little bottle and chugs the lavender liquid back, like it's whiskey. "Return to your room," she commands, without looking at me.

I turn away.

… Seraphim is using her, too.

I step down the hall, past Seraphim's office, and something bright glints on the walls; old staff lockers – odd I didn't notice them before. Each locker is Machinist design, like bank safety boxes – with firm circular locks around the square capsules.

I shouldn't snoop at them, I really shouldn't.

I hunch over, examining the labels over each safety box; Raj, Seacole, Cortez, Gråe, Suri…

Wait…

I frown at the security box labeled 'Professor Gråe'.

I suck in my breath.

…Pa?

He worked here. But that was years ago.

But maybe…

I slip Pa's key out of my dress pocket and wrestle it into the rusty lock.

— *Click*

What – it *worked?*

I turn the key and the lock flips. I tug the handle and the rusty door swings open. I crouch down and peer into the dark gap… a glass object shines beside a square paper. I swipe the glass piece out and turn it over in my palm. It's some kind of… *whistle.* I crack a smile. I loop the little glass whistle onto my necklace chain and fasten it safe around my neck.

I reach into the back again and slide the piece of paper out – I turn it over, it's a photograph of Ma, pregnant. She sits at the candle-shop table and laughs at something outside the frame. I lean into the wall and slouch over the picture, my eyes mist over. Can't remember the last time Ma looked like that; healthy, bright.

My heart twists. God I wish she were here.

I slide out another dusty photograph, and every nerve in me screams: It's... *her!* A photograph of *Seraphim*, standing by Pa, at some Svalbard ball. She's younger than him, shorter, and smiles annoyingly perfectly. I could *rip* the paper.

Ugh! What the *blazes* is she doing in his locker?

I could *scream!* I crumple the photograph and shove it into my dress pocket. If she ever messed with Pa, I swear I will rip her hair out.

That night I dream I stand in Seraphim's office, surrounded by delicate chimes and telescopes.

The white tail of a snow tiger bumps from under the sofa – outside, the moon rises over the glaciers, making them sapphire-blue. My feet are bare and cold on the marble floor. Someone has dripped wax everywhere – in the shape of a large octagon which touches the corners of the room – the same shape as Svalbard's map.

Drowned voices echo along the tile behind me. I turn; Seacole sinks into the corner away from the tiger, shrouded. The red glint of military awards shine from her breast pocket. Her lips don't move, but I *hear* her – the low hum of her internal voice: *Leave us alone.*

In the opposite corner, Anning walks half-concealed in shadow, agitated. She rakes her fingers through swept-back red hair, as though suffering a headache. She grits her teeth at the tiger, frustrated.

I turn again; Cortez, the Artisan, reclines against the wall, leaning into the shadows by a starchy white curtain. He folds his hands snug over his chest. Silver rings line his fingers. He gives a mischievous, approving wink to the tiger.

Beside him, Professor Suri, the Machinist, checks her wristwatch. Her frail features focus, she welds something at the table in front of her – some contraption – she bites her lip, counting the seconds on her watch. "I won't make it," she panics, "not in time."

The tiger roars at her, furious.

"What are you making?" I step toward her.

Beside her, Dr. Laszlo's lab-coat sweeps the floor. He turns in a whirl, and his gold spectacles flash in the dark. He smiles at me with tan, handsome features. He sits, strangely, at Seraphim's desk, going through her personal things; checkbooks, letters, money…

My heart skips a beat.

He shouldn't do that.

It's intrusive.

I hurry, about to stop him – but he raises his finger to his lips: *'shhh'.* He smiles softly, his voice echoes inside me: *Just wait…*

I bolt upright in bed.

What the –

I sit in a ball and rest my chin on my knees, over my nightdress. It felt so real.

But I *did* read parts of Professor Suri's letter when I visited the Machinist lab. The letter *did* ask her to work on something. Some contraption…

Seraphim must have her building something specific.

I pinch my fingers to the bridge of my nose. No. I'm overthinking it. I frown out the tall French windows. It's morning but still dark out. Dim blue clouds smear the mountains.

Grom prods me with a claw, a sign for me to please feed him. I slip out of bed and pour milk onto a tray for him. He laps his tongue at it like a cat –

THUD – THUD – THUD

I snap my head to the front door. Someone knocking… this early?

Only Seraphim knows I'm here.

I carefully step into the living room and peer through the front door look-hole. The freckled servant boy, Eoin, stands outside. He drops my luggage at the door and leaves down the hall.

Slowly, I open the door and heave the cases in. I yank them around the corner to my bed one-by-one and lock the door behind me.

Chills cover my arms; the dragon-mind. It senses something. I listen with every muscle in my neck, but no – nothing could be in here with me. *Blast* – it's cold as death. I slip into the washroom and turn the tub faucet for hot water. I sit on the side and swing my bare feet in, only, and lean back on the wall. A thin layer of bubbles slide along the surface. If Ori were here, she'd whine that I take too long to wash my feet... what I'd give to hear that now. I rest my head against the white stone wall. If only I could sink into the stone.

-whoosh-

Something moves behind me.

I open my eyes. I snap my head in the direction of the soft noise, outside the open door and into the living room. Shadowed curtains drift slightly from the heating vents in the floor.

...It's nothing.

Normally I wouldn't think of it but... ever since the attack, I can't help it.

I clench my jaw, glaring at the curtains until something subtle moves in the shadows. A slight fold in the curtain, crumpling the white cloth.

My heart pumps. *Please no...*

I grip the porcelain ledge. Adrenaline pumps in my arms.

The room spins. It's here. A weapon... I need –

But I have nothing.

The curtain flails – *whoosh* – and the dark head of the shadowed man raises up from nowhere.

TWENTY-SIX

MYSTERY KNOT

I scream.

He runs toward me.

I grip a candlestick – and fling it through the archway at him.

He ducks and the candlestick crashes to the wall where his face used to be – *wham!*

I grab another candlestick behind me. I bend my arm back, about to throw it and his features snap into place. He reaches out. "Oi! Easy – easy!"

I hold the candlestick in the space between us, wide-eyed: Alejandro. *He broke in!*

I drop the gold candlestick and it clatters on the floor. "How'd you get in?"

He holds his hands open at his sides. "Easy, Sunday. *Easy.*"

"You snuck!"

He pats the air with his hands, "I'm sorry, all righ'. You scared me that's all, with your talk of disappearin'. I went lookin' for you – and I spotted the servant boy carrying your luggage n' all..."

I step into the main room, wrap myself in a blanket, like a shawl, and let my heart slow.

"… I followed the luggage boy a'righ?" He puffs his lip and rocks back on his heels, nervous. "I jus' wanted to make sure you're fine and dandy. So I hid in the corner there. I was all behind the curtains, but I heard you pour water for the tub and – well, I didn't want to say nuthin'. I was startin' to think your feet would turn prune." He chuckles, holding his gut.

I roll my eyes. "Did you take care of Rosie?"

"The pig?"

I nod.

"Gave her to Jael. The Warbringer girls had a thing for the pig… I dunno." Alec reclines on the sofa, shoes-on, and Grom curls in the crook of his elbow. Alec's smile fades, "So how come you're in this place, kept away from everyone else."

Grom's belly gently rises and falls. I sit beside him and pet him.

If only I could tell Alec everything.

His eyes narrow, "She really has a tight grip on you, doesn't she?"

"… You promise you won't tell anyone?"

"O' course." His frown deepens. "I won't look *down* on you, Sunday. Whatever it is."

I slide my toes along the blue rug. He thinks my secrets are something embarrassing. He has no idea. The strange things that have happened to me since I've been here – the off interactions I've had with Seraphim – the pressure.

They won't make sense to someone who hasn't lived them.

For Ori. I'll tell him for Ori.

"I think," I lean in, whispering, "I think Seraphim has been watching me since I got here. She's been making the professors do things, and, she's up to something."

His face is close to mine, his hazel eyes intent, "So Seraphim's plotting somethin'?"

"Yes," I press. "It's like she's always monitoring me. Sometimes, she's testing me."

His brows crinkle. His face is long and slim with stick-out cheekbones.

He chews his thin lip.

"Sometimes I don't recognize she's testing me until after the fact," my gut rolls. "I can't tell, am I the one that's so horrible? Or is it her? At the start of the year she wanted to know if I understood the man underground speaking Amafi. She had me translate what he said. But later that day, when I spoke to Ori, Ori thought the man was crazy – like he was speaking gibberish."

He tucks his chin under, "*Was* it a gibberish?"

"Well, no," I splutter. "I understood the message."

"What message?"

The strange words surface to my mind so easily:

> "The ancient order,
> Is not to be found.
> As memory fades, the trace of them is gone.
> Both man and beast,
> tastes air like death – to an animal's mind."

Alec slumps over his knees, staring sideways at the paintings of dragons all around my room. His expression is firm; he's strategizing. "Question," he blurts, "if Seraphim says she speaks this Animalia language – which is something, let's say, only some Animalia understand – why does she need *you* to translate for her?"

I shrug. "Dunno."

"You think maybe she's using you?"

I press my lips together.

Yes.

"So what about this *Eoin*," he stands. "You said he follows you."

I nod. "Sometimes he's just this empty shell walking around... And when I arrived, Seraphim gave me all these gowns and things."

"Seraphim gave them?"

"I assumed it was her."

"Maybe we assume too much."

"I thought, maybe because she knew Pa, she wanted to help me."

"But you never asked her directly." He sits and leans over his knees to me, talks with his hands, "in these meetings with her. You never ask her directly how she knew your father, or if she's been the one organizing these things for you."

"I can't just ask."

"Really?"

"Also, one night I caught Eoin in the Animalia lounge…"

He stands, paces by the table, and stops. "You saw him *inside?*"

"Yeah. He snuck."

"How?"

I shrug. "The door only opens for Animalia."

"Yeah I know that," Alec says, "I tried it before."

What?

Of course he tried breaking in. I shake my head. "…Maybe Eoin is the monster. I mean, *something* is off about him. And it would answer the question as to how Ori was taken, even inside the Animalia dorm."

Alec runs his fingers along his neck. "It could be Eoin."

"And that night in our dorm, I saw white fur on Eoin's pants – from Seraphim's tiger. Like he'd *just* seen her. And then Eoin told us he didn't know who he was, or where he came from. Apparently Seraphim found him, and invited him to work at Svalbard."

"*Huh.*" Alec's jaw rests open. "You ever think it's Seraphim who's behind all this?"

"It's not her. I'd be able to tell if she had attacked me that night."

"But maybe she's smart, and has other people do it for her," he folds his arms. "Maybe *she* didn't rescue Eoin. Maybe she was messin' with his mind, and then convinced him to be an arm of hers."

"Why would she do that?"

"Maybe she wants to be one of the only Animalia. Ever think o' that? Maybe she likes being Dean of Svalbard. Top o' the food chain."

…The apex predator.

The room shrinks, suddenly. "No. She'd never do that."

"Don't be so sure, Sunday," Alec says, slowly. "Not everyone is as sweet as you. Maybe she's giving you these nice things, butterin' you up so she can use you, too."

Chills roll on my neck. "Anning told me not to tell Seraphim about my test results. She said – *'Some people will see you as a threat'.*"

Alec taps his chin. "When are you seein' the dean next?"

"Today." I stare blankly at his hands folded over his chest. "This afternoon."

"Be careful," he presses. "Don't trust everything you see."

TWENTY-SEVEN

DRAGON INSTINCTS

I press my hair back into a braid, folding it down my back. I wander through the hall and pause at her doorstep. I set my jaw.

I don't have to trust her. I only need information. To find Ori.

I knock.

Tap – tap – tap.

I cradle Grom and he bites my crystal necklace. He makes soft growling sounds, like it has a sweet flavor for him.

"Come in," she sings.

I push the heavy double-doors and they creak open.

Justine sits at her desk. A long, painted portrait is lofted on the wall behind her – an image of herself – with her white hair parted the exact same way and her light blue dress strangely similar to the one she wears now. She glances my way with the same thoughtful, porcelain expression as in her painting – I tense. *Holy heaven.* Her presence is so jarring – like standing in a hall of mirrors – I have to look away.

I approach her desk and curtsey. *Remember, she knows more than she lets on.*

Her smile is stiff. "Sit."

I sit.

A model of animals rotates on her desk. It's a Machinist contraption with metal-wires and brass animals that spin in an orbit, chasing each other. "You must wonder what our lesson will be."

"Yes, ma'am."

Grom eyes her from my shoulder.

"Animalia has always had enemies, as far back as the medieval era –" she spreads a parchment over her desk, showing chaotic charcoal drawings and dark symbols.

I cringe.

A sketch of a large, hanging rose points downward on the parchment with dismembered animals sketched all around.

"This," she swirls her finger along the symbols, "is from the Rose Fraternity, a *scientific gentlemen's* society." Her voice is all toxic. She drags her finger along the scroll, like she'd smear it all away if she could. "You see Animalia protects the natural world, while their businesses would exploit it for profit."

"What kind of profit?"

"Resources, control," Seraphim says, flatly. "Control the secrets of Svalbard and you can control nations. The most hateful men in history knew about Svalbard, some of them went to school here, before they were expelled; Rasputin was Apothecary. Napoleon was Warbringer… but even after they were expelled, they were still hungry for knowledge, so they sold their minds to the fraternity."

I clench my arms in my lap.

The casual way she talks about them – like she knew them personally.

"The Rose Fraternity gives their followers false hope, warped knowledge, false cures through harmful drugs…"

Harmful drugs.

The walls shrink in on me. Seraphim talks louder, aggressive. Pa worked at Svalbard briefly, he knew Seraphim. Maybe he didn't trust her, either.

"…They prescribe drugs like opium, chloral, laudanum."

Chloral.

She slumps forward over the parchment and a waterfall of white hair spills over her shoulder. "Chloral is a sedative, and a hypnotic," there's a smile in her throat, "it slows the nervous system with long-lasting effects."

"...Oh."

Her eyes light – there's something... *obsessive* about her.

The snow tiger purrs loudly, like a house cat. "Years ago, your father thought he saw Rose Fraternity symbols in this area, they're spiritualists, remember, so they brand everything with their symbol – the rose."

I risk another glance at the sketched parchment between us. A charcoal man with a dagger in his eye glares back at me.

"I'm telling you this," she pets the tiger, "because there have been signs of the Rose Fraternity in your hometown, Sjosburg, for years."

My throat closes. "You mean –"

She nods.

"Did Pa know?"

"Maybe." She props her elbow on the desk and rests her chin on her fist, frowning at the wall behind me. "In Animalia, our empathy and our subconscious mind allow us to sense and understand animals, and in the same way, we can understand one-another, as well."

I don't admire her like I used to.

Something is off.

"The Rose Fraternity has been following me for some time now..."

"But – what happened in Sjosburg?"

She frowns at me, intense, like she's choosing her next words. "Perhaps you've heard, of men or women who died, mysteriously, carrying roses."

Carrying roses...

Ma's face returns to me, her weeping: '*We found him holding roses... To think he'd gone to get me roses.*'

No, no... I was there that night.

I got lost in the woods. It was my fault.

Heat rises in me. Seraphim could be lying.

Don't listen to her.

I twist my neck – a quick, thrashing movement.

"You all right, Sunday?"

My face is hot and my hand bounces on my knee. "No... It was my fault."

Focus. Let the fear pass through you.

Seraphim's hands spread flat over the chestnut desk. "Someone in the Rose Fraternity killed him, Sunday. My job is to hunt down people like that."

My face burns. Outside, a wolf howls in the wind.

"I'm not here to comfort you," she says with some bite, "I'm here to stop this monster, understand?"

I nod.

"And since you're my apprentice now you must know the truth. We have a real enemy out there."

... You could be the real enemy.

"Will you help me?" she asks.

Ori is still out there. I have to find her.

"I'll help."

"Good," she softens.

I slap tears from my eyelids. I'm hollow inside. I stand on thin legs and on my way out I turn back to her, "Thank you, Ms. Seraphim."

She has a soft, twisted smile. "You're welcome."

TWENTY-EIGHT

MAGNESIUM FOR MR. GROM

Sleep. Just sleep, *blazes!*

I roll in bed, my blasted imagination screams with the screeches of animals in pain, and Ori crying out to me: *"Sunday!"*

Ori.

I bolt upright and clutch my head.

Ori.

Ori.

I'll find you, Ori.

I slip out of bed and stumble into the dark living room.

Something taps my window.

tap... tap... tap...

"Grom?" I whisper, groggy. "That you?"

I turn over my shoulder – Grom sleeps on a blue blanket on the sofa. Odd... I step into my slippers and feel around; dresser, mirror, clock... The clock shows 5:30 a.m. *Ugh.* Misery.

tap... tap... tap...

I turn. That sound again.

Silver moonlight streams in; the furniture is frozen, frosted in cold light. A snowstorm moans outside and one of my windows shakes, ajar – the starchy white curtain beside it flutters. I slide the window shut and watch the icy mountains outside; clouds glide along the base, they're rocky floating islands, like a dream – a land of glaciers, mammoths… who knows what.

The shadowed space behind the balcony curtain, for some reason, absorbs all my attention. The white cloth bulges, suddenly – someone darts out with a lunge –

I scream.

He covers my mouth. *"Shh!"*

I squirm and bolt across the room. I grip the wall behind me: It's Alejandro. He shivers in a thick button-down coat with snow speckled over his shoulders. I grip my nightdress over my heart and let my pulse slow.

What the blazes…

He climbed through the window?

"You can't just do that." I snap.

"Easy, easy," he peels off his jacket and snow dusts the floor. "We can't be too loud shoutin' or someone'll hear." He kicks off his shoes and sinks onto the plush couch. His chestnut hair is disheveled from what I assume was a fight earlier tonight – he flashes me a toothy smile. "I won me boxing match tonight. Got a fist-full of prize money, too."

"So that's why you're here?" I fold my arms.

Grom leaps to the couch, snuggling by Alec's knee. "Nah," Alec sits and pets Grom with two fingers, "we're running out of time and we still got to finish our project – and since you came up with *naught* – I won the bet, remember? We teach little Grommie here to breathe fire like a grown-up dragon. Put a little hair on his grown-dragon-chest."

I suppress my laugh into a snicker. "Dragons need to eat the right *minerals* to breathe fire."

"I see…" Alec scratches under Grom's chin with a finger.

"And Laszlo won't help. I already asked… But, there's a boy who can."

"Oh ya?" Alec says awkwardly. "Do I need to beat him up?"

"*No*," I roll my eyes. "His name is Hikaru, he's Apothecary."

I pour a cup of Irish Breakfast Tea and spoon a dab of honey in.

Alec fiddles with the music box Viktor made, he cranks the little silver handle and the melancholy tune trills behind me. It's odd; Alec playing it. That sad, strange song – it's home.

"Bit o' a creepy song, idn't it?" Alec slides the music box across the table, like it's trash.

I grimace. He'd never understand.

He can be rude sometimes.

I sit by the window in the breakfast nook. The sun rises, glinting off the mountains. Hidden animals are everywhere; an arctic fox leaves tiny heart-shaped footprints in the meadow below. A dove settles on the window rim. They blend in perfectly – most people wouldn't notice them. The dove flaps away and I glance to the meadow again: Someone is down there.

It's *her*.

Seraphim.

I hold my breath.

She glides in a gown of white silk, a floating angel, and pauses...

Strange.

Seraphim turns over her shoulder ever-so-slowly, and her pale gaze finds mine.

My chest tightens.

I start to turn away, but – she hasn't turned away, either.

The moment is frozen. We stare at each other – it's a challenge. Like two wolves staring across a clearing in the woods. My arms tense. It isn't aggressive, but a searching.

She softens, oddly, and waves to me with a wide smile.

I crack a smile, and softly wave at her from behind the frosty window.

She turns away and walks on. Chills prickle my back.

...Odd. Seraphim never smiles like that. She acted that way – artificial – on purpose. It stings – it's an insult, somehow – a smear at my intelligence.

She's sharp. *Too sharp.*

Below, a wolf pack leaps out from behind the rocks and pine branches:

the wolves that pulled our sleighs earlier this year. They surround Seraphim, she runs her hands over their thick gray manes.

… Impossible.

They're huge. If they wanted, they could tear her apart. The pack leader, with a speckled gray mane, walks side-by-side with Seraphim, like equals.

I turn away from the window. I shouldn't watch their interaction. It's… intimate.

If Ori were here, she'd understand these things.

Alec stands with a sleepy smile and shrugs on his overcoat, "Well c'mon with your up-tight self, we'll find Hikaru, a'ight. Can we bring the dragon?"

Alec waves me forward through the complicated Svalbard halls and I jog to keep up. Warbringers have the best sense of direction. I follow him into a tall, circular library just outside the apothecary compound. It's like standing inside a museum garden; mosaic windows, antiques and books litter the walls in a patchwork of green plants and anatomy charts. I crane my head at the towering bookshelves and ladders that roll around the shelves. Tables glow orange from study lamps and Apothecary students slump over textbooks, sipping herbal tea with dark circles under their eyes.

Alec crouches, walking silently among the rows of students. And by some Warbringer instinct he strides precisely to the back corner where a boy with a black bun and glasses sits, surrounded by books: Hikaru.

Alec stands to the side and I pass him, carefully entering the shadowed corner where Hikaru studies. "Excuse me," I interrupt, softly, "we spoke the other day."

Hikaru tenses. He lifts his head from his book.

"I was wondering," I try, "if you might help us with something."

Hikaru's neck turns pink. "Sure," he splutters, "I'll help."

Perfect.

I step closer. "You see, you know a bit about dragon anatomy, and I was wondering if you might help me with Grom."

Hikaru nods and his bun bounces atop his head. He bends over and pulls out a book from a stack beside him. He holds it out to me; *Reptiles and Dragons – Myth and Physiology.*

I pull the heavy green book from him.

Odd… He already had it on hand. I open it and the pages fall flat at a bookmarked section for the Green Tree Dragon.

He'd already tried to figure out Grom on his own.

… *Interesting*.

I skim the inscription, showing various minerals. "I'm wondering, if you might help us find some of these minerals?"

Hikaru frowns with thin lips. "Which mineral?"

"We need Grom…" I hesitate, "to breathe fire."

Hikaru taps his fingers on the wheel of his chair. "You'd need minerals which aren't exactly at our front door," he shakes his head. "Why don't you just ask Dr. Laszlo?"

"I already did. He thinks we *shouldn't* do it."

"Maybe you shouldn't," Hikaru leans back with his arms behind his head, like he's sizing us up. His arms are strong and his features handsome. "You'd need salt for one, crystal for another – which is easy enough to come by. I'm sure he's eaten that. But you need magnesium – that's the key agent. *Magnesium*."

"Where do we get it?" I ask.

"It isn't exactly *around* here," Hikaru says, like it's obvious. "Only Dr. Laszlo has some in the storage lab."

Alec and I exchange a look.

"We can go there," Alec says. "Show us where it is."

Hikaru recoils from Alec like he's a criminal. "You can't just *take* things from the lab."

Alec shrugs. "Why not?"

Hikaru curls his lip, disgusted, and sort of laughs at Alec like he's ridiculous. Right. Apothecaries don't exactly mesh with Warbringers.

Alec rests his elbow on my shoulder in a casually way. "So how much you want. I'll pay ya, a'right?"

I roll my eyes. Alec is having too much fun.

Hikaru sets his jaw. He won't be bribed. I admire that, actually.

"Listen, Hikaru," I rest a hand on his desk. "We only need to borrow a *little* magnesium. It's for *school*. We only need you to tell us where the storage room is. That's all."

Hikaru softens and leans back in his worn wooden chair. "Fine," he sighs. "The door to Laszlo's pantry is the third room on the right down the Apothecary hall. The door is unlocked sometimes at night. I don't know why…" Hikaru's gaze drifts sideways, "… that's all I know."

"Great, thanks." I turn to leave and –

"Wait," Hikaru grips his desk.

"What?"

"That whistle, let me see it," he holds his palms out to me.

I slide my fingers around Pa's glass whistle which I'd fastened to a bit of twine around my neck. I'd barely noticed I wore it. I lift it from my neck and place it, slowly, in his palm.

"No kidding," Hikaru mutters.

I frown.

"It's an animal whistle. Håkon Gråe's fabled invention. Watch," he holds the little whistle to his lips, and blows lightly, once.

Ugh! I clasp my hands over my ears – the sound is sweet, but piercing. Grom leaps from my arms to the table and stands in front of Hikaru, entranced.

"Only Animalia can hear the whistle, isn't that fascinating?" Hikaru says to Alec, thrilled at my reaction. "It's like there's something fundamentally different about their minds. I'd die to figure out why. Any apothecary would."

Hikaru blows carefully again, moving from the right to left.

Grom follows the movement, it's almost… like a dance, like some secret, intimate thing.

"Håkon Gråe made it to call animals," Hikaru says. "Any animal within a few miles would run to that call."

My gut dips. Hikaru knows more about Pa than I do… I swipe the whistle and pull Grom from him. "Thanks. See you 'round."

I dress in dark clothes.

I tie my hair back and wear my shoes with soft soles, so they're quiet as I walk. I pour Grom some cherry snacks and lock the door behind me, moving silently in the nighttime halls. I reach the bottom of the stairs and Alec waits for me, leaning on the wall. He's at ease.

I'm not.

"You can relax now," he nudges me. "No one comes out at night, it's dark as doom down here. Besides, you're with a Warbringer."

We sneak back into the apothecary compound. Around each corner Alec checks to see if it's clear, like some military tactic. I count the doors to my right as we pass – one, two, three, four, "Five – this one."

Just like Hikaru promised – the pantry door stands ajar.

Yes.

Alec and I exchange smiles in the dark. He opens the door with a flat hand, and slips through.

I duck in behind him.

My jaw drops: It's like standing in the bottom of a deep water well; with everything up high, oversized and out of reach. I cup my hand over my nose. The air is stale and awful here, like burnt sulfur. Bucket-sized drawers are labeled alphabetically with all kinds of minerals and herbs. I point to the letters, searching 'M', for magnesium.

"Found it," Alec pulls a wobbly stepping stool over to the drawer, and balances on it to reach the cupboard. He dunks an empty glass into the powder, filling it.

The drawers are dusty and old – barely touched. But the floor, strangely, is dust-free. And on the far end, a trail of boot prints stops over a square door on the ground.

Odd...

I crouch low over the square trapdoor. It's flat and wide, like a cellar door, and has a small rope to open it. Noises echo, muffled beneath it.

No... It's nothing.

Fear stirs the mind, that's all.

Alec fumbles with the drawers behind me, but something pulls me toward the trapdoor.

Focus. Focus.

Heat lights in me; my mind magnifies its details: The rope to open it is worn – the door is opened frequently, from this room. I slip my fingers over the gaps in the sides of the door – cold air gently rises from beneath. It's a cellar. I lower my nose to it and smell the rusty, moist air beneath.

Chills prickle my neck.

Something's living down there.

TWENTY-NINE

CONCERNING ANIMALS

What the blazes – something is just beneath.

My heart pumps in my neck.

I have to find what.

Quick… Do it quick.

I wrench the rope and the trapdoor opens in a narrow square. I lower myself through the hatch – falling through musty, damp air – and land with a soft *thud*.

I turn, but cages lay stacked against the walls.

No, no, no. Blood drains from my face.

Limbs drape around the cage bars.

Not human limbs – animal. The arm of a monkey and the tail of a dog. The feathers of a parrot and the leg of a lion. They hang limp, lifeless.

I slap my hands over my mouth and stumble in the dark, splashing into a puddle. I can't see – *blameit!* A lightbulb flickers down the way. Cages are stacked down the whole cellar.

No…

Adrenaline squeezes my chest. *Focus.* I squint down the dark hall; doors, passageways. Faint footsteps echo around the corner:

Step, step. Step, step.

I listen with every nerve in my back.

Someone is turning the corner.

I turn to the square-shaped light above; the trap door. I jump for the ledge – but my hand slips – *no – blazes!*

My hands shake. *God don't let me be trapped here.*

I leap again, and Alec – like a miracle – appears in the square opening above. He reaches down, grips my arm, and hauls me up like a soldier.

I scramble out and Alec yanks the trap door – and between the closing gap – a shadow darts sideways – and the quick silhouette of a masculine arm swipes the space where my legs were.

We run. Alec grabs my hand and pulls me through the complicated passageways. My heart hammers in my chest; ballroom, library, hallway, stairs. We reach the hall outside my room and I have to stop. I gasp for air and bend over. Alec grabs my shoulder. "Are you hurt? What's wrong?"

"It's doing –" I splutter, "something horrible."

"What did you see?"

"The animals," I press, "it's torturing them."

Alec turns the vial of magnesium with his long fingers... "We got what we need and –"

"We have to go back," I press. "We have to free them."

"Hold up, hold up," Alec pats the air. "There's something down there. And it saw you. It saw… *you.* So we can plan to help the animals, but not tonight."

The way he says it. So casual. Like it's some Warbringer exercise.

"You don't understand," I snap, "they might as well have *me* in that cage. Or *Grom.* They could die. I have to help them *now.*"

Alec's chest raises, firm, but he takes me in with compassionate, hazel eyes. "I get it. I do. But it's dangerous down there, a'right? It's not good strategy. You could tell the dean and–"

"But you said we can't trust her."

"Yeah, but she's in charge of Animalia."

… But if I tell her, she'll know what I've done. She'll know I broke her rule to not go out at night. I'll be expelled.

My chest trembles. I double-over and hug myself. I should tell her.

But I'm a selfish girl. I am.

That night I dream I stand in the dark basement, filled with rusty cages;
I turn in my nightgown, but instead of animals – Animalia students hang,
limp between bars.

Fire flares in me.

No!

The students beg me to free them – they open their mouths, but they
bark like animals; the groan of an ox, the bleat of a lamb.

I clasp my hands over my ears and stumble away. My shoulders hit the
wall and I shiver in the dark – but a slight figure darts in the shadows – a
swift, calculated movement, as though to avoid being seen: The demented
man. The monster.

He holds his position, stiff. He thinks I can't see him. Insane.

Run!

I sprint in a frenzy, slapping around in the dark; wall, cage, hook.

No way out.

It's a trap.

Out of nowhere – the Animalia objects appear around me. The same
ones from my test:

> Blue ribbon.
> Small knife.
> Crystal bell.
> Bowl of meat.

The bell would distract the monster. The meat would appease him…

No. Too late to make peace.

I grab the knife.

The monster slithers and leaps for me – I plant the knife deep into
their chest and they writhe in pain. The monster grips me by the wrists

and I dig the knife deeper into their chest. Hot blood oozes over my hands onto my nightgown. The weight of their body pushes me deeper and lower.

I scream.

I prop my knee beneath me and push the monster off. I stab him in the chest over and over until he is dead-still. A lump of cold flesh. Scarlet blood drips onto the floor and over my knees. My hands are plum-red and tremble. Slowly, I slide the cloth from his face, but instead of a beast's face – it's my own.

The monster is me.

Me...

Sunday.

She stares at me with empty, ghost eyes.

I didn't mean to!

"Help!" I squeal. I clutch her to me – I sob into her hair – and push her away – I hate her.

I hate her!

Her eyes are dark shadows – she isn't human.

She's a monster.

I scream.

My hands squeeze my throat, choking me.

"Wake up!" Alec pries my fingers away from my neck. "Stop that."

I force my fingers to release and push him away. I stand and stumble away from the couch.

What the blazes –

I pace the living room. I must've fallen asleep on the couch. *No, no...*

Ori.

Ori. Ori. Ori.

I dig my fingers into my hair. My knees hit the floor – if only I could push the blasted images from my mind: Students in cages. *No, no, no...*

Alec approaches me, slowly, "Sunday, are you all–"

"NO!" I scream at him. "Don't touch me!"

He recoils. "I didn't!"

"Why didn't you let me go to them?" I sob into my hair. "What if Ori is down there? What if –" my hands tremble, I choke – "what if they'll die without me?" My hand finds my throat again and squeezes.

Fire lights in me: The dragon-mind.

Ori is down there, with the animals, in cages.

I'll save her.

In the mirror, I grit my teeth at my own reflection. I let others influence me. Make me doubt myself.

That was a mistake.

"Something's wrong," Alec backs away. "You need help."

I need help? He needs to get out of my blasted room.

Control it, Sunday. It's the dragon-mind. Forgive – blazes!

Every nerve in me tenses – frozen. I glare at his leather shoes. He has no idea how hard I've fought to keep the dragon-mind down. Not anymore. They'll die without me.

I clench my jaw. *Let the fear pass through you.*

His voice is gentle, but there's warning in him. "You are *not* yourself."

He doesn't know the first thing about me.

Only Viktor really knows.

Forgive – blazes!

I soften. Release the dragon-mind – I let the touch of a thousand needles wash down my skin and dissolve.

Yes. I did it. It's gone. "I'm going to save them. Whether you help me or not."

It's like skating over thin ice, the dragon-mind lives just below the surface but I'm above it.

All my work is paying off.

I glance at the clock above Alec's head. My meeting with Seraphim starts just minutes from now. I'll have to take care of that first. Then I'll save them. I pull a brush through my hair, I twist the ends into a curl, and Alec looks at me with fear, like he's watching some wild animal.

I slap my brush down. "Then don't help me, Alec. Just don't stop me from doing what –"

"But Sunday," he rolls his eyes, as though I were stupid, "you don't *really* know if anyone is down there or –"

"*I know,*" I snap, and fire lights in me again.

"*No,* ya don't," he claps back.

"They're *down* there," I press. Heat builds in me. "I know it."

He looks down at me from his long nose, with condescension, "You're acting delusional."

Something snaps in me and I can't look at him. Fire prickles my mind and screams into every corner. "Get out." I glare, dark. "You don't know me. You never will."

I sit in Seraphim's office. Paintings of tigers surround me.

I wear my face as a mask, like Anning. I won't let my thoughts show. Flashes from my dreams haunt me; animals behind metal bars. *Don't think of it.*

I can never tell Seraphim about the caged animals. She'd kick me out of Svalbard for breaking her rules.

I'll save them myself.

Seraphim sits across from me, reviewing my report on how to access the mind sanctuary. She marks the sides of the paper and slides it back to me.

I squeeze the velvet chair. Her gaze pierces my every flaw.

She softens. "Is there something you want to tell me?"

Yes.

So many things.

I shake my head. "No, ma'am."

She turns away to the windows and white mountains beyond. She pours herself a drink; lavender liquid in a short glass. Honeysuckle fumes in the air. She sucks the rim; like Ma would with her morning chloral.

"Masters of Animalia, like your father, were gifted with Amafi, he could speak with authority over almost any living creature…" She delicately swirls her lavender drink with her wrist. "Machinists can pull genius inventions from scraps. Master Artisans, like Cortez, are visionaries and understand future events. Master Apothecaries create life-saving medicines, as Dr. Laszlo has."

"Is that what you're drinking? Something from Laszlo?"

Seraphim sits across from me again. She slides a marble coaster under her drink and rests a flat hand over a folded note on her desk with words scribbled; *Dear Bjørn –*

"I need to ask a favor of you, Sunday."

My toes curl in my shoes. I nod.

"Tell me anything suspicious you see. Can you do that?"

"Sure."

"…And *have* you seen anything suspicious?"

Yes.

My neck stiffens. I've seen animals in cages.

"I've noticed that…" I bite my lip.

Heat flares in me: *Don't tell her.*

"I've noticed some people… have forgotten important things, like Anning – she forgot about Ori. And Eoin. It's like he can't think for himself. Like their minds aren't working right."

Seraphim folds her arms on the table, "You're right about that."

"So what's wrong with them?"

She leans in. "*That* is what I'm trying to find out."

THIRTY

PRESENTING GROM

I've worn my best dress for the project presentations – an icy blue gown with long bell-sleeves. Grom rests on my shoulder. At least he *looks* ready; he hasn't actually breathed fire yet. This will be his first time. On stage.

My gut sinks beneath the wood floor. *Heaven help me.*

Alejandro ducks into the foyer. His clean white uniform and trimmed hair makes him a tall, formidable soldier. Our eyes meet but he doesn't smile.

He must hate me after how I acted.

I deflate.

He stops in front of me, sticks his hands deep him his pockets and chews his lip. "I forgive ya, you know," he says, softly. "With you bein' all awful to me. I'm not saying you're right, but I'm saying – I'm not lettin' it bother me nah more."

I hold my breath.

He... *doesn't* hate me?

"And," he tilts his head. "I didn't mean to doubt you or talk down at you. And also, I'm not afraid of you..."

My cheeks go hot and I can't look at him. I smear a tear from my nose.

"But," he steps closer. "I still think ya need people who'll listen to ya."

I nod.

He gives Grom a little scratch on the head. "Wha'd you say we get this project done?"

I nod. "All right."

The dining room bustles with energy – a special stage is set at one end.

The happy chattering of students at the dining tables is jarring next to the stillness inside me. We'll have to show Grom in front of all of them.

If only I didn't have to do this now.

Inventions line the Machinist table; the Apothecary students hold potions; sculptures sit beside the Artisans… And I brought Grom.

I slide the little pouch of magnesium from my wrist. It's filled with powder, enough to fill Grom's belly with the minerals at least four times.

"He'll be all right," Alec mutters, "and if we fail and get an 'F,' I don't care anyway."

He's trying to make me feel better. It helps, a little.

The students eye me, whispering; "… Dragon-girl."

"… She's so strange…"

I tune them out. I'm different. It's obvious. Let them think whatever they want.

Alec and I sit at the Warbringer table, by Jael. She was partnered with Ori, so she was forced to find a new team. The Warbringers chat with animated gestures, and I cut through their conversation, "Jael?"

She perks her head up.

"You remember Ori, don't you? My friend."

Jael's dark eyebrows pull together. "Of course," her hazel eyes flick from Alec to me. "Why wouldn't I? … Anning told me she went home."

I lower my head. Anning is lying about her. Some people remember her, others don't.

Why?

The students cheer and Anning calls the teams one-by-one; they stand on the platform: A machinist-made harpsicord is played by an artisan student; a warbringer shoots a crossbow made with apothecary-infused poisons…

Hikaru made a white cream that heals burns instantly. He coats his arm with the cream and holds it over a gas fire burner – to everyone's horror – but he pulls away, unharmed.

Anning calls; "Sunday Gråe and Alejandro OlShield!"

My legs go numb. Alec helps me up the platform. I clutch Grom to my chest and he squirms.

I stand above the crowd. The students stare blandly at me, slumped over the circular dining tables. My fingers tremble as I open the pouch of magnesium and hold it to Grom's mouth, feeding him like a baby.

Grom opens his small mouth and swallows.

Yes.

But he gags and makes a sour face. He looks at me with horror, like I tricked him.

No Grom. I'm sorry.

Adrenaline pumps in my chest.

…No. It's too soon. He's not ready.

Grom thrashes his head.

I pet him, soothing him.

No, no…

Sweat drips down my back.

The room is painfully silent. All eyes stare at Grom, squirming in my hands. He drapes himself over my arms, wheezing.

Please Grom… don't be hurt.

Alec squeezes my arm, to reassure me.

Seated beside us, Dr. Laszlo frowns at the pouch around my wrist and turns away in one sweep of his lab coat.

He knows we took the magnesium.

"Our project was something of an experiment," Alec shouts over the room with big hand gestures, improvising. "We thought to help this little dragon here – *er* – do what he could–"

"*Grnaaa,*" Grom growls.

The artisans in the front row lean away.

... This was a mistake.

Alec cracks a smile at me, like Grom is funny, but I don't smile back. It's all I can do to pin Grom down in my arms. He claws along my dress sleeves, tearing the fabric.

"It's *er* – still a work in progress," Alec announces. "But eventually–"

Grom arches his back like a cat, he groans – and red-hot sparks spew from his mouth, scorching the space between Alec and I – the table edges in the front row fleck with fire. I pull Grom back and he flails his head up and all around, throwing fire in an upward spiral.

I scream and turn him away from the students.

Grom reels like a maniac. He flails his head toward the professors.

No!

The professors stumble back. All but Seraphim, who in the brief, frenzied moment, folds her hands under her chin and smiles softly.

Alec leaps through the fire to me, holding an arm over my face, protecting me.

Grom roars louder and uglier – throwing fire all around, until his flame turns thin and blue, then yellow, and runs out.

My legs shake. Alec grips my shoulders, wide-eyed. Grom hangs limp in my arms.

The entire room stares, silent.

This was a mistake.

Stupid. So stupid.

In the front row, white ash – like snowflakes – flutters in the air. Jael stands, slowly, and claps. The Warbringers join her, one-by-one, standing until the entire hall cheers:

"Bravo!" Jael yells.

"Good on ya dragon!"

"Little dragon!"

"Scorch em' again!"

Alec grabs my hand and raises it in the air with his, like we've won a boxing match.

Seated by me, Seraphim raises a slender champagne glass to me and drinks.

Grom crawls up my shoulder spritely and licks his lips.

I can't help it – maybe it's nerves – I giggle on the stage and can't stop. Holding my hand up, Alec watches me from the side.

I face the crowd with my head high.

I belong at Svalbard.

THIRTY-ONE

ROSE FRATERNITY

I finish dessert – chocolate rhubarb cake with lemon cream – and leave the banquet. I cradle Grom to my chest and Alec slings an arm over my shoulder, still relishing our victory. Warbringers slap Alec on the back:

"Way to scorch them professors."

"Hey-o team dragon!"

Alec walks me back to my room for the night. My heels *click* on the marble floor but – out of nowhere – moisture drips onto my cheek.

…Rain?

I stop.

Students pass briskly and Alec turns back, confused.

My hands go cold. *Something's wrong.*

Grom stands on-edge, his claws grip the fabric on my shoulder.

Slowly, I wipe the cold moisture from my cheek. But as I pull my hand away, my fingers are red and glossy. Crimson. Like… Blood.

I crane my head up.

What the blazes –

A woman's body drapes over a chandelier and dangles upside-down above me.

I clasp my hand over my nose and scream.

She hangs from the crystal spires – the chandelier rotates and her face swings toward me: Agnet, the housekeeper. Her gray hair is a tangled spider-web on her face.

The monster got her.

Alec grabs my arm and pulls me back. Panic flutters the student groups, their shrieks echo up the halls.

The walls spin. I clutch my head.

Breathe, breathe.

The Warbringers organize; one runs for Professor Seacole and another clears the space under the chandelier.

Down the hall, Seacole bellows orders while they form ranks. She charges past us, just as Agnet swings under and slips from the chandelier and – midair – Seacole runs and catches Agnet like she would a child.

Gently, Seacole lays her down, like a ragdoll.

Dr. Laszlo pushes past students. He kneels by Agnet, touches her cheeks and neck, then grips her right arm and turns it over – revealing burn marks – no, *branding* marks. Her forearm has been branded with symbols in the shape of an upside-down rose, with the stem touching her elbow.

The Rose Fraternity.

"What is *that*?" Alec whispers beside me.

"The Rose Fraternity. Seraphim said they hate Svalbard, and especially Animalia. They've been trying to shut down Svalbard for years."

Seacole lifts Agnet and carries her in the direction of Laszlo's laboratory. She turns; "Soldiers!"

The Warbringers stand at attention, including Alec, who faces her with a straight back and firm jaw. She yells; "We're locking down. Escort all students to their houses." The Warbringers run, herding students like sheepdogs into separate hallways.

"I'm taking *you*," Alec turns me by the shoulders in the direction of my room. "We're sticking together."

My mind lights – alert. We walk and I imagine Ori's last message to me, scratched into the wood ceiling beams: ROSE.

What were you trying to say, Ori?

It's nearly audible, Ma's voice whispers; "*To think he'd gone to get me roses...*"

My gut sinks.

I stop walking and stand with Alec in the dark, narrow hall. The furniture spins around me; clock, lantern, chandelier... I clutch my head, dizzy. "I think the person behind these attacks is the same exact monster who killed my father."

"Just breathe, Sunday. You're red as a rose and all flustered."

"*Red* as a what?"

"Bright red."

"It's like I see all these moving pieces. Memories. Details. And if I focus, they connect. They make sense. It's like an instinct."

"Instinct?"

"I almost have the full picture, I'm just missing one last piece."

His eyes narrow. "You think you know who's behind all this."

"Remember how I told you about the monster working in an octagon around Svalbard's houses?"

He frowns.

"Machinist is the next house in the pattern. It's the last missing piece."

Alec stops me with an arm. "You aren't going there alone. I'm coming with you."

I won't fight him anymore. Not after how I treated him last night, "Thank you."

"For what?"

"For believing me."

Alec and I link arms in the dark. We walk a narrow, grease-stained passage into the Machinist lab.

The air is dusty – sharp, like aluminum.

With each step my gut sinks. *Please let this be the right decision.* I squeeze his arm where it links with mine.

Focus...

I only need information. For Ori.

The Machinists would've gathered in their dorms for lockdown, professor Suri would be in her office, or in the lab.

Slowly, we turn the corner. I hold my breath. Dull firelight from a lab burner speckles the awning. The lab is like standing in a clock; the walls are covered in pulley systems with gears and scaffolding. Grom's slit-eyes dart around in the dark.

Strangely, professor Suri sits collapsed over her desk, as if asleep.

The blazes –

Alec sniffs in the dusty air and sneezes, loudly.

But Suri doesn't move.

Alec and I exchange a look. My instincts stand sharp on my spine, rooting me to the spot – something dewy and bitter hangs in the air.

"Don't," I clasp my hand over Alec's mouth, "the air has drugs. Don't breathe too deep."

The monster was just here – they released a gas in the air, with a faint aroma. The monster sedated her, and he'll return. My heart pumps.

Quick.

Alec leaves my side and checks Suri's pulse. "She's alive. Asleep."

The dragon-mind searches for things the eye would usually glaze over. Scuff marks line the arms of Suri's chair – she's been furious about something, but hiding it. A metal contraption sits on her desk; an envelope rests beneath her palm; with ink lettering:

JUSTINE

The heavens –

She was working on this machine for Seraphim.

I pluck the handwritten note, unfold it, but it's blank inside. Odd. *Justine –* so casual, to call Seraphim by her first name.

Alec coughs, dizzy, and waves me toward the door. I stuff the note in my pocket, slide the contraption into my side bag, and join him by the door.

"What's that little machine you got in your satchel?"

"I think… we need it."

"How d'you know?"

It sits in my bones. *I know.*

I jog through the hall behind Alec, coughing, clearing my lungs. "We have to find Seraphim first. She'll know how to help Suri."

"She'll be in the Warbringer barracks. It's the safest place in Svalbard."

Alec runs ahead of me, searching each new area like a soldier. He opens the east door and we hurry into the expansive snowy courtyard toward the Warbringer compound.

Frosty, peppermint air tingles my skin. My boots sink deep into the snow with each step, like trudging through deep water.

The wind moans.

Muuuooohhh….

I stop in the middle of the courtyard. "Did you hear that?"

Alec turns, "Huh?"

Must be the storm. "Never mind."

Alec walks on, but it echoes again – and louder. I listen with every nerve in my back. It's an animal.

I turn toward it. All around me the statues of Warbringer graduates frown down at me; Pharaohs, Czars… Their eyes are sad, like they're warning me. Behind the blur of their gray faces, something large moves on the horizon.

Thump – thump – thump –

Giant feet pound the snow. Whatever it is, it's huge.

My pulse pumps in my chest. The beast stampedes, faster and closer.

"What in the –" Alec pulls his knife from his belt. "What is that thing?"

Fire sparks in me: My senses reach out far across the snow; the animal's rage fills my chest. It will kill. We are less than halfway to the Warbringer compound. The animal is fast – it's too late to run. We won't make it. "Something's wrong with it, it's drugged. Angry." I stumble back toward the school. "We can't fight it."

The shadowed creature charges faster – until its tusks shine ivory in the moonlight. It's at least two stories tall, with brown shaggy fur: A wooly mammoth.

"Run!" I shriek.

Alec yanks my arm and we sprint.

I turn over my shoulder.

The mammoth roars, it charges us, closer and taller as we scramble toward the main gate. My boots sink deep into the snow – Alec passes me – I trip – and fall behind, slogged in the snow with each step. "I won't make it!" I cry, "It's too fast!"

I glance over my shoulder. The mammoth thrashes his head like a dog, its tusks stab the snow behind me.

"KEEP MOVING!" Alec bellows over the storm.

I push through the knee-high snow. The mammoth strikes long tusks into the slush behind me, sending snow flying in waves.

"ALEC!"

I trip with each heavy step.

The mammoth swings its head again – *whoom* – and the heavy wind from its tusks passes behind my head.

This is it.

I will die.

The school doors are still far across the lawn.

The mammoth's tusks slap an Egyptian totem, knocking it clear off the ground – *WHACK* – and the pharaoh falls in front of me, cornering me to the giant creature.

"ALEC!"

Alec leaps over the fallen totem, knife-in-hand, and stands between me and the beast.

The mammoth rears on its hind legs like an angry horse. Its red, manic eyes go wide – it's drugged. Alec holds me back with one hand, with the other he holds his knife.

The mammoth pulls back, ready to strike.

I grip my hands into fists. The mammoth will kill Alec.

It will *kill* him.

No.

Fire blazes deep in me.

I can do this. I'm Animalia.

I breathe, calming myself; I step out in front of Alec. I hold my hands out and speak to the massive creature. I look it straight in the eye: "Stop," I demand. "Hold still."

My voice resounds, stronger than I thought, but still not strong enough for Amafi. Not focused enough. I close my eyes.

I am my father's daughter. I am my father's...

The words slip from my tongue – Amafi – "STOP". The mammoth slows to a stop. It thrashes its head, confused. It's tusks swing at me but I grasp them instead, swift as a bat, I catch the ivory bone – *WHAM* – it strikes my hand – my wrist bends back and – *pop* – my wrist bone pulls from the socket.

I shriek and clutch my hand to my chest.

Alec pulls me back, into his arms – but the mammoth raises its front feet, aiming to stomp us – I scream. I curl my head to his chest. We bend over and in one last movement Alec pulls his arms up to protect my face.

This is it.

Our last moment.

I look up through his arms – above the statues and snowflakes swirling in the wind – and a white flash leaps sideways across my vision – over the fallen totem and onto the mammoth's leg: A white tiger.

The tiger roars, followed by a woman's voice over the storm.

Seraphim.

I hold Alec. Seraphim drops down from the fallen totem and stands between us and the mammoth. She is something from a nightmare, some dark ghost standing there, perfectly still – her hair pulls loose and catches in the snowy wind. The white tiger loops around the mammoth, herding it like cattle. Seraphim raises her hands, edged in moonlight, and commands the mammoth back in Amafi. Her voice – it's intoxicating – like the voices of all the Animalia women that came before. The mammoth thrashes it's head at her. It's a strange exchange, some enchantment. The mammoth swings its tusks – an act of protest – and she grips its tusk with two arms, catching the momentum and swinging herself up on top with the poise and balance of a tiger. In one swift movement she loops a chain around the tusk, leaps off and yanks the mammoth away, as though pulling a dog by the leash.

How in the world...

The mammoth follows her out, into the glacier field beyond.

...She saved us.

I melt onto Alec's shoulder. *Holy heaven.*

We hold each other and my good hand trembles, still gripping his coat.

Alec's cheeks are flushed and his lips are purple. "I've got you."

THIRTY-TWO

MADNESS OF ANIMALIA

I sit in Dr. Laszlo's laboratory, alone with him. Musty herbs hang in the humid air and cling to my skin. Plants surround me; leafy-green vines drape from shelves, filled with all kinds of tinctures.

I swing my legs over the edge of the hospital bed and hold my broken wrist. If I squeeze it, it hurts less.

"Doctor?"

"*Hmm?*"

"Did Professor Suri wake up yet?"

"Ah. Yes. It's the fumes from the engines the *Machinists* made. These machines," he rolls his eyes. "She'll wake soon…" He rummages through jars of silver surgical utensils. He pulls out a flat wrench and twirls it in his hands. "Have you ever dislocated a bone before?"

I shake my head and brace my broken wrist. Ori's purple friendship bracelet droops around my fingers.

"Ah," Laszlo runs his fingers over his mustache. "Well, this will hurt." He straightens his glasses, lowers the tool to my wrist, and encircles it in a swift, mechanical movement. The cold, metal touch gives me chills – he turns it in a twist – *pop!*

I yelp.

Laszlo pulls the tool away.

Blast! I clutch my wrist to my chest, coddling it. My God, it throbs. The skin all around it goes pink and hot.

"It'll be fine," Laszlo straightens his lab coat. He gathers a glass vial with clear liquid. "Drink this and you'll feel good as new," he leans closer, winks, "It'll help with the pain."

"Thank you," I take the vial with my good hand. "It hurts so bad."

Laszlo turns away and laughs. "To get well, one must suffer. Indeed, the suppression of something bad is the definition of health. It is not mercy, but punishment which saves us."

I frown at the back of his lab coat. *What?*

"Off you go," he rummages through his tool drawer.

I slip away into Svalbard's dim main hall; it's early still, like walking in a nightmare. The emergency bell sounds faint in the distance and the Warbringers form ranks in the main ballroom – still locking down the school and sealing it shut.

Which would work, if the enemy weren't already inside.

I swing the satchel around my side, which still has Professor Suri's machine in it. Apothecary students pass me, headed to Laszlo's lab. *Think, Sunday. Think.* I cradle Grom in my arms and he licks my wrist. I start in the direction of my room, but students scream and run down the distant hall.

I freeze. *No. Not again.*

I run in the direction of their screams, turn the corner into the ballroom – and all is chaos; exotic birds swarm the high ceiling, screeching. Animals run everywhere.

Someone broke into the Animalia atrium.

Marsupials swing from the chandeliers. Bats flap along the archways. Artisans duck under a flock of toucans.

"Stop it!" I command them.

The birds ignore me.

Why won't they listen?

"I said STOP."

But they flap wildly, mindlessly, ignoring me.

To the side, Eoin holds a tall pole and opens the high air vents to the ballroom. I set my jaw. "What are you doing?" I snap at him. "Why don't you help everyone?"

His eyes are empty and bloodshot. "School's orders. Close the vents."

Close the vents?

My gut sinks. Someone is manipulating him. "Who told you that?"

Eoin shrugs. His cap dips sideways. "School's orders. Close the vents to the outside air. Open the vents for the inside air."

Ugh. I grit my teeth. *Useless.*

Fire swirls in my belly: The dragon-mind.

Vents. Vents. Vents.

I search up and all around. Air vents line the tops of the ballroom, but they're closed.

"How long have you been closing these vents to the outside air?" I ask Eoin.

His eyes gloss over. "All the vents are closed now for outside air. The vents for inside air are open."

No air…

The man's message underground:

> "The ancient order
> Is not to be found.
> As memory fades, the trace of him is gone.
> Both man and beast,
> Tastes air like death – to an animal's mind."

Air like death.

That's it.

Someone will disperse a drug through the air. The animals have already gotten it, that's why they've gone wild. That's why only some people have forgotten Ori.

I run in the direction of Seraphim's office.

"Help!" someone screams.

I stop. My toes curl in my boots.

Not again.

I turn. Down the hall, Hikaru, the apothecary boy, hangs upside-down from an oil lamp. Artisan girls shriek below him, "Someone help!"

No – not Hikaru.

My chest trembles.

Seraphim. I need Seraphim.

I back away into the shadows and a cold, thin hand grips my arm.

I jump and turn; a curtain of glossy hair spills over her shoulder. Her eyes are blue-gray and terrifying. "This way," she pulls me forward.

My heart pumps in my throat. I run to keep up with Seraphim.

"Help us!" the students shout. "He's hurt!"

I follow her into the west wing.

"Shouldn't we help them?" I splutter behind her. "They need help."

Their cries fade into the distance.

… Where is she taking me?

I follow, quick at her heels, into her office. She locks the door behind us.

"You took Suri's contraption," she says, flatly.

I pull away from her. Her face is twisted, ugly. The angel is gone.

I squeeze the bag at my side where I slid the little machine. "…How did you know–"

Frustration flashes in her eyes, and for a moment it's like she'll hit me, but she shakes her head, "You're going to deliver the contraption she was working on to Bjørn."

"But –"

"I am filling this messenger bag with anything Bjørn would need." Seraphim hands me a stiff satchel. I loop the leather strap around me like a sash, so the case hangs by my side, and I tuck the little cloth bag with the machine into it as well. "Take the case to Bjørn, in Sjosburg. I need *you* to take it, understand? Deliver whatever he's made back here as *fast* you can."

"But – how will I get to Sjosburg?"

She turns away. Her hands clench behind her back. "The school is going into full military lockdown," she turns back to me and hands me a folded note. "Give this to whoever tries to stop you from leaving."

I pull the note from her.

Go to Sjosburg… *now?* But it's impossible.

"Now!" she pushes me.

I run from the room. I clutch Grom to my chest, sprinting down the stairs and toward the west exit.

Speed, Sunday. Speed.

Students clamber over one another, all is chaos. Tropical birds fly overhead and squirrels run between my legs. I fight through the crowd toward the west exit but the students pull together – everyone pushes to leave the school grounds.

I shove through them and reach the Warbringer students guarding the west exit, with Alec among them. They lunge to stop me and I dart past them.

Alec chases me. "*Eh! Sunday!* Where you think you're going?"

I can't waste time with him.

I sprint, but he catches up and grabs my arm. "I'm on an errand for the dean." I push. "I'm going to Sjosburg."

"You can't go there alone," he pulls my arm in his direction.

I rip my arm back from him. "Yes, I *am.*"

"*No,* yer *not,*" he sets his jaw. "We're a team, eh? We said we'd work *together.*"

Professor Seacole guards the west exit herself. She crosses her arms at me. "No one leaves. Emergency lockdown."

I thought you'd say that. I hand her the note Seraphim wrote for me.

She snatches it from me, her eyes flash over the paper. "Fine," she steps aside.

Alec leaps forward, "Commander," he stares at the place above her head. "Permission to accompany messenger on errand."

Seacole looks him up and down, and nods. "Go with her."

She pushes us out the door and slams it shut behind us.

Alec and I stand beneath the school entryway. A snowstorm whips around us – it's a white-out, nothing but fog and snow. I hug Seraphim's satchel to my chest and wrap Grom into my overcoat, shielding him.

No. We can't get to Sjosburg like this.

Think. Think.

Alec huddles beside me, he throws his arm around me to protect us from the slicing wind.

At least I have him.

"What's yer crazy idea?" Alec yells over the wind.

Wide-eyed, I search through the fog; snow, glaciers, mountains… Nothing.

I close my eyes. *Focus…* The dragon-mind rises in me. My senses sharpen. I don't see it – I *feel* it.

An animal is nearby.

The windy basin echoes into me – I sense, without needing to look – the quick footsteps of a pack of wolves, the groan of a distant polar bear, the flutter of an eagle. The weight of wolves' paws sink in the cold slush.

"Wolves," I huddle under his arm. "They're nearby."

The wolves won't have been exposed to the drug. They're our only option.

I dip into my neckline and grab Pa's animal whistle. *Please let this work…*

I blow into the little glass whistle, sending a shrill echo across the snowy meadow. Its song reverberates along the frozen mountains, like the call of some arctic bird. It's song echoes in my mind, and in the mind of animal close enough to hear it. But Alec frowns at the whistle, unable to hear it.

Please work…

I wait. My feet ache from the cold.

Out of nowhere, Alec grips my arm. "Stop."

He's frozen-still. His eyes narrow on the fog. "Did you see that?"

Beneath the moan of the wind a wolf howls, and a huge fur leg steps out of the fog: Deepeyes, the pack leader. He knew the call of the whistle.

Alec steps in front of me and holds his knife out protectively, but

Deepeyes shakes his white mane – he looks only to me.

"Put your knife down," I tell Alec. "He won't hurt us."

Alec gives me cautious side-eyes and sheathes his knife. I step around Alec, slowly, toward Deepeyes. He bares his sharp teeth at me, wild.

Deepeyes is not a tame creature, he is not *nice*.

But *nice* is different than *good*.

I pull my glove free from my fingers and raise my bare hand to the wolf. He sniffs my skin. A friendly greeting. His hazy gray eyes reach into mine. His determination sinks into my skin and becomes my own. I draw deep into myself, thinking of Pa, and whisper to him in Amafi. He growls back at me – he understands.

Alec's jaw drops, "How did you –"

"Come," I pull his hand. "He's going to take us to Sjosburg."

THIRTY-THREE

BJØRN AND JUSTINE

I hold Deepeyes' neck and he runs – flying over the snow. Wind whips us. We lurch forward over rocks and jagged mountainside. Pine boughs snap past us, grazing my shoulders.

I huddle low on the wolf's back and clutch Grom beneath my coat. Seraphim's messenger bag flaps by my leg. Alec hugs me around the middle and wind blusters through the juniper trees with a fresh, green scent – like crushing pine needles and holding them to my nose.

The wolf races along steep cliffs – the sheer drop is just inches from his steps. He's made for this – his thick paws, his balanced tail – his breath surges with every leap.

Deepeyes slows to a walk down a hill. Snow falls in fluffy cotton balls and drifts around my shoulders with tiny firefly movements. I turn over my shoulder. The flakes stick to Alec's hair in a glowing halo over his short brown locks. He smiles and creases appear around his tan cheeks.

We break through the tree-line and Sjosburg appears, nestled in the slopes below. It's tiny next to Svalbard; a gingerbread-town of cookie-cut shops and people. Deepeyes carries us down the slope and through town. Tiny icicles drip along the rooftops like glazed sugar, but the street is hauntingly empty. Windows are dark and hollow.

No one around. Like some abandoned fairy-town.

This had felt normal.

"It's a bit creepy, idn't it?"

We pass Ma's shop – my old brick storefront home. Candlelight flickers in the tiny attic window; my old room. Maybe Ma is there, sewing by candlelight.

We stop outside Bjørn's apothecary. I slide from Deepeyes' back and Bjørn races down the steps to me – he grabs Seraphim's messenger-case and hauls up the steps to his shop. I run after him and push through the store door, smacking the door-chimes. Bjørn sits behind his desk, surrounded by plants and potions – he snatches up the case and flips open the locks with his thumbs as though he'd done it a hundred times. He brushes through Seraphim's case, arranging the bottles with his fingers. A clear liquid glints in one of the glass vials; chloral – chills roll down my spine: Mind control.

Bjørn mixes powders into a pot heating over a burner. Sweat shines orange on his forehead. He frowns at his concoction and creases line his thin cheeks. Purple rings circle his eyes – he stayed awake all night working on this – whatever it is.

I glare at the drugs in the bottles. "What is it?"

"An antidote."

"For what?"

He sets his jaw. "…Chloral poisoning." He pours the steaming violet liquid into the contraption. "And this machine is a diffuser."

So this is the lavender drink Seraphim had before.

If he wanted, Bjørn could poison Seraphim or maybe even control her. He could do it, he's close enough to Svalbard to make trips, and far enough away to avoid notice…

No. It couldn't be.

Bjørn grips the diffuser pump by its two sides and separates the handles to activate it. It's something only a Machinist could dream up. "Will it work?"

"Suri made it. It's for all of Svalbard."

The entire school?

"But Suri didn't finish," he says. "The handles are blocked. You need a Machinist."

"But the Machinists at school are drugged. They won't wake for hours, maybe days."

"You need it fixed now."

"But I don't know any –"

I bite my lip. I do know a Machinist.

Viktor.

"Fine. I'll figure it out."

Bjørn slides the lilac antidote bottle into the case.

Heat fills my chest; the dragon-mind. I study Bjørn: Blushed cheeks. Tossed chestnut hair. He's handsome, with bright eyes and narrow, Nordic features. The room has bohemian décor and renaissance paintings from various countries. Tan lines circle his neck. He recently visited warmer climates. He isn't tidy, per say, but he's clean and regal. I could see him with Seraphim. "You're in love with Seraphim."

He flicks a bushy brow at me, smiles at his shoulder, and lifts the diffuser. "Push down on the center valve first, it takes two people to start the antidote's diffusion from liquid to breathable gas. One person holds each grip, see, while someone pushes the center valve," he mimics the pulling motion in the air.

I take the case and turn away.

"And Sunday," he stops me with a gentle hand, "make sure the diffuser sets off *inside* Svalbard. Understand?"

I nod.

I won't fail.

I loop the messenger case over my shoulder, step outside and a village boy argues with Alec, someone thin with messy hair and dark, accusing eyes: Viktor. He snaps his head toward me with a fixed expression, like I'm the only one he really cares about.

I stop on Bjørn's front step.

Snow drifts between us.

Grom lifts his little green head from my coat and squeals at Viktor, who squats in the snow and extends an arm – Grom leaps from me and scampers in the snow to Viktor.

Dammit, Grom.

"I actually wanted to see you," I tell Viktor.

"Oh, yeah? Actually?"

Church bells drone in the wind.

"Come, Grom," I pass Viktor and stand with Alec but Grom just tilts his head at me in Viktor's arms, confused.

"Your Ma will hear you've been in town," Viktor says, "don't you want to at least see her? Or you're too important now to visit. Too above it all."

"We don't have time," I say. "We're on an errand for the dean."

"Wow. So it is like that," he flicks his head to Alec. "Their lot really got to you. Now you're all hoity-toity, aren't you? You'll just betray your home that quick. You know, we aren't perfect Sunday, but we're your family."

Alec folds his arms over his chest, like he's keeping himself from punching Viktor.

"Viktor, it's not like that," I press. "The students are in danger. We're trying to save lives. Besides, you left without even saying goodbye."

He scuffs the snow with his boot. "...I'm sorry. I am. But I had to protect what dignity I have. Clearly, they stole yours."

"Watch it," Alec growls.

"Alec please," I hold him back with a hand.

"That's right, good boy, stay back," Viktor mocks, and faces me. "I see you're still obsessed with animals. Found yourself a guard dog to do your dirty work, didn't you? Clever girl. I should get me one."

Alec tenses with one hand resting over his hip where his knife hides.

"Look, we can talk but later," Grom leaps back into my arms. "We need your help. We need a *machinist*. Professor Suri was working on this contraption but didn't finish," I open the case and show him the diffuser, "the handles are locked, see. Can you fix it?"

Viktor pushes his jaw forward, satisfied. "*Hmm*," he taps his thin lips.

"My, my, haven't the tables turned."

"Can you help us or not?"

"Easy, easy," Viktor says, smooth, "as I recall, you weren't willing to help me, when I needed it. But that's all right, I'll still help you, I'll help all of those pompous people at Svalbard, whether they deserve it or not."

Alec rolls his eyes.

"Thank you." I hand Viktor the diffuser. He snatches it from me – something flashes in his eyes – I swear he'll smash the diffuser to the ground. But he only bites his lip. "I can fix this, easily, but – what will you give me in return?"

"You can't be *serious*," Alec snaps. "People's lives are in danger."

Viktor turns to Alec, "Oh I'm perfectly serious."

"*Anything*," I say. "What do you want?"

Viktor's bushy eyebrow flicks, he stares down Alec, challenging him. "Anything I want?"

Alec curls his hand into a fist, like he'd punch him if we didn't need him.

Viktor smiles at the ground, "Oh. I know what I want," he squares his shoulders at me. "You."

THIRTY-FOUR

VIKTOR'S ULTIMATUM

I do a double-take. "What do you–"

"I want you, to spend the summer here with me and your Ma. And *not* with the dog."

Alec steps forward, itching to fight.

"Fine," I cut. "I'll do it. I'll stay with you and Ma. Now will you fix the machine?"

Viktor's mouth twitches into a wicked smile. He spins a few cogs on the contraption and tightens a screw. "Done," he hands it back to me and brings his arms out, pulling me into a hug.

I stand there, awkwardly, as Viktor holds me and rocks me a little. His hair smells like warm cigars and bar soap. It's comforting, strangely. But the moment is too long – and I pull away. "Thanks," I say, stiffly, "we have to go."

Alec helps me up onto Deepeyes and we take off – out of Sjosburg. I turn over my shoulder – Viktor disappears into the maze of wood cabins and brick shops.

Holy heaven... What did I just agree to?

Deepeyes leaps over cliffs, iced-over lakes, and forests. He lurches up the mountainside to Svalbard – it's all haunted-looking, with parts of the school swallowed in fog so it floats in the sky, detached, with drifting spires…

We slide from Deepeyes' back and he disappears into the fog.

I clutch Seraphim's messenger bag to my chest and gape up at the high, broad wall which blocks us from entering the compound. "If it's locked down, how do we get in?"

"We'll break in," Alec nods at the frozen wall. "I'll go first and unlock the gates from inside."

No. That'll take too long.

I turn to protest but – too late – he crawls like a frog up the divots and mouths of the stone wall – he slips over the edge – gone.

I stand alone, in the white wasteland.

My spirit stirs like fire in my chest. Something isn't right.

I should know who the monster is by now.

Who is it?

I close my eyes.

Shut out the wind… Listen deep into yourself…

Forgive.

I open my eyes and I stand in my mind sanctuary – like Seraphim taught – I'm alone in the same white wasteland, but it's odd… like standing in a dream.

In the distance, a graceful man with light hair and honey-eyes strides toward me. My heart twists: Pa.

If only he were real.

A lump turns in my throat. Pa stands above me, his tall frame edged in light. I reach out and hold his warm hand. My vision goes glossy, *"Papa…"*

My cheeks go hot – I curl over and cry through my teeth. "I didn't mean to hurt you."

"I know."

"I didn't mean to kill you."

Pa tilts his head an interesting way, "You didn't kill me, Sun. I saved you."

I wipe my cheeks and tears smear on my fingers.

Pa kneels, takes my hands and presses them to his forehead. He shuts his eyes.

He's only in my own mind, of course.

"Even if you're only in my mind. At least I can ask if you'll forgive me." I rest my head on his shoulder. His hair smells like peppermint and sunshine. "Pa please forgive me."

He pulls away and smiles down at me with hazy eyes. He kisses my forehead with thin lips, and disappears. *Where did he –*

I stare at the white, empty space where he stood.

He forgave me.

My body melts, soft, like I can breathe again.

I open my eyes and my surroundings shift and change: I sit on the floor of Svalbard's main hall. Tall cathedral-windows and renaissance paintings drift into place like puzzle-pieces from my memories. Red-carpeted, grandiose stairways peel off in different directions.

A woman's voice echoes in the lofty room. *"Think, Sunday."*

I whip my head around. Seraphim sits at a desk on a pedestal behind and above me, with a wood gavel – like a great judge. "There's not much time," she folds her hands under her chin. "The students will die if they're exposed to more of this drug. They need the antidote, soon. You need to find out *who* is behind all this."

My heart pumps. "But how?"

Seraphim nods at the ascending stairways. "Ask them."

I turn. The stairs are filled with students now, professors, and house staff.

Who is the monster?

I bite my lip. *Who, who, who?*

"Start with elimination," Seraphim calls behind me.

My mind buzzes – I've noticed too many inconsistencies over the months here.

Ugh. Fine. Elimination. It's just like cards. I'll get inside my enemy's mind.

The monster is older. Strong. Smart. The disappearances have happened for over a year. I point to the various harmless first-year students from other houses; "It's none of you," I call to them, one-by-one. "No, it's not you, no." The students sit as I call them. "Not you…"

I walk along the stairs. Ori stands among them. Her dress is pressed, face full and fresh. My gut dips. Her gaze reaches past me, "Do you think the person drugging everyone is different than the one who attacked me?"

"No. They have to be the same. Sit down, Ori."

Ori sits.

Who?

The professors. It has to be one of them. No student would have the authority to tell the house staff to close the vents. Eoin would only obey a professor.

Unless… It *is* Eoin.

The white fur on Eoin's pants – Seraphim watched him closely. *Why?*

I raise my voice; "All students, sit down."

The students sit – only professors and house staff remain.

Agnet stands beside Eoin. Poor Agnet, the way she fell from the chandelier…

I cringe at the Norwegian woman.

"Not you, Agnet."

She sits.

Eoin stares blankly at my throat. His green eyes glaze over, empty. His sideways cap is worn. He's gullible, not smart enough to drug all of Svalbard. Someone told him to close all the vents, so fresh air would not get inside, and the students would be drugged.

Eoin spoke with the killer.

Perhaps he'll tell me. I come close to him, "Who'd you speak to?"

Eoin's nose twitches, his eyes gloss over.

Ugh.

He's useless. Just like the man I saw in the dungeon, who spoke Amafi…

That's it.

I turn, searching, and spot him in the back of the room. "You."

The aged man hobbles down the stairs to *me*.

I frown at him. "You know who the killer is."

He nods.

"But Seraphim couldn't speak to you, she had to use me. Anning set it up, didn't she? She knew Seraphim couldn't speak to you. But for some reason, you *wouldn't* speak to Seraphim, even though you both speak Amafi, why?"

Seraphim clears her throat at the judge's seat, uncomfortable.

She could be the monster.

But the man only repeats the riddle:

"The ancient order
Is not to be found.
As memory fades, the trace of him is gone.
Both man and beast,
Tastes air like death – to an animal's mind."

Memories reel in front of me:

Ori's message to me, scratched on the wood floor: R O S E

"At first I thought she meant her pig, Rosie," I tell Seraphim. "But I think she meant the Rose Fraternity."

"Which means…?" Seraphim raises her brows.

"She identified her attacker – and was trying to tell me about it. She noticed something about the person, so she sent that last message to me…"

The Book of Animalia appears on the red carpeted steps and I pick it up, I flip through, finding the diagram of the Rose Fraternity sketched inside. The pages surface to my memory and color themselves with black and gray ink, the drawings float in front of me until I find the symbol of the ancient order; the upside-down rose. "What was it you told me," I squeeze my eyes shut, "about the signs of the Rose Fraternity."

"… That everyone in the Rose Fraternity receives *that* mark on their left arm."

So the killer is someone whose… *left arm* I haven't seen.

"You haven't seen *my* arms," Alec teases beside me. I turn to the ghost of him. He wears a fresh-pressed white uniform and his brown hair falls in short, handsome waves.

"*You* are distracting me. Besides, I was with you when Ori went missing, it couldn't be you." He gives me a big wink and I brush my hands through him, smearing his image until he dissolves from the hall.

I turn back to the stairs – a small circle of suspects remain:

Professor Cortez, Suri, Seacole, Anning, Laszlo, and Eoin.

Anning frowns at me and checks her wristwatch. She scowls at Seraphim, bitter; she doesn't trust Seraphim.

Why?

I smirk. I don't trust Seraphim, either.

I've never seen Anning's arms, even in the heat of the atrium she always wore long sleeves. Odd…

No. She's modest.

I move to Professor Suri. Her elegant green kimono swishes when she moves. The day I visited Machinist, she received a letter from Seraphim. Of course… Now it makes sense why. Seraphim asked her to design the diffuser. But also, that day her sleeves were loose and hung back to her elbows, exposing her bare arms.

"Not you," I tell her.

She disappears.

Professor Cortez gives me a mischievous, curling smile, like he sees through me, "You always knew a bit more than you let on, didn't you?" He bites his lip like he's hiding something.

"You have an interesting secret," I reply, "but you aren't the killer. I remember you rolled up your sleeves while painting in your studio class."

He shrugs, like he's sad to be called out of the game.

I slide my hands through him and he disappears.

I turn to Seacole who stands in full-clad military dress with her hair slicked back in a bun. For some reason she hates Animalia, she'd have enough reason to want them gone. She sways, as though slightly drugged.

"You were the first target of whoever drugged the compound. They didn't want warbringers around. Because you would've stopped them, wouldn't you? So it can't be you."

Seacole sits and dissolves from the room.

Leaving Laszlo, Seraphim, and Anning.

Laszlo situates his gold spectacles. He wears his lab coat, concealing his arms.

I turn over my shoulder to Seraphim at the judge's table. "But when the boys went missing, Laszlo took care of the survivor and —"

I clasp my hand over my nose.

No.

No one ever saw the Animalia boy after he went to get care from Laszlo. My gut dips… *No…*

"But it couldn't be Laszlo," I tell Seraphim. "He was there the night Pa died. He helped Ma and I find him."

"Did he?" Seraphim counters.

"But he was nice. I trusted him because he was a doctor."

"*Nice* is different than *good*, isn't it?" Seraphim replies. "You can't just trust someone because of their assumed authority. Like being a doctor, or a professor. And so it's possible Laszlo is the culprit."

"It's more than possible." I hang my head. "He could have killed Pa and pretended to help Ma and I."

He offered me tea once, and I never touched it. That was probably drugged, too.

My heart pumps furiously. My cheeks go red-hot.

"It's Laszlo. It has to be."

I open my eyes.

I stand outside Svalbard's wall in the white wasteland. It's like waking from a dream, into a worse, darker reality. Svalbard's wall is too tall to climb, only a Warbringer could do it. I can't wait for Alec to come back. Ori is trapped inside, somewhere. One of the compound's balconies hangs just over the wall, in the apothecary wing.

Yes…

That's my way in.

I'll set a trap for my enemy. Laszlo is arrogant, he wouldn't expect anyone to sneak up on him.

He trapped animals in the apothecary wing and who knows what else. I set my jaw. The Animalia students.

I'll save them.

A snow bank piles high beside the wall, high enough that – if I jump for it – I can reach the low-hanging balcony.

Adrenaline squeezes in my arms.

I can do this.

I climb the snow bank. With all my strength, I leap for the balcony ledge – I grasp the iron rail, slip, and fix my grip again. I swing beneath and hoist my legs over the edge, and pull up the messenger bag behind me. Slowly, I approach the glass French doors.

I press my hand to the door.

It creaks open.

Good.

I step inside.

It's Dr. Laszlo's study; a small library with mahogany chairs and red carpet. Candlesticks burn on his desk, wax spills over the sides; freshly lit – someone is near. Toxicology books sit stacked on the desk beside a letter in ink scrawl, addressed to Paracelsus, Laszlo's old friend.

My gut clenches. If Laszlo catches me here…

He won't.

I step through his office and the wood floorboards creak underfoot. I duck under the archway and into a fork in the hall with two diverging paths. The wider path is polished and meant for public use – but not the other – Laszlo must hide things there on purpose. A curtain hangs over the narrow path and I push it aside, revealing the pantry door Alec and I found the night I saw the caged animals…

I set my shoulders. I can save the animals.

I'll be quick.

I slip into the pantry and Grom pokes his head out from my overcoat.

His lizard-nostrils flare, sniffing the pantry minerals. He leaps out – a lime-green swipe – and climbs the dusty drawers into the magnesium box like a lizard. I stand on a stool and pull the drawer open; Grom swims in the fine magnesium powder, scooping the soft mineral into his mouth.

I pull him up from his sand-box and he curls his tail under like a gecko.

"Not now," I whisper.

I secure Grom to my shoulder and kneel over the trapdoor, bolted to the floor. I listen with every nerve in my back; the room is dark and silent.

Slowly, I lift the trap door. Cold, dusty air fumes from the shadows beneath.

I shut my eyes. *Be brave.*

I jump – and slip through the trapdoor in one clean motion. I land with soft feet on the metal floor. I squint – my eyes can't adjust to the darkness – I feel my way through the shadows; shelves, candlesticks, table, chairs, matchbox. My fingers tremble and I spark a match, lighting a candle.

Adrenaline pumps in my neck. *Please let me be alone in here.*

With one hand I hold out the candle, with the other I clutch the antidote case to my chest. I inch down the narrow room but my boots step into the slosh of a puddle. *What the –* I lean over with the candle, but only cage bars reflect the light.

My heart hammers – a fox lays behind the bars, its eyes open and close, like a dazed child. Drugged.

A lump turns in my throat. *Quick. Move quick.*

I turn the iron clasp – *clunk* – and wrench open the cage. I pass cage after cage, releasing them; fox, goat, tortoise, otter. The animals roll from their cages, panting. I turn, about to open the distant door when something – no – *someone* – moans in the distance.

I freeze.

That voice – it's… human.

THIRTY-FIVE

HUMAN VOICES

I slap around in the darkness until my hand hits iron cages. A pale, hairy arm hangs from the gap between bars.

No...

I hug myself.

No, no...

The faces of Animalia students stare at me, empty; the older students Anning told me had 'graduated'. My fingertips brush the rusty bars, my face burns and tears slip over my nose. I pass cage after cage until a girl with curly locks and olive skin moans at me: Ori.

Ori!

I bite my fingers to keep from screaming. My hands tremble as I slap open the lever of the cage and pull hard. Ori's head lolls at an angle and she stares past me with glazed-over brown eyes. My arms tremble and I pull her to my chest. "Hold on," I hook my arms under hers and pull her from the cage. I sob aloud.

Accept what is real.

This evil is real.

I clench my jaw. I'll save them. I slide Ori onto the damp floor but her face smudges in the dirt. She is a ragdoll, limp. I open the cages one-by-one, but I can't pull them all out. Not all of them. I need Alec.

I sling Ori's arm over my shoulders. She's shorter than me, lighter, but I groan as I heave her up and carry her. My back aches as I haul her, searching around in the darkness for a way out, but she's too heavy and my arms bend.

She falls to the floor – *thud.*

No!

She lays on the filthy floor – bent at an angle.

Adrenaline surges in my chest. Alec. I need Alec.

The dark silence of the room swallows me. I hold my breath to keep from sobbing.

Quiet. Keep quiet.

I reach into the dark, inching forward. My hand trembles in the cold empty air until it touches the wet, smooth surface of a doorknob.

A way out.

I crank the handle and shift my body weight into the old, stiff door. I pound my shoulder against it –

Open, dammit!

I toss my weight into the door and –

WHAM!

I stumble through, trip – and fall forward, landing with my hands planted into a plush red rug. Mahogany chair-legs frame my hands.

What in the – I'm back in Dr. Laszlo's study.

My reflection frowns at me through the same glass balcony doors I first entered through.

I listen with every nerve in my neck. My instincts stand sharp – sensing the presence of someone – but all is quiet.

I'm not alone…

Slowly, I stand.

It's an intimate library. A fire crackles beneath a chimney on the opposite wall.

Beside me, a glass case of human skulls shine – all strung up like a trophy closet. Beneath them, metal surgical instruments gleam in the candlelight; medical pokers and saws – like something from a horror show.

My toes curl in my boots.

Out. I have to get out.

I reach for the same balcony doors I'd come through earlier. I turn the handle but – *click* – they're locked.

My insides twist.

Someone locked these doors behind me, and recently.

There must be another way out.

I search around but – odd… An idle gray blur in the far corner draws all my attention. The blur shifts slightly – *what in the* –

The edged silhouette of a man crosses his legs, poised on the library chaise, reading a letter. He reclines with a blanket over his lap, cigar-in-hand, and a book balanced on his left knee. Gold, octagonal spectacles hang on the bridge of his nose; his honey-brown eyes flick up to me from behind the glassy shine. He's kept so still, so silent I hadn't even noticed him. "Ms. *Sunday*," he snaps his book shut and I jump. His voice resonates with a romantic Hungarian lilt. "You're a *smart* girl, aren't you?"

My heart slides up my throat.

No.

I stumble away and my back hits the wall.

Trapped.

Grom crawls and hides in my coat.

Laszlo smothers his cigar on a silver plate, stands, and folds the blanket on the chaise.

"What *are* you?" I splutter. It's a strange question, but it doesn't feel strange.

"Relax. It's me." He glides toward me and lights candles on the coffee table between us, one-by-one.

I suck in air and hold it.

He can't be the monster. He just can't.

He's controlled and kind. I twist Ori's friendship bracelet around my wrist nervously. He's a doctor.

With him this close, he's two heads taller than me. He racks a hand through his thick, chocolate-brown hair as though he's just woken from a nap. His smile twists, "No need to fear, love. I'm a doctor."

The blood drains from my cheeks. He's cunning – I can't let him outsmart me. I step sideways, slowly, expanding the space between us; "What kind of doctor?"

"Alchemist – researcher of toxicology, chemical-neurology, pharmacology, colleague of the Rose Fraternity. Pioneer of the neuro-chemical mind-network," he says it like he's rehearsed it a thousand times – and his tongue flicks behind his polished teeth as he speaks, quick and sharp, almost pointed. He busies himself with a glass beaker on his desk, swirling it, "as an alchemist, I research the evolution of things to become better. Just as gold must be purified, so the human body must be purified – and especially, the human mind." He speaks with this relaxed, calculated manner that's interrupted only by the intermittent gasp-choke of his throat – his allergies, like he mentioned. He chokes on and off, it's a strange tick, and it's worse with stress.

"Indeed," Laszlo chokes, "it's *lower* thoughts which must be suppressed. We strive for *perfection*, not merely survival. The things of survival are lower. Animal instincts, if you will." He chokes again – his hand trembles over the various surgical instruments at his desk. His voice is strangled, almost drunk. "Might I tell you the story, of a patient I treated once?"

He sits at his desk.

I clench my hands behind my back. As long as he's sitting there, I'm safe.

"My patient's name was Paracelsus," he mixes an orange liquid in a beaker, "Paracelsus confessed to me dark deeds he did. So dark. In confidence, Paracelsus told me everything he had done. He had *killed*."

My hands go cold behind my back.

Help, Alec. Help me.

Find me.

"Paracelsus was, in fact, a monster, devoid of morality. A sensual being," his hands shake as he withdraws a bottle of lavender liquid and pours it into a syringe. Everything about him is clean and manicured, everything except his feet on the plush red carpet: they're filthy, all bare with no shoes or socks – his toenails are long and yellow.

My lip curls. Disgusting.

Laszlo flicks the lavender-filled syringe. Veins bulge in his neck, purple and bruised, like he's shot up with his own drug.

"You're sick," I mutter, "aren't you?"

Laszlo coughs again, sways like a drunk. He rolls up his sleeve and injects himself with the lavender liquid. He exhales with a sigh of relief, almost pleasure, and the serum surges his bloodstream.

He licks his lips, like he tastes something sweet. "I always liked you, Ms. Sunday," his voice is a hum, almost a purr, "always so observant about everyone around you – everyone except yourself," he laughs, chokes, and waves a casual hand, "Paracelsus, changed everything for me. He changed the way I view the human condition. Because Paracelsus existed only within the deep animal instinct we all must suppress, I realized *he* must be suppressed and sedated to exist within society. I realized something universal in every patient I treated – that illness comes from a lower mind and must be… *persuaded*."

The door out is far behind him. I'd have to run past him to reach it.

Not now. Wait. When he's not looking.

His eyes shine strangely at Pa's animal whistle dangling from my neck – he stands, comes close to me, and extends his hands to me, palms-up, offering them to me like a gentleman.

Why is he –

It's a rehearsed reaction. Polite. Shaking hands.

I return the gesture – out of habit – and I hate myself for extending my hand back to him.

No.

His rough, cold fingers touch my bare skin.

I lean away, but too late.

He bends over, and gently kisses the back of my hand. His thin lips are cracked and dry, his breath warm.

Chills roll down my legs. My insides squirm.

I've been taught this. Manners.

Fire flares in me: *Think. Break free.*

Grom hears my heartbeat. He crawls from my coat and growls at Laszlo.

Laszlo releases my hand and returns to his desk. I don't know why – it's like he's stolen something. "You are a prodigy of animals," he snaps his equipment chest shut.

My gaze narrows on the chest. "What is that drug you took?"

"It's an *antidote*," he says it with a smile in his throat, as though I were a fine lady. "It's all in the dosage, love. An antidote is only a poison we *want*. A little poison can save a man, a lot can kill him. But I think you know these things, don't you? You know by... *instinct*."

I set my jaw.

He's teasing me.

Laszlo laughs, his eyes water. "My dear, you know nothing about your condition."

He comes closer and reaches out to me. His fingers brush my chin, they're long and dry. I turn my face away.

"You are Animalia," he mutters, "you're torn between a human mind, and a monster's."

"I am *not* a monster."

Laszlo delicately steps to the side, so I face him. He sweeps a few strands of hair from my face and his hand hovers by my ear. "Justine tells you nothing about yourself," he frowns and leans back on his desk, away from me. "You'll have no help from her. She's the alpha. She's threatened by you. Actually, I would be too, if I were Animalia."

Grom snarls at Laszlo.

"You've chosen the perspective of a *monster*," Laszlo side-smiles, leans forward, and tucks my hair behind my ear, "You share a mind with a dragon. You love a monster. And slowly, you're becoming a monster yourself."

I step away from him, toward the balcony doors, and his hand falls aside.

"*Ohhh*, she didn't like that," he sniggers at the wall. "You have no charm,

Paracelsus. No charm."

The way he speaks to himself – as though there were two of him.

Insane.

My fingers grip the balcony doors, but they click – locked in place with a bolt.

No...

I turn back to him. The door opposite me is the only exit, and he stands between it. If I ran now, he'd block me. I'd have to fight him –

My advantage: He underestimates me.

His advantage: His size.

I should use the element of surprise. Beside me, there are sharp needles and surgical knives in a glass case. I could break the thin glass with my elbow, but it would injure my arm. If I wait for the right moment, and move fast enough, I can stab Laszlo's gut.

"Don't look at me like that, Sunday," Laszlo's face crumples, it's uglier now, his breathing strains, "*you* have the mind of a monster. Not me."

"Grom isn't a monster like that," I snap, "and caring about animals is different than becoming one."

Laszlo cackles to his shoulder, "You think you know what a monster is?"

You're the only monster here – "A monster is someone who sees everyone only on how he can exploit them – who thinks others are 'lower' than him."

Grom hisses. Laszlo steps closer, he lowers his head the way one would when trying not to scare off a child. "You are so young now and know nothing. But one day, you'll understand. You'll need to suppress the instincts inside you. And who will teach you? Justine? She'll kill you when you're a threat."

I set my jaw. "She's taught me things."

He cackles. "Did you think she was an angel? She's a predator. A killer through-and-through. A few years from now, mark my words – you'll need *me* – not her. That dragon will burn you from the inside-out. But I can help."

His eyes are sincere, he believes everything he says, and that's what's confusing. "You can look at me that way, Sunday, with all your hate, but it's Justine who's the real threat. And deep down, you know that, don't you," he leans on his desk, crosses his legs. "You can feel the monster inside."

"I am *not* a monster."

Laszlo chuckles, approaching me. "But you *are*," he inches closer. "And you'll be the most ruthless of all I think." The way he says it, with fascination in his eyes. He *desires* it… He desires… *me*.

"It was you who attacked me that night."

"Not me," he says in a whirl of defense, and he taps his desk as though to make it understand. "It was Paracelsus."

"You *are* Paracelsus."

His smile twists.

He stirs orange liquid in a beaker, above a burner; he rolls up his sleeves, revealing thick, hairy arms, with markings: Branding lines from a hot iron pressed to his skin in the shape of a rose.

I squeeze my eyes shut.

It's confirmed then.

Every muscle in me screams: *Murderer.*

He stirs his orange tincture. "It's nothing personal, little dragon. When we kill Animalia, it's for the good of the world."

Run! Now!

My fingers brush the glass case of surgical knives behind me. He isn't close enough now, but at the right time, I'll stab him.

I search for the exit but it's blocked by a metal contraption with a tube that leads up to a vent in the ceiling – it's pumping vapors into the entire school.

He's drugging all of Svalbard through the air.

Laszlo stirs his poison. "I'm only helping you, just as I've helped myself." He pours the orange liquid into a syringe with a sharp, long needle. "This remedy impacts Animalia differently – imagine that – normal students were only mildly affected by the drug – but Animalia," he laughs, "they go rabid, as the lower beings they are. So I brought them in, one-by-one, to test the effects." He twirls the syringe in his hand. "They're like *animals*, Sunday. Beasts. Minds torn in two."

My face twists into a snarl.

"Oh she didn't like that, did she?" he mutters to himself. "I think not, Paracelsus."

"Animalia isn't double-minded – it doesn't work like that."

"*Tssk, tssk.* She takes it very *seriously*, doesn't she, Paracelsus? Did you know," he inches closer. "I've been waiting for *you*, Ms. Sunday. You are the missing piece to my studies." His tone is all fascination, like he wants to drink me in. He stands only an arm's length away.

I back away and my shoulders hit the wall.

"Don't be afraid," he says in a small, intimate way, inching closer. "The moment I met you, I knew you *needed* me to suppress the monster in you."

"I don't need you."

"But as the monster –"

My voice thunders in my chest – Amafi – one-thousand voices in one: "I AM NOT A MONSTER." Tears burn my cheeks.

Laszlo stumbles away. "For the moment, you're fine," he reaches out to me and runs his fingers along my arm. "The time will come when you'll need me. And I will rescue you. And I will be with you then. When no one understands…"

His brown eyes reach into me. There's a sickening familiarity to him. He's so confident, I listen so intently, I barely notice his hand rest on my cheek. He's taller than me, much taller. His shirt is unbuttoned around his neck and loose. Dear God. Outside, the wind cries. My chest goes numb. God save me.

… He killed Pa. He's a *killer*.

His thin face is slack, sad.

He leans to the side, like he's grief-stricken, drunk. "When no one understands," he strokes my cheek, "what it means to live with a monster inside."

His eyes are bloodshot. His breath is sour with pine and cigar. His lips are heart-shaped and plum-colored. I think he will kiss me.

THIRTY-SIX

LASZLO'S OBSESSION

Laszlo holds my cheek. His fingers are cold, calloused.

Now. Stab him.

His face hovers over mine. He sways like he's drunk – his nose brushes mine.

Behind my back, I clench my hands into fists above the glass knife case.

Outside, snow whips the windows, and beyond it – Alec yells:

"Let go of her!"

His voice is muffled, distant.

I close my eyes.

Laszlo's forehead rests heavy against mine, slick with sweat. He grips my arms, pulls me closer...

No, no –

NO!

I twist my arms out of his grasp – like Alec taught – and shove Laszlo on his chest. He stumbles away, slaps around his desk, and grabs the orange, poison-filled syringe – he holds it needle-out, like a knife. But he bursts out laughing at the floor. "Little dragon has some bite in her doesn't she, Paracelsus? She is a monster yet. We don't mind, do we? We have some bite as well."

Alec pounds the glass doors.

THUD – THUD – THUD!

His voice distorts behind the window; *"Stay-away-from-her!"*

I turn and run but Laszlo darts in front of me, blocking my way. He corners me to the wall like a predator. He steps slowly toward me until my back bumps against the metal ventilation contraption.

Alec pounds the glass.

THUD! THUD! THUD!

My hand bumps Laszlo's diffuser. It's shaped like an hourglass, with liquid in the base that boils into vapors above, filling the school with poison gas.

Fire flares in me. If only I could smash the contraption – but I can't. It's filled with chloral and if I break it, it'll spill all over me. I twist Ori's friendship bracelet.

Think, think…

The small glass tube in the middle of it – strangely – is just the right size for the clay beads of my bracelet. I can clog it.

That's it.

I rip Ori's bracelet from my wrist. Beads spill everywhere.

I take one of the little beads and push it deep into the spout of the glass contraption – *snap* – it locks in place, blocking the vapors from rising into the castle.

Laszlo leaps toward the contraption, "NO!"

I stumble aside.

Alec slams into the glass with his shoulder.

THUD.

Laszlo swears at the clogged contraption – he pinches the bead to pry it loose, but it won't budge. It's lodged tight into the apparatus.

Yes.

He inches closer to me, feigning kindness, but the orange-filled syringe glints in his hand behind his back. "Easy, little dragon."

"Stay-away-from-me," I snarl.

"One day you'll understand," he presses in, closer, "what I'm about to do."

Alec pounds on the glass:

"Stop!" THUD – THUD – THUD – *"Get-away-from-her!"*

Laszlo stands close – if he wanted – he could hit me.

Grom growls weakly, retreating into my neck.

"Easy. It's just a *little* medicine. To make you relax," his face is so gentle – he believes his own lies.

I swing my elbows down onto the glass case with all my weight – it shatters and slices my hand. I grip a surgical knife with a bloodied hand, and hold it out to Laszlo –

Do it.

Kill him. Now!

I stop my hand mid-air.

No. I don't have to be a monster, like him.

Laszlo stumbles aside, away from my knife – I hardly notice him slip the syringe from behind his back, holding it up like a dagger and in one quick movement – he swings it down on my neck.

I scream.

He plunges the needle – sharp – into me.

"SUNDAY!" Alec cries behind the window.

Laszlo squeezes the syringe, pumping the poison deep into me. The stabbing acid-burn oozes into my chest and flows inside me – toxins stream over my neck, into my heart… Laszlo holds me under my arms, keeping me from falling to the floor.

The floor rotates to the side and I sway, dizzy. My legs are numb. My head lolls and I jerk it upright. My vision speckles; blue, white, red…

Grom roars in a frenzy, jaws-open, and crimson fire spews sideways across my vision – burning Laszlo's face – he drops me –

WHAM.

– I slam onto the wood floor, on my side.

Alec tackles the window and glass shatters around him – his leather shoes run toward me. His arms bear under me and he pulls me to my feet.

The walls spin. My pulse pumps in my ears.

Alec's lips move, but his voice distorts.

Drugs boil inside me.

Wake up, the dragon-mind snaps. *Focus. Judging from the side-effects, you have only minutes before the drug stops your mind completely.*

Grom growls on the floor – sparking fire at Laszlo – but his thin blue flame runs dull. He's out of magnesium, and his slender green body darts around the corner, running away.

Everything is hazy, underwater. "The case," I mumble. "We need... the case."

Alec holds me to his side and I hobble beside him to where I dropped the case on the floor.

Laszlo rolls on the ground, smothering fire from his clothes.

Alec lifts the case – but the wrong way – the antidote and diffuser roll on the rug near Laszlo.

No. He'll destroy the antidote.

Focus! What must be done?

My breaths slow – strained.

The diffuser. Diffuse the antidote into the castle before he breaks it.

It takes two people to activate the diffuser; one pulls the handle, the other activates the diffusion.

We can do it if we hurry.

"Get the handles," I tell Alec.

I lodge the serum into the valve, twist it into place, and lunge for the first handle. I run the length of chord to the end of the room. I stumble, trip – and crawl, stretching the handle to its full length and – *click* – it locks into place: Ready.

Just start the diffuser, Alec.

Alec grips the other handle, to activate the diffusion – but Laszlo rises from nowhere and in one swift, calculated movement Laszlo grabs Alec's arm and bends it back – *pop* – and dislocates Alec's shoulder.

Alec yelps out in pain, but he bounces back, like he's in a boxing match.

The air between them is charged, like two bulls staring down before a fight.

The dragon-mind focuses me; Alec's hands twitch into fists, he shifts his feet under him: His advantage is his experience. His weakness is his youth.

Laszlo lights a cigar and takes a long drag. He blows smoke into the space between them: His advantage is his medical knowledge. His weakness is his rage. Laszlo smokes, "I should tell you I'm less of a monster than you think, and after we're done with our conversation, I won't kill her. I'll find a more *productive* use for her. In my experiments."

Alec's face twists. He knows he needs the element of surprise – he grips one of the candlesticks behind him and throws it at Laszlo – a distraction.

Laszlo swipes the candle aside while Alec advances and uses the heel of his hand to thrust upward at Laszlo's nose.

But Laszlo is fast – he turns aside and uses Alec's momentum against him. He grips Alec's outstretched arm and pulls down, making Alec double-over. Laszlo jabs his knee into Alec's gut.

Grom peels around the corner – a green flash – he climbs and claws Laszlo's eyes.

Yes!

Alec reacts with jabs to Laszlo's gut –

one – two –

Alec is experienced, but uncontrolled.

Laszlo's defense is calculated – cold, medical – he twists Alec's wounded shoulder. As expected, Alec is predictable. But he's also quick – he shifts his tactic, using footwork – and changes his weight under him – he uppercuts Laszlo's chin.

Wham –

There's my fighter.

Laszlo's jaw cracks out of place – Alec lunges forward with his fist – *jab, uppercut, jab –*

Laszlo scrambles away and slaps around for a syringe on his desk. Hands shaking, he presses the needle to his forearm and pumps clear liquid into his veins. He holds it there, flexed, until his body softens with relief, almost pleasure. And he stands tall again, as though he feels no pain at all.

What the –

He turns to me and his face is a snarl; the professor is gone – he is the monster. He lunges and clambers on all fours like a dog – swift and frantic – and runs for me with dark eyes. He pins me down with thick arms and legs, pressing me to the floor – I pull away – but his hands catch hold of the slippery ends of my hair and he wrenches it – my head jerks at an angle.

Across the way, Alec finds the diffuser and locks it into place.

The toxic serum pulses in my skull. The room swirls.

Get up. Fight back.

I strain to turn over – Laszlo kneels over me with hungry eyes, he rips the neckline of my dress down my shoulder and arm. He drags me across the floor. The room blurs; fireplace, rug, floor…

Laszlo pulls something from the fireplace flames. He sweeps toward me – over the exposed skin on my back – the end of the fireplace poker is rose-shaped and bright.

A branding rod.

God help me…

My gut turns – my mind slows – Laszlo presses the red-hot iron into the tender flesh on my back – it's one thousand searing needles into me. I shriek and writhe on the floor. The sour tang of melting skin burns the air.

The branding rod clatters to the wood floor beside me.

The blur of Alec's frame tackles Laszlo and pins him to the ground. Alec beats him repeatedly with his good fist, punching; face, body, face.

I shiver and sweat – my skin is fire.

Alec sprints back to the diffuser and shoves it into the pipe Laszlo had created to connect to the school's ventilation system; "Now, Sunday!" he yells, "Pull the handle!"

I can't breathe. The handle for the contraption is right at my fingertips. But too far.

… I'm… dying.

Pull the handle. Do it.

God give me strength.

I groan and strain, pulling the handle in.

Click.

It worked.

My head falls to the floor.

Lilac fumes spurt from the diffuser in fluffy clouds, floating all around and up the pipe into the school ventilation system.

It's done.

My heart turns.

If only Ma were here, to hold me before I die. I'm a child again, weak, helpless. Why did I have to leave home? My heartbeat fumbles – slower and slower until my vision darkens, and I'm swallowed in a hole of shadows. All around me is… dark.

THIRTY-SEVEN

THE STORY BEHIND THE STORY

Snow falls in a moonlit slush outside the hospital windows. The dim chatter of students wakes me.

I lay in a hospital bed. Glass bottles and gauze are scattered on the bedside table.

I'm... alive.

Bandages cover my back – the skin beneath burns where the branding rod pressed into me. The ghost of its blazing touch hovers there, prickling my skin. Everywhere I look is a bright blur, like I'm newborn again, using my eyes for the first time. I roll my head aside. Hospital beds line the wall, students sleep in them. Candlelight flickers on my bedside table, and behind it – sits *Seraphim.*

She's here for me?

Alec sleeps in a chair, slumped over the foot of my hospital bed. His right arm is bandaged in a cast. Across the lantern-lit room, apothecary Bjørn carries medicines down the hall. He gives orders to the house staff.

I roll my head to Seraphim. "How long have I slept?"

"About two weeks," she mutters. "You were poisoned. Still, it's good you checked Laszlo's lab. Otherwise Oria may not have made it."

Ori?

My gaze wanders back to Alec, and behind him – Ori sleeps. Her clothes are clean and her complexion bright. Her corkscrew curls splay on my bedsheets as she rests. Tears brim my eyelashes.

Thank God.

She's safe.

"They're all right?" Moisture creases around my eyes.

Seraphim nods. "Thankfully, all the Animalia students survived," she sighs, more relaxed and more human than ever. Her tiger lays on the floor by her feet, licking its paw. She rests a hand on my starchy bedsheets. "What you did was courageous." Her icy eyes are sincere – she is a marble sculpture. Thank God she was my teacher, and not Laszlo.

"Thank you," I say. "For believing in me."

The sheets lift by my legs and something moves like a ball rolling beneath the cotton sheet, toward me, until Grom pokes his head out from the covers. He grins at me, showing his curled pink tongue, and climbs up my arm to my shoulder. He nestles by my neck in a familiar curl. I press my cheek to him.

Across the room, Bjørn speaks to a hunched man: The man from the dark underground room. The man who spoke Amafi.

I tense.

Wait a minute –

He wears gentlemen's clothes now, with a sash and long blue coat, all regal-looking. Bjørn watches me with side-eyes as he speaks to the man. They're talking about me.

Seraphim follows my eyeline. "I believe you've had an unconventional first meeting with Dean Raj."

"Who?"

"Dean Raj. Dean of Svalbard, before I replaced him."

My mouth hangs open. *The man underground was… the former dean?*

Seraphim smiles gently to her shoulder. "Let me tell you my story then, from the beginning," she flattens her hands on the bedsheets. "A few years ago, Dean Raj, who is Animalia, was the first to feel the effects of Laszlo's drugs."

Dean Raj carries a snub-nosed tortoise as he speaks with Bjørn. The same tortoise I saw caged in Laszlo's lab.

"Raj had psychological symptoms," Seraphim leans a shoulder to me, "everyone thought he was ill, but I thought it was something else. Now we know he had a reaction to Laszlo's serum, as all Animalia do. It forced Raj into a protective, instinctual state of mind, which is why he resented me for replacing him. Laszlo had slipped chloral into Raj's morning drink repeatedly, testing the effects on him. And so Raj's symptoms worsened, until his mind was jumbled – he could speak only Amafi. He hated me and barely spoke to me and acted tormented, still aware of his surroundings, still thinking at a high level, but unable to cope with himself... So I hid him underground. Unfortunately, he blamed me for everything."

Seraphim props her elbow on the bedside and rests her chin in her hand. "More Animalia students went missing – no one knew why. I only found one stray Animalia boy – Eoin – I set him under Agnet's supervision. But he, too, couldn't remember his past. He'd even forgotten his animal companion, an Irish Wolfhound."

Of course... Eoin was Animalia. That's why he could enter the Animalia dorms...

"Eoin had been poisoned by chloral. More students went missing... and Seacole started to work with me to hunt down the culprit."

"So that's why you're dean? Because the alumni wanted you to hunt him down?"

Seraphim softens. "Yes... I'm part of a... *special* society," she leans in. "A sorority of exceptional women... So the alumni chose me for my skills, yes."

I sit upright. "Did Anning send me to Raj on purpose?"

She sets her jaw. "I could scarce understand Raj and his Amafi. He refused to work with me – but I still needed crucial information from him..."

"But no one else spoke Amafi..." I mutter. "You told Anning to take me to him."

"…Yes, I did."

"You tricked me."

"With reason. I banned all students from the west wing, where he stayed, to keep him a secret. I'd thought perhaps Raj ordered Eoin to do these strange errands at night, but it was Laszlo all along."

Seraphim stares hard at the wall with pale eyes. "I also experienced mild symptoms, which worsened when at Svalbard. And my symptoms disappeared whenever I went outside or left to travel. I wondered if it were possible that some allergen was in the castle. That's when I discovered traces of chloral everywhere – I didn't know Laszlo had dispensed it through the air, evaporating the toxin into gas. Nearly everyone in the castle had been affected."

I cradle Grom to my chest.

"I had Bjørn develop an antidote for chloral poisoning – a lavender mixture which I drank to keep myself unaffected… It's the same tincture I had you give Seacole. She was more maliciously poisoned by Laszlo."

"How come?"

"She's Warbringer. She suspected Laszlo early on. He drugged her to keep himself hidden. His hallucinogen had a horrible smell, by the way, like rotten meat. The same was true of Agnet – while cleaning the Apothecary wing, she found Laszlo's secret room of caged animals… So he drugged her severely, attempting to wipe her memory of the place. He strung her upside-down – attempting to scare Svalbard into a lockdown, so the students would stay inside, afraid, isolated, breathing bad air. He knew fear was his greatest weapon. What better way to control everyone? Think of it, one man controlling all of Svalbard. He knew under a lockdown no one would be allowed to leave, to save themselves, to refuse his 'treatment' as school doctor. And there would be no group of students outside who weren't harmed. The castle would be sealed, vents closed, and his chloral vapors would slowly drug everyone inside. If you hadn't arrived in time, his plan would've gone through."

I hold Grom to my chest. "It was Laszlo who released the animals from the atrium."

"Laszlo's alter-ego, this *Paracelsus*."

Chills prickle my neck. "Is he Paracelsus or Laszlo?"

"Does it matter? In my sorority we'd heard of Paracelsus. We all had. Paracelsus was a notorious murderer. He'd killed Animalia before and had created all kinds of diseases, 'accidents', leaving odd symbols behind. It was rumored he'd retreated to the Swiss Alps. I never imagined he was hiding in plain sight, collecting students as test groups for his drugs."

I chew my lip.

I was almost in one of those cages.

"Laszlo was obsessed with everything Animalia. He'd asked me, multiple times, for Håkon Gråe's whistle – he wanted to run tests on why Animalia students could hear the whistle and others couldn't…"

I pull the sheets to my chest. That's why he came after Pa. And after Ori in our dorm.

"It was Raj's hint about death coming through the air, remember?" she says. "That's why I wrote to Suri to have her make a diffuser for Bjørn's antidote."

Dean Raj rocks his tortoise in his arms. He wears a colorful scarf; he's a polite, meek sort of man, the type of person you'd expect to be academic.

"Will you still be dean, or will Raj come back?"

"… I'm sure you're exhausted," she pats the sheets. "The school year is nearing an end this week. We're stopping short this year, because of everything. And I'd like to offer you something special. As a thank you gift."

I sit straight. "Sure."

"I'd like to introduce you to my sorority. A place where you can spend the summer safely, and practice Animalia. The Sorority of Exceptional Women."

"All summer?"

Seraphim smiles knowingly.

"If you don't mind my asking," I hesitate. "Who were you, to my father?"

She draws back a bit, "Håkon was…" she smiles at the floor, "my brother…" She stands, abruptly, and turns away.

She's... my *aunt?*

She walks to Bjørn, brushes her hand against his, and the blur of her white hair disappears around the corner. Grom curls into a ball in my hands, using them as a nest. My body sinks into the pillows, and Ori squeals; "You're awake!" She rushes to my side and hugs me over my good shoulder. "Thank God you're all right, what with your back and everything."

My eyes mist up. She's healthy, safe. Her chattering wakes up Alec – his face is purple and splotchy. He sits up and holds my hand.

Ori holds my other hand.

My chest swells.

It's all I wanted.

They chatter over me; excited, teasing – and it's worth it – the whole struggle; all my time at Svalbard; studying, learning the dragon-mind – it's worth it to have them as friends.

They banter, leaning over the hospital bed to me. Ori's cheeks are round and healthy as she smiles – as though she were never poisoned at all. They pause, waiting for me to respond to one of their questions. Pressure builds in my chest. "I love you both so much."

Ori wraps her arms around me and places her chin on my shoulder. "You're my best friend."

Alec squeezes my hand.

And I know in my heart. We'll be friends forever.

It's only the beginning of all we'll accomplish here, at Svalbard.

THIRTY-EIGHT

THE HOME THAT'S NO LONGER HOME

I step down from the sleigh into the springtime street, outside Ma's shop. Sjosburg is one of our stops on the way to Seraphim's sorority, and – well, I promised Viktor I'd come back to visit, at least. It's only a quick overnight stop.

I carry my trunk in one hand and Grom in the other. Seraphim brushes the manes of the reindeer who pulled our sleigh.

"Are you sure you don't want to meet Ma?" I ask.

Seraphim feeds the deer dried berries, her eyes are hazy. "We live in a different world than them, Sunday. You'll see," she pulls gloves up her hands, leaves in a swish of her blue dress and turns the corner toward Bjørn's apothecary.

Wind moans through the empty street. It's a ghost-town.

I'd never noticed the emptiness before. The buildings are old, faded, with worn wood and flaking paint. A schoolgirl watches me from a storefront window.

Perhaps she sees me how I first saw Seraphim, walking down this road in an elegant gown.

Gray smoke rolls from Ma's chimney.

I knock on her wood door with a clean gloved hand.

Footsteps scramble inside, and the door swings open.

Ma's brown eyes look confused, her eyebrows draw in. She claps a hand over her heart. "Sunday!" She hugs me.

I nearly drop my luggage.

She holds me by my shoulders, at arm's-length. Tears form in her eyes. She looks me up and down. "Look at you! I barely recognized you. Such a refined young lady."

I smile to my chest and step inside; the candle shop is a glorious mess, with reams of candles draped everywhere. Ma's been working hard. Herb vines curl over the fireplace mantle. Soot seeps from the fireplace floor into the little dining area. Melding wands are scattered on the living room table.

I follow Ma into the small kitchen area. She ties up her disheveled hair to hide the tangles. Her skin is dry and her hands are smeared with wax stains. I'd never noticed those things before – it had felt normal.

Ma sorts through pots and pans, starting breakfast. She has a wry smile, "Look at the lady who's come to our home. My little Sun, so grown-up."

I set my things on the floor and sag into the worn kitchen chair. "I missed you so much."

She cracks eggs and they sizzle as she drops them in the pan.

I roll my head back onto the chair and close my eyes. Familiar fumes of salt and oil froth over me. She sets a plate in front of me. Eggs and blood-pudding. I used to love this breakfast, but it's sparse next to how I've eaten at Svalbard.

"Your favorite," she turns off the fire and pours herself a coffee.

"Thank you," I say gratefully.

She sits, cups her mug in-hand and leans over the table to me. "Well go on," she huddles over her coffee. "How's school? Did you make friends? …How are classes?"

It's like asking me to explain heaven. Even if I told her, she wouldn't believe me.

"Everything's fine," I say, stiff. "I've learned a lot. I even have an allowance now, I can help pay for the shop, so you can stay open."

She pets my hand. "Meet any nice friends?"

"*Nice* isn't exactly the word I'd use."

"Do you like classes?"

I nod, and tilt my head. "Ma, your eyes are so clear. They're not all bloodshot anymore. You have more energy now, too."

"Ah, yes… Well. While you were at school, there was something wrong with my shipment of that medication I was taking, that drug – chloral."

My grip tightens on my water glass.

"The doctor who I was ordering it through just fell off the map, and well, Bjørn wouldn't give me any, so."

My gut dips. I stare hard at the wood table. "Ma, who was the doctor you ordered that drug through?"

"Well, Dr. Laszlo, you remember him. He was our town doctor here. He was the one who originally recommended it for me. But he just stopped responding to my prescription…" she cups her chin in her hand and bites her lip. "I hope he's all right."

I grimace.

"Turns out I never needed drugs that much, at all," she softens and her thin lips spread into a smile. "There's something different about you, too. You seem… Quiet."

"I'm just tired."

She has a warm, knowing gaze. She rubs my arm. "I'm so proud of you."

God it's good to be home. I eat my eggs – they're salty and delicious – I tell her about Ori. And my room. And how hard we study. As instructed, I say nothing about Animalia. Nothing about Seraphim or the other programs.

"Ma… Did Pa ever tell you about his family?"

"He was an only-child, you know that. He lost touch with his parents overseas when he came to Svalbard as a teenager. He never found them again, even though he looked."

"But did he ever say –"

Ding!

The shop doorbell rings. Ma rushes down the room to answer it.

I bite my toast. Footsteps thud down the entryway and Viktor swings around the corner to me. "You're back," he runs and hugs me from the side – a faint aroma of chimney smoke and candy – and he sits opposite me. Everything about him is familiar, comforting. He rolls up the sleeves of his old tunic, showing long, strong arms. He's handsome, and he knows it. "So what'd I miss?"

I chew my toast. "Ma and I were just catching up."

"And you're staying here this summer, then?"

"Well, for part of the summer, actually, tomorrow I'm visiting the – *um*, somewhere else, first. And I'll stay there a bit."

He rolls his eyes, taps his foot. "Sunday, you trust too easily."

I spread Ma's salmonberry jam over my toast.

"That woman, Seraphim," Viktor presses. "She's not all she's cracked up to be. You need to watch out for her. Already I can tell she has a hold on you."

Of course. I roll my eyes. Viktor thinks he's the saint and everyone else is the villain. "So what have *you* been up to? Helping out in your parent's shop?"

"Kind of," he straightens. "I'm building something. What – is that not good enough for you now?" His voice is loud. Loud enough for Ma and the customer in the front of the shop to hear. The customer glances our direction.

Ugh. Viktor.

He taps the table between us. "Tell me what's happening at Svalbard."

"You know I can't tell you about school. It's the rule."

"But I *went* there."

"Then why'd you drop out?" I snap. "You should've stayed."

His cheeks turn plum-colored. "Stay to be brain-washed and turned into one of their little *pompous minions?* No thanks."

I stand.

"Where are you going?"

I turn at the bend in the stairs, "I'm going upstairs to my room, if that's all right with you, you know, because I'm a pompous minion."

"Sunday," he stands, "that's not what I meant."

I frown down from the step above him.

"Look, I just wanted to stop by and say I'm glad you're back. I know I don't always say things perfect, but, we have to stick together, right?"

"Sure," I soften. "All right."

He pulls me down a step and hugs me abruptly. He holds me tight, rocking me a little. My chin rests on his shoulder. Down the shop, Ma eyes us from the side, there's an approving look in her, she smiles at us, and – for some reason – it scares me.

THIRTY-NINE

THE SORORITY OF EXCEPTIONAL WOMEN

I step down from the sleigh, at an unfamiliar stop.

I clutch Grom to my chest and crunch through the half-melted snow behind Seraphim's tiger. Her blue gown sweeps the snow as she walks.

What if she isn't related to me, and she's lying?

But we do look alike.

No… There must be some mistake. We reach the top of the snow-speckled hill, and patches of lime-green grass sparkle in the sunlight; the horizon is skylark blue. Oddly, a red brick mansion is situated, alone, atop the hill. *Blazes.* It could belong to a queen, with three stories of tall windows and peaked columns. Lanterns cast an orange glow along the windows and inside, the silhouettes of women chat, holding wine glasses.

…Must be a party.

I step up to the brick porch and scuff the snow from my boots. I lift the hem of my moss-colored velvet dress, and step inside.

Warm, smoky-cedar air encircles me, like a fireplace.

A butler bows to Seraphim and I; he takes her coat first, then mine.

I gaze up and all around at the intricate woodwork of the place; archways and dovetailed stairways. I follow Seraphim through a ballroom and we pass under marble statues – we hike up a curved stairway into a library. Ladies gather in groups, chatting in animated conversation – dressed to the nines.

Amazing.

I follow Seraphim. We must look strange, us walking as a pair, as though I were her daughter. We pass women playing chess; reading; pouring wine; striking business deals. As I pass, they take me in – glancing from Grom, to me.

Their stares aren't accusing, per say, but curious…

Seraphim leads me to the opposite end of the library and ducks under a low archway into a narrow, intimate map-room.

An aged woman sits by a fire, sipping a glass of red wine in one hand, reading a map with the other. She frowns at Seraphim – "This the girl?"

Seraphim nods.

The woman sets down her paper and rubs her forehead; "You'd like to see him, then?"

"Thank you, Maurice," Seraphim replies.

The gray-haired woman, Maurice, lifts an odd lever on the floor and a metal gate slides open from the nearby wall, revealing a small cage-lined room.

Seraphim sweeps into the tiny room, it's the size of a closet. She waves for me to follow and I shuffle into the cramped space with her. The metal grill of the door shuts behind me – *snap* – and I jump.

"It's called an elevator," Seraphim cranks a lever by the side which turns a dial above the door. "Professor Suri designed it."

Seraphim's tiger purrs by Maurice, watching us through the grill of the door.

The elevator locks into place – *clunk.*

My gut flips. I grip the railing.

"Hold on," she pulls the lever.

The floor drops and the library slips up and out of view – replaced by a thick stone slab, darkness, a series of tunnels, and chilled, musky air from an underground cavern engulfs me. I hold my breath.

The elevator stops again – *snap* – and the doors swing open. We step off.

My shoes clatter on the rough stone surface. It's uneven underfoot. Like granite.

It's so dark. I peer up and all around at a vast underground cavern – empty and cold. Bats screech in lofty places. As I walk my boots strike puddles on the ground.

...*Odd*.

Why would Seraphim take me down here?

My heart dips.

No. Everything is fine.

A man stands in the distance ahead of us. He is thin, the skeleton of a lost coal-miner; like the shell of someone who's spent too many hours underground for too long. He holds a lantern in one hand, and the other side of his body hangs limp. Shovels and digging tools are splayed on a table behind him.

Who in their right mind would live down here?

My hair stands on end.

This place is meant to be forgotten.

She's just taking me to see something. That's all.

My pulse pumps in my head.

"This is our grave-keeper," Seraphim mutters to me.

I step quickly to keep up with her and avoid the man.

"Madam Seraphim," the grave-keeper says, flatly. "Here to visit the dead?"

"Only Paracelsus," Seraphim replies.

What in the –

The grave-keeper swings his lantern, walking us down a carpeted, dark path in the cavern.

Paracelsus had been declared *'dead'* by Seraphim.

Only... We hadn't killed him.

Neither had Seraphim. Not really.

I follow her a distance, until the silver glint of metal bars – jail cells –

reflect from the grave-keeper's lantern. The cells are dark pits built into the stone cavern wall.

Imagine spending your life down here...

I shiver. *Imagine what you'd have to do, to deserve it.*

Behind the metal bars, the beady eyes and contorted faces of strange men watch me. Their faces are haunting; some are apathetic, some scurry around their cages like insects. They reach out through the bars, drawn to the lantern-light of the grave-keeper.

Living in total darkness.

"When I told you I had killed," Seraphim whispers beside me, "I meant it. They're dead to the world."

Seraphim checks stall after stall of men. She mutters something faintly; she's counting them. Counting them like trophies, like a coin-collector.

...These are her trophies. Men.

But horrible men.

The grave-keeper drags his boots as he walks, like a weary mannequin.

"We declare them dead to the world," she explains softly, "and we seal them away in here."

I grow quiet. We pass cell after cell of strange men. I shiver.

"Don't be afraid," she whispers. "They'll never get out. This cavern is the most secure place in the world," there's a smile in her throat. Pride. "The Sorority protects this place. We created it. It's our little secret."

She turns to me, in the dark. "I'm counting on you to keep that secret."

I nod quickly.

"Good."

With the light behind her, her face is slim, ghostly. "We're here," she gently places her hand on my back, leading me toward the nearby cell.

I stop, confused.

No one is inside this cell.

My gut sinks beneath the rock floor.

Is she... taking me inside?

No. Ridiculous.

She walks me forward, to the jail cell – and his presence tingles my spine: It's an instinct, the tiny hairs on my arms stand on edge. I *feel* him, hiding in the dark corners of the cell. He shifts behind a shadowed rock, inching closer to the bars of the cage.

Laszlo.

His voice purrs, "… a little dragon."

That voice lives in my nightmares.

"This is for your own ease, Sunday," Seraphim whispers to me, strangely, "you have to look into his eyes and know you are superior."

I do?

"You must confront your fears," she whispers. "Show them your strength."

I step forward, once.

Paracelsus chuckles – two beady eyes glint in the shadows. His figure slumps forward, bent at a demented angle. Without his drug, he is Paracelsus in full. The doctor is gone.

"Couldn't stay away from me," he purrs, draped in darkness, "could you, little dragon?"

Seraphim glares at the slumped edges of him, and the grave-keeper raises his lantern, showing Paracelsus in eerie orange lamplight.

Paracelsus huddles beside a rock. His head is bent at an off-angle, he inches closer to me. "One day," he mutters, soft enough so only I hear him. "You'll come back for me. You'll realize I alone have what you need. *I am* what you need."

"Done, madam?" the grave-keeper interrupts.

"You'll realize she's betrayed you," Paracelsus whispers, suddenly desperate, and louder. He doesn't move, but his eyes shift, manic, as he stares at Seraphim. "*She* is the dangerous one. She is the one who you can't trust. It's only a matter of time before you're a threat to her. You'll be locked down here, too. She's the killer!"

I recoil. I stumble backward and into Seraphim, who places her hands on my shoulders. She steadies me.

"That's enough," Seraphim cuts, turning me away with a gentle hand on my shoulder.

We walk away and my heart drums in my chest.

I'm safe. He's locked up. He can't hurt me.

We head back through the cavern and pass the rows of trapped men. As we walk, I watch the back of Seraphim's silky head... *She is the killer.*

Is she?

We board the elevator and rise again, back through the layers to the sorority house; the warm lamplight, the dim chatter, the tangy scent of wine is jarring next to the dark hole of criminals. I step out of the elevator, deflated.

"All well?" Maurice eyes me, smoking a pipe by the fireplace.

Seraphim nods. "Sunday and I have agreed she'll stay here this summer, in a private room, to continue her Animalia studies independently."

Actually... I never really agreed to that.

I said I would visit. I said it was a kind offer.

Maurice raises a brow at me, half-impressed. "Have you decided that, now?"

I lower my eyes.

Maurice exhales cigar smoke. "We'll be sure to take care of you then, little sister."

I bob with a little curtsy. "Thank you, ma'am."

"Though we certainly can't teach you much about Animalia," Maurice laughs, and gives Seraphim a meaningful look, she tucks a wisp of gray hair behind her ear. "But we can teach you trade, investments, all matters of money and society."

"I would appreciate that very much," I keep my eyes lowered.

"Such sharp manners," Maurice says, keen on Seraphim. "Have you scared the girl half-to-death, Justine?"

"I'll be close by," Seraphim says. "And I'll check on her now and then."

Maurice's sparse eyebrow flicks up. "Sure you will."

"I'll leave you now," she unties a blue ribbon from her blouse, "this ribbon was given to me by someone special, years ago. I'd like you to have it."

"Oh... thanks," I cup my hands for her to place the blue ribbon inside. It's beautiful. Silky smooth with threaded sides. I glance up – but she's gone.

Maurice grunts. "Well she certainly likes you, doesn't she?" she stands, using a ladies' cane to steady her. "I've never seen Justine so warm to anyone here."

I wrap the silk ribbon around my wrist.

I wouldn't call Seraphim's manners toward me... *warm.*

Maurice hobbles past me with her cane. "Let me show you your room, then." She leads me down a long hallway and I stand in a new bedroom.

"I'll leave you to get settled then," Maurice shuts the door behind her, leaving me alone in the bedroom: It's dark forest-green with crimson carpets and oil paintings all around. My new bed has blood-red drape curtains all around, suited for a sophisticated woman. A basin of pears sits on the table and Grom leaps for them, pattering on the wood table and sniffing them.

I step up to the full-length dressing mirror.

I wonder if it's healed yet...

I shrug my shoulder out of my dress and turn to see my scar reflected. The rose branding is puffy and white, still sensitive to the touch. *Ugh.* I sag. If only I could rip the burn marks from my skin. I press my forehead to the cold surface of the mirror. At least with it on my back, it will stay covered. No one will know.

I fix my jaw at my own reflection – it doesn't bother me the way it used to – seeing myself as a monster all the time. I don't have to fight her anymore.

I lean in close to my reflection – I press my hand to the cold mirror surface and make her a promise: "I am going to be the best Animalia that ever lived. And your suffering won't be for nothing."

I stand back from the dressing mirror and smile at myself.

Sunlight filters through the French balcony doors. Beyond, the sky is springtime blue. I shrug my sleeve back over my shoulder and open the doors. Outside, the air is crisp and floral. I lean over the stone railing and – *smack!*

What in –

Something strikes my sleeve; a tiny snowball.

What in the world... I peer down at the courtyard below and all around, and I spy him; dressed like a lumberjack, with tossed chestnut-hair and his left arm hanging in a cast: Alec.

My jaw drops. "What are you doing here?" I hiss, keeping my voice low.

"Your place here is naught but a half-hour ride from my own house ya know," he slaps his mitten on his pants to remove evidence of his snowball.

"Well this is a *ladies'* house," I tease. "No boys allowed."

Alec scoffs with fake-hurt. "Wha' about servant boys, I seen 'em around here carrying things."

I smirk. "Servant boys are allowed."

He beams up at me. "Sign me up," he gives a quick nod and runs to the side of the building, he climbs the brick and ivy exterior with his good hand.

"Careful!" I hiss at him. "Are you mad? You'll fall."

"I'm yer servant boy!" he laughs loudly, climbing the ivy. "I gotta report fer duty!"

"Shhh," I press, helping him over the railing.

"Shhh," he presses back to me, as though I were the noisy one. "You can't let them know," he whispers, teasing. His face is flushed with cold; pink and splotchy – he smiles, showing a puffy bruised jaw from his fight with Laszlo.

We've been through so much.

I hug him and he holds me with his good arm.

After everything we've been through, at least we have each other. He's tall and I have to stand on my toes to get my chin over his shoulder for the hug.

At least I have someone here who I trust.

He holds me by the shoulder, "It's gonna be allrigh'. Ori and I are gonna be around."

I hold his fingers where they rest on my shoulder. I wish it were that simple, but part of me knows; this is only the beginning.

The beginning of Animalia.

Of Grom growing stronger.

Of strange happenings and prisoners locked deep in the belly of this place.

Grom scurries onto the balcony patio – a flash of lime green – and darts between Alec's shoes and mine. He crawls up Alec's pant leg to his shoulder, rubbing his snub-nose on Alec's cheek affectionately. Ever since learning to breathe fire, Grom is less timid, more loving.

Alec laughs at the tickle of Grom's scaly nose. He blushes when he laughs and purses his lips at Grom, teasing him. Even Alec is calmer now, like he has nothing to prove.

More monsters may come, but when they do, we'll face them together.

DISCUSSION QUESTIONS

1. Sunday struggles with double-mindedness, just like the antagonist. What do you think makes Sunday different than the antagonist?

2. In having forgiveness for her father's death, Sunday is able to be herself again, instead of forming her identity out of a reaction to the event that hurt her most. Do you think many people form identities around the things that hurt them, instead of who they are? Consciously or unconsciously, have you ever formed an idea of yourself around your own anger or hate of something?

3. Why is it dangerous to hold hate in your heart? What advantage does forgiveness have in allowing someone to be free from their pain, and to become who they truly are? Discuss.

4. In Animalia, there is a special way of speaking with certainty, called Amafi. Are there moments in your life when you spoke from your heart with certainty and truth? What happened when you did?

5. Sunday describes the voice in her mind that condemns her as, "the monster." Have you ever felt accused by something or someone without much cause? How did you overcome and recover from that?

6. Seraphim teaches Sunday that nice is different than good. What do you think? Are 'nice people' different than 'good people'? Have you met any 'nice' people who did you wrong? Have you met others who were rough-tempered, but did the right thing?

7. Alec says, "Ya don't find yerself by diggin' a crazy hole in your own mind. You find yerself when you enjoy others and serve 'em with your life – that's what makes ya whole." In what ways have you served others? When you did, which of your special abilities or characteristics naturally came forward?

8. When talking about her father, Ori says, "He was only hitting me some of the times." In what ways can we normalize wrong things that often happen to us? If you had a friend who this was happening to, what would your advice be to them? Discuss.

9. Sunday desperately tries to control her mind without much success. What do you think? Is self-control something that can be forced? Or as Alec suggests, is it the outcome of forgiveness and mercy?

10. Have you ever been bullied by someone, maybe even someone you used to trust? In what ways did you forgive them? Also: In what ways did you stand up for yourself? If someone else were bullied the same way you were, how would you stand up for them?

11. Animalia uses empathetic abilities to understand animals and one another. Do you think caring about others makes you a more capable person, or less? What happened to convince you one way or the other?

12. The antagonist of the novel is both a teacher and a doctor. Can people abuse positions of authority? Do certain positions warrant more trust, or does that trust have to be earned? In what ways can we be wise about boundaries that must be set with people in special positions?

13. Has someone ever been diminishing of your voice? How did your perspective change after that experience? Did you stand up for yourself? If you didn't, what would you do differently next time?

Q & A
with
SHAUNA C. MURPHY

What Svalbard house would you be in?
Artisan. But if not, Animalia.

What do you think makes someone a monster?
I agree with what Sunday's mother said: Monsters are people who see others based on how they can benefit from them. I think monsters can also be chaotic and controlling – both at the same time.

Why did you design the abilities of Animalia the way they are?
I love the natural world so much, and I like feeling as though I'm part of something larger. Personally, I relate with the wonder that is found in the natural world, and in everyday relationships, more than any other type of fantasy.

Why create a protagonist with so much grief and trauma?

Sunday's uncertainty about her trauma is something that over time acts like this agitation, and creates these miraculous abilities in her as a result. I think all survivors of trauma or abuse are forced to create some kind of superpower to endure what they go through and process it, and her character is a way for people to understand not only the paradigm of grief, but also how traumatic life events can evolve us into more resilient individuals and grow us in positive ways, as well.

Amafi is a way of speaking with authority, why did you include this in the story?

Amafi is about speaking the truth. There are moments in life when we speak out of a firm conviction with absolutely no fear, with full confidence in who we are and perhaps even with a kind of faith in God. I think when someone speaks in Amafi they are really speaking from their true identity and the core of something that is kind of larger than life, and that is always powerful. I put it in the novel because speaking truth is part of what heals trauma and allows someone to be who they truly are.

ABOUT THE AUTHOR

SHAUNA C. MURPHY

Shauna C. Murphy spent her school years in Los Angeles, surrounded by theatre and the arts. She spent her summers in the country, exploring the outdoors, and developed a love for nature, hidden wonders, and stories that inspire hope.

Shauna has a MS in Multimedia Journalism / Filmmaking, and a BS in Multimedia Publishing and Writing. She is a producer and recently produced a documentary which examines the psychology behind how young people create fictional worlds for themselves, and the corresponding best practices for commercial storytelling. She helps others embrace their imagination and understand the benefits of living with wonder.

SPECIAL THANKS

To my family who indulges my imagination. To my friends who love my wild ideas. And to the extraordinary people who picked up these ideas and ran with them. I am grateful to have you all in my world.

Printed in the USA
CPSIA information can be obtained
at www.ICGtesting.com
JSHW021948210124
55618JS00001B/9